NOT ALL THAT GLITTERS

★

*An LGBT Literary
Fiction Novel*

By Elizabeth R. Ashfield

Producer International Distributor
eBookPro Publishing
www.ebook-pro.com

Not All That Glitters
Elizabeth R. Ashfield

Translation: Elana Kieffer Ginsberg
Editing: Mathew Berman

Contact: Elizabethashfield176@gmail.com
ISBN 9798877708310

★ *Part One* ★

CHAPTER 1
Manhattan, Early May

The sun rises over Manhattan. Tom Gold, the owner of "Olympia," the largest shipping company in the United States, is standing on the balcony of his Park Avenue penthouse watching the city come to life.

Another ordinary day awaits him, the highlight of which will be standing here tonight, on this same balcony, watching the flickering lights illuminate the sky.

He has about an hour to get ready before his driver, Arthur, will take him to yet another meeting with other young Jewish millionaires, most of whom, like him, inherited their business empires from their parents. This meeting was arranged as part of an annual trip by Israel's minister for Diaspora affairs, who is visiting New York hoping to persuade the younger generation of businesspeople to donate money towards Israeli security.

"Good morning, Tom," his housekeeper, Maria, greets him. "Your breakfast and newspaper are in the breakfast nook."

"Good morning, Maria," Tom replies, smiling. The sight of Maria's kind face always lifts his spirits, especially at the beginning of the day.

Maria basically raised him on his family's Connecticut estate; she was his surrogate mother whenever his parents were off working on their prestigious careers. His relationships with his two siblings had seen highs and lows. Maria was the only one who was always there for him. She was a good friend who guarded his secrets, dreams, and aspirations. She has always taken care of him and given him a sense of belonging and security.

"Music," Tom says, and as the room fills with the sound of electro-swing music, he feels slightly more energized.

The cozy breakfast nook is tucked between two walls essentially comprising wooden cubbies that hold row after row of wine bottles that Tom brings home from his business trips around the world. *The New York Times* sits, ready and waiting, on the side of the table, and Tom is leafing through it, trying to guess the latest headlines generated by the small Jewish country in the Middle East. He wants to come prepared for his meeting with the Israeli minister.

Arthur stops the Jaguar in front of the Plaza Hotel on Fifth Avenue. Ed Leibowitz, one of the biggest names in the American Jewish Alliance, hurries over to greet me. He is an extremely friendly guy who favors faded polyester suits and outdated ties, as if his sense of style stopped developing sometime in the 1970s. Tucked under his arm, as always, are a stack of cardboard files; why he has to lug them around everywhere I will never, for the life of me, understand.

"Hello, my friend," he calls over to me as I step out of the car. "It's good to see you. I always enjoy reading about what you're doing to help fight childhood hunger in Africa."

"The children are our future," I respond. "It's true that the past is important, but the future of the world lies with the generations to come." This is my way of telling him that talking about the Holocaust will not get any donations out of me this time. Ed signals with his eyes that he gets the message. Not that he has much choice; he knows that the tone I set at this meeting, and the size of my donation, will influence the other donors in the room.

We make our way down The Plaza's wide, magnificent corridors, towards the Columbia Conference Room, a private room where the meeting will take place. Inside, there is a long, ornate mahogany table that looks as if it could have been taken straight out of some European palace. The table is surrounded by about forty matching chairs with round bases, all upholstered in dark green leather that let you sink in comfortably when you lose interest in what's going on around the table.

As soon as I walk in, a heightened awareness settles over the room. It's coming primarily from the corner where the spoiled Jewish American princesses, or JAPs, are sitting. Most of the people who have been invited are already there in their expensive suits, and I say hello to them. Nicholas Stern, who inherited the Penko trading firm from his father, wants to hear more about my business, and is saying something to me about some collaboration. In keeping with the rules of etiquette, I agree to meet with him, even though I'm not the least bit interested in his, or any other, proposal. I scan the faces around the table, making sure I know who everyone is. I then settle back in my chair, ready for another predictable and boring meeting.

There is an empty chair across from me; the name plate on the table in front of it says "Richard Silverman." I wave Leibowitz over so I can ask him about the missing attendee.

"Richard Silverman is a successful, young entrepreneur from Chicago," Ed tells me. "He single-handedly created a thriving company that focuses on groundbreaking water technology. He is considered one of the top experts in the U.S. who'll be able to help find a solution for the global water crisis, and he invests a lot of money in Africa. He's currently in New York to set up a branch here, and he recently joined the American Jewish Alliance. That's why we decided to include him in the "Young Supporters of Israel" club and the "Corporate Heirs" club – even though he hasn't actually inherited any corporations," he adds earnestly.

A few seconds later, the very same Richard Silverman enters the room, along with a glowing aura that seems to surround him. As he takes his seat, I find myself sitting up straighter. I steal glances at him from the corner of my eye, careful not to give myself away. I instantly notice the fine tailoring of his suit, which he has matched with a blue tie and elegant sunglasses that are perched atop his head. He's a little wide set, but with his black hair and blue eyes, he's extremely attractive. There's something youthful about him, and his eyes exude warmth, honesty, and genuine simplicity, in the best sense of the word. All of which seem incongruent with his prestigious and well-groomed appearance.

When the minister of the Diaspora enters the room, Richard's eyes meet mine. We nod to each other, then turn our attention to the minister. I've been at meetings with him before, and I know that he's not going to waste too much time with niceties but will get right to the point. Indeed, he quickly begins speaking about the security threat looming over Israel, and how crucial it is for American Jews to help fund a security budget that will allow Israel to stand up to its enemies. Then, just as I predicted, he unleashes his secret weapon – the Holocaust. When will the Israeli government finally learn that if they want to enlist us as young donors, they're going to have to come up with justifications from the twenty-first century? I can't help myself, and I cut him off.

"Honorable minister," I say, noticing through the corner of my eye that Richard is looking right at me. "The State of Israel is extremely important to us. Many of our parents are Holocaust survivors, or the children of survivors. Even though they decided not to live in Israel, their hearts are with Israel, and they are committed Zionists.

"Our generation, on the other hand, is more open-minded, more cognizant of what's going on around us. The world is facing many problems right now besides the security situation in Israel." As I speak, my eyes keep drifting towards Richard. He's listening closely, a satisfied smile playing on his lips, and I find myself more concerned with this Richard Silverman guy and how he's reacting to what I'm saying than with conveying my message to the minister.

"At this very moment," I continue, "innocent people are being slaughtered in Africa. Women are being raped. They face constant humiliation and violence. Most of the continent has no access to clean water. And yes, there are Palestinians living under occupation, and I'm not convinced that Israel is doing enough to resolve the conflict, and let's be honest, Israel doesn't carry the same cache among young American Jews that it used to. I love Israel, but I need to hear more reasons why I should invest in Israeli civilian or security concerns instead of, say, fighting child hunger in Africa."

I look at Richard again; our eyes meet. We exchange quick smiles, and my body trembles with an excitement that I don't think I've ever felt before. The minister is responding to what I said, but his voice is like distant background music, and it feels like everyone has left the room except for Richard and me. I look at Richard's profile.

I am brought back to reality by the sound of applause directed at Ed Leibowitz, who's making his way towards the podium for his concluding remarks. He pauses on the way, urging me to announce my contribution publicly, but I refuse, leaving him to simply thank the minister and reiterate the importance of our support.

After the meeting, we all gather in the hotel lounge where a festive brunch awaits us. This is but one of many events that take place several times a year in fancy hotels across the country. Among the people dispersed throughout the lounge, engrossed in dull conversations, I spot Richard and make my way towards him.

"Nice to meet you," I say. "Tom Gold."

"Richard Silverman," he responds, shaking my hand warmly.

"Ed told me about your accomplishments with water technology. He says you're setting up a branch in New York."

Richard smiles. "I'm pleased that that's how Ed speaks about me. And yes, I am opening a branch in New York. I moved to Tribeca a few days ago."

"In that case, Mr. Silverman," I say, "we should talk. I'd love to meet with you sometime soon."

We shake hands again before parting ways. A piercing look

passes between us, catching me off guard. I choose not to address it.

"Tom, my friend, can I get you a drink?" It's Nicholas Stern again. Richard is still standing next to us, so I have no choice but to respond politely.

"I'm afraid I've got to get going, Nicholas. I have to be in Connecticut tonight for my mother's birthday party. My father has planned a dinner in her honor."

"Where he'll try to fix you up?"

I smile, gesturing helplessly with my hands. I give him my standard response – "My father never gives up" – and walk away.

Arthur drops me off in front of Rockefeller Center, where Olympia's legendary offices are situated. For some reason, even though nothing actually happened, my unexpected encounter with Richard has put me in a great mood, and I enter the building satisfied. It feels as if the statues in the lobby are smiling at me.

Alexandra, my secretary, welcomes me warmly as she straightens her blue pencil skirt. We say "hi" to each other and I head into my office. I'm immediately followed in by Adam Schultz, a former Israeli who's my personal assistant; Alexandra comes in right after him.

"Please order something expensive from Chanel for my mother," I say to Alexandra. "And arrange a card, too. Adam, please have the CFO arrange a donation to Israel. Five million dollars."

Adam is stunned. "You're donating five million dollars to Israel?"

"Yes, Adam. Five million dollars." Even though the minister's speech was unconvincing, so much so that I considered forgoing the donation altogether, I ultimately changed my mind. I want to help him and Ed, and this is the best way to do it. And aside from that, I'll be seeing my father tonight, and I'm sure he'll be happy to hear about this.

★

I leave my office in the afternoon and head to my parents' house. Arthur exits the I-95 towards the New Haven countryside, and drives to Silver Bell, my parents' estate. It is named after Olympia's first cargo ship, which my father named in an effort to immortalize his childhood landscape in Austria, where silver bell trees were ubiquitous. When we arrive, the large front gate swings open to greet us with an aristocratic slowness. After driving down a long, winding road, we reach the front entrance, where everything is all set up on the sprawling grounds.

"We've arrived," Arthur announces when he sees that I've remained in my seat.

"I'll get out in a bit," I tell him. I lean my head against the window and look out at my childhood home, and the despondency that strikes me every time I come here quickly greets me this time as well.

I spot my father among the throngs of people on the lawn. In addition to being a savvy businessman, he is a seasoned politician who was considered a leader of the Democratic party, and he had even served as Connecticut's senator some time ago. He suddenly seems older than his age. He has white hair, a stiff smile, and constantly flushed cheeks. He is well-dressed, but as always, there is something a little off about his appearance. Unlike my mother, who also appears on the lawn in a flattering, tight-fitting black dress with black heels and a drink in her hand. She always looks happy and is always smiling, radiating the sense that everything in her life is perfect. She has goodness and purity, even though her paranoid, controlling, and anxious personality compels us – even now – to do what she wants. Only then will she be satisfied.

Also on the lawn are my niece and nephews, Elizabeth, Jonathan, and Jeremy. They are the children of my brother Benjamin and my sister Diana, both of whom studied medicine. Neither of them showed any interest in taking over my father's business, and sometimes I wonder if they made that choice precisely to keep their distance from my father and all the family complications. When I look at my family standing in front of my parents' estate, I feel completely disconnected from this seemingly idyllic existence; it's as if I'm on the outside, looking in. And even though I know that what I'm looking at is just an illusion, I can't help but feel a twinge of jealousy. Here, everyone lives in denial. Here, nobody gets to the truth. Here, everything is always fine.

I take a deep breath and get out of the car.

"Hi, Tom my love," my mother greets me. "Your father invited Rita and Ted Zimmerman, and they brought Emily with them. Come, let's go say 'hello.'" I trail after her like a good Jewish boy, putting on my most winning smile, winding my way through the crowd of guests and the dozens of servers – all so I can say "hello" to the Zimmermans, which is to say to their daughter Emily, without delay.

Rita Zimmerman is actually a wonderful woman. I know her as an active member of the American Jewish Alliance, which is why I can't understand how her daughter Emily turned out as idiotic as she did.

"Hi, Emily," I say, leaning towards her with a mischievous, sardonic smile. I kiss her on the cheek and think about the fantasy that is no doubt running through her head – how I'll be won over by her charms, buy her an engagement ring, marry her, strip off her magnificent wedding dress on our wedding night, swoop her off to the Caribbean for our honeymoon, buy her diamonds and a house, and we start a family together. *Oh Emily*, I think to myself, *You skinny, blonde, airheaded Barbie doll, if you only knew my plans for tonight.* I quickly find an excuse to slip away, help myself to a glass of champagne, down it in one big gulp, and go over to my father to say hello.

"Hello, Tom," he says, shaking my hand.

"How are you?" I ask.

"Tired. I spent the whole day getting the tent ready for your mother's party. It would have been nice if you'd have come to lend a hand."

These sorts of comments would have riled me up in the past, but in recent years, I've learned to live with them. I try not to get too worked up, although I don't always succeed.

"I was busy negotiating a deal with Hong Kong," I tell him. "It should net hundreds of millions of dollars for Olympia. You'll be pleased."

My father nods, signaling that his interest in our conversation has run out. My brother and sister join us, and the discussion turns to the security situation in Israel.

"Oh, and by the way, Father," I chime in, "earlier today I donated five million dollars to the Israeli army." Again, he nods. This time, I can see that he is pleased. I can't remember the last time he offered anything more than this nod, the last time he showed any warmth or affection, much less love.

We are invited to enter the huge white tent that has been set up in the middle of the lawn. It is decorated in the signature style of "Henry and Odette," the only event planners that the top one percent on the East Coast would ever consider hiring. The theme of the party is France, and the tent is adorned with dozens of round white tables with matching wrought iron chairs, all decorated with delicate parasols. The tables hold small bouquets of purple, pink, and white flowers. The white porcelain dishes are meticulously arranged alongside sterling silver cutlery, which my mother uses at every opportunity.

Mother is always trying to prove to her fellow East Coast one-percenters that nobody can throw a better party than she can, and indeed it feels like we're at a fancy French ball where every last detail has been scrupulously planned out. My father may have made the actual arrangements, but he did so only after receiving explicit instructions from her.

The first course is served, and I see that "Henry and Odette" decided to go with the cuisine of the Burgundy region. Three-tiered silver serving platters are piled with mini spicy cheese puffs, miniature pastries, and escargot cooked in tarragon butter and sparkling wine. As someone who uses food as an escape at these kinds of events, I take a quick scan of the pastries and decide to choose the darkest one. I take a bite and discover that it's stuffed with lamb and cumin.

After the first course, my father asks for everyone's attention and calls my mother to his side.

"My dear, beloved Susan," he says, "Happy birthday. I love you. You are my whole world. You only improve with time, and as far as I'm concerned, you get more beautiful every year." Applause comes from every direction, and my feeling of not belonging intensifies. Again, I take refuge in the pastries.

"Thank you, Joseph, my love," my mother says. "As with every year, I am so moved to be here with those who are our nearest and dearest: our beloved children and grandchildren. My birthday wish is that by my next party, Tom will be married, too, and we'll be blessed with a grandchild from him as well." Again, the tent fills with the thunder of applause, only this time, everyone's eyes are on me. I have no choice but to smile, raise my champagne glass in the air, and pray for this nightmare to end.

After dinner and dancing, my mother blows out the candles on her cake and the party starts to break up. I say goodbye to my family, get into the car, and tell Arthur to take me to Soho. I pour myself a glass of bourbon from the bar in the back of the car.

The Jaguar flies down the I-95, back to New York. Once we're in Soho, I start to come back to life.

"Thanks, Arthur. I'll get a taxi home. Good night."

"Good night, Tom," Arthur replies, and hurriedly drives away as I take out my phone and open the app I use to find other closeted men who, like me, are looking for something quick and casual. Photos of men who happen to be in my vicinity start popping up on the screen, one after the other. This is a popular time of day for the app, and the number of nearby men keeps growing.

I see someone about two hundred yards away, an attractive young man named Daniel, and together we walk towards my favorite club, The Silent Bartender. Amy Patriot and her band are about to begin performing songs by Abba.

The Silent Bartender is a speakeasy for successful, closeted men. Its design – from its expensive leather sofas and its opulent bar to its stylish tucked-away seating areas – is reminiscent of a British men's club. There is a secret entrance. You go into an old phone booth and punch in a password that opens a side door in the wall leading to the club. The club's owners and staff know me. They know to leave me alone, and I never have to worry that my name will show up in the gossip columns in the next day's newspapers.

Daniel and I go inside and sit at the bar.

"Bourbon, please," I call out to the bartender.

"Make that two," Daniel adds.

When the show starts, we turn around to face the stage. Amy Patriot walks onstage wearing a blonde bob wig and a tight red dress with a corseted top. Two long, gold cones protrude from her chest. The entire atmosphere in the club is charged with excitement the moment she appears, and everyone starts clapping.

She starts moving her body in exaggerated motions, and she even manages to elicit a small smile from me. With Abba playing in the background, her bandmates join her onstage in extravagant red dresses. They, too, are wearing blonde wigs and over the top makeup, and they all start swaying to the rhythm in a unified, slightly ridiculous manner. With a wave of her hand, Amy Patriot strips off her red dress. Wearing only black sequined tights and a corset, she pulls out a cigarette lighter and ignites the two cones on her chest; they turn into fountains of sparkling light. The audience breaks into applause and excited cheers.

"Another glass?" Daniel asks, and I nod. It's my fifth drink tonight. I wasn't planning on getting drunk, but that's what seems to be happening as the medley of Abba songs picks up speed. The band starts singing "Waterloo." Amy Patriot jumps off the stage and walks among the crowd, pushing the microphone towards people's mouths and making them sing along. Four muscular dancers in tight, shiny black pants and close-fitting tank tops climb onto the stage. Behind them, sparklers are going off, and another singer named Dorothy Wood comes out. She's wearing heels that transform her into six solid feet of woman, along with her dramatic makeup, her glittering orange wig, and her preposterously large chest. She starts to sing "The Winner Takes It All," and people start waving their arms with cigarette lighters in their hands. Everyone in the room is swaying to the rhythm of the song, and soon the hugging and touching and fondling begin. It's easy to see who's going to spend the night with whom.

Unlike the other people in the club, I remain frozen in place, and Daniel, who I think wants to jump me right then and there, has to follow my lead and play it cool. Over the years, I've learned to close myself off, to protect myself, to act as if the entire world is my enemy, even though I try to believe what Judith is always telling me: "The world is love, you just have to choose the best things it has to offer." But I know that I still haven't internalized this message, and that I don't live accordingly, not even at this very moment.

The show is over. Everyone goes back to their private little conversations. I order us a couple more whiskeys and offer Daniel a cigar from the box of Cohibas that I keep at the club. We sit at the bar and smoke, barely exchanging a word. After a while, we head out into the chilly evening air and walk drunkenly through the streets. Even though we are pressed against each other, our hands are in our pockets, and we are immersed in our own separate worlds. I feel like I might vomit but the cold night air is helping me feel better.

"Your place or mine?" Daniel asks.

"Mine." I raise my hand to hail a taxi. We climb into the backseat, and the cab lets us off in front of my building.

"Hello, Mr. Gold," the doorman says, holding the door open for us. I nod to him and make my way across the red carpet leading to the elevator. Daniel follows. The elevator attendant punches in the code for the penthouse. I show Daniel to my bedroom and then go into the bathroom. When I come out, I find Daniel lying in my bed, naked. I strip and lie down next to him. I grab his head and push my cock into his mouth. Then I flip him over onto his stomach, pull on a condom, grab his ass, and fuck him from behind until I come.

"I think you'd better go," I tell Daniel after our second round. He stands up and gets dressed. I sit at the edge of the bed and wait patiently until I hear the door close behind him.

CHAPTER 2

Manhattan, Mid-May

Arthur drops me off in front of Rockefeller Center. The building is surrounded by flags from all around the world. As I enter the building and head to the lobby café, the sound of the flags flapping in the wind is a reminder that we still have so much work to do for this world of ours. I pick up a copy of *The New York Times* from the newspaper rack and find a table. Florence, my favorite waitress, brings me my usual coffee. My phone buzzes, signaling an incoming text. It's Adam, my assistant, informing me that there is a strike at the Israeli port and that as a result, Olympia's ships can't enter to load and unload. Since most of them are refrigerated cargo ships, this could mean a significant loss for the company. *Good morning to you, too,* I think to myself, leaving a twenty on the table and rushing towards the elevator.

I storm into my office and ask Alexandra to get me Israel's Cabinet Secretary on the phone immediately.

"What kind of loss are we talking about here?" I ask Adam.

"The big and pointless kind."

Sometimes I understand our president's attitude toward Israel, I think angrily. Those people in Jerusalem can really drive you crazy.

Alexandra's voice comes through the intercom. "Arik Gonen on line one."

I take a deep breath. Adam gestures to me to calm down, and I pick up the phone.

"Hello, dear friend," Arik says affably.

"Arik, have you lost your mind?" I seethe. "I'm going to lose a huge amount of money today because of this damn strike by your damn port union, and you say, 'Hello, dear friend?' What the hell is going on in Jerusalem? Is anybody home? Listen closely, Arik – I'm only going to say this once. If I lose money today because of this strike, I'm taking back the donation I just made to Israel. I've had enough of these games. The minister of the Diaspora came crying to me about how big the deficit is, how bad things are, and that you need donations. Of course there's a deficit in Israel! Your unions and your treasury officials are ordering you around! You have one hour to confirm that my refrigerated cargo ships are entering the port to unload their cargo and will leave by the end of the day. I'm not interested in hearing about collective bargaining or nepotism. Have I made myself clear?"

"OK," Arik responds after a long silence. He sounds bewildered.

"Listen, we're talking about a huge ship of mine that came from Port Said. It's a joint commercial venture with international shipping companies, and it's flying an American flag." I read out the details that Adam has just handed me. "And another thing, Arik," I add, "It's not just the Olympia ships that are going to be allowed into the port; all foreign ships will be allowed to unload. I don't want to read in tomorrow's papers about how you only let Olympia's ships in because of our donation."

When I've said everything I wanted to say, I slam down the phone. I lean back in my chair, close my eyes, try to calm down – and am filled with remorse. I meant every word that I said, but Arik is an old friend. We met at a Jewish Agency summer camp when we were teenagers, and we've been close ever since. I shouldn't have used that tone with him; it's no wonder he sounded so surprised. I buzz Alexandra to come in.

"Is everything alright, Tom?"

"What do you think?" I snap at her. I ask her to see if Jessica has time to talk on the phone. "Cancel all my evening meetings and instead schedule a meeting for me with Judith," I add.

"OK," Alexandra replies. "And by the way, Richard Silverman called to schedule a meeting with you."

I sit up straight, surprised.

"When did he call?"

"His secretary called this morning. I scheduled a meeting for you with him for next week – he has to visit his mother in Chicago. My sense is she's not well."

"Thanks, Alexandra. That's all for now."

She wishes me a good day and leaves my office. Adam hurries out after her.

I sit back down on my chair and start to play with a perpetual motion toy on my desk. For a moment, I forget about ships stuck in the Israeli port, and an adolescent smile plays across my face. Now I have a reason to get through the coming week.

"Jessica's on line one," Alexandra tells me over the intercom.

I pick up the phone.

"Hi, Jessica, how's it going?"

"You tell me."

"I just exploded at Arik Gonen, the Cabinet Secretary of Israel, who also happens to be a good friend."

"Yes," Jessica said. "We've spoken about him in the past."

"Every word I said was true, and I don't regret the content of what I said, but I do regret the way I said it. I need to process this with you if I'm going to get through the long day ahead."

"Take a deep breath," Jessica says. "Later, when you're done with your meetings, call Arik or send him an email. Get back on the same page. Your relationship with him is strong enough to withstand this." We speak for a few more minutes and agree to continue this discussion during our next weekly meeting.

Jessica is my personal coach and mentor. She helps me think more clearly and be a better manager, and a better person. She's not the only one. There's also my psychologist, Margaret, who recently decided to go back to London, where she was born. And there's Judith, my neo-humanology therapist. I have surrounded myself with supportive women, and that's the paradox of my life: I trust them completely, but I can't manage to be sexually attracted to them.

★

"Our situation is grave," the Angolan Ambassador to the United States is telling me. With us in the conference room are Adam and Olympia's CFO. "Millions of Angolans live on dry, barren land. The tribal conflicts are violent, and many people are dying. Our water sector is in trouble. We desperately need purification systems to treat the wastewater flowing from the cities right into our water sources. Water companies around the world have expressed interest and are considering investing in projects that would provide drinking water to the region and support local agriculture."

I gesture for him to continue. He looks at me, confused.

"If water companies from around the world want to invest," I say, feeling my patience running out, "and I assume local contractors are prepared to help, why are millions of people still without proper drinking water?"

"It's hard to get money from the government for these kinds of projects," the ambassador replies.

"What's the lowest possible cost for one of the projects?"

"Four million dollars."

"The Angolan government can't commit to four million dollars, and you want me to do business with you? First show me that you're capable of carrying out a small planning project, then come talk to me about business."

"Mr. Gold," the ambassador cut me off. "We've come to you because we can't raise the funds. You're a well-respected man, known for helping our continent. That's why I'm appealing to the goodness of your heart. I know you're a good man. We need investors. I'm sure that a businessman like you knows how to leverage these projects to your benefit, even if it requires an initial investment. If you build a sewage system in the cities, you'll be able to develop tourism, and you'll be able to get your investment back and more. We won't stand in your way."

I almost blurt out, *What in God's name does tourism have to do with my shipping business?* but I restrain myself. He clearly doesn't understand business. Still, there's something to what he's saying. I have committed myself to donating and investing in Africa, for the sake of the children.

"What do you suggest?" I ask the CFO.

"I suggest that we take everything into consideration and see if Olympia stands to gain anything by investing in Angola."

"That's not the answer I'm looking for," I tell him. "We have to partner with the seed and fertilizer companies that export their goods on our ships, the companies that specialize in water reclamation for agricultural purposes, and the water technology entrepreneurs. We need to come up with a formula for providing cheap water for agriculture, water that is suitable for all the crops in all the regions. At the same time, we have to strengthen the agricultural sectors that already exist there. I'll donate the seeds and grains. We'll also pay for the farmers' education and training, and we'll export the products to the rest of the world. As for water reclamation, we'll have to find a solution.

"I want it to be perfectly coordinated," I say to Adam. "If necessary, you can recruit people who think outside the box." I can't stop myself from taking this jab at my CFO, who thinks like an administrator and has no imagination whatsoever. "And find out which countries have the most expertise in water reclamation. I'm taking this on as a personal project, and I am committing, in front of the ambassador, to ensure that things will move forward."

The Angolan ambassador shakes my hand and thanks me profusely.

"Millions of Angolans drink water that you wouldn't even wash your hands with, and millions wash their hands with water you wouldn't mop the floor with," he says, quoting a well-known African aphorism. I can't help feeling excited about this decision that I just made.

In the afternoon, Adam presents me with a list of countries that lead the world in water reclamation for agricultural purposes. At the top of the list is Israel, which reclaims 80% of its household-use water for agricultural purposes, mostly through its Greywater reclamation company. Next on the list is Spain, which reclaims less than half of what Israel does.

"Get Arik Gonen on the phone for me," I say to Alexandra over the intercom. Then I turn to Adam. "Has he gotten back to us about the ships?" He shakes his head no.

"Arik Gonen on line one," Alexandra tells me a few minutes later.

"Tom," Arik says nervously.

"Arik, I'm sorry for how I spoke to you this morning. The way that country of yours runs drives me crazy sometimes."

"I know what you mean," he says, and I can hear the smile in his voice.

"I hope you know that your friendship means more to me than anything else," I say. "I mean it. I'm planning to be in Israel this summer, and I'll make it up to you."

"You don't have to make anything up to me," Arik assures me. "I know that our friendship comes first. And your ships have unloaded their cargo, so you can rest easy."

"Thank you. I really appreciate it. But I'm actually calling about something else. What can you tell me about your Greywater reclamation company?"

"A national treasure. It's doing very important work in the water industry. It's just a shame that it's a government monopoly. It wouldn't hurt to make it more efficient, or to privatize it."

"It's profitable?"

"Yes."

"Then why would you want to privatize it?"

"The United States privatizes a lot of things, too," he responds.

"True," I say, "but it doesn't make sense for you to privatize these kinds of companies. If you do, the prices will go up and the quality will go down."

"I still don't understand. What do you want to know? What are you getting at?"

"I want to be part of the solution to the global water crisis, particularly in West Africa. I did some research on your company. You guys know how to do good work when you want to. I'd like you to set up a meeting for me with the CEO of the company, and I want you to allow it to work in Africa," I say. "And regards to your wife."

Arthur drops me off in Greenwich Village, where Judith, my neo-humanology therapist, lives. After my psychologist, Margaret, decided to go back to London, a friend of mine told me about Judith. "Nobody really understands what Judith does," this woman said, "but everyone agrees that she could dramatically improve the quality of a person's life." She teaches her patients how to master any situation by using the rational mind, which is located in the frontal cortex and produces ever-changing amounts of energy, an open information system that constantly absorbs new information and enables us to look at the world objectively and make decisions. I later found out that the entire New York establishment goes to Judith, and that getting an appointment with her is not as easy as it sounds. Needless to say, I got an appointment, and I finally feel like I'm starting to understand her approach and how to apply it to my life. At the stage I'm at now, she's been teaching me mantras. When I remember to repeat them, I truly do feel my energies rising, and I can feel everything becoming simpler and better.

The blue door to Judith's townhouse is always unlocked. I knock on it and go inside, walking past the kitchen and living room, where I can see her statues of Buddha and other ethnic deities, and I find her husband Jeff in the back garden. He invites me to join him, and we exchange a few pleasantries until Theodore

Lewis, the television host, comes out of Judith's office. Unfazed, we shake hands – we're both here for therapy, after all – and I walk in.

"Hello, my dear Tom," Judith greets me. I smile and sit down on her green armchair. Judith is tall and formidable. She has thick lips that are always painted with burgundy-red lipstick, and her brown hair reminds me of Katherine Hepburn.

"How has your week been?" she asks, lighting sticks of sage-scented incense.

"I'm trying to digest and understand your philosophy. It's not easy, but I think I'm starting to get it."

"Tom, darling, you are standing at the precipice of a magical journey, at the end of which your worldview will be completely transformed. Our feelings are a result of how we look at the world. If you view the world negatively, you'll feel bad. All you need to learn is how to allow the positive pole of your emotional brain to control your worldview through the rational mind. The rational mind will play the role of therapist, allowing you to neutralize the negativity that's shaping your feelings. Transmitting information to the rational mind will allow you to take charge of your emotional system. Then you'll be able to find the emotional stability that you're looking for." "If you learn to conserve energy in your brain, you can overcome your fears, your anxieties, and your depression." She takes a sip of lemon water, then continues.

"In order for us to move forward, I have to know what you remember from your childhood. I see from your map that you experienced at least one severe crisis when you were around six or seven, and that this memory affects the way you live your life. Can you tell me more, Tom? If I'm going to clarify for you the source of your current emotional experiences, I need to know more about what happened."

I listen carefully to Judith and try to decide whether I even want to continue the conversation. After five years of psychotherapy, I'm tired of rummaging through my past. She can sense my distress. "We don't deal with problems here; we deal with solutions. But if we want to get to the solution, I need to know what the problem is."

"Drama created by my father," I say breezily, trying to lighten the heaviness that has settled over the room. I have absolutely no desire to talk about this right now.

"What exactly happened?" Judith doesn't let up. "I have to know what happened so that we can do regression exercises."

"Regression?"

"Yes. I'm going to put you into a state of deep relaxation. Your emotional brain will fall asleep and will, briefly, let down its defenses, allowing you to go back in time until you encounter an event that has had a negative impact on your life. After the memory is revealed, we will clean it by radiating it with light. The negative memory will be replaced by positive information that will support the positive axis of your emotional brain. We'll be able to neutralize the information that supports your patterns, to allow you to bypass them."

"Wow," I say. Judith laughs.

When I leave her house, I can't decide what surprised me more today: Judith's regression exercises or the Angolan ambassador who wants to do business with me and can't come up with four million dollars.

Friday is packed with meetings, discussions, and consultations. Finalizing yet more major business deals that will bring in more revenue for Olympia. About five years ago, after much deliberation, my father decided to step back from running the company that he'd built with his own two hands, and he transferred full control over it to me. Although we barely speak, I know that he admires my business savvy, as well as my political involvement with the Democratic party.

I glance at the clock. Time is creeping by so slowly today, not that I have anywhere to rush off to. The despondency that seems to accompany me wherever I go doesn't take a break on the weekends, so I decide to repeat some of Judith's mantras. A light knock on the door brings me back.

"Ed Leibowitz wants to know if you're going to the Corporate Heirs annual weekend in Maine," Alexandra says. "He asked me to remind you that the date was chosen to accommodate your schedule, and that your attendance is very important. Senior members of the Israeli government, the American Jewish Alliance, and the Democratic Party are expected to be there."

I lean back and gaze at Alexandra. Do I really feel like spending a weekend filled with endless small talk and unnecessary social nonsense? Alexandra, feeling uncomfortable with the contemplative gaze that I have unintentionally directed towards her, looks down and straightens her pencil skirt.

"Please get me the confirmed guest list," I finally say.

Alexandra, who always anticipates my needs, hands me a few sheets of paper stapled together. I leaf through them: forty people are expected. As I scan the list, I notice the name Richard Silverman.

"Is this list up-to-date?"

"Yes, it's the final list. It just came in a few minutes ago. That's why Ed is so eager for an answer."

"Tell him I'm coming," I say. "Please prepare a file with everything I'll need for the meeting."

Alexandra leaves the office. I close my eyes and feel something that I can't exactly name, but I think it's something good.

Maria welcomes me home with her usual heart-warming smile.

"I packed your bag for Maine," she says.

"What would I do without you, Maria?" I ask in amazement. "I didn't even remember the trip myself until half an hour ago."

When I close the door behind her, I feel a bit sad that my patterns and emotional barriers prevent me from showing my affection towards her more openly. I throw myself down on the living room sofa, grab one of the purple pillows, and start tossing it in the air. Tomorrow morning I'll head to Maine. Until then, I still have some time to myself, and a short while later, I'm sitting on a barstool at The Silent Bartender, browsing the morning paper for the first time all day. A club member – someone I don't recognize – sits down next to me.

"Brandon," he introduces himself.

"Tom," I reply curtly. I'm happy sitting here alone, with my newspaper and my bourbon. Brandon can tell that I'm not in the mood for small talk and gets straight to the point.

"What are your plans tonight?"

"What do you suggest?" I ask instinctively.

"Your place or mine?" He puts his hand on my back.

I close my eyes, look down, swallow. All I want, I realize, is for him to leave me alone. I shake off Brandon's hand and, for the first time, look him in the face. He's actually a handsome guy.

"Not interested," I respond.

CHAPTER 3
Maine, May

I love driving by myself. I love the quiet that settles upon me when I drive long distances, just me and my car. Music. Nature. My thoughts. Very soon, I'll be doing just that. For now, though, I'm still driving down Fifth Avenue. Spring is in the air, and I've let the roof of my Porsche down. I grab a coffee at the Corn Bake café, and head out of the city feeling excited.

I head north, towards the open roads that lead to Maine. At the last minute, I decide to take side roads so I can enjoy the spectacular scenery. My Porsche and I have the roads almost to ourselves as we wind around the enormous maple forests. The signs along the road are the only thing indicating the small towns hidden among the trees. My favorite Israeli band, Orphaned Land, is playing over the speakers, and I am filled with a tremendous sense of calm. I stop at the side of the road to look at the rustic scenery that surrounds me, then continue on my way.

In the afternoon, after several hours of driving, I pass through Kennebunkport on my way to Tiffany Manor. The town's main road, which is paved in carved stone, branches off into a series of meandering paths, all leading to houses surrounded by manicured gardens. I turn onto a side road that takes me to a large stone building resembling a fort, a boutique luxury hotel right on the beach.

As I drive up to the main entrance, I catch sight of Richard. He's leaning against a black car, holding a glass of beer; he looks like he stepped right off the cover of GQ magazine. Dressed in jeans, a blue polo shirt, brown moccasins, and a baseball cap, he exudes the same boyish simplicity that won me over the first time I saw him at The Plaza. The excitement I felt back then strikes again, with a vengeance. He's standing some distance away, but I can tell that he has spotted me, too. I park the car, take my suitcase out of the trunk, and walk up to the hotel entrance, but by the time I get there, Richard is gone.

"Hello, my dear Tom," Ed Leibowitz calls out. He's wearing one of his outdated suits, as always, and he's carrying his usual stack of frayed cardboard files. "We rented out the entire resort for the weekend so we won't have any interruptions," he tells me, following me to the front desk. "Go upstairs and rest. At seven, we'll all have dinner together, followed by our traditional party. I hope you'll celebrate with us."

In the evening, I go down to the reception room, wearing a grey suit with thin white stripes, a white shirt, and a red tie. I spot Richard right away but decide to sit with my acquaintances from the American Jewish Alliance, and from the Democratic Party. *Maybe it's all in your mind,* I caution myself. *He's probably just a straight guy who was only looking at you so penetratingly to see if you might be a potential business partner.*

The waiters start serving the food, and so the celebratory dinner is officially underway. Despite its elegance, the hotel restaurant has a homey atmosphere. The bar is near the back wall; across the room, the DJ is getting ready for the dance party. I pour wine for the people sitting near me, help myself to fresh pasta with chili butter and sardines, and start telling jokes. I want to make it clear that I'm not in the mood for serious conversation.

At the end of the meal, Emily Zimmerman – the blonde Barbie doll whose parents send her to all the best conferences with the hope that she'll find a husband – tells us to choose between two options: a dance party or an evening of games. I don't voice an opinion – neither option appeals to me – but everyone else at my table is eager to play games. They sit in a circle on the carpet, and, reluctantly, I join them. Richard is there, too;

our eyes meet, and we nod to each other. Emily puts an empty wine bottle, a bottle of whiskey, and a stack of shot glasses in the middle of the circle.

"We're going to spin the bottle," she explains. "Whoever it points to has to name something he's never done. Anyone who *has* done it has to go into the middle of the circle and drink a shot."

The game begins. Everyone seems to be enjoying themselves. I have no choice but to resign myself to the situation. Apparently, games like this one are designed to break the ice between people who don't know each other well. I hope, with all my heart, that the bottle won't end up pointing at me. As it turns out, it ends up pointing to Richard, who mulls over his answer for a few minutes before speaking.

"Never have I ever driven a Porsche," he finally says, looking at me. I run into the circle and drink a shot; then I drink another. I wink at Richard, and he smiles back.

When the game is over, I sit down on a bench outside the room. When I see Richard come out, I call his name, spinning my key ring on my finger.

"It's all yours," I say, tossing him the keys, and together, we walk to the parking lot. Richard sits behind the steering wheel, and I climb in next to him. He puts the top down, and we head out of the resort and onto the winding roads of Kennebunkport. It's hard to talk with the wind smacking our faces, but the silence doesn't bother me, and I sense that Richard feels the same way. It's as if we've known each other for years.

Richard pulls over on the side of the road, and we get out and walk. The wooded paths are illuminated by the pale light of the moon and stars.

"When I was a boy," Richard says, "we used to go to New England this time of year. We would visit my mother's friend in Rhode Island. I used to love watching the trees changing color from one season to the next. I was mesmerized by that deep red in the fall – there's nothing else like it in the whole world."

"I came here with my parents, too. They have a house here in Maine. We'd go to Maine one year and Eilat the next. Have you ever been to Israel?"

"No," Richard replies. "But I have family there."

"How's your mother doing?" I ask.

After a long pause, he answers. "She's sick. Alzheimer's. I was supposed to stay in Chicago until next week, but there's not much I can do for her right now, and she has a caretaker."

"What about your father? He's not in the picture?"

"My father died when I was ten." After a pause, he adds, "He worked for Olympia."

"Your father worked for Olympia?" I blurt out. "When? Doing what?"

"After surviving the Holocaust, he moved to Israel, and lived there until 1948. Then, after the war, he moved to America and got a job working as a sailor for Olympia. He spent years sailing the world and served as third officer on a ship. After twenty years at sea, he transferred to Olympia's Illinois branch, overseeing the export of refrigerated commodities."

"Maybe we've met before after all," I say to Richard. "At least that's how I felt when I saw you."

We smile at each other and walk on in silence.

After a few minutes, I ask, "How did your father die?"

He answers with a question. "How do sailors always die?"

"Alcoholism."

"It's rampant. They drink all the time, and it messes with their health."

"So do you feel like Olympia killed your father?"

"Not at all. I'm just telling you what happened," Richard says softly. "I read about you in *Time Magazine*, when you were voted Man of the Year." I smile but stay quiet. We continue walking, looking into each other's eyes. Richard loosens his tie. He smiles bashfully, and I smile back. Then his smile turns to laughter, and I find myself laughing along with him.

"I've never been with a man," Richard says without warning. Now I'm the one keeping quiet. *The world is not your enemy,* I tell myself, evoking one of Judith's mantras. *The whole world isn't against you.*

"I have," I say. I've never admitted this to a straight person before.

"A one-time thing?"

"Way more than one time, and way more than one man."

"You're still in the closet though?"

I consider how to respond and decide to tell him the truth.

"I'm scared of my father."

"Do you want me?" Richard asks with a confidence that surprises me. He smiles.

"Would you be into that?" I ask, confused.

"I was seeing someone until recently. A girl. We were together for a few months. The thing is, I haven't felt a real connection with anyone in years. It's just been one fling after the other. Some were longer than others, none of them were serious, all of them were with women. But then, when we were sitting across from each other at that meeting in The Plaza, I felt attracted to you. It's true, I've never been completely indifferent to men, but to go from that to finding myself here with you, saying these words ... I don't really understand what's happening to me."

I can see that Richard is flustered, so I suggest that we head back to the car. This time I take the driver's seat. We drive back to Tiffany in silence. By the time we arrive, it's late. I put the top up and turn on the stereo. Classical music plays softly in the background. We look into each other's eyes and start moving closer to each other. Gently, I put my hand on the back of Richard's neck and pull his head towards mine; we start to kiss. I wrap my other hand around him, too, tightening my grip, and our mouths seek each other frantically. After a few minutes, I pull away from Richard and gaze into his eyes for a long time. I decide to be brave and invite him up to my room.

Richard nods. We walk on tiptoe, laughing at ourselves, but the truth is we're afraid someone will see us together. Once inside my room, I take off my jacket and tie and remove my shoes. With my hands in my pockets and a small smile on my lips, I approach Richard, who seems to be frozen in place. I lead him, slowly, to the edge of the bed and caress his face and we find ourselves kissing once again. I start undoing his tie and unbuttoning his shirt, but he stops me.

"I'm a little overwhelmed," he says. "I need to be alone for a little while. Can you understand that? It's not that I'm running away or having regrets or rejecting you, I'm just confused. Two weeks ago, I saw you for the first time, and now here I am in your bed – my first time in bed with a man." He smiles. "And not just any man – the most desirable bachelor in the country."

I give him an understanding smile and take my hand off his shoulder.

"Of course. I understand."

"I'll see you at breakfast," Richard says, getting up. I walk him to the door, and we part ways.

The next morning, the dining room is buzzing. Richard is standing by the buffet; when he sees me, he nods. I nod back. I get the feeling that we're both completely embarrassed.

At the end of the meal, Israel's minister for Diaspora affairs begins his lecture about Israeli-Palestinian relations. Needless to say, he recycles his government's familiar slogans: no negotiations with preconditions, no right of return, no dividing Jerusalem, and a few other no's.

"Have you considered any possibilities besides political ones for resolving the conflict?" I ask.

"What do you have in mind?"

"Economic agreements. You could set up a deal that requires both sides to meet a set of predetermined conditions that will stabilize the Palestinian Authority's economic infrastructure without damaging the Israeli economy. That way, the Palestinians will have something to lose – and they won't want to lose. They'll discover that living with abundance is much more comfortable, and much more interesting. After they can prove the viability of economic agreements, once mutual trust has been built, you can move on to political agreements. For an initiative like this, I would make an initial donation of, say, twenty million dollars, and I would spearhead an effort to raise even more funds further on. I'd help the Palestinians, say, build a modern commercial port in Gaza, and open up an Olympia U.S.-Ashdod-Gaza-Africa line. As you see, I'm not trying to undermine the Israeli ports, even though my feelings about their unions are no secret."

"Well, that's certainly an interesting approach," the minister responds dismissively. I know that his reaction is meant to provoke me, but I don't lose my cool, probably because of Richard's presence and the looks he's directing towards me.

"I'm glad you find my approach interesting," I say. "When can I transfer the twenty million dollars?" I can hear people chuckling. The minister for Diaspora affairs mutters something under his breath; he doesn't know what to say beyond the catchphrases he'd been spoon-fed before coming here, and at the moment, none of them can help him. "Mister Minister," I add, "it's not my intention to embarrass or amuse. It's just that sometimes I wonder if you're actually trying to maintain the status quo, for whatever reason. If you want to keep getting money from us corporate heirs, though, you'll have to make some serious strides. I'll be watching, I promise."

Ed Leibowitz thanks the minister and invites us to break into discussion groups. Suddenly, I'm cornered by the spokesperson for the Maine Democratic Party, who tells me that the chairman of the Democratic National Committee wants to meet with me in New York next week. The moment the words are out of his mouth, he disappears, almost as if to make sure I don't have a chance to refuse. While the rest of the guests disperse into their different groups, I have meetings with various political leaders, which were scheduled in advance. Afterwards, I plug in my earbuds and go for a run along the beach with rap songs playing in my ear.

Dinner is served on the lawn, under a big white tent. Outside the tent, huge cuts of beef are sizzling on grills. When the meat is done, it is sliced and carried to the buffet. Inside the tent are large, square wooden tables. There's some Irish music playing in the background. Richard is standing next to one of the tables, his hands in his pockets, nonchalantly watching the proceedings. I can't take my eyes off him. When he sees me, he smiles, and I walk over.

"We haven't had a chance to speak today," I observe.

"That's true," Richard says, continuing to watch what's happening in the tent.

"It's boring here."

"Very."

"Do you want to come up to my room?" I immediately regret my crudeness and my urgency. I can see that he wants to come, but he's still confused. "Even just to talk," I add. Richard nods.

But the minute the door closes behind us, it is Richard who takes my face in his hands and starts kissing me. He leads me to the edge of the bed, and I take off my shirt; then I reach under his shirt and gently lift it over his head. My hands glide over his chest and his hips, then back to his chest where I can feel his heart beating. I tear my lips away from his, stand up to remove my pants, reach out to Richard and pull him up from the bed. He takes off his pants, and we stand, pressed against each other. As the experienced one, I take it upon myself to take the lead.

I lay Richard down on the bed, lie down next to him, and stroke his chest. He returns my caress and we kiss again, fondling each other – the way I used to back when I was younger, before sex had become the technical, even exploitative thing that it had turned into for me over the years. After a while, I go down on him, surprised by the intensity of my excitement, and when he comes, I immediately do too. I rest my head on his chest and gaze at his face. His eyes are closed.

Richard has to leave for Manhattan early the next morning – he has some business in the city. When I wake up, he's already in the shower; I lie back down, somewhat perplexed. Never before have I allowed a man to stay the night. I watch him as he gets out of the shower, a towel wrapped around his lower body. He looks at me, and when he sees that I'm awake, he drops the towel, a beguiling expression on his face. But before I can do anything about it, he's quickly getting dressed.

I get up, naked, and although I haven't even brushed my teeth yet, I find myself kissing him again. Afterwards, he takes his wallet and cell phone from the dresser and walks towards the door. We agree to meet at the front entrance of the hotel in half an hour.

As I'm walking towards the hotel entrance, I feel a hand grasp my shoulder. Richard pulls me into one of the corridors. The expression on his face tells me he's scared and a little confused. I smile. It's hard for us to say goodbye.

"I'm going back to Manhattan tomorrow," I say. "Should we meet up in the evening?" Richard nods.

When we reach the entrance, we shake hands like a couple of pals. Richard walks towards the door. When he gets there, he turns around and waves goodbye. I wave back, and the next thing I know, he's gone.

CHAPTER 4

Manhattan, Late May

Another week begins. The office workers greet me as they do every morning. They have no idea that after the weekend I had with Richard, I am no longer the same person I was before.

"What will today bring me?" I ask Alexandra, smiling.

"I understand Maine was a success."

"Much better than expected."

"You're going to have two big meetings about the trade routes to China, Japan, and Korea. I have also scheduled a meeting for you with Adam, who will be able to give you a preliminary overview before the meetings." And just like that, she is back to managing my day, just like she has always done. I thank her, enter my office, and begin planning for the roundtable discussion I have coordinated with potential business partners from the water and agriculture fields, hoping to promote my business in Africa. A thought occurs to me: I can invite Richard to the meeting. I debate whether or not to text him and offer him a spot at the meeting but decide to leave it for another time.

"Turn your thoughts elsewhere," Judith would surely say. "When you think about Richard, you feed energy and information to him, and then he won't notice your absence."

The Angolan ambassador to the United States could be a wonderful distraction, I think to myself; so could Israel's Cabinet Secretary, or the chairman of the Agricultural Wastewater Reclamation Company, or even the chairman of the Democratic National Convention, for that matter.

"Try to schedule a call for me with the chairman of Israel's Agricultural Wastewater Reclamation Company," I ask Alexandra over the intercom. "Ask Arik for the contact details."

I need to figure out the best way to conduct my business in Africa, the right formula that will be profitable for Olympia and will give me control over the continent while helping its people develop more suitable sources of water for drinking and for agriculture.

About an hour later, I enter the conference room. The large screen in the middle of the wall shows me the Israeli side getting ready for the meeting. I enjoy watching them when they aren't aware that I am there, and I know enough Hebrew to understand what they are saying.

At long last, a handsome, light-haired man sits down in the large chair at the head of the table facing the screen. I sit up and straighten my jacket and tie. "Hello, Mr. Herman," I say. "Thank you for your quick response."

"With pleasure," he replies, inquiring whether I come from the well-known Gold family.

"There are so many branches of the Gold family; I hope we're talking about the same branch," I respond.

His body language tells me he is a matter-of-fact, decent man who I can definitely do business with.

"I am the owner of Olympia, the largest shipping company in the United States. Naturally, my ships also visit ports in Africa. In addition to my business, I've decided to move forward with a project that will attempt to solve the water crisis in West Africa, to improve the quality of life for the people living there. I won't hide the fact that my main motivation here is business, and that is why I wanted to have infrastructure officials from all over the world sit around a table together to formulate a plan for cooperation. According to my data, the State of Israel is the world's leader in wastewater reclamation, and most of this reclamation work is done by your company. I would like you to join the roundtable forum that I have put together, along with global entrepreneurs, leading companies in water technology, and some of Olympia's clients who supply fertilizers and grains to Africa along the U.S.-Africa shipping route."

"That's incredible," Herman says. "Just this morning, I had a meeting about our global business development. Africa is one of the business goals we set at that meeting. We are trying to promote projects in Uganda, South Sudan, Angola, Ghana, and other countries that have a great deal of business potential."

"At this stage, I plan to invest in West African countries that have seaports," I say. "I am willing to hear about projects in other countries in the continent; maybe I'll find potential to build land ports."

"Sounds interesting," Herman says.

"Are you authorized to work abroad, unrestricted?" I ask.

"There are some regulatory restrictions about the scope of activity and investment abroad, but I am sure it can all be dealt with," he replies, and we end our conversation warmly, agreeing to meet as soon as possible in order to draft an outline for our cooperation.

"Get me Angola's ambassador to the U.S.," I tell Alexandra.

When we speak, he invites me to visit Angola again. I accept the invitation and promise to move forward with our plan.

My phone beeps, announcing a text message, and this catches my attention. It's Richard. My distractions had kept me so occupied that I hadn't thought about him for some time, and in one moment he comes back and fills me with excitement and worry. I open the message and brace myself, ready for anything.

"A Holocaust memorial is being dedicated today," he writes, **"and I'm the main donor. It was my first donation. I'd like you to be there with me.**

I respond: **I need to teach you what you should be donating for…I'll be there.**

Richard: **Four o'clock, in the garden of the Jewish Museum.**

Me: **I can't wait.**

★

I walk up Fifth Avenue towards the Jewish Museum, which is built like a French castle, and I take a minute to enjoy the fresh air while trying to organize my thoughts. I see Richard from afar. He is speaking with three older men. People start taking their seats in the brown wooden chairs arranged on the museum's large, shaded garden. The monument, designed to look like a ship, stands at the center of the garden, and for a moment I think Richard must have chosen the ship design for me. I walk over and signal to him that I've arrived. He excuses himself from his conversation and walks over to me. We shake hands, smile awkwardly, look down in embarrassment, and laugh. No one here knows our secret.

"Mr. Silverman, with your permission, we'd like to begin," the ceremony director tells him, and we go towards the stage. An usher guides me to a reserved seat in one of the front rows while Richard is seated at the dais for VIPs. One by one, the speakers go up to the podium and say their piece, and finally Richard is invited up. He glances at me and begins to speak.

"Today is very important to me," he says. "I am dedicating a monument in memory of my father, Moses Silverman, a Holocaust survivor, who lived through four years of the horrors of the Holocaust in Austria, immigrated to Israel as a sworn member of the Beitar movement, fought in the War of Independence, and ultimately came to America without a penny to his name, to be with relatives. When my father arrived in New York, he started working as a sailor for the Olympia shipping company. As co-designer of this monument, I wanted it to be built in the shape of a ship, since it symbolizes for me the adherence to a goal, correct navigation, courage, and foresight, qualities that can withstand the difficult situations that life hands you."

Richard pauses a moment and takes a deep breath. He's moved by the occasion and the words about his father. I am also moved by his mentioning the company that my father founded, which enabled his father to rebuild his life after the Holocaust.

"Today, I am commemorating my father, who passed away from serious illness after having dedicated the majority of his life to working in the sea. He loved the sea, and the ships were his second home, if not his first."

When the ceremony is over, we leave together, walking, our hands fluttering towards each other's again and again. We cross Central Park, walking quietly, talking about the weekend in Maine, but neither of us says what's truly on our minds. When the conversation drifts towards more intimate topics, we both escape to silence. It's not a threatening silence, though, and it seems to actually indicate more than anything else the brave intimacy that we have managed to create so quickly and naturally.

In the middle of the park, an amateur baseball game starts to pick up. We buy a couple hot dogs and a Coke and sit, amused, on the makeshift stands. Our legs rub against each other's. When the game starts, we decide to support the team that's already behind.

"Should we buy the team if they win?" Richard asks.

"I really need to teach you about your purchases and donations. It's getting worse and worse," I say.

We cheer when "our" runner makes a complete run of the field, even though our team is losing 8 to 2. After about an hour we decide to leave. Our need to touch one another is way too strong, and I invite Richard to my place.

At the entrance to my building, the doorman greets me happily. "Hello, Mr. Gold," he says, and I respond with a smile. We wait for the elevator. Richard leans against the wall facing me, his hands in his pockets, and he doesn't take his eyes off me. "You are devastatingly handsome," he says suddenly. "If you're brave enough to come out of the closet, you'll be the most wanted man in New York, or probably the entire world." He gives me a kind-hearted smile.

"After you," I respond, and we enter the elevator. I lead Richard toward the balcony so he can see the view of Manhattan. The look on his face reminds me of how amazed I felt the first time I went out on this balcony myself. I put my hand on his shoulder and start caressing him. He pulls me close, and we kiss. For the first time in my life, I don't care if anyone sees, and after a few long minutes, we finally manage to pull apart and go inside.

I lead him to my bedroom and undress him. Unlike last time, he takes the lead. He lays me down on the bed, undresses me, pleasures me, and I once again find myself so overtaken with passion that I can't stop myself. As soon as I come, it's Richard's turn. When we are done, we lie down on the bed spooning, with my back against his chest, and we fall asleep.

"Who's the hottie walking around here at this hour?" Richard asks me.

"That's Maria," I answer, "my housekeeper. She comes every morning to organize whatever I need. Did she see you? Like this? Shirtless and in your underwear?"

"She seems lovely," Richard says.

"She really is lovely," I say. "She raised me since I was a small boy in Connecticut. She's the closest thing I have to family."

"I'm going home to get myself together," he says. "I have a long day ahead. Can we get lunch together?"

"I'll make the time," I tell him, and I walk him out to the elevator.

When we say goodbye, I go back inside and see Maria. She winks at me, and I wink back.

An hour later, Arthur drops me off at Rockefeller Center. I sit in my office feeling a sense of inner peace, a feeling I've never had before, and I realize that this is what it must feel like to be happy. Maybe my time has finally come, maybe Mother was right to say patience pays off.

There's a knock on my door. Jessica enters.

"Jessica, my darling," I say, as I get up to greet her, "what a pleasure to start the morning with you."

"Tom," she says with a hint of suspicion, "it's a pleasure to see you like this, too. What's the reason for your wonderful mood this morning?"

"Everything is wonderful," I respond, and even though for the first time I want to tell her all about Richard, I panic and stop myself. Maria was enough for me this morning. But I can't help but speak about Richard. "I am moving ahead with the initiative in West Africa. During the meetings of the Corporate Heirs, I met a successful young entrepreneur. He did not inherit an empire but he built one himself, and now, at the age of 38, he is a millionaire in his own right."

"To gain control of a family empire and quadruple its profits," Jessica cuts me off, "is just as big a challenge as starting a new empire. Don't you forget that, Tom. And don't waste your time with that kind of thinking. You are a creative businessman, and I am sure that with your skills, you'd be able to start your own business or lead processes that could impact all of humanity, if that's the direction you choose."

"What would I do without you? I'm so lucky that you are here to remind me of all this. Still, I'm sure Richard will help me; I feel it. Our connection, our understanding of each other, he is a simple and wonderful man, with a simplicity that comes from within, with a lot of power." I suddenly fall silent, startled that I had let myself get so carried away, and I buzz Alexandra on the intercom, "Aren't you going to offer Jessica anything to drink?" I ask too loudly, and at the same time, I am repeating to myself, *Calm down, Tom. Calm down, Tom. Calm down, Tom.*

"Jessica, would you like something to drink?" Alexandra asks after entering my office.

"Cappuccino," Jessica answers.

"Order us some small sandwiches as well," I say.

These distractions help calm me down.

"I have never heard you speak like this about any of your partners," Jessica says after Alexandra leaves the room. "I understand that he is trustworthy in business. What exactly does he do?"

"He works in water technology. He started an incubator in Chicago for startups in that field. He chooses the companies and when they finish developing their technologies, he sells them at a profit and receives royalties." I get up from my chair and start pacing the room, trying to organize my thoughts.

"I'm thinking about a joint venture for Richard and Olympia to start working together. A profitable initiative that will also help solve the food and water crisis in West Africa."

"Wonderful," Jessica says. "By the way, I can sense something personal when you speak about him, and I haven't heard you do this before in business. As always, Tom, you surprise me. I am actually happy that you exposed this side of yourself to me."

Alexandra enters the room holding a tray with coffee mugs and sandwiches. Afterwards, Jessica and I go over the week that passed, and when we are done, I lead her to the entrance floor. The elevator doors open, and I see Richard waiting for me next to the café. We walk over to him.

"Jessica, this is Richard Silverman."

"Pleased to meet you," Jessica says. "I have heard a lot of good things about you today."

"How nice," Richard says with a smile. We say goodbye to Jessica, sit down at my usual table, and order lunch.

That evening, Richard comes over to my place and we sit on the balcony, sipping whiskey and smoking cigars. I excuse myself, go inside, and come back out with an old folder.

"I brought you something," I say, and I hand him the file that has grown yellow with years.

"What is it?" he asks.

"Your father's personal file from Olympia," I say. "I found it in the company archives. It lists every voyage by Moses Silverman on board Olympia's ships, until he came to dry land." Richard's fingers quiver a bit as he opens the file. There is a picture of his father glued to the first page. Richard gently passes his finger over the picture. "I bet this was taken right after he came to America," Richard says with emotion. "His first picture here."

Together, we read what is written on the next page, and tears stream from Richard's eyes.

"This was the first time he set sail for the company," I say, "on board the Gold Lady, a cargo ship that brought goods to Liberia."

Richard's emotions are contagious, and I find myself wiping some tears away from my own eyes as well. We read it all, page by page, learning about the journeys he took over the twenty years that he sailed for the company. We peruse the yellowed pages in a silence that stems from the immense intimacy of the moment. When we are done, Richard closes the file and hands it back to me.

"No," I say, "it's yours."

He stands up, hugs me, and thanks me again and again for the gesture. We then order something to eat and continue our evening together.

In the morning, I wake up and snuggle into Richard's arms. I take advantage of his deep sleep to gently pull the blanket away from him and study him – his face, his body – and thank the universe for this gift that was sent to me. I get up from the bed, cover him back up, walk on tiptoe to my study, and begin sending emails with tasks to my team.

"Good morning, dear Tom," Maria greets me. I say "hi," and signal to her that Richard is asleep in my room, and wink. Once he wakes up, I hear him speaking with Maria in the kitchen.

"Would you like something to eat?"

"I'd love exactly whatever it is you're making for Tommy."

"Right away," Maria says. "Toast with butter and cherry jam, and black coffee."

We sit at the kitchen island, eating and reading the New York Times. Richard scans the sports section, and I check whether the press release my spokesperson issued about Olympia's expansion plans has made it into the news.

"I'm going to London next week," Richard tells me. "Would you join me?" He explains that he is going to look into the possibility of selling water technology to the United Kingdom. "Some of the time, I'll be busy," he says, "but we'll be able to find time for fun, too."

"London is my second favorite city in the world, after Manhattan," I say. "I haven't been there in a long time, and now I see that I have no choice but to be in London right when the Kingdom needs advanced water technologies." We laugh, and then finalize the details of our first trip abroad together.

CHAPTER 5

London, England, Early June

A pleasant summer morning slowly wraps itself around Manhattan. My black Jaguar, driven by Arthur, speeds towards Tribeca to pick Richard up on our way to JFK Airport. He gets in and we sit next to each other in the back seat. Richard places his hand on my knee, and I rest my head on his shoulder.

Arthur glances at us from time to time through the rearview mirror. I trust him. Shalom Hanoch is playing over the stereo. I pour us some fine cognac and we clink our glasses. This is my first time flying abroad with a boyfriend. Until now, I've only flown for business or political purposes, or as part of a delegation. And I've also flown to Berlin to have some quickies far from Manhattan. We'll be far from Manhattan on this trip, too, and we'll be able to be together without worrying about bumping into anyone we know.

For the first time in my life, I am feeling cautiously optimistic that in the battle being waged between my inner truth and my family's conservative views, I might actually win, and the mere thought fills me with a sense of immense liberation.

Arthur stops at the entrance to the airport, and we enter the terminal. Our hands grasp for a moment, and immediately separate.

"I have sort of a tradition of buying my mom and sister perfume whenever I travel abroad," Richard says.

"I never bring my family gifts when I travel, but maybe the time has come to start," I say, following him. Richard buys large packages of Juicy Couture perfume, and I follow suit.

We board the plane and take our seats in first class. Once the plane takes off and we finish our lunch, Richard falls asleep, giving me some time to look at him and have fun thinking about how sometimes, dreams really do come true.

After landing at London Heathrow Airport, we go outside to catch a cab.

"The Four Seasons on Park Lane," I tell the driver. We sit in the back and look at each other. We're in a safe space now; we can start our "freedom tour" here in the cab. But a quick glance at the driver tells us he's a religious Muslim, so we control ourselves out of respect.

English baroque music is playing in the hotel lobby. The clerk at reception smiles at us.

"Your rooms are ready," she says, handing us keys to two separate suites – with a connecting door between the two – overlooking the park. Even though we are far from home, we were too nervous to make the reservation as a couple.

The next morning, we take the elevator down to breakfast in the garden terrace. I feel like the guests entering the elevator from other floors are staring at us. I know we look good, but I'm beginning to think that the aura that surrounded Richard the first time I saw him is contagious and has attached itself to me too. For a moment, our eyes meet. Richard lowers his head, his arms folded, as he tries to keep himself from laughing, but I can't help it and I drag him into a laughing fit with me.

When breakfast is over, we part ways. Richard leaves for his meetings, and I decide to walk the streets of London. I had considered offering to accompany Richard to his meetings, but I remembered what Judith said: "A good relationship is based on fulfillment of the terms of the contract, which include mutual devotion and loyalty. An attempt to control the other person stems from fear of abandonment or rejection, which leads to feelings of suffocation and stress. Positive thinking – containing love, trust, joy, and pleasure – creates a sense of choosing the relationship rather than searching for proof of love in order to feel safe." I once again understand how my fear of rejection and abandonment controls my common sense, and I decide to release Richard, or rather, to trust myself and recognize that I am worthy of love. How strange. As soon as I let go, Richard stares at me inquisitively.

"Maybe you should come with me?" he asks.

"Not this time," I answer.

I walk outside to Park Lane, towards Hyde Park Corner. Hyde Park stretched out in front of me, green and clean, its paths already crowded with people. I enter the station and board the Piccadilly Line towards Covent Garden. I spend an hour wandering aimlessly among the stalls and boutique shops, thinking about life. I run a vast empire, and the entire world presents me with business opportunities. But looking at these merchants whose entire world starts and stops at their stalls, for a moment I can't help but think that their lives seem far more fulfilling than mine. The sweet smell of baked potato with cream and mushrooms draws me towards a stall in one of the corners. I order one, along with a beer, sit down on a concrete bench, soak up the sun's rays, and enjoy the simplicity of my first day in London, without any commitments – business, social, or political – other than my commitment to Richard.

In the afternoon, I return to the hotel and get ready for our date at the Royal Opera House, where Puccini's "Tosca" will be performed in the evening. I decide to surprise Richard and put on my tuxedo and a black bow tie, as if I were part of Britain's high society. He sees me from afar, adjusts his jacket, raises his right arm, and gestures for me to walk arm-in-arm with him. We enter the Royal Opera House happy and still entwined, and we take our seats in the private box we reserved. Soon, we're holding hands, and I can't tell whether I'm moved by the music, by the libretto story, or by our story, mine and Richard's, which brings tears to my eyes.

Once the thunderous applause subsides, we leave the Opera House and wander around SoHo holding hands. We sit at one of the small tables on the sidewalk in front of a quaint pub. We drink draft beer, clinking our large glasses again and again, smoke cigars – me in my tux and Richard in his fine business suit – and we seem a tad out of place in the simple pub setting. I can feel a lot of attention on us from passers-by, but right now, perhaps for the first time in my life, I don't care what they think about me.

By the time we are back at the hotel, we are drunk, and I find myself sitting on the couch as Richard kneels before me, reaching his right hand forward as he rests his left hand on his heart, and sings – in what I can only assume is Italian – parts of the opera we had just seen. When he is done, he draws us a bubble bath, strips down, and invites me in with him.

I take off my clothes and get in, but my long legs make it hard for me to find a comfortable position. Richard pulls me towards him so that I'm sitting in his lap, with my back against his chest. He wraps his arms around my stomach and rests his chin on my shoulder. "When did you realize that you were attracted to men?" Richard asks me after a long but pleasant silence.

"It wasn't something I needed to realize," I respond. "I always knew. Even when I was a little boy, I was never interested in girls. When I was six years old, my father caught me kissing the neighbor's son. I was only a little kid, but my father lost it. He took off his belt and beat me with it like ten times, all the while yelling that I am never to kiss a boy ever again." I get a bit choked up, and Richard hugs me tighter. "I've never told anyone that, other than my psychologist," I say in a trembling voice, and I quickly apologize.

"It's fine," Richard says, and holds me tighter.

"Several years passed in quiet after that. I swore to myself that I would never kiss another boy. I wanted to please my father, and it wasn't too hard at that age. But when I was 12, I fell in love. His name was Sean. He was in my grade, but we'd only met on a school trip. Later, we found out that his father had some senior job at Olympia. He was short and handsome, and even then, he had a unique style. During the trip, we immediately became friends, but it was clear this wasn't just friendship. There was something more. Later, a few days after we returned to school, after Biology class, I found him sitting on the back stairway in the school. He asked me to sit next to him and he lit a cigarette for us to share. After a long puff, he let out some words that had me completely amazed. 'For me, everything is just meaningless when I see girls,' he said, and I immediately knew what he was talking about. So, when I was 12 years old, I figured out, meaning, I recognized, even though I didn't want to, that I was attracted to boys. Next thing I knew, I was kissing Sean.

"I was afraid someone would see us, so I told him he should come over to my house after school. I waited with bated breath for school to end. We used the back entrance to the house, and I took him to our garage because I was nervous that if we went to my room, Maria or one of my parents might enter. We kept the lights off, so no one would know we were inside. We were a bit scared but we both wanted it so badly, so we started making out. We did the same thing the next day, and the day after that. Then it was the weekend, and Sean came over again. We couldn't stop ourselves, and even though my parents and siblings were home, we snuck out to the garage. Then, while we were in the middle of making out, my father opened the door. When he walked inside, the light from outside fell right on us. There was a look of dread on his face, and he walked out without a word. Since then, he has been looking at me with that same look of contempt and revulsion, and that is how he looks at me to this day."

"So how do you explain the fact that your father handed control of Olympia over to you?" Richard asks.

"It suited him from a business perspective. For him, the company has absolutely nothing to do with emotions. Maybe he thought that this would also help him turn me into a real man, somehow." There is a long silence in the bathroom. "And you?" I finally ask. "How do you explain the fact that in your late thirties, you suddenly discovered that you're attracted to a man?"

"It's hard to explain," Richard replies. "There were always only women in my life. I was with one girl for six years, in Chicago, but I didn't really love her. There have been men I have met throughout my life, who I knew I was attracted to. It wasn't anything special. Or sometimes, in the changing room at the swimming pool, for example, I'd find myself looking at some men with interest. But I told myself it was just curiosity, nothing more. When I met you at The Plaza, it was something totally different. I felt a very intense longing that I had never felt towards any woman in my life. And that's it. You know the rest of the story."

Richard tightens his embrace again. My body surrenders to him and I snuggle up inside his arms. The bathwater has already cooled, so Richard turns on the hot water faucet and we warm back up.

"What would your father have said about this?" I ask.

"He's definitely turning over in his grave right now," Richard responds, and we crack up.

"So your father was tough, like mine?" I ask.

"Yes, in his own way. They actually do seem similar. Their families went through the Holocaust, went to America without anything, and Olympia was their entire world. For many years, I thought that he was simply a man who was stuck in one job all his life. It was only later that I understood I was mistaken, that he had worked for a big company, loved what he did, saw the world, learned languages, understood what made people tick, moved up in the company, and even got a management position. Maybe, if he hadn't died, he would have climbed even higher."

"I would have appointed him CEO," I say.

Richard smiles. "He was very closed off. The Holocaust never left him. My mother was also a Holocaust survivor. They loved each other, but it wasn't easy for them together. I mean, as long as he was out sailing, they actually lived well," he smiles. "They dated for a really short time before they got married, and then my dad went back to sailing, so they never really lived a shared life. But when he stopped sailing, they suddenly needed to deal with the routine of everyday life. They fought a lot.

"My mother would have these crazy outbursts and mood swings. One minute she'd be laughing and the next she'd be yelling. We always needed to do whatever she wanted. I think her brain was short circuiting, and I wouldn't be surprised if even back then, in her early forties, her Alzheimer's was beginning to take root. She took care of everything for us, made sure we got a good education, that we always had whatever we needed. That much is true. But she didn't really function as a mother, and when my father passed away, her world fell apart. Suddenly, she was all on her own, without a husband, without a job. What's good is that he left her money and property, so she didn't have to worry about those things, but she had her anxieties. She always felt that my father's family discriminated against her, both in terms of how they treated her and also regarding money. She had complaints, and ultimately, she cut them off from any contact with me and my sister. I haven't seen them for over twenty years, and we only recently got back in touch."

"Why?" I ask.

"I realized that the truth is always somewhere in the middle, and that they also have their own truth. Ever since my father died, I've really been identifying with all the difficulties my mother had to deal with. My sister left Chicago at a very young age, and I stayed to live close to my mother, who wanted to keep me to herself so she wouldn't be alone. I was influenced by her worldview, her paranoia, her fears and anxieties that she had after everything she went through during the Holocaust. And despite it all, she was a good mother. Now I understand that a lot of her behavioral problems stemmed not only from her PTSD from the Holocaust, but also from the slow degeneration of her brain, and so I forgive her."

"Are you in touch with your sister?"

"Me and my sister? Yeah. Are you in touch with your siblings?"

"Yeah. We're in touch. They're both doctors. Diana is a pediatrician and Benjamin is an OB-GYN. They're both married with children and they both live near my parents. They have a good relationship with my parents, much better than mine. I always feel like an outsider when the family gets together. But all in all, we love and respect each other."

"But let's say you have some sort of problem. Could you pick up the phone and call them, and know that you can trust them?"

"I've never tried. I'm used to only trusting myself."

Richard smiles to himself.

"It turns out you and I are a bit alike."

"Do you realize you have completely stolen my heart?!" I say after a short silence.

"What we have here, this is fate," Richard replies.

We fall silent again, and shortly after that, we decide to get out of the bath.

"Do you know the story of King Richard the First of England and his mother?" I suddenly ask when we're toweling off.

"No."

"I'll tell you about it some other time."

In the morning, we make love. After last night, we feel closer and even more intimate with each other. We order English breakfast and enjoy fried eggs and bacon, pastries, butter, and French cheeses. We sip our coffee and read the morning paper. As usual, I'm looking for news about Israel, my little country in the Middle East.

"What's happening today?" Richard asks.

"When you finish your meetings, text me. I want to take you on a journey in the footsteps of King Richard the First.

"And his mother," Richard adds.

"Yes of course, and his mother."

When Richard leaves the suite, I turn on my laptop. I haven't touched it since I arrived in London, and I force myself not to be tempted by the countless emails that I'm sure are awaiting me. I Google "Richard the First," because I do remember that there was some story with his mother, but I don't actually remember the details. I then get ready to leave. I text Richard: **Two o'clock at the House of Lords**, and then make my way to the Portobello Market. I wander around the stalls and shops. At the top of the street, just after Westbourne, at the entrance to a covered passageway, there is a sign that says, "Licensed Dealers in Art and Antiquities." I have found what I'm looking for, and I go inside.

Later, I buy a rum cake at Gail's Bakery and sit on the curb, watching a street performance of a priest and a nun meeting for the first time and trying to figure out how they can make love without actually telling each other that they want to. The witty dialog has me cracking up. When the large clock in the square grabs my attention, I'm pleased to see that it is almost time for me to meet up with Richard. I hurry to catch a cab and manage to get to the House of Lords only a little bit late. Richard is already there. We walk towards each other and share a long, brave embrace, and it feels like the entire world is standing still. I have never been hugged like this by anyone in my entire life.

I hold out my hand to Richard, and he places his in mine. "Close your eyes," I tell him, and I lead him along the courtyard of the House of Lords – which we got special entry to thanks to my connections – until we reach a statue of King Richard the First. Once there, I let Richard open his eyes.

"This is a statue of Richard the First, King of England, also known as Richard the Lionheart," I say. "He was given that nickname because of his bravery on the battlefield. You and he are similar in a number of ways."

"Oh, I've heard about Richard the Lionheart," Richard says.

I shush him and continue.

"Like you, he was a good, kind, and beloved man. They say that on his way back to England from the Crusades, his ship sank, and spies working for the Austrian Duke Leopold captured him and handed him over to the German Emperor Heinrich the Sixth. The emperor asked England for a ransom of one hundred thousand pounds sterling. He was so beloved that the entire nation rallied together to pay the ransom. He is considered a brave and benevolent king, a true nobleman, and you, my love Richard, are also a true nobleman. And so, I find it fitting to give you," I say, playing with a ceremonious tone, "on this special occasion, the pin of the Lionheart." I open an elegant box and take out the antique golden pin that I bought this morning, and I put it on the lapel of Richard's jacket.

"Wait a second," Richard says after thanking me for the pin. "What's the story with his mother?"

"As it turns out, my love, the mother of Richard the First, King of England, was also a dominant figure in his life. His parents, Eleanor of Aquitaine and Henry the Second, separated when he was a little boy, and like you, he stayed with his mother, who was kept as a prisoner of his father's for many years. They say that Richard was her consolation prize."

I switch over to a British accent. "But now the plot thickens, listen carefully. They say that Richard the First, King of England, the one and only, was bisexual. And that he had a gay relationship with Philip the Second, King of France."

Richard gasps and claps, as I bow before him. From there, we walk to the Victoria Tower, all around the gardens. I take a blanket out of my backpack, and we lay down to rest.

"You've thought of everything," Richard says.

"I am known for my attention to detail, and I hope I've made this summer afternoon in London nice for you," I respond.

"You've gone above and beyond," Richard says right as a waiter appears out of nowhere in a very fancy uniform. Without saying a word, he spreads out a white tablecloth, and puts down a bottle of champagne, two glasses, a bowl of strawberries, and a bowl of chocolates.

Richard looks at me in disbelief. We sit on the blanket sipping champagne and eating strawberries. He looks up at the sky and the treetops with a smile of utter happiness on his face, and I think to myself that I have never felt this sense of belonging before.

"Thank you for a wonderful afternoon," Richard suddenly says. "I love you and I am in love with you, Tommy. I think you're amazing. You make me laugh and you are one of a kind. A limited edition." He thinks for a moment. "No, not a limited edition. A rare edition, with only one copy left, and I am the one who's lucky enough to have it."

"I love you too," I say. "Very much, my Richard the First."

It is our last morning in London. Richard has left for his meetings, and we've arranged to meet up in Piccadilly Square in the early afternoon. In the meantime, I leisurely read the morning papers and find out that my friend Arik Gonen, Israel's Cabinet Secretary, is considering resigning in order to run in the next Knesset elections. I text him, telling him he should join my water business ventures.

You are needed more in politics, he replies, and he invites me to join the Israeli delegation that will be accompanying the President of the United States on his upcoming visit to Israel. I decide not to respond to his message, but this only strengthens the temptation to check my hundreds of emails.

I tell myself I'll be back in Manhattan tomorrow and I should probably start reconnecting with the world after the past few days. I hurriedly skim the subject lines and the names of their senders.

My eyes spot an email sent by the chairman of the Democratic National Party. "We want you back as a political activist in the party," Bill Black wrote. "Only talented young people of virtue can become the chairman of the Democratic party in New York City at such a young age, while also doing excellent work at their job. Very few succeed in carrying out the tasks that the party gives them, and you did it with flying colors. It is so rare to be able to deliver the party's reaction speech, as you did when the Republican president gave his famous speech after the terror attack at the beginning of the millennium. We need your mind and your soul now," he wrote. After some brief deliberation, I decide to wait until I'm back in New York to read the entire message. I must admit, it is nice to know that both the chairman of the Democratic National Party and the Cabinet Secretary in Israel had the same message for me on the same day. I close my laptop, go out to the balcony, look over at the park, light a cigar, and smile to myself, excited for what awaits Richard and me later today.

"The Bathhouses of London" reads the sign leading to a side road, and from there to a mysterious nineteenth century castle that holds the most luxurious sauna in London for the gay community.

"You rented out a private sauna and spa?" Richard asks. I just smile, confident that with my Richard, my boyfriend and best friend, there is nothing I can't do.

"Come," I say, and we walk through a special private entrance that leads straight to a tucked-away bar. Richard is taking in the impressive structure, reminiscent of a French Gothic castle. I am also feeling the splendor and power of this place, with its large columns, ornamented arches, and enchanting lighting. It's all working together to sweep me away into my fantasy. In a side stall, next to a small table lit by candles and a small wall lamp, there is a picture of an evil sorcerer standing completely naked. Richard and I sip the house cocktail and look at each other with penetrating eyes.

"Yes," I say, knowing exactly what Richard is thinking. When our host arrives, wearing nothing at all, I hold Richard's hand and the three of us walk to the private room I reserved. "Enjoy," the host says, leaving us alone. I go over to Richard, take off his clothes, undress myself, and kiss him lovingly and tenderly. Then I open the door, which leads right to the steam room where dozens of gay couples, now including Richard and me, are having sex.

CHAPTER 6
Manhattan, Mid-June

A rthur picks us up from the airport. The black Jaguar enters Manhattan and Richard suggests we go to his place. I am buzzing with excitement. I follow him in what I would almost describe as a sort of fear accompanied by joy and happiness, longing with my entire being to finally see my love's private space. Like me, he also has a doorman who greats us, and an elevator attendant who leads us up to the seventh floor. The apartment door opens, and we enter an enormous living room. A large window in the middle of the wall looks out onto the street. There is a long, low bookcase full of books next to two brown, legless armchairs with corrugated backs. When I walk over to the chairs, I can tell that they are not made of wood, but some other material I don't recognize.

"Can I sit down?" I ask.

"Of course," Richard says. "In fact, I insist."

I sit down on one of the armchairs, sink in, and it feels like the chair is hugging me.

"Who designed these chairs?"

"I ordered them myself," he says. "I drew up a hybrid design of two armchairs I saw at an exhibit."

I look out at Manhattan through the window, and I quickly doze off. The smell of something cooking wakes me. I go to the kitchen, where I find Richard standing by the stove with an apron tied around his waist.

"So do you cook," I ask, "or do you also have a Maria who prepares everything for you in advance?"

He glances back, smiling. "I don't have an anyone, and I'm glad you're awake. The food's ready. American Vichyssoise soup and pasta in olive oil and squid sauce. And yes, I cook. I've been told I cook well, but I don't really get a lot of opportunities to cook."

We sit down and begin eating. He really is a great cook. I compliment him. He thanks me and I compliment him again. "It's nothing," he says, embarrassed.

We finish our soup and Richard serves the pasta. "My parents usually invite friends to their vacation home in the Hamptons," I say, after complimenting the food once again. I pause for a moment. "Would you like to come with me? I can introduce you as my business partner for the water venture in Africa, an entrepreneur from Chicago who's in Manhattan on business for the week. That way we can spend the weekend together. It will be much easier for me to get through it if you're there with me."

"Since when do you go to family events like that?"

"I usually don't, but I promised my mom I'd come this time. She's pressured me into it. It's like she wants me to be near her this weekend, at any cost. If it feels like too much and you can't come, that's fine," I add, because the look on his face shows me that he is really weighing his words.

"I would actually love to meet your parents," Richard says, "but I don't love the idea of doing it as a lie, with you introducing me as your business partner. I don't want us to need to pretend the whole time."

"So how would you want to do it?" I ask, somewhat reproachfully.

He looks at me in silence and says, "That's it? You're ready to come out to the world and declare that you're gay?"

"Not yet. But it's only for the weekend and I promise it won't be too hard. I've been doing it for years. Some of the time we really will pretend," I say, trying to organize my thoughts, hardly believing that I'm actually trying to convince Richard to meet my parents, "but other times, we'll just be together, just the two of us.

We can go down to the beach, or we can make love in one of the millions of rooms in the mansion."

"What if your mother is planning on setting you up with another JAP?"

"Not 'what if.' She definitely is. You don't want to see my mother trying to force me to propose to some pious Jewess? She might even have someone to set you up with, too." I approach him, holding his hands. "And what better way to spend your weekend than with my rigid and emotionless father and my anxious and overbearing mother? And anyway," I add, "I don't see any other way for you to meet my family."

"Maybe one day, when we come out of the closet together."

"Don't fool yourself," I say. "It'll never happen. Maybe we'll come out of the closet, but my parents will never accept you as part of the family. My father will never be okay with it, and my mother would never go against him, certainly not openly. At any rate, I can guarantee that the weekend will not be boring."

"Are you sure this is what you really want?"

"Definitely."

"OK, I'll come," he says.

I text my mom: **I'll come to dinner on Friday night, and I'm bringing a business partner.**

"Where's Richard?" Maria asks me when she opens the door for me the next morning.

"What about, 'Hi Tom, how are you?'" I smile. "That's your first question for me after we haven't seen each other for a few days? I'm fine, by the way, thanks for asking."

We laugh.

"He already seems like your other half," Maria says. "It's not right for someone to come home without their other half."

I sit at the kitchen island and Maria serves me breakfast.

"I'll be going with him to the house in the Hamptons this weekend for a party my parents are throwing."

"Are you going to tell them?" she asks, astonished.

"Maybe someday," I answer. "Who knows. For now, I want to tell you about the trip so you can help me get everything I need."

After a morning run and some mindfulness meditation – which helps the leaders of countries and companies understand events in the best way and deal with them optimally, without negative impact – I get ready to return to the Olympia offices. Arthur lets me off at the entrance to Rockefeller Center. I am light footed and relaxed as I enter the building, greeting everyone kindly, and I can't ignore the surprise I see all around me from this display of warmth. But I no longer care what other people think. Uncharacteristically, I enter my office without asking what the day ahead will bring, and Alexandra rushes in after me.

"Was it quiet here without me?" I ask.

"Yes, actually," she smiles. "But we missed you."

"Great, here's another reason to miss me," I say as I hand her the box of chocolates that I bought for her in London. She is taken aback and thanks me. I have a hard time with such open displays of emotion, so I ask what meetings I have that day.

"I've arranged a light schedule for you today," Alexandra says. "Jessica will be here soon, and then you have two big meetings about deals in South Korea, China, and India." Just then, with perfect timing, Jessica knocks on the door, and I get up to greet her, guiding her to the armchair next to my desk.

"That's all for now, Alexandra," I say, thanking her with a bow of my head. Alexandra says "hi" to Jessica, kisses her on the cheek, and leaves the room.

I take out the bottle of perfume that I bought for Jessica in London.

"Juicy Couture?" she asks in shock.

"Indeed," I say with a sheepish smile. "I bought this perfume, which Richard always buys for his mother and sister when he flies abroad, for all the women in my life."

"You were with Richard in London?"

"We had business meetings in London."

"I remember you telling me you were flying to London for business, but I didn't know you were going with Richard," she looks straight at me, smiling. "What's going on, Tom?" she asks. "You are showing some qualities that I never knew you had." She thinks for a minute and suddenly says out loud, "You look like you're in love. Have you found a girl?" Discomfort shoots right through me. I straighten my tie to buy some time, but some uncontrollable impulse has me answering, "Yes, Jessica. I am in love."

"That's wonderful, Tom! I am so happy to hear! I definitely think you're ready for a relationship. I'm sure she's amazing."

I remain still, once again straightening my tie, with a slight smile on my lips.

"Yes, she's amazing."

"Can I ask who she is?"

"It's Richard," I respond, in a defeated tone.

Jessica's expression is one of shock. She looks half surprised and half disappointed, maybe because I have destroyed her image of the young, rich Jew from New York.

"I've been in the closet for years, Jessica," I whisper. "My lifestyle hasn't enabled me to come out, but this thing I have with him is stronger than me. I can't stop it. I'm definitely still afraid, but I've decided that my life doesn't depend on other peoples' opinions, and I'm just going to go for it."

"I must confess I am surprised, but it is so important that you know that I love you and accept you no matter how you choose to live your life," Jessica says in her characteristic gravity.

"I only ask that for now, this stays between us."

"Of course," she says. "Not a word."

★

When Jessica leaves my office, I sink into my own thoughts. Alexandra's voice pulls me out quickly. "Arik Gonen on line 5," she says over the intercom. I pick up the phone.

"My friend," Arik says, "how is it back in Manhattan?"

"Fascinating," I say sarcastically, and we both laugh.

"You haven't told me whether you want to come to Israel to join the delegation that will receive the President of the United States."

"I'm not sure," I answer. "I've known the president for years, from my involvement with the party." I share with Arik something I have never told anyone else. "When we were at Harvard, me at the beginning of my time there and the president for his graduate degrees, both of us energetic and fully believing we could change the world, the party tasked us with finding 'political talents' on the east coast to recruit. Anything was considered a legitimate place to recruit, including nightlife spots. That's how the New York nightlife scene became very familiar to us. Our friendship grew closer even outside of our political activity. We know a lot about each other, but over time, we've grown apart. I don't know what he'd think if he saw that I was invited by the Israeli side."

"That was then, this is now. I'm sure he'd be happy to see you," Arik says. "You're Jewish, a big donor to Israel, a citizen of the United States – but first and foremost you're a proud Jew."

"Extremely proud," I say. I decide then and there to join the delegation, because it means I can fly to Israel with Richard. "I'll come with another proud Jew."

"He'll also join the delegation?"

"No, he's a water technology entrepreneur. He'll come so we can have meetings about this. I also want to remind you to arrange a meeting for me with the chairman of the Greywater Reclamation Company. I spoke with him, and we agreed to meet in Israel at the first available opportunity."

"I'll take care of it," Arik promises.

"So I guess I'll see you in Israel," I say. We say goodbye and hang up, and I text Richard: **Think about what you want to write on the note that you'll put in the Western Wall.**

That evening, we meet at Club 52. The bouncer at the club escorts us to the bar. Richard clasps my hand, and we find an intimate table off to the side where we can speak quietly. We order an aperitif and wait for our first course.

"Jessica knows," I say.

"Jessica knows what?" Richard asks.

"I told her today. After I gave her the perfume, I told her that I'm in love. With you."

"How did she react?"

"She had quite a shock, which looked almost as big as your surprise the first time we kissed in Maine."

"If it's the same shock, then a few hours later she'll realize that she's in love, as a mentor of course, with the idea of Tom Gold – the Jewish billionaire shipping tycoon, known donor to Israel, Democratic party activist, peace worker in Africa…who is *gay*," Richard says with emphasis, and we both crack up.

"What about your parents?" he suddenly asks.

"Please don't think that what happened today with Jessica has any bearing on what I can do with my parents. It's much more complicated. And anyway, what are you even talking about? Last time we spoke, you yourself said you needed more time."

"Well, it turns out I didn't really need that much time. Since our last conversation, I've been thinking about things, and I realized that I don't care. And you, Tommy, isn't it time for you to stop thinking about your parents and start thinking about yourself?"

I fall silent. I have no idea what to say. Richard considers his words carefully. "Everyone has always said that I resemble my

67

mother. So I assumed that I must also resemble her personality. But ever since I got back in touch with my father's family, I've started to see how similar I actually am to him. My mother tended to only see the good in herself, and when I became the only man in the house, I started putting myself last. I always said "yes," always worried what she would say. It was only years later that I decided to change this and learn from her. Since then, I've been making sure to take care of myself first. I love myself as I am, and I don't care what other people think. Since then, I have also understood that only someone who loves himself can truly love others."

"I really don't love myself so much," I say after a short silence. "Thanks to you, I'm getting better at it, because I am loved by someone whom I love, and so I guess there is something in me to love. But still, I think there's a long way for me to go from that to having an outright clash with my parents about who I really am."

"I'm not criticizing you, Tommy," Richard says. "I just want you to be happy. I want us to be happy. I don't want you to feel ashamed. I want you to love yourself for who you really are. At least think about it."

"I'll certainly think about it. I think about it all the time, but in the meantime, we can be a couple in the closet. There are plenty of couples who are successful in business, who live our kind of lifestyle, and who remain in the closet so as not to change their status."

"If it's in the meantime, I can wait," Richard says. "For 28 years, ever since my father died, I've cut myself off from my feelings. Under my mother's guidance, I gave a false impression of myself, as if everything was perfect for me. You could say I was in my own kind of closet. I was the king of society, a night owl addicted to clubs, affairs, fun, but nothing was ever emotionally deep. Now, I'm looking for something else entirely. I guess fate wanted it to be with a man, with you, and this feels right, and I am not willing to keep hiding. I'm no longer fighting against reality; I am accepting it for what it is."

"Do you really think you're gay?" I ask.

"I'm bisexual. Remember Richard the First?"

"And you can see yourself living like this, forever?"

"With you, yes," Richard says. "But we can never really know where life will take us."

Moved by his answer, I put my hand in his, but quickly pull it back when the waiter appears next to our table with our orders.

"You see why I don't want to live like this?" Richard asks once the waiter leaves.

"Richard," I say, "I don't want this to stand between us. Can we agree not to speak about this until we return from Israel?"

He thinks about it.

"Fine. If that's what you want."

We change the subject and talk about our trip, and when the meal is over, we leave the club on foot. Without realizing where we're headed, we find ourselves right in front of the Plaza Hotel. "Twenty bucks for a ride all around the park," the driver of a touristy horse-drawn carriage calls out to us, and the next thing we know, we're sitting inside it, being led through the street lit paths of Central Park, sitting quietly, each lost in thought.

I wake up to the sound of the alarm clock. It's seven in the morning. I turn it off and look at Richard. He's sleeping. My head hurts. I know I should hurry up and get to the office, but I decide to continue dozing for a few more minutes.

"Tom," Maria calls from behind the closed door, and I open my eyes with a start. "It's ten o'clock. Arthur's been waiting downstairs for you for a while." I jump out of bed, sit on the edge, and hold my head in my hands. I then wake up Richard gently, but he refuses to get up.

"Get up. No indulging after ten in the morning."

"It's ten?" He squints at me.

"10:03," I say, getting up and starting to get ready. Breakfast is waiting on the kitchen island. I wonder why Alexandra hasn't called to find out where I am, and I realize my cellphone is turned off.

"Way to go," I mutter to myself.

"For what?" Richard asks, suddenly appearing in the kitchen.

"I was speaking to myself. Way to go for waking up at ten, for having my cellphone turned off, for enjoying a leisurely breakfast. Way to go for all of it. Maybe I actually have begun loving myself."

"It's a start," Richard decides, quickly downing some coffee.

"You're not going to eat anything?" Maria asks him.

"Unfortunately, I don't have any time," he says, kissing her on the cheek.

"I'll see you this evening," I call after him, already missing him.

In the afternoon, I meet with Bill Black, Chairman of the Democratic National Committee and the Governor of Ohio, for lunch at Renaissance. It's been a while since we last met. We used to meet here at this same restaurant once a week back when I was active in the party. Back then, I hadn't yet inherited Olympia.

"Hi Tom," Bill smiles at me, having arrived a bit late.

"Hi Bill," I say as I get up to shake his hand. "Always good to see you."

"Even though we went through a period where it was a bit hard to schedule meetings with you," Bill teases as he sits down.

"Busy with work, you know how it goes. Ever since I took over Olympia, I basically haven't done anything else, making myself totally available for the company."

The waiter comes over to hand us menus.

"Let's get straight to the point," Bill says once the waiter has taken our order. "How can we get you involved with the party again?"

"Get me involved again? I don't think you can."

"Maybe give it a second thought," he insists.

"On second thought," I say, acting thoughtful and rubbing my chin, "even on second thought, it's impossible."

"How about this," Bill offers, determined. "We'll agree that you'll take some time to think about it during your trip to Israel. We'll set up a meeting for after you return, and then we'll talk about it again."

"How did you know I'm going to Israel?" I wonder, even though the answer is obvious.

"I saw your name on the list of the Israeli delegation," he immediately answers.

I wonder why Bill is so adamant about me being active in the party again. What does he want to talk about after my trip to Israel? It's been almost five years since I was involved. It's true, I do have "the bug." In the past, being active in the party really did fill my life with meaning, but I have proven to myself that I can live without it, too.

"OK, so I'll see you when I get back."

From Renaissance, I go to my weekly appointment with Judith, and I feel like I've arrived in her neighborhood too soon. I need to organize my thoughts. Make decisions. Calm down.

"At the end of our last appointment, I asked you if there had been an event during your childhood that was significant in your life," Judith says once we've begun. "This is something that is very prominent in your birth chart, and it is important for me to know about it in order to make sure the regression exercises are accurate."

"When I was six, my father whipped me, exactly as you would a horse. Ten precise lashes on my back, in order to suppress my urges," I blurt the words out. I no longer care how it sounds; the main thing is to rid myself of this burden.

"What urges was he trying to suppress?"

"My attraction towards men."

71

"When you were six years old?" she asks, astonished. "What urges does a six-year-old boy have?"

"Ask my father."

"What happened?"

"He happened to walk into the room when I was kissing Brad, the neighbor's son, who was ten at the time. Actually, to be precise, Brad had kissed me, and it was a surprise to me, too. He was a boy with a crazy head and, it turns out in retrospect, he was gay. I was in shock and I froze. I didn't just go with it, but I also didn't stop it. Anyway, my father walked in and that's what happened. But the whipping didn't help, and when I was twelve years old, I understood that I wasn't interested in girls. Since then, I've only been with men," I say, feeling a sense of release. *Now Judith knows,* I think to myself, and I am full of hope that my therapy will be much more effective from now on.

"Tom, my dear, I am not surprised. Your sexual orientation stood out in your star chart. I have treated men and women who have hidden their sexual orientation, but I must confess, you've been the biggest challenge for me. You have such a strong fear of rejection and abandonment. That's what's responsible for your moods and it's impaired your quality of life. The regression exercises will neutralize these negative patterns and imbue your brain with new, positive information, which will miraculously improve your quality of life and enable you to connect with yourself and the new information systems within you. Like a rebirth. A system reboot. Your life will change at our next appointment," Judith concludes, walking me to her door with a smile.

I pick Richard up near Wall Street in the Porsche and we head to my parents for the weekend. I'm wearing a baseball hat, sunglasses, and a sporty suit that I bought in London. The car roof is down, and when I look at Richard, all sewn up in a suit after a long day at work, I burst out laughing.

"It isn't our wedding day today," I tell him.

"And yet, my darling," Richard answers. "Your mother should get used to your boyfriend's style."

"If you want, there's a hat in the glove box," I say, and we head out.

When we get to my parents' Hamptons summer home, the electric gate slowly opens, and Richard looks around in amazement at all the well-kept gardens unfolding before our eyes.

"Yes, Richard, this is where I spent a lot of weekends growing up."

"This explains a lot."

"Like what?"

"Like why you employ Maria."

"Are you bothered by Maria?"

"No. But it's not always easy to wake up naked and then bump into her."

"Well here, you'll meet Marta."

"There's also a Marta?" Richard laughs. "I see that the Gold family likes to follow patterns."

We continue driving along the path, which is now adorned on both sides by long lines of tall trees that I don't remember seeing before. The water fountain built right where the paths meet is also new to me, and I realize that these are my mother's newest additions since Feng Shui entered her life.

"Do you think we'll reach the house at some point today?" Richard asks as we continue driving along expansive lawns and large colorful flowerbeds.

"Here, look to the right," I say, thinking to myself that we're lucky he has his own money, and I park the car near the front door.

We get out of the car and walk towards the house, built in a rustic style in an attempt to make the enormous house feel somehow like a home. Right by the door, we run into my father.

"Hello, Tom," he says, distant.

"Hello, Father," I respond. "This is Richard Silverman, a water tech entrepreneur from Chicago who's in New York for business."

"Hello, Mr. Gold," Richard greets my father. They shake hands and my father leaves us without another word, even though he usually likes to speak to young entrepreneurs. "Tom," Mother calls as she approaches us. "This must be Richard. Hello, Richard," she says. "It's nice to see a friend of Tom's in our home. It's been years since I've seen any of his friends. He is so busy and hardly ever comes here. We'll find some more time later on to talk about him," she winks at him, leading him by the hand to see the pool. Richard follows her with a tight smile on his face, and I can tell that Mother is up to something. Generally, when she's sweet-talking to someone, she's got some sort of an agenda. In the meantime, I go inside and say "hi" to my parents' friends. I then go to the kitchen, where I see my father once again.

"Can I help with anything?"

"Marta and her husband have taken care of everything," he says, walking away. He is acting even more severe than usual. He's more rigid, more withdrawn, at least towards me. I enter the living room, sit on the couch, and start reading the weekend papers. Through the glass doors from the living room to the swimming pool, I can see Mother and Richard wandering around the garden immersed in lively conversation.

The festive Friday night dinner is served in the garden. Mother welcomes everyone as my father gazes at her with a look of admiration that, despite all their years together, has never waned, remaining as fierce and sincere as I remember from my childhood. Twenty people were invited to dinner, and Marta is preparing to serve the meal. The meat has been grilled outside by a chef my father brings in for these kinds of evenings. A large bar has been set up next to the pool.

The chef comes over to the table with a large tray loaded with juicy slabs of meat. "Albert, you're the best," my father calls. Good food has always managed to improve his mood.

The guests attack the serving dishes, and the festivities are underway. Albert pours beer from a keg into pitchers, and with my father's encouragement, we also remember to drink from the full case of fine wines that he specially ordered for this meal.

When the meal is over, Mother disappears, and she comes out a few minutes later dragging out a large bingo machine. "Surprise!" she cries, to the delight of her guests, who are used to going along with her surprises. I glance at Richard in embarrassment, but he actually looks intrigued. A few minutes later, everyone is deeply immersed in the game, and I console myself by drinking an excessive amount of wine.

"One more and I win!" Richard cries, and I can see he's enjoying himself.

"Wonderful," Mother replies. "If I could, I would make sure it falls on the number you need." She bursts out laughing and my father looks at her in surprise. Ten minutes later, Mother announces that Richard has won, and the game is over.

"I hope you're not suffering," I tell him.

"Suffering? Are you insane? I'm having the best time. I love your mother! Come on, when can we tell her about us?" And I realize that Richard is drunk, too.

"Don't misjudge her," I say.

"You're exaggerating," he replies.

"Can we not talk about this right now?"

"I'm sorry, Tommy, let's forget about it."

"Who wants dessert?" Albert calls out.

Richard has his way with a respectable amount of the fine petit fours, announces that he is finally done, and I congratulate him on joining the refined Gold family. Two hours later, my parents say goodbye to their friends, and the party is over. "Come, Richard. I'll show you to the guest room that Marta has set up for you," Mother says.

"It would be my pleasure, Mrs. Gold," Richard replies, as she drags him up the steps that lead to the second floor, where the guest wing is. I gesture to him that we'll meet up later on and go up to my room. The room is steeped in my childhood memories. I am beginning to feel the drunkenness from all the wine taking hold, and I decide to doze a bit to gather my strength so that I can steal away to Richard's room later.

I wake up with a start and look at the clock. 8 a.m. I pull back the window curtains and the bright morning light bursts through the blinds. I leave the room and realize that my parents are still asleep. I tiptoe into the room my mother showed Richard into. He is still sleeping, and he looks like an angel. I sit there as the minutes tick by, just gazing at him. I finally leave the room, letting him continue sleeping.

I drink coffee on the edge of the pool, as is my habit. In the past, when I would sit on Saturday mornings alone next to the pool, I'd sink into my thoughts, generally depressing ones at that. But this time, I don't want to think about anything at all, and to my surprise, I manage to enjoy the moment. Nothing is bothering me. I sip my coffee, light a cigarette, and look around, actually feeling happy.

In the afternoon, Richard and I walk on the sand until we get to the beach, far away from my parents' eyes. We lie down on the beach and breathe in an intoxicating sense of freedom. About two hours later, after reading books and dozing, we start playing catch, and I throw the ball at Richard with all my might. He hardly catches it.

"Are you jealous that I won yesterday?" he asks.

"I'm definitely not jealous. Having that kind of chemistry with my mother is something to admire, not to envy."

We finally grow tired of playing catch and start wrestling in the sand like a couple of kids. In the late afternoon, we return to the house and get ready to go back to Manhattan. My father remains silent and ignores us, and my mother continues flirting with Richard.

"Mrs. Gold, it's been an absolute pleasure," Richard says.

"Please come and visit us in Connecticut as well," she replies. "Tom, bring Richard with you next time you come."

"Yes, Mother," I answer, like an obedient child, not understanding this strategy of excessive friendliness she's decided to adopt.

We get in the car and start driving.

"Truly an idyllic family picture," Richard says with a small smile.

The car passes through the gate. I step on the gas and speed away from my parents' vacation home, towards freedom, towards Manhattan, escaping from the family weekend to the small family unit that Richard and I have built for ourselves.

CHAPTER 7
Israel, Late-June

Richard and I have been together for almost two months now. When we go into the airport shops, I already know which chocolates and cigars he likes, and we buy them in abundance. The plane takes off, and about half a day later, we land at Ben Gurion Airport. A representative from the car rental company is waiting for us in the arrivals hall. Arik had offered to arrange for a chauffeured car to pick us up, but I politely declined.

We get the keys to a black Infiniti and drive to Tel Aviv, toward the suite we reserved at the Dan Hotel. The GPS guides us through the congested Tel Aviv streets until the sea suddenly unfolds before us. Ignoring the navigation instructions, we continue along the road parallel to the bustling beachside promenade down to Jaffa, after which we make a U-turn and head back to the hotel.

At the reception desk, I say I am Tom Gold, and I've reserved a suite for two. *If only I had the guts to do this in Manhattan*, I think to myself. The bellhop accompanies us to our suite, with its enormous window looking out over the water. Unable to resist the temptation, we hurry into our bathing suits and go down to the beach. In the late afternoon, we go back upstairs, and in the evening, we go out to wander the streets of Tel Aviv.

We walk up Dizengoff Street to the national theater, and from there we continue on Rothschild Boulevard. We find a bistro in the Neve Tzedek neighborhood and sit down to eat dinner.

"Tel Aviv is amazing," Richard says.

"It really is a special city. Small and special. In one day, you can see all of it. There are clubs where everyone goes, bars, some prominent restaurants and cafes that the locals love going to."

"Just like Manhattan."

"You can't compare the two. Manhattan has many more options. Israel is a small country and Tel Aviv is a microcosm of it."

"Would you ever live here?" Richard asks.

"No," I say with certainty. "I love to come visit. I also like to go to Jerusalem and Eilat, even a few times a year. But for living, for business, and for going out, Manhattan is the only place for me."

"When we drove to Jaffa," Richard continues, "I remembered my mother telling me that when my father had arrived in Israel, he lived in Jaffa's Old City. It used to be called "the big territory," because that was where the Tel Aviv prostitution scene was. The homes there had originally belonged to Arabs who fled during the War of Independence, and my dad found one of the abandoned houses and brought his family there. After the war, they immigrated to America."

I decide to hail a taxi and take Richard to the Old City. Amongst the narrow alleys, we look at all the homes, trying to guess which one his father had lived in.

"Let's decide that it's this one," Richard suddenly says. He stops in front of a small stone house with a narrow staircase and old window shutters painted turquoise.

"Seems about right," I say.

"We sit down across from the house and stare it at for several long moments. I know Richard is thinking about his father, and I give him the time and space he needs to do so in quiet.

"Shall we?" he asks finally, getting up to stand.

"We shall," I say.

On the way down the steps leading to the port, we find a small bar overlooking the fishing boats tied to the docks. Rows upon rows of them. "I need a drink," I tell Richard after a long silence. "You know, my heart always beats faster whenever I see a port, even if it's a small one like this. Look where my father was able to go, thanks to the ports. Ports are a gateway for saving weak cultures, a gateway to freedom, a source of employment for hundreds of thousands of people, who bring billions of dollars in for the owners of the companies that employ them," I add with a wink.

Richard and I leave the port and walk along the boardwalk towards central Tel Aviv. It's late now. The beach is dark and empty, and it feels like the black horizon and the line of stars are looking at us. Swimming naked, we reach the breakwater.

In the late morning, we leave Tel Aviv and head towards Jerusalem. We'll be in the capital city for the next few days. I'll be spending most of my time in business and political meetings, and Richard will have time to discover the city.

"Look to the right," I say, pointing to the road that weaves through the Jerusalem mountains. "This is my favorite part of this drive. Look at how the trees are arranged, just like in a picture. When I was younger and we would come on our annual trip to Israel, I could never decide whether the trees were an illustration against the sky, or were actually real."

"What are those?" Richard asks, pointing to the shells of old armored vehicles standing along the side of the road.

"I think they're from Israel's War of Independence. They used those to bring equipment into Jerusalem."

"My father fought in that war," Richard says, and even though he's already told me the story, the skeletons of the old, armored cars turn it into something much more tangible. "He received the badge of war. I have the certificate at home," he adds, his voice trembling a bit with emotion.

We arrive at the American Colony Hotel, where suite number 6 is registered in our names. The reception manager takes us to our room.

Towards evening, Richard and I make our way to the Western Wall. In preparation, I have made sure to have two notes and a pen ready. In the Armenian Quarter, next to some small shops filled with art and ceramics, a religious procession passes by. A priest in traditional dress holding a large cross is followed by a large crowd from his congregation. We continue walking towards the Zion Gate and enter the Jewish Quarter. From there, we walk to the Western Wall.

"Write something short and to the point," I tell Richard, "So whoever is up there can make your wish come true."

"Should we show each other?" Richard asks me.

"No, that's between you and God. Even when the president visited the Wall a few years ago, before he was the president, someone took out his note."

"I can see Israelis doing that."

"Definitely."

"Well, as luck would have it, you're not the president yet."

Evening is upon us. From the Old City, I decide to take Richard to a restaurant in the YMCA building that I remember from my previous trips. The atmosphere is hypnotizing, and when we finish eating, I drag Richard all the way up to the top of the tower there, where there is an observation point looking out over all of captivating Jerusalem. The magic of the night closes in on us from all sides.

The next morning, I leave Richard and head over to the prime minister's office.

Arik comes to meet me at the security checkpoint at the entrance. "You never change," he says, after we've greeted each other warmly and patted each other on the back.

"Manhattan does me good," I respond.

Arik leads me to his office. The entire Israeli press corps is spread out in the corridor that leads to the Israeli government's meeting room. The U.S. President's delegation is already in Israel, and Bill Black suddenly appears.

"Surprise!" Arik says to Bill Black.

"Half a surprise," Bill responds. "Tom and I had lunch a few days ago in Manhattan. I'm trying to get him involved in the party again."

"An excellent idea," Arik says. "I would love to see Tom in American politics. The United States needs people like him, and we Jews need him, too. The Gold family's contributions to the government in Israel are priceless."

Bill continues walking, and when we get to Arik's office, we find the chairman of Israel's Greywater Reclamation Company waiting for us.

"I'd like to introduce Tom Gold, owner of Olympia, the largest shipping company in the United States, a precious Jew, and a true friend of Israel," Arik says with pride.

"Hello, Mr. Herman," I say. "We've actually already met."

"Yes, but we couldn't shake hands through the screen," Herman adds, shaking my hand.

After some small talk, we move on to the ways we can advance our common interests in Africa.

After the meeting, Arik takes me out to lunch. "The usual," he tells the waitress.

"And for you?" she asks me.

"Arik's usual."

"So you said that Manhattan does you good," Arik says when the waitress leaves. "That's clear to see."

"Thanks. I'm in love," I tell Arik with a smile.

"I'm so happy to hear. The truth is that I had begun to worry. I even spoke about it with my wife, and she said maybe you were gay," Arik laughs. But when he notices that my expression remains serious, he falls silent, examining my face, and I put on an amused look of being resigned to my fate.

"Really?" he asks after a few moments.

"Yes," I say with a smile.

"Well, that is really a surprise," he says, after thinking it over a bit. He puts down his fork, sits up straight, and a little smile plays across his face. "Wow," he cries. "Where did that even come from? I would never have guessed. Tom Gold, my perfect, handsome, rich friend from America – is *gay?*" he whispers.

"Arik, I consider you a close friend, and this information is to stay between us. I have only just started telling people who are close to me. I am with someone, and we're talking about coming out of the closet together. I'm still on the fence about it, but I feel like I want to know what the people closest to me think. Anyway, your reaction was the most surprising yet."

"I really am surprised," Arik replies. "Why haven't you come out until now?"

"I was afraid. Afraid of my parents, afraid of hurting the company, afraid of the party. But I'm sick and tired of acting out of fear. In other parts of my life, I'm not afraid of anything."

"I'm with you," Arik says. "It's the 21st century, and I think the U.S. can figure out how to accept someone like you."

"My boyfriend's name is Richard, in case I haven't mentioned."

"Oh, your business partner for your Africa ventures, the one who came to Israel with you? Another surprise."

"I've never been in a serious relationship with a man before. For years I've spent my time and money on therapy to make sure I don't go back to my old patterns with men. Now, I finally feel wanted, and I want to be able to protect our relationship."

"A rich, Jewish, handsome businessman, who is active in the Democratic party, donates to the State of Israel, and is involved in extensive volunteer work in Africa is coming out of the closet," Arik says in the voice of a news broadcaster. "Be brave," he adds. "It suits you to be brave.

Arik wonders whether Richard is in the area and tells me I should invite him to join us for lunch. I text Richard, and it turns out he's just about to leave the Israel Museum, right next door to where we are. He comes to meet Arik. It's the first time that I openly introduce Richard to anyone as my boyfriend.

Everyone is waiting in the room that has been specially set up in advance. It has two podiums where the president of the United States and the prime minister of Israel will deliver their joint statement after their one-on-one meeting. The room is full of local and foreign political reporters.

"The president of the United States and the prime minister of Israel will deliver a brief statement. No questions will be allowed," the prime minister's spokeswoman announces. Once the statements have been delivered, the two leaders leave the room, and we are invited to attend a meeting of the delegations, which the two leaders will also attend. I know most of the people here quite well on both the American and Israeli sides.

The prime minister welcomes us and reiterates his diplomatic agreements with the American president, who is in Israel as part of a Middle East tour. When he is done, everyone raises a glass of champagne to toast the strategic partnership between the countries.

Bill comes over to me. "Tom, I want you to come meet the president," he says, and we cross the room to where the leader of the free world is chatting with Israel's ambassador to the UN.

"Hello Tom," the president says.

"Hello, Mr. President," I respond, and we shake hands and exchange the look shared between people who know each other well.

"Bill really trusts you," the president says in an official, obligating tone. "I believe in you, too. I understand you met. We want you to come back to the party," he declares, and then quickly walks away. Bill also hurries off and I am left standing there alone, holding a glass of champagne, pondering what I had just heard.

"Tom," Arik calls, motioning for me to come over, "come say 'hi' to the prime minister." Once we find him in the room, we walk over. "Hello, Tom," the prime minister addresses me in Hebrew.

"Hello, Mr. Prime Minister," I respond in Hebrew as well.

"How's your father?" he asks.

"He's fine," I answer.

"Your father's uncompromising commitment to the State of Israel, as a donor and otherwise, is admirable," the Israeli leader continues.

"Tom just donated five million dollars himself to the defense establishment," Arik notes.

"I really appreciate it," the prime minister tells me. "These days, the State of Israel truly needs the support of the American Jewish community."

"I understand the need," I look directly into the prime minister's eyes, "but, unlike my father, I think that donating to starving children in Africa is no less important, and perhaps more. That's why it's important to me to see steps taken by Israel on issues like agreements with the Palestinians."

"Don't be naïve, Mr. Gold," he says. "The Palestinians do not truly want peace. They want to maintain the status quo. They do not want to renew our negotiations, and we are fighting a war for our principles."

"As long as we keep saying we are 'fighting a war,' we'll never manage to break through the deadlock and the closed patterns of thinking," I tell the prime minister cautiously, but with a degree of firmness and straightforwardness that is characteristic of me, even at the cost of clashing with him. I re-emphasize that I expect much more regarding the Palestinians. "I need to see that Israel is ever-present at the negotiating table, not stopping for a minute, because this will give hope to both sides."

"When you make deals for your shipping empire, do you agree to preconditions?" the prime minister asks me. I reply that in my estimation, any solution that depends on economic agreements in its first stage could serve as a basis for diplomatic agreements in the future and that I would be willing to contribute a great deal of money for the sake of such agreements. "Your position is clear, Tom," the Israeli leader concludes our exchange with a pat on my shoulder, and we shake hands.

Later that same day, Richard and I travel to Eilat.

"Wake me up when we get there," Richard says, reclining his seat.

"What's the matter with you?" I scold him. "I simply will not accept you not seeing the road to Eilat your first time there. You think you can just not see the Dead Sea? Masada?" Richard relents.

When we reach the middle of the Arava desert, I stop on the side of the road. We get out of the car, open a beer, and look out at the desert. About a half hour later, we are back in the car, opening the sunroof, and heading out again. At dusk, with the pleasant desert wind beginning to blow, we race into Eilat, my third favorite city in the world. The first thing we see are the hotels, immediately followed by the blue water of the sea, surrounded by the rugged desert mountains.

In the evening, I take Richard to a restaurant I know. We sit at a table for two on the inner section of the boardwalk, quietly sipping wine. I sneak a smile at him, and we laugh. We light cigars and watch the passers-by. I love being a tourist in Eilat. Richard looks at me, enjoying seeing me enjoy myself. Afterwards, we return to our hotel suite, and I sit on the straw sofa overlooking the sea, watching the lights of the big ships anchored at the ports of Eilat and Aqaba.

Richard kisses me softly, removes my clothing, and then undresses himself. I lie on my stomach with Richard on top of me.

About a half hour later, we start all over again, this time with me at the command. Finally, we fall into a deep sleep.

On our last day in Eilat, we spend time on the beach, lying on our sunbeds, ordering beer, and soaking up the sun's rays. My mind is free of all thoughts, worries, fears. We look at each other, happy, trying to capture each moment of our time together, just us, and we feel like the entire world belongs to us alone.

CHAPTER 8

Manhattan, Early September

Today is Richard's birthday. We've been together for four months now – long enough for our relationship to become a part of our intensive lifestyles. Richard's been spending a lot of time setting up his New York branch, and he's been traveling all across the country to promote his water tech incubator. I've been busy running Olympia and moving forward with my enterprise in Angola. But for Richard's birthday, I have taken the day off from work. I spend the morning running and practicing my mindfulness meditations, and in the afternoon, I meet again with Bill Black, National Democratic Party Chairman and Governor of Ohio. He is waiting for me at the entrance to the party's offices, and he introduces me to the new party secretary of New York, his deputy.

We then enter his office for a one-on-one meeting. "I take it all your excuses to push this off have run out?" Bill asks.

"Yes. Today will be the last postponement and then the case will be closed," I respond with a smile.

"Don't be so sure you'll say 'no,'" Bill says. "It isn't easy to reject an offer from the president himself."

"An offer from the president?"

"Yes, Tom. On his behalf, I am making you an offer you can't refuse."

"Speak," I say, sitting on the guest chair. Bill begins and I listen intently. A slight tremor courses through my body, and I am not sure whether it's from excitement or fear, but it's clear that this is huge.

"On behalf of the president, I'm offering that you serve as his special envoy in the Middle East, to promote diplomatic negotiations between Israel and the Palestinian Authority," Bill finally declares. "We think you're the man for the job for a number of reasons: your contributions to Israel, your status among senior officials in the Israeli government, your empathy for the Palestinian side, your rich background managing complex negotiations, and of course your many achievements for the party in the past. Anyway, right now, the party doesn't have anyone else for the job. And by the way, your father is pushing us hard to get you back into political action."

"My father? What interest does he have in me leaving Olympia?"

Bill evades the question. I know that I need to talk this over with Richard. I can't make any decision like this alone. Although my gut reaction is to politely decline, mainly for fear that my relationship with Richard will come out, something inside me doesn't let me, and I know that I need to think about this offer carefully.

"At some point next week, I'll give you my final answer, Bill," I say. "I'll take the weekend to think it over and consult about it."

"No problem, just be discreet," Bill asks.

"Of course. Discretion is my middle name."

I smile and shake his hand with genuine excitement; this is no trivial proposition. We agree to speak again on Tuesday. Bill walks me to the door, and we part ways. I'm still in the elevator when panic starts to overtake me and I'm having trouble breathing. I try to steady my breath. I loosen my tie and wipe the sweat from my forehead. The distance from the elevator to the door leading outside the party offices seems endless, especially now, when I hunger to come out and live in freedom.

When I get out onto the street, I realize that it's not the role I've just been offered that's filling me with anxiety – I've already held significant positions within the Democratic party and in the business world, after all – but the fact that Richard wants us to come out of the closet and live life openly as a couple. I have no idea how he'll react to the proposal, but one thing is clear to me: if it comes out that I'm gay, not only will this proposal be taken from me, but Olympia will too.

A repetitive honk catches my attention. Coming out of my confused daze, I realize that I heard that honk as background noise the whole time, and I see that it's Arthur. He's been waiting for me in the Jaguar and honking to get my attention. I race across the street and leap into the car.

"Hello? Earth to Tom?" Arthur asks with a smile. "Where'd you disappear to?" I smile back, turn on the radio, and pour myself a large glass of cognac. I then call Richard to make sure he's on his way to Picasso, where I made lunch reservations for us to celebrate his birthday.

The waiter shows us to our table for two in a private room, and once we're seated, I hand Richard the gift I've brought for him. He carefully opens the wrapping paper, takes out a box, and inside is a miniature, silver model of a water desalination plant, sitting atop a small gold ship, which I had specially ordered from a craftsman silversmith.

Moved, Richard gets up, and I get up and go to him, and we kiss. A knock on the door makes us jump, and as the door opens, we dash back to our seats to receive the waiter.

"I met with Bill Black today," I tell Richard once the waiter has left the room, "and I was offered to serve as the president's envoy to the Middle East."

"You were offered what?!" Richard asks.

"I was offered," I repeat quietly," to serve as the president's envoy to the Middle East."

"That's a big deal!" Richard exclaims. "It's a huge deal. A once in a lifetime deal. Do you know what a big deal this is?"

"I know. And as each moment passes, I understand it even more."

"I hope you said 'yes.'"

"I told Bill I'd give him an answer next week. I wanted to know what you thought first."

"If you decide that you want this job, I'm with you. In principle, I think you should take it, but the decision is yours," Richard says, smiling.

"You understand that I'll need to fly to Israel a lot over the coming months."

"I'll join you when I can," Richard replies.

"Richard, Arik knows I'm gay. I trust him, but it could leak."

"You know what I think about that," Richard says quietly.

"I almost threw up in the lobby of the Democratic Party offices today. I felt like I was suffocating. I had a panic attack. I realized that my panic was coming from the idea of being an open couple, coming out of the closet, and not from the actual job I was being offered."

"Well, what do you suggest?" Richard asks.

"I think I should take it. The job is for three months. After that, I promise, we can come out and make our relationship official."

"I have a feeling you'll always find some excuse to push it off," Richard says. "You need to make a decision. I didn't want to bring this up while we were celebrating but be real with yourself and with me. Don't lead us on."

In one moment, our festive mood is spoiled, and we sit morosely facing each other. The waiter comes into the room, serves our first course, and leaves. We look at our plates in silence; we both seem to have lost our appetites.

"You're right," I finally say. "I guess I am leading us both on. The thought of living life openly gay terrifies me. It's been terrifying me for thirty years already."

"But you claimed that it's different now," Richard says.

"Yes, of course it's different. Completely different. And yet, the idea of taking that step has me paralyzed with fear." I fall silent. "And your love can't dispel this fear," I add, unable to look him in the eyes.

"You should tell Bill 'yes,'" Richard says. "You cannot give up on this offer..." He's weighing his words, and finally adds, "even at the cost of our relationship."

We ask for the bill before we've gotten our main course. We don't feel like eating anymore.

"I'm sorry," I tell Richard when we're standing on the sidewalk outside the restaurant. "It's your birthday. We're supposed to be celebrating."

"It's fine," Richard says. "I've never really made a big deal out of my birthday."

We look at each other for a few moments.

"I think I'll go home now," Richard says. "I need to be by myself for a bit."

I feel like I'm suffocating all over again. I don't know what to say. I feel lost.

"Yeah," I reply, choking on my words. "I also need to sort out my thoughts." I get into the Jaguar.

"Won't Richard be joining us?" Arthur asks.

"Not for now," I answer, looking out the window as the car drives away.

When I get home, I burst into tears and begin drinking to dull the pain. But the more I drink, the stronger my sadness grows, until it fills my entire world.

"You look awful," Maria says the next morning.

"I feel awful."

"What's wrong?"

"It's Richard. I don't know. I think we broke up."

"Don't give up on him. Everything will work out," she says. Her wisdom is simple, true.

I decide to go out for a morning run, and while I'm out I try to practice my positive mantras that Judith taught me, but they're not really helping me right now.

The day passes, and neither of us tries to contact the other.

The next day, I decide to go over to his apartment. On the way there, I buy a bottle of wine, some chocolate, and a bouquet of roses. I enter the building and am stopped by the doorman.

"Where are you headed, sir?" he asks, as if he doesn't recognize me, even though he's seen me many times before.

"To Richard Silverman's."

"Mr. Silverman left the building last night and hasn't come back yet."

"Where did he go?"

"He didn't say," he replies indifferently.

I walk outside and sit down on a bench by the building's entrance.

I sit there for close to an hour, ostensibly waiting for Richard to return, but I know he might not come back for days. Once I devour all the chocolates I bought him, I suddenly get up, run to my Porsche, and speed towards the vacation village in Tiffany, Maine. Something tells me Richard is there, where our story began.

If he is actually there in Maine, I'll take it as a sign that our relationship is important to him, and that I must make brave decisions and get over my fear. The road is almost empty, and I drive like crazy between the giant trees with their leaves in shades of orange and red.

Late-autumn in New England is absolutely beautiful, and I feel my senses getting sharper. I am aware of what is happening all around me, of everything contained in this moment. It all becomes clear and focused before my eyes. The lyrics to Metallica's "Nothing Else Matters" playing on the radio suddenly take on special significance.

When the smell of the ocean begins to fill the air, I just know that I'm in the right place. Just like that first time four months ago, I'm traveling into the unknown. But now, my excitement is different. Everything just feels much more fateful.

I drive into the parking lot. Richard's car isn't there. Still, something tells me not to give up. I walk towards the ocean, getting close to the water's edge. Ships and sailboats are bobbing before my eyes, and it looks like a painting. I walk all along the beach. Some isolated travelers pass me, as others sit on chairs looking out at the ocean. Richard is not among them. My heart feels like it might crack. I wasn't prepared for this disappointment. I have never failed like this before. My instincts always lead me to the right place.

By the afternoon, I start losing hope. Half a day has already passed without any trace of Richard. My fear of abandonment and rejection overwhelms me, reminding me of harder times. How could I have let someone I love so much, someone for whom I waited for so long, leave me just like that. I lie down in the sand in despair. The wind beats against me but isn't able to shake my sense of utter emptiness.

Two hours pass, and I wake up with a start on the beach, a bit wet from ocean spray. My emotional exhaustion had won, and I had sunken deep down inside myself into a sort of wakeful sleep. I try to figure out where I went wrong. I remember what Judith says: if feelings are rooted in my heart and in Richard's, our connection will continue. What is meant to be will be.

I cover my eyes with my hands and I try to calm myself down; I repeat my mantras and try to raise my energy level. My eyes, slowly recovering from the massage my hands gave them, suddenly notice a figure lying on a wooden bridge leading to a harbor for small boats.

It's Richard, sitting there on the edge of the bridge, staring into the water. I breathe out a sigh of relief. I approach him, full of apprehension; I have no idea how he will react to seeing me.

I stomp loudly on a pile of shells and Richard turns around. Surprised and sad, he walks towards me, and we embrace. Tightly. We ignore everyone around us.

"How did you know I'd be here?"

"I just knew."

"I hoped you'd come."

"I hoped you'd be here. But where's your car?" I ask

"I came in a rental. I didn't want anything that was mine," Richard responds.

Silence.

"We need to talk," I say.

"We've spoken a lot recently, and look where that got us," Richard says. "I've had a really tough few days."

"Me too."

"It's impossible to find a solution to a problem when you're still inside it. You need to remove yourself in order to find a solution, and that's what I did."

"And what have you found?" I ask.

"That I love you."

"I love you too. After managing to pick up some of the pieces of myself, I realized that I can and must deal."

"With what?"

"With the truth. With however people I do business with will react, with the leaders of the Democratic Party, with my parents. I don't know how this adventure will end, but I am ready to take this step, for our sake."

"And what about the president's offer?"

"It's a tad more complicated," I answer. "But I thought about that, too. I'll tell them I'll take it, and we'll start a slow process of coming out. In the beginning, we'll just tell our mothers."

"I can go first," Richard says. "It won't be so complicated with my mom. But you come with me when I go."

"OK. And then I'll tell my mother. And when I finish the job in the Middle East, we'll get married."

Richard is taken aback. His expression shows me that he is excited, but he stops himself, unwilling to surrender yet.

"When does the job end?"

"It's supposed to be about three months."

"So in December we'll make it official?" he asks.

"Yes. In December, we'll get married," I reply.

Something big is about to happen; something that I can't even begin to comprehend, but I feel it, and it is accompanied by a sense of power the likes of which I have never known before, along with a great deal of curiosity.

We go up to Richard's room, clinging to each other. We undress, and Richard leads me to the bed.

"Let's spend the night here," I say.

"Definitely," Richard answers. "When should we go to Chicago?"

"You're very decisive."

"I am. Someone needs to make some decisions around here, and you have a tendency to push things off when it comes to your private life."

"Let's go to Chicago next weekend," I say.

"Great. I'll book us tickets for a baseball game," he says, while grabbing my neck and kissing me passionately. I surrender myself completely, holding Richard's head and kissing him back, passion and desire rising inside me. I gently kiss his chest, feeling his heart beating fast. He lies down and surrenders to the pleasure. We pleasure each other until we both come, and then sprawl out on the bed, side by side, in silence.

At the entrance to Rockefeller Center, I say 'hi' to everyone I see. In a few more months, everyone will know I'm gay. Along with this thought comes the familiar fear, but it's different now, under control.

"Good morning," I greet Alexandra, who follows me into the office. "Please schedule a dinner for me with Bill Black this evening."

When Alexandra leaves the room, I sit on my chair, close my eyes, and think about my life: This evening, there is a chance that I will be appointed the president's envoy. By next week, I will be out, at least with Richard's mother and mine, and in December, I will be openly married to a man, for all the world to see. It's hard to believe that only a few months ago, I thought my boring life was going to just keep repeating itself over and over again.

I am convinced that I'm the right man for the job. My main goal will be to bring the Israelis and Palestinians together to the negotiating table without any preconditions. I'm sure it's possible. I know I'll be able to bring them together for economic agreements as a first stage. This will be my direction if there isn't any diplomatic breakthrough.

Adam enters my office, shaking me out of my thoughts, and I look at him. *He is the best person to replace me at Olympia in my absence,* I think. *He should take the reins over the next few months.*

That evening, I meet Bill Black at Renaissance. We sit at our usual table. We order our usual wine. "I accept the offer," I tell him, extending my hand.

"You've made the right choice," he answers, with a firm handshake. His two hands wrapped around mine remind me of the great deal of trust he has placed in me, going as far back as when I was a young party activist and he a senior official. It also makes me think of how much he expects of me. He gives me a wink, the kind that says everything will be fine. We unclasp our hands, and start finalizing the details of my mandate letter.

CHAPTER 9

Chicago, IL, Mid-September

"Are you OK?" I ask Richard. We're waiting in the first-class lounge for the boarding call.

"I'm fine," he assures me.

"You don't have any concerns? Not even something small?"

"Obviously I have concerns about the future, but not about this visit. My mother's very sick. She can't process any new information, and she's basically completely out of touch with reality," he says, as his eyes well up with tears.

Richard escapes into his newspaper, and I pick up a paper, too. My eyes scan the headlines, but nothing grabs my attention.

"If you really want to know," Richard continues, "what scares me the most is the feeling that you're here, not because you want to be but because I want you to be. I don't want you doing anything for me unless you're sure you want to."

"Enough, Richard," I'm annoyed but trying to be considerate of the emotions that came up when he was talking about his mother. "I can't do any more than I'm doing already. I'm as sure about my decision as anyone who's been living a lie for years can be."

Richard doesn't respond. We sit there in an oppressive silence until salvation comes in the form of our boarding call.

That afternoon, we land in Chicago's O'Hare Airport and pick up the rental car that Richard had reserved. This time he takes the driver's seat.

"It's been years since I was last in Chicago," I say. "Back when I was working for the Democratic Party, I'd go to Chicago at least twice a year. From my desk at party headquarters, I organized huge demonstrations against the Republican president's domestic policy. All across the country, we took to the streets. The protests always caused chaos, and people called them "Tom's Gold-en demonstrations." Wherever we went, the police chiefs knew I always got what I wanted. The rallies were enormous – hundreds of thousands of demonstrators, young, passionate Democrats, liberal activists who I enlisted into action. They'd shout out slogans calling for changes in the country's educational and welfare policies.

"Back then," I tell Richard, "I had this tone of voice I'd use in speeches, and without noticing, I started using it in my everyday life." We both laugh. Then I sigh, remembering the discord I used to feel between my professional success and my emotional emptiness.

After my outburst of nostalgia, we resume our silence. I think about the things that Judith taught me, and blame myself for the murky atmosphere in the car. I'm the one who doesn't trust people, who interprets Richard's every movement or word or expression as a rejection or proof of imminent abandonment. At the same time, I still haven't completely deciphered Richard's negative emotional state. I think about what Judith says: "Listen to what he's actually saying to you, that's where the truth lies, not in what your emotional mind is telling you."

"Chicago's changed," I say, breaking the silence again.

"For the better, I hope."

"Definitely. I'm seeing a lot of skyscrapers that weren't here the last time I came."

"When was that?"

"More than eight years ago."

"And you're surprised?"

Richard laughs, and I join in. The heaviness starts to dissipate. Richard talks about Chicago's unique gift for reinventing itself, and how the cultural and culinary scenes here are thriving. He promises to take me to one of the city's hottest new restaurants for dinner. I think about how I'm about to see where Richard grew up, where he developed his personality, and I'm excited.

"Let's just hope you're not disappointed," he says. Again, we laugh.

"So how do you want me to introduce myself?" I ask him.

"It really doesn't matter. Just say whatever feels right, and lovingly follow her lead."

"'I'm Tom, Richard's boyfriend.' Is that OK?"

"That's perfect."

Richard drives towards the suburb, known to be a home for many Jews.

"This is one of the biggest Jewish communities in the country," Richard boasts.

"Even your mayor is Jewish," I add. "I emailed him to let him know I'm here. I'm going to meet with him, if we can make it work."

"You know the mayor?"

"He was at the Jewish Agency camp with Arik and me."

"Is there anyone you don't know?"

"Your mother," I say. Richard laughs.

"It's too bad you didn't get to know her in her heyday. When she was healthy, it was great spending time with her." Then he sighs. "Not that it happened very often."

"If I'd have known her back then, I would have known you, too, at a much younger age. My life might have turned out completely differently."

"Maybe. But what difference does it make? Our lives went the way they did, and now, here we are, on our way to visit my mother."

We turn onto a small side street.

"Did you always live here?"

"Yes. My father bought this apartment when he married my mother. She's lived here ever since. I lived in this neighborhood, too, until I was 28."

"Did you like living here?" I'm trying to imagine Richard as a little boy, running down the street on his way home from school. "This is where everything happened to you. You and I grew up in such different places."

"Very different," Richard agrees. "I liked the neighborhood, and the kids. When I was little, there were lots of Jewish families living in our building, and we'd go on trips together. We'd even celebrate holidays together. It was wonderful."

"So you kept that up until you were 28?" I'm trying, unsuccessfully, to lighten the tone, because Richard is parking the car, and I realize that the moment of truth – the moment I've been fearing my whole life – is coming.

"No," he answers earnestly. "High school, lots of friends, going out, Lake Michigan, parties, vacations. Studying, not so much. I didn't actually enjoy learning until college."

When we reach the top of the stairs, Richard rings the doorbell to one of the apartments. A petite woman with short chestnut hair opens the door and greets Richard. He returns her greeting and kisses her affectionately on the cheek.

"This is Rosa, my mother's caretaker."

"Nice to meet you. Tom," I say, shaking her hand.

"Just to be on the safe side, you probably shouldn't say the word 'caretaker' in front of your mother," Rosa tells Richard. "Tell your friend, too."

"Got it," I assure her.

We walk into a pleasant, modest living room. Richard's mother comes over to us.

"Look who's come to visit!" Her voice is full of joy.

"It's wonderful to see you," Richard says, hugging his mother. She doesn't return his hug, but pats him on the back instead. We sit down in the kitchen, and Richard gives his mother the bottle of Juicy Couture perfume that he bought in the airport. It is clear from her expression that she's pleased, even if she doesn't know exactly what to do with the big glass bottle in her hands.

"Are your parents still alive?" she asks Richard. For a moment I'm confused, and then connect her question to her Alzheimer's disease that Richard described to me.

"Mom," he asks gently, "who are my parents?"

"Who are my parents?" she answers.

"You're my mother," Richard explains patiently, "and your husband Moses, who died many years ago, was my father."

"That's right, Moses. Do you remember him?"

"Of course I remember him."

"I remember Moses," she says, and it is clear that she is trying to process what Richard just told her. "It's confusing, all this stuff."

"It really is confusing," Richard agrees, trying to make her feel better. He makes us coffee and a plate of cookies, and we carry them into the living room.

"Did you notice that Tom's here?" Richard asks.

"Of course I noticed," she says.

"Do you remember him?"

"Of course I remember him."

"Tom is my boyfriend, and we're going to be living together. As a couple."

"You've been together since you were young," she affirms.

"Yes," Richard says, flashing a smile at me.

"Speak quietly," she suddenly says. "They can hear you through the TV. We don't want them to think we're talking about them. Yesterday, some people came into the living room through the TV. I hosted them," she adds, gratified. Richard sighs and looks at me.

We spend about an hour sitting in the living room of the home where Richard grew up, talking to his mother, who seems to be constantly shifting back and forth between clear-mindedness and incoherence. When Richard decides that it's time to go, his mother walks us to the front door. Richard hugs her. I shake her hand, and then, on the spur of the moment, hug her and kiss her on the cheek.

"How you've grown," she says to me. We say goodbye. Rosa closes the door behind us, and we go down the stairs and out of the building.

"Well?" Richard asks once we're on the sidewalk.

"Sad."

"Very. But there's nothing we can do beyond what we're already doing."

"Why did you insist on coming here to tell her? It seems unnecessary, given her condition."

"You might be right, but deep down I still think of her as the woman she once was. In my mind, I see her the way she was back then: beautiful, vibrant, with yearnings and desires and a lot of love. Also, I want her to know, even subconsciously, that she still has value, so I treat her like I would anybody else."

"I understand," I say quietly, unable to find the words to describe the sadness and pain I feel witnessing the pain of my beloved. Richard pulls me closer, hugs me tight, and kisses me on the forehead. We stay in each other's arms for a long time, then drive away.

Richard stops near a crowded jazz club, where there's an afternoon concert of Chicago Blues covers of soul music. We get pushed inside. Richard clears a path for us, and we find ourselves standing at a tall bar table. We order beers.

"I once thought about becoming a talent agent here." Richard has to speak loudly to be heard over the noise. "I spent a lot of time in the Blues clubs in the city, and even thought about opening my own agency to find young talent with potential."

"That's basically what you're doing now," I tell him, "Only in the water industry."

We order another round.

"And you?" Richard asks. "If you hadn't inherited Olympia, what would you be doing?"

"Politics, I think. I'd be much more politically active."

The band takes a break, and we applaud. Quiet jazz pipes through the speakers.

"If you hadn't grown up in Chicago," I ask Richard, "where would you have liked to grow up?"

"Connecticut, I think. Right next to you." He pauses for a moment. "Actually, I have no idea. Chicago's a fascinating city. It has everything."

"I used to think that Connecticut had everything, too. I got to live in a fancy town, on a street where every family owned an estate as big as a neighborhood, where money flowed like water, and nobody worried about getting by. But at a certain age, I realized that it was just an illusion, and I began to feel like I was trapped in a golden cage. Manhattan saved me. When I got there, I felt like I'd been let out of jail. Manhattan is a bastion of freedom and self-realization. It's hard for me to imagine living anywhere else."

"Manhattan really is the embodiment of freedom," Richard agrees, "but every place has its pros and cons. I don't think where you live matters all that much when you're at peace with yourself."

When the show is over, we leave the club and go to our hotel suite. The hotel clerk escorts us to the elevator that opens directly onto the suite. The windows overlook the entire Chicago skyline. From the design of the suite, and the brochures neatly stacked on a small table, it's clear that we are in the hotel's honeymoon suite. We're pleased – we're celebrating our honeymoon a few months before the wedding.

We order breakfast up to our room and stay in bed until noon, at which point we need to get out of bed because Richard has arranged for us to meet with his good friend Wendy Tuchman.

"Wendy's a curator. She's currently showing an exhibition of giant globes designed by artists from all over the world, all relating to the international water crisis," Richard explains. "I promised her I'd see it."

We head over to the covered exhibition space at Grant Park. Wendy waves to Richard, and we walk over to her.

"Richard," she's excited to see him. "You look fantastic."

They share a warm embrace and she clings closely to him, making me a tad jealous. I quickly tell myself to calm down.

"Wendy, this is Tom," Richard says.

"Hi, Tom." Wendy looks me over from head to toe and shakes my hand, offering me a small smile. Then she unfolds a map of the exhibition and tells us where we should begin. "Text me when you're done," she tells Richard. "I have to go meet with some potential buyers now."

"The globes are for sale?" I ask.

"Yes," Wendy says. "We're selling them to increase awareness of the global water crisis. Wherever they're displayed, they'll raise people's awareness."

Since the water crisis is one of my top priorities, I wonder whether I could display one of the globes at the entrance to Rockefeller Center or some other central location.

"How much does a globe cost?"

"A lot."

"Try me."

"The cheapest one is about a hundred thousand dollars," she says.

"And the most expensive?"

"Five hundred thousand."

"Sold to Tom Gold," I announce.

"That's you, I assume?"

"In the flesh."

Wendy turns to Richard. "Your friend is rich, I gather."

"A billionaire," he laughs.

"A billionaire who is passionate about the global water crisis," I add. Wendy again studies me with interest.

We leave Wendy after she shows us where we'll find the globe I just bought, and we start wandering through the exhibition. The globes are impressive. I'm pleased that I made this decision. We stop next to my globe; it's beautiful. Unable to restrain myself, I text Adam.

Find out if the management at Rockefeller Center will let me put a sculpture in the lobby. It's about eight feet tall.

He texts back immediately. **Checking.**

"It was a great idea, coming here today," I tell Richard.

"I knew we had to come. I trust Wendy's taste. She does great work."

"By the way, what's the deal with her? I saw how she was clinging to you."

"Yeah, we had a fling once," Richard confesses. "She wanted more than that, but I was too afraid of intimacy. We stayed in touch after we broke up."

"Is she married?"

"No, but she'd like to be. Do you want me to fix you up with her?"

"Of course. Didn't you see how she looked at me?"

"What did you expect? You're her ideal man: hot, nice, tall. And now that she knows you're a billionaire, it's even better."

"So she likes money?"

"No, I'm just being mean. She's a wonderful, talented woman. But like all American Jewish women past the age of 35, she's feeling the pressure to find a Jewish husband. And a rich one, if possible."

"Does she know about us?"

"Not yet," Richard says. "But she will very soon."

When we meet up with Wendy after our tour of the exhibition, I give her my business card so we can make all the arrangements for the purchase and transfer of the globe by tomorrow.

Then, Richard begs my pardon and pulls her aside.

They talk quietly for a while. Richard's doing most of the talking. Wendy's back is to me so I can't see her expression. Finally, they hug. Richard leaves her and comes back to me, and Wendy waves at me, smiling broadly.

"She was stunned," Richard said, "but she has an open mind, and she's happy for me."

"And you?"

"I'm over the moon."

In the taxi, on our way to the baseball game, we hold hands. Richard buys us hot dogs with a lot of mustard and a giant cola, and we find our seats. The Cubs are high in the standings, and every seat in the stadium is packed. I'm not a huge baseball fan, but I enjoy a good game, especially when it's an important one.

"Number seven is my favorite player," Richard informs me.

"Then he's mine, too."

As soon as the game begins, Richard is up on his feet. He joins in with the other fans, singing the team song, calling out to the players, and shouting out encouragement. I stand next to him and find myself watching him more than the game. He's shouting, singing, jumping up and down; I've never seen him so uninhibited. He's as excited as a little boy. I look at him with tremendous love, and a little envy. I have never allowed myself to let loose like that.

Our team wins. Number seven really did stand out. We leave the stadium happy. Richard buys some souvenirs and asks me to take his picture with a group of fans.

"How much do you think it would cost me to buy the Cubs?" I can't figure out if he's joking or not.

"You don't need to try and impress me with your money," I tell him, and he laughs.

Back at the hotel, we have dinner in the bar next to the lobby. Then we go up to our suite. After we shower and have sex, Richard falls asleep quickly, but I lie awake. I know that once we're back in New York tomorrow, it will be time for me to fulfill my part of the deal and tell my mother about us.

Still naked, I get out of bed and look out the large window at the illuminated Chicago night sky. I stare at the few stars I can see and am reminded of something my grandmother used to tell me when I was a boy. If you counted seven stars for three consecutive nights, she said, on the third night, you would dream about the person you were going to marry. I don't need to count stars anymore. I go back to bed, lie next to him, wrap my arms around him, and fall asleep.

My mother is currently curating an exhibit at MoMA, so we meet for lunch at a nearby chef's restaurant. I know she's not going to make a scene there, where everyone knows her, but I reserved a quiet table off to the side just in case. Apparently, my fear of an outburst is far stronger than any rational consideration.

"Mrs. Gold is already waiting for you," the hostess says, leading me to the table. Mother stands up to greet me. I kiss her on the cheek, we hug, and sit down.

"Are you ready to order?"

"I'll have the Sunday special," my mother says. "Same for you?" she asks me. I nod.

"What's new with you, Tom?"

"I just got back from an art exhibition in Chicago," I tell her after the waitress leaves. With my mother, it's always best to start the conversation with something from her own world.

"Who was the curator?"

"Wendy Tuchman."

"A great girl."

"You know her?"

"Yes, she's quite known. A fine young Jewish woman."

I tell her about the show, about the globe I bought, and about my plans to display it in Manhattan.

"Where in Manhattan?"

"The lobby at Rockefeller Center. Or maybe Central Park."

"Maybe you should put it at the entrance to the U.N. After all, the water crisis is an international issue."

"Excellent idea. Lucky for me, I have a mother who is not only beautiful, not only smart, but also a curator."

Mother smiles. She looks pleased, or at least as pleased as she can.

"So what brought you to Chicago?"

"The exhibition."

"Since when do you go to exhibitions?"

"I went with a friend," I reply.

"Richard?"

"Yes."

"You've been together a while?"

"Yes," I answer, without thinking about the implications of her question. Then it hits me: she knows. My mother knows. I'm too shocked to speak.

"I know, Tom," she confirms. Her expression is serious and sad.

"What do you know?" With tremendous effort, I manage to keep my voice down.

"That you and Richard have been a couple for months. I knew that weekend, too, when you brought him to the Hamptons."

"You guys have been following me?" I feel like I'm about to explode.

"Keep your voice down," she says, glancing from side to side. "We don't have to follow you. We have Arthur."

"*Arthur?*" I bang my fist down on the table.

"Be quiet, Tom," my mother says, using her authoritative, aggressive tone that has always managed to silence me. "People know me here." She takes a sip of water. "You know that Arthur was your father's driver for years at Olympia. He's the reason your father was able to keep tabs on you." Her voice is too calm, and I feel like I'm about to lose it. "We know about

The Silent Bartender, and also about Richard. Your father found out everything he needed to know about him."

The fury rising inside me is about to burst out, but – as always – all it takes is one look from my mother to convince me to restrain myself, to keep my feelings buried deep inside, to keep my mouth shut.

"Your father's crushed, Tom," she says sadly.

"Let him be crushed," I finally reply. "I don't care. I don't care! I'm gay, Mother," I blurt out. My voice quivers, but I feel an enormous sense of relief. "I've been in the closet for years. I didn't come out because I didn't want to hurt you and Father, to destroy the illusion you built of a rich, perfect Jewish family in Connecticut. Until now, I've been so worried about what people would say, about what it would mean for you. But I'm coming out. This is my decision. The son of Susan and Joseph Gold is a confirmed homosexual. He has a boyfriend named Richard Silverman, and in December, they're going to get married."

After a long silence, she says, "Your father won't stand for it."

"And what about you?"

Another long pause. "I'll try, Tom," she says quietly. "I really will try. I know that a mother is supposed to love her children and accept them as they are, and I really will try my best."

I feel like I can breathe again, that I'm back in control. Now that this secret that's been eating me up inside for so many years is finally out, I feel like, for the first time in my life, I'm in a position of power.

"If you knew all this time, why didn't you try to talk to me about it? Why did you keep trying to fix me up with girls? At your last birthday party, you told me – in front of hundreds of guests – that what you wanted for your birthday was for me to be married by your next one."

"And now you're granting my wish," she says bitterly. She can't bring herself to look me in the eye.

"Will you come to the wedding?"

"I tried, I really tried," she says, ignoring my question. "I tried to accept the fact that you date men. I wanted to embrace you, to show you how much I love you, to comfort you. I know you, and I know that you're sensitive, that you care about family. But I couldn't do it. I kept thinking about how hard this was on your father, how his heart was breaking, and I couldn't find the strength or courage to talk to you about it. But I'll keep trying, Tom. You just need to give me some time." And in these words, I manage to find some solace.

"When you brought Richard over for the weekend," she continues, "I tried to accept him and love him, just as if you were bringing a serious girlfriend to meet your parents for the first time. It was hard, but I tried. I was nice to him the whole time, even though I felt like I was going off the rails. I wanted to befriend Richard; I thought it might help me understand why the two of you are together. I wanted you to be happy and to know that you are wanted no matter what, even if you date men."

"Gay, Mom. I'm gay. I don't 'date men,'" I say with some measure of satisfaction. I am aware that on some level, I am saying this to myself as much as to my mother.

"This whole thing is a lot for me. I'm worried about your father - he's like a dead man walking. He doesn't know how to keep you and Richard apart. He's been using all his political connections to get you appointed as the Middle East envoy, in the hopes that the job and all the traveling will drive a wedge between the two of you."

None of this surprises me. My father has no boundaries.

"Did he ever tell you what happened when I was six years old?" I suddenly ask her.

"No." I can see she's telling the truth.

"You should ask him."

We ask for the bill, even though neither of us has touched our food; we've both lost our appetites. Outside the restaurant, we say our goodbyes. She heads back to the museum, and I go off in the opposite direction. I walk for a long time. Finally, I arrive at home, where Richard welcomes me with open arms. He hugs me, and I burst into tears.

CHAPTER 10

Manhattan, Late-November

This week will be my last trip to Israel. Over the past few weeks, I've been coming and going, flying roundtrip between the Middle East and Washington. During all these trips, I've come to the realization that it's all futile. Each side has dug into their positions. The most dramatic move I could hope to achieve would be getting the Israelis and Palestinians back to the negotiating table based on the hazy idea of a two-state solution, with all the main topics of dispute remaining unchanged. The absurdity is that even that would be considered a huge achievement.

At the same time, I'm also running Olympia and moving forward with my private ventures in West Africa, with the help of Adam, who has been a champion for both of these large projects.

But the bulk of my attention is dedicated to something much more important to me – my upcoming wedding, on December 31st.

Richard told everyone close to him about our decision and was rewarded with blessings and congratulations. I, on the other hand, haven't told anyone. I haven't heard a word from Mother since we met. It's been difficult for me, and I'm having mood swings. Richard is full of understanding and consideration, and Jessica and Judith have been trying to be as supportive as possible.

Judith suggested that before starting with the regression exercises, I should do some positive thinking exercises using my rational mind, in order to train it to handle my negative emotional mind, which has been working overtime lately, sending me back to my old habits, patterns that I am trying as hard as possible to break. The thinking exercises have helped me overcome my feeling of rejection and my inability to trust. I am learning to observe the world from the inside, as if I'm standing at the center of the universe looking out at infinite possibilities, rather than doing so from the outside, the way I've always observed the world until now, which made it seem like I didn't have any good options. The anxiety I live with has definitely decreased, and I am better able to deal with the decision to come out of the closet and get married.

Richard wants us to get married somewhere small, only with family and close friends, but he hasn't ruled out the idea of a small wedding at home with only family. I have a hard time imagining either of these possibilities, since there is no one from my family who'd come anyway. Even if I were to invite my mother, I don't think she'd come, and I don't think she'd have the nerve to tell my father or siblings that I was marrying Richard. Life is all about making decisions, and the toughest ones to make are the ones that push us forward. We don't always know or understand the destination, but we can feel it in our gut when we've made the right choice, something that will lead us to the right place. My decision to live together with Richard was an intuitive one, and I tend to trust my gut feelings. They are what has led me to my most important decisions for my business empire. Unlike Richard, I like to imagine a wedding where there is only me, him, and someone marrying us on my penthouse balcony.

In the meantime, I keep up my daily routine, trying to divide my energy equally among tasks, giving each of them my full attention, and when the weekend arrives, I welcome it with open arms, because that's when I finally get to enjoy my time and my quiet with Richard.

The stereo is playing Neil Young, and I relax as I look at the view from my balcony. A hand caresses my head as another hand gently takes my headphones off me. I stand up and hug Richard. He breaks away first and looks at me with a seductive smile. He slowly brings his lips close to mine, his eyes closed, and I follow his lead. He tightens his grasp around my neck and kisses me.

"I missed you," I tell him.

"I missed you too."

"I've been thinking about the wedding," I say.

"And what have you concluded?"

"Let's get married, just the two of us, here on my balcony, with someone from the 'Tomorrow Organization.'"

"I take it you still haven't spoken to your mother."

"Nope, and I don't plan to. I told her we were getting married at the end of December, and I haven't heard a word from her since."

"And your siblings?"

"I don't think she told them."

"Maybe you should go see them?"

"I don't think it'll help. They'll never go against my father and come stand by my side at our wedding."

"Still, I think you should go see them before your next trip to Israel. It's important for them to know, and it's better for them to hear it from you, not your mother. Who knows? Maybe they'll surprise you and come. Then we could have a small ceremony with family from both sides. If not, we'll do it with just us and then we can celebrate with my sister and brother-in-law after."

That afternoon, I call my brother. Based on the conversation, I can tell he doesn't know a thing. I ask if we can have lunch together on Monday. We arrange to meet up at a restaurant on the beach in Bridgeport, and he promises to invite our sister Diana. I then sit down and write a short letter to my father, a letter that I'll send by courier to make sure he gets it. But my hands have turned to stone and my brain is totally empty, so I decide to leave it for now. I'll write the letter when the time is right.

Sunday passes nicely. We go for a morning run in Central Park, and then we walk around the park holding hands. From time to time, the thought crosses my mind that I might bump into someone I know, but then I remember that I'm prepared to deal with it if it happens. We go back to my place and Richard cooks up some Chinese food for lunch. He makes corn soup with egg noodles and vegetable beef stir-fry topped with crushed peanuts. I help, following his instructions.

"Have you thought about where we should live after the wedding?" I ask him.

"I think this place is great. It feels like home when I come here."

"I'd love for us to live here together," I say. "I really feel connected to this apartment."

"Do you want me to buy half of it, so it belongs to both of us?"

"No. This place is yours, even without you paying a penny. Later on, we'll buy a home together."

"In Connecticut?" Richard asks.

"No. I don't want to live behind walls. I was thinking more like a townhouse in Chelsea."

"So we'll be hipsters," Richard laughs.

That night, after Richard falls asleep, I go into my office with a glass of cognac, sit down at my desk, and write to my father:

Dear Father,

I don't even know where to begin. It has been so many years since we exchanged any loving words. Our emotional disconnect is so deep and painful. You should know that I feel it every day, every hour. For years, I lived a life that was disconnected from my feelings, seeking out the father I knew from the past, my father from before I was six years old, the one who spoiled me, hugged me, loved me unconditionally. I was living something that was almost but not fully a life. Living a big lie. But recently, ever since I met Richard, something's changed. I will never let myself go back to the pain and the fear that made me so miserable.

I'm getting married, Father. To a man. I know that you know, and I can only assume what you've been going through. But I also know that in the years to come, you will regret not finding the strength to accept me, to understand me, and to love me unconditionally. I am finally able to feel, to experience emotions, and I am asking with all my heart that you try, despite your basic objections, to stand beside me on my wedding day, and to join in my happiness.

I have been on a long journey, an endless one, seeking peace and quiet. I recently found peace, and I also found that I have the inner strength it takes to accept and forgive you for how you tortured me when I was a child and then a teenager. That is why I am begging you, Father, to find your own inner strength and try to accept my life choices, my decision to live my life with my soulmate. I dream about you standing beside me at my wedding, smiling at me, loving me unconditionally.

I love you,

Tom

I haven't been using Arthur's services since my conversation with my mother, but the truth is I can't really feel mad at him. I know how hard it is to withstand pressure from my father. And also, somewhere deep down, I feel grateful to him for telling my parents what I had wanted to tell them for years but never found the strength to. Still, I can no longer trust him. I put my faith in him, and he betrayed me. But I haven't fired him yet.

On Monday afternoon, after finishing up some work I needed to do at Olympia, I go with my new driver Philip to an authentic Tuscan restaurant in Bridgeport to meet up with my brother and sister. I arrive a half hour early, sit down at the table I reserved, and quickly order a bottle of Chianti so I can try to calm my nerves before they arrive. The three of us have never made plans like this. We've never taken our relationship outside the framework that Mother and Father put us in. We are always polite towards each other, we celebrate holidays and birthdays together, we buy each other presents, we speak about politics and sports, but we haven't actually had a real relationship for years now.

"Tom," Diana calls to me from the door, waving. My sister is the female version of me, with her toned build and her aristocratic looks. And then there's our brother, who's turned into a short, chubby man.

"How's it going, handsome?" Diana asks, hugging me tight.

"It's going good," I answer. "Actually, much better than good, but I'll get into that when Benjamin gets here. It would be a shame to have to say it all twice. And how are you?"

"I'm doing less good," she responds. "David and I are getting a divorce."

"What happened?"

"We fell out of love."

"What does that even mean? After 11 years together, you suddenly fell out of love?"

"It's been happening for the past year and a half," she tells me. "We started to grow apart. David kept working for his insurance company, I'm at the hospital and my clinic, everything basically stayed the same, but something had changed. We were speaking less and less, sharing with each other less and less about what we were going through. Sometimes I feel like we sold our souls for our careers and money, until we had nothing left inside. I told him a number of times that we were drifting apart, and I suggested couples therapy, but he kept pushing it off. One day, I felt like I couldn't take it anymore, and I told him I wanted a divorce. He got nervous and tried to please me, but I realized it was too late. There was no appreciation left. There was no friendship left. I think he was also having an affair. And that's it. That's how we fell out of love."

I reach out for Diana's hand and hold it tight, trying to comfort her.

Benjamin joins us. We hug and laugh, sip wine, and eat the food that Benjamin, our confirmed foodie, has chosen for us.

After about an hour spent mostly talking about what's going on in Diana's life, I gently tap my fork against my wineglass and ask for their attention.

"Even though we're all catching up on Diana, I would like to remind you that I am the one who asked for this lunch," I say in a silly tone, managing to make them laugh. "Do you know why I asked you guys to come meet me here?"

"No," they both answer.

"Has Mother spoken to you guys?"

From their expressions, I can tell that they don't know anything about it.

"OK, so I'm getting married at the end of next month."

They attack me with hugs and kisses, surprising me with this display of real warmth.

"Tell us about her!" Diana asks. "What does she do? What's her name? How old is she?"

"I told Mother," I reply. "I was sure she'd tell you."

"You weren't surprised that we didn't call to congratulate you?" Benjamin asks.

"I finally realized she must not have told you, and that's why I wanted us to meet."

"Does Mother not like her?" Diana asks.

"She doesn't like the idea."

"Because it's a quick engagement?" Benjamin asks.

"Because I'm marrying a man," I say, lowering my face, having a hard time maintaining eye contact.

There is a long silence at our table. Benjamin fidgets, one hand playing with his short beard while the other rests on his belly. Diana looks out the window.

"What's his name?" she asks.

"Richard."

"Since when are you gay?" she blurts out, with a directness that is almost scathing, but her tone is actually full of sensitivity.

"I've been for many years." I answer. "For years, I've been in the closet, afraid to be found out. I didn't want to hurt Olympia, or our parents' feelings, or my political career. But Richard made me believe in myself and gave me the courage to do this."

"How long have you been together?" Benjamin asks.

"Seven months, and we're getting married at the end of December. I asked you to come here because I want to invite you to my wedding. I would be so happy if you'd come stand by my side on this important day in my life."

"Are Mother and Father coming?"

"I haven't spoken to Father. I'm sending him a personal letter tomorrow, and I hope it will help. I told Mother, and you can guess what she thinks about it all, seeing as she didn't tell you anything."

When we say our goodbyes after this conversation that has brought us closer, my siblings hug me warmly. They promise to do whatever they can to try to help me with our parents.

I wave goodbye and get in the Jaguar. I pour myself some cognac and notice Philip looking at me through the rearview mirror.

"What is it?" I ask.

"You look different from the Tom who got into this car in Manhattan a few hours ago," he says. "Is everything okay?"

"What do you mean different?"

"Just different. I don't know how to explain it. But it looks like a good change."

I thank him and smile to myself. I know exactly what he means.

"Who did you hand the envelope to?" I ask the courier, who has returned to my office after delivering the letter I wrote to my father.

"An older man with white hair and red cheeks. The guard at the gate called him out, and I asked him if his name was Mr. Gold, just like you told me to. Only after he said yes and I saw that he fit the description you gave me, I handed him the letter."

"And then what happened?"

"They wanted to close the gate, but they saw that I was still standing there. Your father thought I was waiting for a tip and took his wallet out of his pocket, and I said this might sound strange but I was asked to make sure he opened the letter and read it."

"What did he say?"

"He didn't say anything. He looked me in the eyes suspiciously and looked at what was written on the envelope. I guess once he saw your name, he decided to open it, even though he didn't seem pleased about it, and he read it."

"How did he react?"

"He looked like he saw a ghost," the courier answers. He leaves my office after I pay him.

I sit down, still as a rock. Thankfully, Adam comes in, forcing me out of my thoughts to deal with company matters. He updates me on the newest developments at Olympia and I tell him I'm going on my last trip to Israel as the President's Envoy to the Middle East tomorrow. I know that the chances of reaching any breakthrough are small, so long as the current generation of leaders isn't replaced with young, pragmatic, creative ones. When he leaves, Alexandra comes in and updates me about the rest of my day. Finally, with a bit of embarrassment, she mentions the dinner I've scheduled for her, Adam, and me.

"So, what are we eating?" I ask Alexandra and Adam when I get to the restaurant, trying to lighten up the mood.

"The Tuesday special looks great," Adam says.

While we eat, he asks me if this meal was scheduled to celebrate my achievements in the Middle East. The question makes sense; after all, the three of us have never gone out for a meal, so why should we tonight?

"If we take a closer look at my achievements in the Middle East, I think we'd find that they don't even warrant the Tuesday special," I laugh. "No, I invited you to dinner because I wanted to let you know that I'm getting married next month."

"Congratulations!" they both cry out.

"You're worse than a CIA agent," Adam says. "How could you keep something like this a secret?"

"It's a bit more complicated than you think," I answer, and I add, quickly, so I don't have time to change my mind, that I'm marrying a man. The joy on their faces that I saw a moment ago turns into astonishment.

"You're what?!" Alexandra asks loudly.

"I've been gay for many years," I say, and I realize that this word, "gay," which I could never associate with out loud before is starting to feel more natural for me to say.

"Seven months ago, I met someone who gave me the strength and courage to come out of the closet, and we've decided to get married. You guys know him."

Adam and Alexandra exchange glances, trying to guess who I'm talking about. I tell them.

"Richard Silverman is gay?!" Alexandra calls out loudly once again, and immediately quiets herself.

"No, he's a straight guy marrying a gay guy," Adam answers mockingly, and we all crack up.

The Wedding, Late-December

When I fly home from Israel, Richard comes to pick me up at the airport and we go to meet his sister at a chef restaurant in Manhattan. We don't let go of each other's hands for even a second. Our time with Richard's sister, Rachel, and her husband, Ben, is really pleasant. They're a wonderful couple. I think to myself how easily I've been fitting in at these personal social gatherings. What once seemed to me a burden, suffocating, a threat to my privacy and freedom, now seems light and full of positive significance. At night, we return to the apartment. I ask the doorman whether I've gotten any mail from my parents. No. Neither Father nor Mother will come to my wedding.

I go inside the apartment and sprawl out on the couch. Richard sprawls out next to me. I move closer to him, gently grab his face, and kiss him. We feel ourselves getting hard. My body is up against his backside, and I gently penetrate him. Our hands are tightly clasped together. I look at him, and his eyes are closed. We change positions, and I am lying on top of him. He lifts his head and our eyes meet, and we stay like this until I lose control and come inside him. Richard pulls me onto his lap, and we lie down, embracing, without saying a word. We can't fall asleep. We don't want to let each other go. We're relishing our bubble of sweet intimacy.

Daylight shines through the blinds.

"The big day is two days away," Richard says, trying to find the strength to lift his head and get out of bed. "Who would have believed?!"

It really is hard for me to believe, especially given everything that I've been through over the past eight months. "It really seems like science fiction," I smile at him.

"We're science fiction that is becoming reality against all odds," he says. "I love you, Tommy. I'm going to do everything I can to make you happy."

"Against all odds, you are my whole life, Richard. You are my lover, my friend, my parent, my confident, my advisor, my chef. Everything I've ever wanted I have in you. You have changed me for the better, and I promise to keep working on improving."

Richard is moved and hugs me tightly. "What do you want to do this evening?"

"I feel like going to a club," I say.

"A club," Richard repeats, amused. "Since when do you go to clubs?"

"Never, actually," I answer, not mentioning The Silent Bartender.

That evening, Richard reserves a spot for us at a Karaoke Club near Times Square. I am surprised to discover a well-known club that I had never heard about before. In the past, I always knew which were the popular clubs in the city. But on second thought, since I spent most of my nights in recent years at The Silent Bartender, it makes sense that I didn't know about this place.

Richard booked us a booth off to the side, away from the rest of the club. The booths are acoustic, and the singers only hear themselves. Our deep intimacy allows us to do the one thing that embarrasses me most in front of other people – sing – and even to enjoy it.

On our wedding day, Richard has ordered us a light lunch, and then I ask for a little alone time until Cliff, the man who will be marrying us, arrives. I settle myself into one of the rooms and focus on staring into the horizon that I can see through the enormous penthouse windows. I have managed to find the point of balance that helps me clarify my thoughts. I am able to understand the emotional place that I am in today. I feel like a changed man. As if I was reborn. I think about Judith, the woman responsible for this change, with her neo-humanology methods.

After staring out at the horizon for two hours, a soft knock on the door manages to center me again. Richard urges me to get ready, it's time.

An hour later, we meet in the living room. Richard straightens my jacket and runs his hand through my hair to fix it. I straighten his blazer, and we kiss.

When Cliff arrives, we exchange niceties, and then he walks us through the ceremony.

As befits an alternative wedding, Cliff lets each of us make a personal declaration as part of our love contract. After his concluding blessing, we place wedding rings on each other's fingers.

Since we're both Jewish, we take Cliff's advice to end the ceremony by breaking a glass, as a reminder of the destruction of Jerusalem. We each break a glass and are declared married on behalf of the State of New York. When the wedding ceremony is over, Cliff takes a picture of us, and we warmly say goodbye.

At night, we go down to Fifth Avenue for our first night stroll as a married couple, to celebrate our freedom and liberation. Hand in hand, we go down to the ice-skating rink at Rockefeller Center, rent skates, and go around each other on the ice in endless circles.

On Sunday morning, we wake up late and rush to get ready for our guests who will be coming that afternoon to celebrate. Richard's sister and brother-in-law, my brother and sister, Adam, Alexandra, and of course Maria and her son Jose.

We raise a glass and enjoy one of the boutique wines I brought from Israel.

In the late afternoon, once everyone has left and our wedding party is over, I feel happier than I ever have in my entire life.

In the evening, we snuggle up together on the couch. Richard's hand rests on my shoulder. My head rests on his chest, like a child cuddling on his father's broad chest.

CHAPTER 11

Manhattan, Early January

"Tom, my friend, how are you?" Bill, who's asked me to meet him for an urgent one-on-one, enters the restaurant like a tornado. We sit across from each other, and he gives me a big smile.

"I got a good report from the president about your work in the Middle East. Both he and the party thank you."

"Thanks, Bill. But what's with all the urgency? What's going on?"

"I think you can probably guess," he answers with a wink.

"Honestly, I don't have a clue."

"Tom, the way the party is now, with all the rifts and the bickering, we're going to lose the election. I have no intention of allowing that to happen."

"I agree with you. We can't afford to lose this election."

"That's why, in light of your impressive track record in general and your accomplishments in the Middle East these last few months, we'd like you to announce your candidacy for president," Bill gushes.

"You'd like me to *what?!*"

"I'm serious, Tom. You've got everything the American people want. You're rich, successful, bright, with political experience. You're a successful businessman, an impressive philanthropist, and now you have these important diplomatic achievements under your belt. Young voters will support you – you'll fire them up with your charisma. You have the right last name, and I'm sure you'll be able to win over the country's liberal factions."

"You forgot to mention that I'm Jewish," I point out wryly.

"Yes, you're Jewish, but bear in mind that the Jews are the most well-organized political minority in the country. They also have high voter turnout. We've managed to put a Catholic in the Oval Office, and a black person – twice – so I don't see any problem. You wouldn't be the first Jew to run in the Democratic primaries, and we won't let your connection to Israel get in the way either. It's true, Tom, anti-Semitism may rear its ugly head every now and then, but it would be underground, and we'll know how to take care of it.

"Anti-Semitism has been plaguing the American Jewish community since the thirties. People even accused F.D.R. of being born Jewish and changing his name, and fascist groups incited attacks on Jews. Surveys taken in the forties showed that Jews were considered one of the biggest threats to America. So what?" Bill asks angrily. "We got through all that, didn't we? We have more influence over American leadership than any other minority in this country. If there are anti-Semitic responses, we'll quash them." His voice is firm.

"American Jewry is fractured," I say, insisting on getting into it deeper with Bill. "Are you aware of the reciprocal disgust within the Jewish population?"

"There have always been disputes among the different Jewish organizations, making it hard for them to work together," Bill says. "They didn't come together in the past, when it came to saving the European Jews' lives, and they won't unite now either to support you. Israel's first prime minister, David Ben-Gurion, called American Jews cowards because they laid low during the Holocaust. Some Jews might choose to lie low and support another candidate. It's nothing to get worked up over, Tom. And I don't see anti-Semitism as anything that should bother us, either."

I take a moment to get my thoughts in order and catch my breath. "Bill, I really don't know what to say."

Bill's expression is determined and serious. "Tom," he says, as if he's read my mind, "I'm the chairman of the Democratic National

Committee. I'm going to tell them that I'm backing you as a candidate. I have no doubt that other senior members of the party would do it too, even if I didn't. Take a few days to think it over."

He fixes his piercing eyes on me. We drink red wine, and about an hour later, we part ways with a long handshake. He leaves, and I am left in a state of complete shock. One thought keeps running through my head – a gay Jewish president. I stifle a chuckle, and my mind runs rampant.

"Tommy, why was your cellphone off?" Richard asks when I finally pick up. "I called to see if you were free for lunch, and Alexandra told me you were at a meeting. She said she had a hunch that something big was happening."

"Alexandra was right," I answer, "something huge has just happened."

"What happened, Tommy?"

"Meet me for lunch at Corn Bake, and I'll tell you everything."

When I get back to Olympia, Alexandra is sitting at her desk. She studies me anxiously, and I realize even though I have a huge smile plastered across my face, my eyes are red and teary.

"It's from laughter, not sadness," I reassure her, and I ask her to send Adam into my office. She stands up, adjusts her red pencil skirt, glances at me once more, and goes out to find Adam. Meanwhile, I duck into the bathroom to splash water on my face. When I get back to my office, Adam is already there. I sit on the edge of my desk.

"Sit," I say.

"Did something happen?" Adam asks. He, too, scrutinizes my face with some apprehension.

"Oh, something definitely happened. I'll give you three guesses."

"You're getting your nose pierced, you're dying your hair blonde, or you bought the most expensive penthouse in Manhattan."

I quickly remind him that I already own the most expensive penthouse in Manhattan. "Anyway, Adam, you're way off." I smile, letting my words hang in the air, relishing the wary look on his face.

"Well? Tell me already!"

"I met with Bill Black a couple hours ago," I finally say. "He's convinced that I should run in the Democratic primaries. For president of the United States. He promised to back me as chairman of the DNC, along with other senior members of the party. Even though the party can't officially support any candidate until the convention this summer, I think this is his way of telling me that the party believes I'm up to the task."

"Wow! That's huge, Tom. Whether you accept or decline, this is huge. So speak! What do you think you'll tell him?"

"I have no idea." I straighten my tie and walk towards the door. "Come, walk me to Corn Bake. I'm meeting Richard there for lunch."

We head down Fifth Avenue. I get lost in my own thoughts as Adam walks next to me with pride, smiling at the passers-by as if he's already walking next to the country's next president.

When we get to Corn Bake, Adam says "hi" to Richard and leaves. We sit at our usual table and order the house sandwiches – corned beef – which I consider the best lunch in Manhattan.

"Richard, Bill Black wants me to run for president of the United States."

"He wants you to *what?*" Richard shouts.

"You heard right." I can hardly believe the words coming out of my mouth.

"And what are you going to tell him?"

"I have no idea. What do you think I should tell him?"

"I think this is huge, Tom, and I think you need to do it. That's just my gut feeling, without thinking about all the implications."

"I'm assuming Bill doesn't know that I'm gay or that we're married," I tell Richard. "If he knew, he'd look for another candidate."

"You'll have to ask Bill Black about that," Richard says seriously, and in response I am filled with an anxiety that's all too familiar.

"I don't understand why it's so easy for you to tell the whole world about your sexual orientation," I snap, frustrated.

"It's not easy at all," Richard says, "but that's my way of dealing with it. I made my decision, and turning back now would defeat the whole purpose. And the supportive reactions I've been getting have only strengthened my resolve. I think you'll be pleasantly surprised like I have been."

"I don't know if I can handle the party's rejection."

"What makes you so sure you'll be rejected?" he asks, and I don't have a response.

After a long silence, Richard graciously changes the subject. At his initiative, we start discussing our honeymoon plans, but a text from Adam brings the elephant in the room trampling right back into focus.

Bill Black wants to meet with you next week, he writes.

I read the text out loud to Richard.

"Say 'yes,'" he says decisively.

Say yes, I text Adam, and then I decide that I'm not going back to the office today. I'm too distracted and I won't be able to get anything done. Richard also tells his secretary that he's knocking off for the day.

We go back home and jump into bed with a desire so fierce it feels insatiable. When I sense Richard's desire to pleasure me – a pure and selfless desire – I am filled with an ecstasy that is both physical and emotional. He lowers his head between my thighs, and I close my eyes blissfully. He loves me. I can feel it just as strongly as I feel the warmth that rises deep inside of me. I can't hold myself back, and I collapse on the bed, empty and thrilled. I pull him towards me, kiss him, and plant my head between his thighs. Afterwards, we lie in bed in each other's arms, my back against his chest. We curl up with each other, and he plants small kisses on my back. I feel safe and wanted, and that's how we fall asleep.

Later that evening, I get ready for my appointment with Judith. While Richard continues to sleep, I get in the shower and stand under the stream of hot water for a long time, reluctant to leave. Eventually I go back to the bedroom, my hair wet and wild, a towel wrapped around my waist, and I look at Richard. I wouldn't object to another quick round, but he's sound asleep and I decide to leave him be.

Philip is waiting for me in front of my building, as usual, and takes me to Judith's. She comes out of her room to greet me.

"Tom, dear, how are you?"

"All good," I answer, and follow her into her room.

Judith asks me about the wedding, and I tell her about the ceremony on the penthouse porch, with the New Year's Eve fireworks in the background. Then I describe the celebratory lunch we had the next day, with Richard's sister and her husband, my brother and his wife, my sister, Adam, Alexandra, Maria, and Maria's son, Jose.

"I want to do a regression today," I say. "I just met with the governor of Ohio who also happens to be the chairman of the DNC. He wants me to announce my candidacy for president of the United States, and to run in the upcoming primaries." I say all this as if it were the most natural, commonplace thing in the world. "I want to generate enough energy to be able to withstand the challenges and surprises that await me."

It takes Judith a few minutes to digest this information. "He wants *what?*" she shouts, dumbfounded, as if she's trying to make sure she heard it right. "Tom, that's incredible." To prove her point, she rolls up her sleeves to show me her goosebumps.

"Remember," she says, "you create your own reality."

"Judith, I've decided to do whatever I can to neutralize my fear of abandonment and the patterns of fear that have been a part of me for as long as I can remember. I need to clear some space for rational thought."

"Wonderful!" Judith says.

"Yes, it *is* wonderful," I confirm. "I've been asked to announce my candidacy for president of the United States." I repeat these words, hoping they'll help me absorb this new reality.

"Yes, Tom. I heard you. It's tremendous and it's fantastic, and we will indeed do a regression exercise, to neutralize the rejection that you experienced in your previous life. But first, you have to understand why we do it. Your problems are based within your soul. The soul feeds the brain all kinds of information, based on events that occurred prior to your birth, in what some people call 'past incarnations.' That information shapes your earliest perceptions. That's why children who grow up in the same family can have such different approaches to life. Neutralizing this information will help you overcome the patterns that were ingrained in you during your childhood."

When she finishes her explanation, she gives me instructions that help me enter a state of relaxation.

"Sit comfortably in your chair and close your eyes. Relax your body, arms, legs, neck, shoulders. Try to push away any troubling thoughts and stay as relaxed as you can. I'm going to slowly count backwards from ten, and you'll feel yourself growing calmer and calmer until you enter a state of deep relaxation. Ten…nine… eight…seven…six…five…four…three…two…one. You are now feeling relaxed and calm. You're drifting into a light sleep."

Her quiet counting calms me, and I feel myself losing control and allowing her to lead me to the depths of my tormented soul. A strange feeling envelops me. My heart starts beating faster, and I begin to sweat.

"Stay calm," Judith instructs me. "Treat this as if it's something you're watching in a movie."

After a little while, the pictures evaporate and disappear, as if they had never existed.

"I'm done," Judith announces.

It feels as though a camera flash has wiped out all the images that I'd seen, one by one, erasing them from my mind. I feel a tranquility that I've never known before. Judith continues speaking. "Now, instruct the emotional system inside you and above you to download new information through your energy channels, information that will replace the information you just released."

Something is streaming gently through my body. "It's the new information," Judith whispers. "Keep it concentrated in the area around your heart. Instruct your brain to create electrochemical bonds with this new information."

I feel a wave rush from my brain into my body, closing the circuit.

"Three, two, one – and you're back in the room, quiet, calm, balanced, and full of new energy."

When I open my eyes, I'm still a little hazy, but I do feel serene.

"Well done! You did it! Now you need to understand the connection between what you're experiencing right now and your emotional memory." Judith takes a deep breath and begins.

"The human is an extraordinary system."

I nod.

"I want you to understand the relationship between the feelings of rejection and abandonment that you experienced in the past and the problems you're struggling with today. The memories that just flooded your consciousness explain the urges that drive you today: to save the world, to trust only yourself, to live as if there's no tomorrow, to squeeze out as much as you can from every minute. Neutralizing this information will enable you to let go of the negative thought patterns of your childhood and replace them with new thought patterns and feelings. Remember: positive thoughts lead to positive feelings, and positive feelings lead to a positive reality. Negative thoughts, on the other hand, lead to negative feelings, and so on."

"You're saying that these regressions will enable me to rid myself of the painful feelings that have accompanied me throughout my entire life?" I can't hide the skepticism in my voice.

"Yes," Judith answers. "Remember, your emotional mind will do everything in its power to maintain the old thought patterns, and you may feel dizzy, sad, and lonely for a little while. Just keep using these techniques to neutralize the negative information that controls you."

★

A week later, on the morning of my meeting with Bill Black, Richard pulls me into the shower. He grabs the sprayer hose and points it at my face. I collect the water in my mouth and spit it back in his direction. He's in a great mood and I wonder whether he's forgotten about my meeting, or maybe he's just certain that things will turn out the way he wants: I'll say "yes," and Bill Black won't be the least bit troubled by the fact that the next Democratic presidential candidate is gay and recently married another man. Finally, I decide to be the responsible adult – a role that is usually reserved for Richard – and turn off the water.

"I'm meeting with Bill Black again today," I say.

"I haven't forgotten, Tommy. And I want you to go to the meeting feeling upbeat and full of positive energy. You know everything will be alright, don't you?" I nod, even though I know no such thing. "You *are* going to say 'yes,' right?"

"I'm not really sure if that would be best, and that's totally unrelated to my sexual identity. What do I need all this craziness for? What's wrong with Olympia? Why shouldn't I just keep focusing on my business? I can keep working on my Africa project, earning billions of dollars, traveling around the world with you, having a blast, maybe even adopting a child. The world is our oyster. Why should I jump headfirst into the flames?"

"Because it's your destiny," Richard replies. "Because you care about what happens in the United States and around the world. You have strong convictions and agendas about pretty much everything, and there's nobody else who could do it all better than you. You have so many qualities befitting a statesman – you have an eye towards the future, and you care about the welfare of future generations. The free world needs a leader like you. It needs *you*. This proposal didn't come out of the blue. Clearly, the world wants you, and it's ready to accept you as you are: a gay Jew."

"We still don't know that, Richard. All we know is that Bill Black wants me to run in the Democratic primaries. Right now, it's just him and a handful of other leaders who believe that the American public can come to terms with a Jewish president. They have no idea that their candidate also happens to be gay."

"It's all up to you." Richard's voice is full of confidence. "It's all about how you decide to market it. If you accept the fact that you're gay with love and understanding, the American public will accept it, too. And if you give off the impression that you're afraid or ashamed, that you don't believe in yourself, everybody else – Bill, the party, the voters – will feel that way, too. Your faith in yourself, your self-acceptance... those are what will determine your future – for better or for worse."

"You should have been a neo-humanology therapist."

"Is anyone hiring?"

"I'll check," I say, smiling. We get dressed and walk over to the nook where our breakfast is waiting for us. Maria's there, too, and we take turns kissing her on the cheek.

"Maria, darling," Richard says. "Have you heard what will soon be the biggest news in the country?" He smiles at me.

"No," Maria answers with her characteristic seriousness.

"Tommy's been asked to announce his candidacy, to run for president of the United States. They want him to run in the Democratic primaries." Richard's voice is filled with pride. He waits for her response.

"I'm not surprised," she says, but the quiver in her voice betrays how excited she is. "Tom is made of the same stock that presidents are made of. When he was a little boy, maybe ten, he would go out to the balcony at Silver Bell and deliver speeches as if he was the president giving a speech in the Rose Garden. He thought nobody could hear him, but I heard every word. Even then, I found his firm convictions quite convincing."

Richard looks over at me, and I smile, embarrassed.

"I hope you say 'yes,' Tom," Maria says. "I've always dreamt of managing the household at the White House." The three of us burst out laughing.

Richard leaves for work, and I head off to Renaissance for my meeting with Bill Black.

"It's just like the good old days," Bill says, shaking my hand. "Our usual table at our usual restaurant on our usual day. Have you recovered from your shock?"

"That *was* quite a shock. It really did come as a complete surprise."

"The party can't afford to lose this election," he says, "and as of now, there are no other natural, attractive candidates for the job. You're the right man for us, and I'm going to position you as the leading candidate. I know there are others who will announce their candidacy, but so far, we haven't found anyone other than you who could defeat the Republicans, and you're the only one the party leaders can agree on.

"I have inside information that the Republican party is pushing for Robert Taylor. He's young, rich, successful, and attractive. He's bright and captivating, and we need to strike back with someone equally impressive. That someone is you, Tom. You're a successful and bright businessman with sound ideology, and you have political, entrepreneurial, and diplomatic experience. Plus, you have the charm and charisma needed to win over young people, students, liberal minority factions. They'll generate the buzz you need, and the next thing you know, you'll have the winning formula for a presidential win. The person that the Republican party is supporting was also a factor in selecting you. Moreover, according to an internal survey, both the Democratic Party and the American people are ready for a Jewish president. There's only one problem," he says. He pauses for a moment, and his silence sends a bolt of fear through my body. Does he know?

"You're not married, Tom, and we have to emphasize family values. Our candidate needs to be married. From where we stand, it's a solvable problem. We even have a lovely woman to fill the position. Go out with her for a few months so your story will be believable, then get married. You understand this is important, right? For the citizens of the United States, for the whole world. If you don't like her," he adds with a chuckle, "you can leave her in eight years."

"And who's the prospective bride?" I ask playfully, trying to put off the moment of truth.

"We were thinking of Emily Zimmerman, Rita and Ted's daughter. She's a terrific young woman, and she'd be the perfect First Lady. I assure you; her parents would be thrilled."

Emily Zimmerman, I think to myself. How on earth did she manage to insinuate herself into my life once again?

"Bill, my friend," I say. "Fixing me up with Emily Zimmerman is not an option. Believe me, my mother's already tried."

"Why not?" he asks, surprised. He can't understand how I could possibly reject his million-dollar idea.

My heart starts beating fast and I feel a knot of fear in my stomach, but I understand that despite everything, I am in control of the situation. Bill's phone rings, granting me a few moments' delay. He gets up and leaves the table to finish his conversation in private, and as I sit there waiting for him, a wave of sadness washes over me. Why must it all be so complicated? Why aren't same-sex marriages accepted without question? Why is it anyone else's business whom I choose to marry? If only we could do away with the categories of normal versus deviant, we could just legitimize everything.

Bill returns to the table, cutting off my line of thought.

"So why in the world won't you agree to marry someone as wonderful as Emily Zimmerman?" he asks again.

"Because I'm already married."

"Oh!" Bill says. "That's wonderful news! When did you manage to do that? You didn't betray a single hint. Was she with you when we met up in Israel?"

"Yes, we were together in Israel. We'd been together for seven months and we just got married a little over a week ago."

"Do I know her? Who is she? Is she Jewish? Will she be a good First Lady?"

"Yes," I say, "she's Jewish. That is, *he's* Jewish." He looks at me, perplexed. "Bill, I'm gay. I married a man, and according to the laws of the State of New York, we are officially a lawfully wedded couple."

"You're *what?*" Bill shouts, furious, an expression of contempt and repulsion spreading over his face. His lips tremble, and I know exactly what's going through his mind: I screwed up his plans. To him, I've just turned into something that must be discarded because it's no longer useful. He glares at me with furrowed brows. Suddenly he shifts in his seat, and his tight expression relaxes a bit. He looks up pensively, glancing at me every few seconds.

"What are we going to do with you, Tom?" he asks. "What are we going to do with you?"

"You don't have to do anything with me, Bill." Now that I've gotten past my initial panic, I'm feeling my usual confidence. "That's just how it is." He sinks back into his thoughts.

"What's his name?" he asks, after a few minutes. "I should at least know what to call the next First Lady." He laughs.

"Listen carefully, Bill. I'm a gay man, and my husband and I are both Jewish. I'm proud of myself and the choices I've made, and I have a rich and satisfying life with or without the party. I'm not the one who asked for this meeting. Tell that to whomever you need to tell, and get back to me within a week. Needless to say, I will accept your response no matter what it is, and then at that point, I'll tell you his name."

★

In the late afternoon, as I make my way over to Judith's house for another session, a text message shakes me out of my ruminations. It's Bill Black. He wants to meet with me next week, same day, same time, same place.

When I get to Judith's, I wait for her in the garden. I am bursting with positive energy. I realize that I no longer care what the Democratic Party or the Jewish community will say about me, or what my father will think or feel. It's their problem. Judith calls me in. I tell her about my meeting with Bill Black, about how I chose to relate to him on my own terms, and how my response was dictated by my logic and not my emotions. This positive, rational approach neutralized the negative feelings that had controlled me in the past, and I felt a peacefulness I'd never known before.

Judith is pleased.

"But," I tell her, "I still have trust issues. I often feel like I'm being chased, and I'm so afraid of getting hurt that I avoid any kind of emotional closeness with people. I don't like all this fear, all this distancing myself. I want to live a life based on trust and love."

"Have any of the people you loved ever betrayed your trust?"

I think for a moment. "Aside from my father, who basically ignored me, no. That's kind of surprising, isn't it?"

"No, not at all. Let's take a deeper look." She suggests we do another regression exercise, and I acquiesce enthusiastically. I close my eyes.

"Relax your body, release your neck and shoulders, and take a deep breath." Judith counts backwards from ten until I once again sink into a light sleep and dive deep into another world. Through the fog I can hear Judith's instructions as if they're coming from some parallel dimension. A sharp pain rises through my neck and shoulders, and Judith can sense it.

"Relax, Tom," she says. "Cover the images that are cropping up with a bright white light."

And once again, I am bathing all these images in light.

"Instruct your emotional system to relay the new information I'm giving you, so that it can influence your negative emotional mind. I'm going to count backwards from three, and when I'm done, you'll be back in the room, quiet, calm, balanced, and full of new energy." Minutes later, as I lie there calmly, Judith recaps the regression for me.

"You're experiencing distrust because of an old memory from a previous incarnation, of a grown man beating his son to death," she explains. "Your relationships will always include some measure of suspicion, distrust, and fear of being hurt. It is important that we continue neutralizing the negative pole in your emotion mind, using positive information."

"I don't understand how positive thoughts can neutralize negative information patterns."

"The information in your negative pole is survival information that is activated when you're in danger. Whenever the mind's electric energy level goes down, it sends out danger alerts and quickly operates these patterns in order to replenish the electricity. The new positive thoughts that we're planting in your mind will neutralize this survival mode."

"I'm meeting with Bill Black next week. How can I increase the energy in my mind so that my automatic responses don't control me?"

"Instead of feeling afraid of Bill Black, you'll need to think positive thoughts about him. If you think positively, you'll feel good," Judith says. "Your communication with him happens through electromagnetic waves that carry information. They bounce off him and come back to you. Any information that you send out into the world radiates back to you. That's what we call 'reality.' You must conserve energy. When you tell yourself 'It's all for the best,' two things happen: first, the positive thought creates a positive feeling. Second, you're instructing your mind, the creator of reality, to create a positive reality. If you emit fear and anxiety, even if you don't say a word, Bill will start to question your ability to deal with difficult circumstances. That's why you have to keep repeating positive mantras to yourself. Transmit to Bill Black that you're the only candidate up to the task, that you're the party's best chance of winning the White House, that your sexual identity will actually increase your votes drastically."

"Sure," I say bitterly. "What could be easier than convincing people to vote for a gay Jew?"

"Reality is a direct product of how we think about ourselves. In our system of communication, every thought we send out comes back to us. Maybe what you should be thinking is 'It's time for the world to see that everyone is equal.' Now, I want to remind you that for the next few days, you may feel sad and dejected, and you may have headaches and bouts of dizziness. These are natural symptoms of the process. The negative force in your emotional mind won't give up without a fight; it will do whatever it can to hold on to the old emotional balance from your childhood. Make sure to maintain positive thinking and a positive dialogue with yourself."

When I stand up, I feel dizzy and grab on to the bookcase to steady myself. Judith helps me back into the armchair and puts a tall glass of lemon water in my hand. When the dizziness passes, we say goodbye and I go on my way.

CHAPTER 12

Manhattan, Mid-January

Serenity increases your serotonin levels and makes you feel happy. That's what's happened to me ever since I met Richard. He and I go for a morning run through Central Park to lift my spirits even more, so that I can put my best foot forward at what I know will be another fateful meeting with Bill Black.

At some point, Richard starts walking instead of running and tries to steady his breath. I do two more legs of the running path and then I meet up with him. Richard's physical fitness is far from peak levels. As he leans forward trying to steady his breath, I can't help but laugh at his poor fitness, and he is forced to agree. Once he straightens up, I hold out my hand and he takes it in his. We walk hand-in-hand along the paths of the park on our way to Corn Bake for breakfast.

As we pass the Plaza, I notice Ed Leibowitz in the distance. My first instinct is to let go of Richard's hand, but I stop myself, and immediately understand that I've finally gotten to the point where I actually hope to bump into people like this when I'm with my husband. We walk, still holding hands, towards Ed. I tell myself he must already know, that the rumors that have certainly been spreading among party officials have reached his ears. Or maybe they're trying hard to keep this a secret and he doesn't know a thing. Either way, Ed has now noticed us too. To my surprise, the way he looks at me doesn't make me feel anxious at all, and our hands together don't garner any reaction from him. His eyes open a bit wide in surprise, but he raises his head and looks back at us with a small, sincere smile.

We walk over to him. We shake hands, and I introduce my husband, Richard, even though they already know each other. We exchange some niceties and go our separate ways. Richard smiles at me, and I hope this nice chance meeting with Ed is a good sign about how my meeting with Bill Black will go.

At Corn Bake, once we've ordered breakfast, we're each busy with our own things. Richard reads the Sports sections in the morning papers, and I read the front pages. Richard takes a work call, and I text instructions about Olympia to Alexandra and Adam. When we're done, we go back home and Richard gets ready to go to work, but not without first enveloping me in a deep, loving embrace and wishing me success for my meeting.

When he leaves, I walk out onto the balcony. I am tense, excited, but I calm myself with the thought that everything I am feeling is normal, and that everything is under control.

"So no work today?" I hear Maria's voice. I turn to face her. She has come out onto the balcony and seeing her brings a big smile to my face. I tell her about the meeting that I'm having in a couple hours, and excitement spreads across her face. Her whole body stretches in pride, as her palms press together to her lips in a prayer gesture. For the first time in my life, I give her a warm embrace, and she hugs me right back, asking me to let her get my clothes ready for the meeting.

I get out of the shower and walk over to where Maria has placed the outfit that she prepared for me: a pink tailored shirt with a black suit, which will make me look elegant, serious, but also liberated. I go out to the street feeling festive, get into the waiting Jaguar, greet Philip, and ask him to take me to Renaissance.

Bill Black is already waiting for me at our usual table. We shake hands, and I notice a slight smile on his face. He looks relaxed. I, on the other hand, am having a hard time loosening up.

"How are you?" he asks.

"Wonderful," I reply.

"We're going for it," he says, without skipping a beat.

"Can you please explain the words you just said?" I ask, having a hard time digesting what I heard.

"Over the past week, I've had endless discussions about this with senior party officials. We analyzed your candidacy from every angle, and we concluded that despite your sexual orientation, you will submit your candidacy at the presidential primaries."

"Did you back this decision up with any sort of a polling?"

"We did, and as it turns out, a gay Jewish candidate could actually be a great gimmick."

The word "gimmick" pisses me off. I try to calm myself down, but I guess my face betrays me.

"Of course, it's not only for the gimmick," Bill tries to walk it back. "Your charisma will win America over. You're made of the stuff of winners. We believe this will outweigh everything else, and will give Americans a sense of something new, something that will give them hope. They'll vote for you because they should, but also because they'll want to be a part of history.

"Tom, you have nothing to be angry about. I just wanted you to know that according to the polls, the public – particularly young voters and liberal minorities, like Jews and the LGBTQ+ community – can see something wonderful in a candidate who is young, Jewish, gay, and married. It isn't coming from anywhere negative. It's from something positive. It's about openness, equal opportunity, something new and modern. This could generate fantastic momentum.

"The young voters will think of you as one of them. To them, you don't symbolize the rotten establishment in Washington. The positive results really stand out with what's considered the "creative class," and it's important. It's true, there may be countries that will welcome you with a protest against same-sex marriage, but gay marriage has been a fact of life here since the federal court ruling. Displays of anti-Semitism are not something we expect to see. Maybe they'll be underground."

"OK," I say, regretting a bit how angrily I reacted. After all, Bill isn't the bad guy here.

"But we do have one request," he continues. "We want you to come out first in an extensive interview with one of the big daily newspapers in New York, so that your sexual orientation isn't suddenly discovered during the campaign, and so that we can better understand the general mood. A personal interview, nothing more. You can also talk about your work as the resident's special envoy to the Middle East, but for now, no mention of your presidential candidacy. For now, we'll just put your gayness on the agenda. I'm sure you understand, Tom, what a mess they'd make of it if it only came out during the campaign."

"I understand," I say. "And I agree. I hadn't thought about doing it any other way. I'd also understand if you decided to drop the whole idea altogether if the interview doesn't get good responses."

"I have no intention of dropping it. We know that responses will be more extreme in the beginning, later they'll balance out, and then finally the actual trend will be clearer. But anyway, we're going for it."

"That's what I don't really understand," I say. "I don't get why other senior officials think we should do this, at any cost. Why this determination? Why me? Why at any cost? And what if it turns out you're wrong, and this isn't actually a good gimmick, like you say? Why not find another candidate who's more typical, married with children, charismatic, with a rich political background?"

"Tom, I think I appreciate you more than you appreciate yourself."

"Don't you worry about my sense of self-worth. This is no small thing. Gay marriage is still a complex issue, definitely one that goes against what's considered "family values" in America. That's what I mean. But beyond that, it is completely clear to me why I am your candidate, and I even know that you're not making a mistake."

"We believe that the country is ready for this," Bill says, "and that you'll be able to sway significant demographics of voters. Besides, we're building on the fact that your charm and personality will help hand you a decisive win. We reviewed all the potential candidates for this run for hours and hours. The board in my office has tables upon tables of analyses. There is no other candidate who'd be able to defeat the presumptive Republican nominee. You're the only right fit, and we're comfortable with you."

"You're comfortable with me?"

"In a good way," Bill quickly explains. "We trust that you'll be able to find the right balance between cooperating with us and advancing your own agenda. The right balance," he repeats, and I understand what he means. I don't love the idea of needing to tow the party line, but maybe I can try to live with it.

"One more thing," I say before we part ways.

"Talk to me," Bill commands.

"What about everything I did in my twenties?" I ask nervously.

"Does anyone know about it?" he asks, alert.

"I never told a soul."

"So then everything will stay between friends. We have nothing to worry about," he says, and I agree.

When our meeting is done, we decide to bring back our tradition and meet once a week, like we used to, at our usual table in our usual place, and we go our separate ways.

I text Richard: **Bill says we're going for it, no matter what, he wants to go for it. He just wants me to come out now, in one of the big papers.**

A short while later, I am walking into Olympia's offices and I greet Alexandra. I offer a mysterious smile, figuring she can understand whatever she wants to from it, I take the papers she has prepared for me from the counter, and I ask her to send Adam in.

"Congratulations," I tell him.

"What for?"

"You've been appointed chief of staff for the elections headquarters, for the Democratic Party's favored candidate for president of the United States."

Adam's face remains serious, but I can tell he is just trying to maintain a professional expression.

"Thank you, Tom," he says. "As usual, you are unpredictable."

"And here's your first assignment as chief of staff," I say. "I agreed with Bill Black to give an interview to one of the leading daily papers in New York. He thinks, and I agree, that my being gay shouldn't come out later on in the campaign."

"Of course," Adam answers. "There's no doubt that we need to control the story, like chess players looking a few moves ahead, and each move needs to be planned out in advance." He thinks for a minute. "If you want my opinion, I think we need to go with the New York Times. And let Ellen Mack do the interview. She's trustworthy, influential, humane, and not at all like the young, eager writers out there. Anyway, we'll need to hire a team of advisors first. I think we should hire them as soon as possible, make a final decision, and then tell Bill Black about it."

"Go for it," I say. "But something that's really important to me is that the strategic team, the people who will be making these decisions, should include some unconventional people, not only people with a background in politics or media: people who think differently than us, people who work in fields that are foreign to us, in addition to the typical professionals you'd normally need on a campaign."

"I'll start putting a team together," he says, and then considers his next words. "What are you going to do with Olympia?"

"I'll have to talk it over with my father, but that's on me. You can take it off your to-do list."

I excuse Adam. He leaves, and I remain in my chair, and then decide to call my father right now. There's no point in pushing it off. The phone rings eight times, and just as I'm about to hang up, I hear my father's stern voice on the other end.

"Hello Father. It's Tom," I say quietly. There is a long silence, and I realize that my father isn't planning on saying a thing, that he expects me to continue running this call. "I need to speak to you about Olympia," I finally say.

"That's not something to discuss over the phone," he says in his usual icy tone. "Come to Silver Bell this evening."

The sound of the quick disconnection hurts, and I realize he's probably already in the know, as an expert who's always acting behind the scenes in the party's moves.

I look around at my office, which has been my home away from home for so long but will no longer be mine, at least for a while. I have pictures hanging on the walls, alongside framed awards and certificates from international organizations. The shelves in my bookcases hold model ships, awards, and trophies that Olympia has won over the years. I get up to look at them, and then I walk over to the door and open it. I look back at my office and the view from the large window on the lefthand wall, and I close the door behind me.

The black Jaguar drives past the electronic iron gate. Out of habit, I find myself counting the gold ornaments that adorn it. We drive along the road to my parents' house. Through the window, I can see Mother's latest additions. This time, it's some impressive garden lighting guiding Philip and me on our way to my father.

I get out of the car, take a deep breath, straighten my suit and hair, and walk towards the front door, which the housekeeper Helena opens for me with a big smile. She walks me to the office, where I find my father sitting behind his ancient Italian desk. Near him is another chair, and I sit down there. I can't remember the last time I sat this close to my father, the last time we found ourselves in a situation where we couldn't avoid eye contact.

To my surprise, I feel like I'm in total control. The anxieties that controlled me in the past are powerless now.

"How are you?" I ask

"Good," he answers, and I can tell he wants to have an honest conversation with me, but that his old patterns of strictness towards me are making it hard for him.

"Have you spoken with Bill Black lately?"

"Yes," Father responds, and he stirs a tumbler of whisky, not offering me a drink. The look in his eyes tells me he knows what Bill's been up to.

"I'm going to do it, Father. I came here so we could talk about who should run Olympia in the coming months."

"Who've you thought about?" he asks.

"David Woods, the VP of Finance. I think he'd be the right man for the job in the coming months."

He thinks this over for a few minutes.

"That's fine by me," he says.

"Do you think you'll be more involved in Olympia in the coming period?"

"No," he says. "I trust David Woods and the Executive Board. As far as Olympia is concerned, we'll get through this period without any difficulty." He gives me a look that is hard for me to interpret.

"And if I win?" ready for any answer that might come, even one that undermines my belief that I can win.

"We'll find a solution," he says with serious consideration. He looks at me again and this time I notice a small smile start to spread across his face. I smile back and the two of us get up and leave the room. He walks me to the door.

I find myself standing close to my father in the narrow foyer. I study his face up close. His age is starting to show, seemingly weak-ening the harshness he tends to show the world. Without thinking too much about it, I put my hand on his shoulder. He looks me in the eye, and I can see pride, for the first time in my life. As I leave my parents' home, after saying bye to Mother who was tending the flowerbeds in the front garden, I look back at my father, who remains standing by the front door, following me with his eyes.

From my meeting with my father, I go straight to Club 52, where Richard should already be waiting for me. The hostess takes me to the table we reserved, and sure enough there he is. He gets up to greet me. We hug, and I think about the last time we were out together in a club, when we were still keeping our relationship a secret. We sit down, and I suddenly remember a quote by the Greek philosopher Heraclitus. *Panta rhei.* Everything flows. The world is in constant motion, there is never a still moment, and no moment is identical to the one before it. The same person cannot do the exact same thing more than once because he will never be the exact same person. The same is true for us. We are light years away from the people we were when we last went to a club, only a few months ago.

I kiss Richard on the cheek without even thinking twice. As always, we get looks from people around us, but now I simply don't care, and I'm even amused thinking of the astonishment they'd feel if they only knew that in a couple more weeks, these same two men they see sitting with them will be the presidential candidate and his husband. "The presidential candidate." I repeat these two words to myself, realizing that I'm starting to get used to them, maybe even to enjoy thinking them. Panta rhei.

"So how'd it go with your father?" Richard asks once we sit. I smile.

"It went really well. I can't stop thinking about it."

"It really does look like something has changed in you."

"Panta rhei," I say. "Everything flows. But there is something I need to say. With all due respect to recent developments, I am not willing to let anything come between us. I want us to swear to each other that our relationship will always come before everything else."

I raise my hand as if taking an oath in court, signaling for Richard to do the same. Amused, he raises his hand too.

"I am yours and will stand by you, always and forever," I improvise, and Richard repeats after me. Our hands are intwined. We exchange looks and feel a strong, almost uncontrollable urge to touch each other, and we hurry home.

CHAPTER 13

Manhattan, The Interview

Adam has finished putting together my election campaign
team. For our media advisor, he's chosen Pete Mandelbaum,
an experienced guy with "a spark in his eyes," in Adam's words.
To help me with my communication skills, Adam hired Barbara
Mitch, a beautiful woman from Chicago who's published best-
sellers on the topic. Cliff Burton, a chemist by training and talented patent inventor, has been selected to lead the campaign's
creative, original viewpoint. Joe Green, a well-known clinical psychologist in the Jewish community, was brought on to analyze my
colleagues' and opponents' behaviors patterns. Maria's son Jose, a
social activist involved in New York's Hispanic community, will
serve as my advisor on that politically diverse population. Richie
Cohen will serve as the LGBTQ+ community relations advisor,
and Roy Brown will be the African American community relations advisor.

We've also hired the author Robert Gardner, who specializes
in writing biographies of politicians and world leaders; Professor Michael Smith from NYU, who heads the Administration
and Public Policy department and will advise me on everything
related to how I'll position myself as a statesman; entrepreneur
Amanda Rich, economist Mark Kurtz, pollster Peter Harris, and
social media expert Roy Terry. Jacqueline Stern will be my foreign
policy advisor, Ted Kravitz will be our Democratic party liaison,
Leo Donaldson will manage the field work, Lauren Lanter will
run operations, and Simon Nelson will be responsible for the
PR campaign. In addition to all these people, our best move was

to hire the services of Nathan Glenn, a strategist and publicist whose resume boasts maximum precision and zero mistakes.

Until the election, these members of my campaign team will be the closest people to me.

I invite everyone to my apartment so we can all get to know each other. Nathan Glenn is the first to arrive, showing that his maximum precision applies to his timeliness as well. The rest of the team come right after him, and we all sit down around the table. I purposely sit along the right side of the table, next to a chair placed at the head. I do this for two reasons. One, to present myself as an equal among peers, open to hearing the team's opinions and advice, and two, in order to see who will decide to sit at the head of the table. I notice Nathan Glenn hurrying to grab the spot.

After a short introductory conversation, in which everyone says a few words about themselves, I suggest we get straight to the point, and I ask everyone which newspaper and which journalist I should give my interview to. The look of surprise on Adam's face shows me he thinks I'm challenging his suggestion to go to *The New York Times* and to the journalist he had suggested, Mack, but I signal to him that he has nothing to worry about. I turn to the author Robert Gardner first, and he suggests going to *USA Today* because it has high circulation, but I explain that I'm not sure circulation numbers should be our main consideration here, and what's more, the circulation numbers are generally exaggerated. Cliff Burton, the patent expert, suggests *The New York Times* and thinks we should go with a female journalist.

"She needs to be young, beautiful, someone who'd be able to broadcast your personal charm and present your story in a positive light." He also notes that *The New York Times* is identified with the Democratic party.

"*The New York Times*," Glenn announces. "The journalist should be Mack. She'd be the best. Check out the articles she's written in the past, and you'll see reliability, matter-of-factness, and fairness. Besides, I know her, and I'd be able to control it all behind the scenes."

"*The New York Times* with Mack, it's decided," I say, glancing over at Pete Mandelbaum, who's having a hard time hiding his displeasure with the fact that I didn't actually ask him directly. "Finalize everything with *The New York Times*," I instruct Mandelbaum, and then I wink at Adam, who knows me better than anyone else does and understands what I'm doing.

"From now on, no more speaking freely with reporters," Glenn says. "From now on, you will only speak according to the messaging we lay out, regardless of what you're asked." I nod and tell him and Mandelbaum to get talking points ready for me to use in my interview with Mack.

In a private room that Adam reserved at the Plaza, two black armchairs sit facing each other on a large oriental rug. The photographer asks me to sit on the chair facing the fireplace and he carefully checks the angles of how I'm sitting. He tells me how to best position myself and takes a few pictures. I straighten my tie, check my watch repeatedly, and wait impatiently for the interview to begin, wishing that it was already behind me so I could meet Richard at Corn Bake for lunch.

My team worked hard preparing for this interview. I am equipped with all the tools, techniques, and tricks I need, and I have committed all my talking points to memory. And now, the moment of truth has arrived. Adam is standing near the wall next to Pete Mandelbaum, my media advisor who, as far as I'm concerned, is authorized to stop the interview at any given time. He's standing in my eyeline, so I'll easily be able to see if he signals to me with any of the signs we agreed upon beforehand. In order not to arouse suspicion, the rest of my team is sitting in an adjacent room. Afterall, Mack doesn't know that I'll be running in the Democratic primaries, and she still won't know by the end of this interview. Adam has a microphone in his pocket and they're all wearing earphones, so they'll be able to hear the entire interview.

Everything is ready. The makeup artist has finished her touch ups. The photographer, who is supposed to be taking authentic photos during the interview, is holding the camera in his hands. And now, Mack is here in the room with us. She greets everyone in the room, and we shake hands. Her warm smile and kind eyes manage to calm my nerves, which have grown tense in the last few minutes. She sits down across from me and looks over her papers, while I observe her and find her to be extremely likeable. I sense a hint of embarrassment in her movements, and I realize she also seems a bit excited about this as well.

Finally, she looks up from what she's been reading, asks me how I am, and thanks me for granting her this exclusive. The interview begins. We start by going over the questions that were agreed upon in advance, and I tell her about my childhood in Connecticut, growing up with Holocaust survivor parents, my achievements at Olympia, my volunteer work, my involvement with the Democratic party, and my time as the president's special envoy to the Middle East.

"And where does your commitment to Africa come from?" Mack asks me.

"First and foremost, I'm a businessman," I say, trying to convey credibility about my motivations. "Currently, there is a lot of economic opportunity in Africa. Average growth is high and government capabilities have increased, with many countries' governments now able to guarantee fulfillment of economic agreements. Trade between Africa and the rest of the world is on the rise, and external debts and budgetary deficits have gone down. But there are also places where there is a great deal of public outrage at the elites, who are tied to the governments and exploit laws intended to improve the lives of the locals, and these same elites are making a lot of money at the expense of the poor population. This injustice harms the children and perpetuates poverty and corruption. My commitment to the continent, the money I have invested there, is meant to give hope. My dream is to be able to map out the problems that plague each country throughout the world, and then be able to connect countries to others that can assist them; to open the world up to collaborations based on real discourse."

"As a Jewish man, a political activist, and a known contributor to the State of Israel, what is your position on the establishment of a Palestinian state?" Mack asks, changing the subject to more sensitive political questions that I'd rather avoid at this stage.

"My opinions on this are already known," I answer. "I expressed them even recently, as the president's special envoy to the Middle East. The State of Israel needs to free itself from the Palestinian issue. Economic agreements can be an initial basis for future polit-ical settlement. The Palestinians will have something to lose when they live with abundance and a better quality of life. The bitterness and frustration will decrease. When the sides are ripe, the right statemen will come and help formulate political agreements.

"The main thing is that we need to start by laying a practical foundation. In the organizations that I belong to, I see Israelis and Palestinians cooperating in local coexistence initiatives, as part of their daily routine, without questions of nationality taking center stage. The people are ready, but their leaders – with their external considerations and political interests – are preventing the general public from achieving what it wants."

After some sensitive questions about politics and diplomacy, Mack quickly switches over to personal matters, the main reason why we're here. "You are a successful businessman, you come from a well-known and well-to-do family, and you used to be active in the Democratic Party. This must have all made it objectively difficult for you to come out as gay. Tell me, how did you manage to live your life in secret until now?"

I brace myself. The Silent Bartender. Berlin. One-night stands. Sex for pay. All these thoughts race through my mind, and I know I can't say any of them out loud.

"The same way anyone lives a life in secret," I respond, using her own word that she planted in the question. "With emotional detachment and escaping from reality. Living something that feels like half a life, never quite able to fully be yourself."

"Can you give some examples? Where did you hang out? Where did your sexual orientation find expression?"

"I had relationships just like anyone else, but instead of doing it out in the open, I kept it quiet."

"How did you deal with keeping this secret for so many years?"

"There were many struggles and many thoughts," I respond. "Quite a lot," I add, to buy myself some time. I look at Mandelbaum. He signals to me to keep talking, and I decide to tell the truth.

"I had thought about coming out many times over the years. Every closeted gay person thinks about it. Like you said, I am a successful businessman, from a well-known and rich family, and active in the Democratic Party. All of these facts made my decision difficult to make, but I guess there's a right time for everything." Mandelbaum signals to me that this is enough, and I stop talking.

"And what about the emotional struggles?" she insists, and I decide, despite Mandelbaum's concerned expression, to continue answering honestly.

"I've gone through therapy, but even after that, I couldn't find the right time or the strength to come out. For years, I prayed to God to redeem me from what I felt was a stain. I fluctuated between joy, stemming from my own self-discovery, and shame. Ever since I came out of the closet, I've felt like I'm celebrating my life after so many years of living like half a man. This has been a slow process for me. For years I tried to convince myself that I could live with a woman and start a family with her, but in the end, I really couldn't betray my inner truth. But there is a right time for everything, and that's what happened in my case, too."

"Why? What happened?" Mack asks.

"A few months ago, I met my boyfriend, Richard. We dated for a few months, I felt at one with myself, and we got married."

Now Mandelbaum is pleased. My answer came straight from my talking points.

"How did your parents receive this news? After all, they are the one and only Gold couple. I'm sure it's not easy for them to deal with such a sharp curveball in their lives."

"Yeah. It's definitely not easy."

"And what about kids?" she asks. I'm taken aback and offer an embarrassed grin, and once again decide to be honest with her.

"If that is something that becomes relevant one day, we'd be happy to adopt a child and give them a great life. There are enough children in the world who are suffering, and it is important to show them grace. A long time ago, I had a dream," I add, finding that I'm enjoying speaking about this, "to draw up a list of children from every country in the world waiting to be adopted, and to make another list of all the families from all over the world who meet the criteria for adopting, and to match warm families with parentless children. It probably sounds naïve, but that's what dreams are after all, and maybe one day I'll be able to fulfill this one."

"So, you believe in God?" she asks, turning the conversation over to the fact that I'm Jewish.

"God is in each and every one of us, and we are the creators of reality," I say, leaving her speechless.

"Thank you very much, Mr. Gold," Mack says, smiling. We shake hands and the interview is officially over. Afterwards, we exchange a few words, thank each other, and I promise to provide her with other interesting stories in the future. She laughs, thinking I'm joking. If she only knew what scoop I'm going to be providing her and all the other journalists soon.

When the news crew leaves, I'm alone with Adam and Mandelbaum. For the first few minutes, silence takes over the room. I look at them and feel a bit concerned. Why are they so quiet?

Did I say something I shouldn't have? Adam goes over to the door, looks out, and takes the microphone out of his pocket.

"They're in the elevator," he whispers into the microphone, and a few moments later, our whole team enters the room clapping, whistling, and cheering. In seconds, all the tension that I'd been feeling over the past few days has dissipated, and I let myself unwind, celebrating with them and hugging them all one by one.

We finally calm down and share our general impressions of the interview. We'll do a more thorough analysis once it's published. I text Richard that it went well, and that he'll hear all about it over lunch.

As we leave the hotel, I invite Adam to join me and Richard at Corn Bake. He's pleased but I can tell he's feeling a bit awkward about it. He's not used to us having such a friendly relationship, but the times have changed.

Richard is already waiting at the restaurant when we get there. We sit down, and I let Adam tell Richard how the interview went.

A text from Bill Black brings me back to reality: **We're in suspense here. We hope you managed to control the story.**

We'll have to wait and see in tomorrow's headlines, I reply, and I turn off my phone.

"BILLIONAIRE TOM GOLD IS OUT OF THE CLOSET," screams the headline of *The New York Times*, and underneath that is the byline: "The billionaire has married multi-millionaire Richard Silverman from Chicago, ending decades of living life in the closet."

To my surprise, the headlines don't bother me. Sure, a few months ago something like this would have led to a nervous breakdown, but now, I'm actually pleased, and I think to myself that the headline and byline are actually quite informative. The article itself is printed on an inside section, where I find a large, flattering picture of me and Richard that the media advisor gave the newspaper. In addition to this, there are pictures that were photographed during the interview interspersed throughout the text.

I refrain from reading it and hurry to wake Richard up.

At first, he can't understand what I want from him.

"Billionaire Tom Gold of Manhattan and multi-millionaire Richard Silverman of Chicago, on their wedding day," I read him the caption under our wedding photo, and Richard immediately sits up and grabs the paper from my hand.

"The picture is stunning," he says, and we both laugh, arranging the pillows against the headboard so we can lean on them as Richard reads the article out loud.

We're pleased to discover that a large part of the article is devoted to my management of Olympia, the projects I've been promoting in Africa, my past political involvement, and my role as the president's special envoy to the Middle East. After this is a respectful and matter-of-fact description of my years in the closet, how I got to know Richard, and my decision to come out and get married.

We agree that the article is fair and even flattering, and all that's left for us to do now is to see what sort of reactions it gets, mainly from Bill Black and the other senior party officials who are supposedly going to back me as the party's candidate. I know I need to call my parents. I assume their phone hasn't stopped ringing. I leave Richard in bed and go into my office.

I still haven't heard a word from Bill Black. A struggle is underway in my mind and I'm unable to think positively. Scenes are playing in my head. I can see Bill Black and the party officials coming together to inform me that regretfully, the responses to the article have been too negative and they need to withdraw the offer. The phone rings, making my heart skip and I try to calm my nerves with Judith's words that I repeat to myself before any meeting, that I must do everything in my power to get this job.

My sister Diana's name appears on the screen and I'm relieved. "Tommy, why didn't you say anything?"

"Yeah, I know, I'm terrible, I should have told you and Benjamin about it beforehand. With all the tension surrounding this, and the marathon preparations, it completely slipped my mind. But what do you think?"

"The picture of you and Richard is amazing, and if you were ready to come out, then why shouldn't the whole world know? You guys really look like a presidential couple."

My phone buzzes, telling me I have another call coming in. I look to see who it is, nervous it's Bill Black, but it's my brother Benjamin, and I decide to make it a conference call for all three of us.

"Hi Benjamin," I say. "Diana's on the line, too."

"You could have said something," he chews me out, and I know he's already read it. "Just like your wedding. Everything's a secret, everything in hiding. You should have been the head of the CIA. Your talents are being wasted at Olympia." The three of us crack up.

"Well, to make sure we don't have any more secrets between us," I tell them, "there's going to be another bombshell from me soon: Gay, Jewish billionaire Tom Gold," I announce like a newscaster, "is running in the Democratic primaries for resident of the United States."

Benjamin bursts out laughing and Diana screams. "I'm so proud of you! My cute, little brother!" I can tell from her trembling voice that she's crying. "This is amazing, Tommy. You deserve it. You were born for this. I hope everything will be great."

"Are you serious, Tom?" Now it's Benjamin's turn.

"It's hard for me to believe, too," I answer. "But yes, I'm serious. I was offered to submit my candidacy, and one of the conditions was that I needed to come out in a major newspaper so we could avoid it coming out some other way during the campaign."

"You're actually serious?!" Benjamin asks again, like he's trying to make sure his siblings aren't pranking him.

"I'm completely serious, Benjamin. Do you think I would have done this big interview and come out just because, for no reason? You know me. I wouldn't have done it if I didn't need to. Bill Black convinced me that it was necessary, and my campaign advisors agreed."

"Campaign advisors?!" Benjamin yells, still trying to process this.

"It's wonderful, Tommy," Diana says, her voice still trembling slightly.

"Anyway, let's talk about this more later on. I'm going to want you two to be involved. We'll talk more when things are final. Just like me, Bill Black and the party officials are waiting to see what sort of reactions the article gets."

"Does Father know?" Benjamin asks.

"He knows."

"What does he think about the article?" Diana asks.

"The truth is, I didn't let him know about the article. I'll call him in a bit."

We end the conversation agreeing to meet soon. As soon as I hang up, I take a deep breath, count to ten, and call my father.

"Father?" I ask apprehensively.

"Yes, Tom," he replies, and there is actually a softness to his voice.

"Did you see the article in *The New York Times?*"

"I saw it," he says, not adding another word. I wait a few moments in case he decides to say something after all.

"Bill insisted I do it," I finally say.

"I know. To prevent problems during the campaign. He's right."

I realize that my father was likely in the know before the article was even published, but I decide not to get into that, not yet at least.

"What did you think of the article?" I ask.

"You come out well," he answers. "Mack is fair." My father understands how the media works. He could have been my campaign's best strategist, but he's always working behind the scenes and I wouldn't be surprised if he had heard about my choice through Bill Black and sent a message to the bigwigs at *The New York Times.*

"I've been waiting to hear from Bill since the morning."

"Don't call him. Let him call you," my father says, and we end our conversation.

I decide to heed his advice and prepare for my day at Olympia. *Who knows,* I think to myself, *it might take days or even weeks for the party to make a final decision about me.* Until then, everything needs to be business as usual with the company and my Richard, who I find alongside Maria at the kitchen island watching a morning news program with two presenters discussing my interview.

"Why didn't you call me?"

"You were closed up in your office," Richard answers. "I was sure you were talking to Bill Black."

I join them to hear what everyone's saying. A text from Adam has us change channels to another popular show, and from there to yet another one, and I see that the *Times* article has made waves. All of New York media is discussing it. We're happy to find that all the programs we've seen have been fair, and it seems that the tone of the article itself has controlled the online news. I'm getting requests for interviews from all the media companies, but I decline.

We eat breakfast, say bye to Maria, and go out to the street. A paparazzo manages to snap a shot of us talking next to the Jaguar where Philip is waiting for me. He quickly flees on his motorcycle, and I understand that my life has now entered a new era – that of the paparazzi.

"Did you see that?" Richard asks in shock.

"From now on we'll have to be careful."

I enter the company's offices and Alexandra hurries over to me with a huge smile. "The most important thing is that they used a great picture, and there weren't any typos in your name," she says, managing to make me laugh. We walk into my office, and she goes over my schedule for the day. Once she leaves the room, I occupy myself with business matters, trying not to think about the fact that Bill Black still hasn't called.

In the afternoon, I join a large meeting about trade exports to Southeast Asia. When I enter the meeting room, the conversation that was taking place is cut short, and everyone looks at me. I say 'hi' to everyone and sit down, deciding not to interpret what just happened in a negative way, and I signal to the VP of finance to continue the meeting. I devote my full attention to what he's saying and the way he's saying it, wanting to be sure that I can hand control of the company over to him if I run in the primaries.

Like most VPs of finance, he's quite square in his thinking. He's always guarding the cash register. But I know that's exactly the type of person Olympia will need while I'm gone – someone to manage everything from a technical standpoint, without jeopardizing the company's stability or profitability.

When the meeting's over, I return to my office and Bill Black pops into my head again. It's been almost a full day since the article was published, and I've still had no contact from him. I try to relax, stopping myself from sending him a message. I decide to keep following my father's advice and act as if nothing's changed. Unless I hear otherwise, Bill Black's offer still stands, as far as I'm concerned. So in the late afternoon, I go to the café in the lobby of Rockefeller Center, for a meeting that Glenn requested.

I bring Adam with me to the meeting. From the expression on Glenn's face when he sees Adam, I can tell he's not pleased he's there with me. Glenn wanted this to be a one-on-one, probably to help him get closer to me. But I don't need that kind of intimacy and I want the team to get used to the fact that Adam will be at every meeting I'm at, and they'd be better served trying to establish that intimacy with him instead of me.

"My sources tell me that a lot of the other big papers will be doing follow-ups about your interview, tomorrow," Glenn says once we've all sat down. "This is our chance to add anything we want, before it goes to print."

"Why isn't the media advisor here?" I ask without looking at him, making it clear that I'm not pleased he decided to come to this meeting alone.

"Because this is a strategic matter," Glenn says.

"No, it's a media matter. It's also a strategic matter, but it's undoubtedly a media matter. At a meeting like this, the media advisor needs to be here. I know you're maneuvering and trying to cut him out." I know what he's doing. He's trying to get close to me and become the most influential person on the campaign team. I debate saying something to him about this, too, and I can't help myself. "I'm a very practical, matter-of-fact person. I have zero patience for manipulations and cheap politics," I say. I know I'm being direct, but my gut tells me it's better this way. Best that things are all out in the open.

"From now on, I'll make sure the media advisor is looped in on these kinds of things," Glenn says quietly.

"Great. I have nothing to add to what was in the article."

Glenn nods and I decide I'll keep my eye on him. Trustworthiness is the most important quality for me to have in a campaign strategist, and I hope Adam chose the right person.

Philip lets me off at the entrance to Judith's apartment. The blue door is open, and I go out to the garden to wait for Judith to finish her meeting. I close my eyes, breathing in the night air. Her footsteps bring me back to reality. She says, "hi" and invites me in.

"What did you think of the article?" I ask without waiting.

"It was wonderful. You come off amazing. The article tells the simple truth – the story of a successful Jewish businessman who decided to marry a man, unapologetically and without shame. It's wonderful."

"That's good," I tell her, "But what's bothering me at the moment is, why hasn't Bill Black called me yet?"

"Your question is out of place. There could be a million reasons I could tell you why he hasn't called you, and none of them might be right. We'll wait and see."

"I spoke with my father this morning. He thinks I shouldn't call Bill, but there's a battle being waged in my head right now. My negative emotional mind won't shut up: 'That's it, it's over. You're gay, and no one wants a gay president.' I'm trying with all my might to overcome my mind's negativity, I'm repeating mantras over and over, I'm thinking positively, but this effort isn't easy for me. I've already taken Tylenol for the pounding headache it's caused."

"What did Bill Black say during your last meeting?" Judith asks.

"That I should chose a leading daily paper and let the truth come out before the campaign begins."

"Did he say he'd want to speak as soon as the article was published?"

"No, he said that after it comes out, we'll know how much my homosexuality would affect my chances of winning."

"In moments like these, it's best to think simply," Judith says. "Hear what is said without offering our own interpretations. If you remove your interpretation, which isn't connected to reality, the picture becomes clearer. Bill said that you're the candidate he's backing. As far as I'm concerned, everything else is the invention of your mind."

"You're right, but you know it's not easy," I mumble, looking for Judith's support, but she stays quiet. "Judith," I continue, "the panic attacks have basically disappeared, but I still feel like my mind is trying to control me through my old fears and patterns. I am struggling not to go back to my old ways."

"Enjoy the process. Don't work too hard. It goes against the flow."

She decides to do another regression exercise with me, to help rid me of my fear of rejection that controls me. At the end of the exercise, she suggests that I call Bill and ask him what he thought about the article.

"The simplest way is to get your answers first-hand. You waste so much energy imagining all the countless disasters that might await you, or alternatively, trying not to think about what might happen."

I leave Judith's and make my way over to where Richard is waiting for me at a neighborhood bar on Thompson Street.

"I've had a day," I say when I see him.

"I imagined so," Richard replies, and as he reaches out to caress my cheek, we are blinded by a camera flash.

"That's the second time today," I say angrily, but I know that exposure in *The New York Times* comes at a cost.

I tell Richard about the reports that will probably come out tomorrow and my worries that they won't all be favorable.

"What if they want to make me pay for giving *The Times* the exclusive?"

"Ask Mandelbaum to check with the reporters how the articles are leaning," Richard suggests, and I regret not speaking with him after my meeting with Glenn. I take out my phone to send a message about this to Adam.

"What are you doing?" Richard asks.

"Asking Adam to schedule a meeting with Pete."

"Not everything needs to go through Adam," Richard says, and I don't understand what he means. "People want to get closer to you, to create trust, to voice their opinions without there always being someone else there to disturb them."

"But Adam doesn't disturb them. He never even gets involved in the meetings."

"Right, but then afterwards, he tells you his opinion, and that automatically wins in your eyes, and they all feel it. Adam's opinion is important, and I don't suspect him of foul play, but still, I think you should at least every so often give other people the sense that you trust them and listen to them, without any intermediaries."

I have to agree with him.

When Philip drops us off at the entrance, Richard thinks it's funny to check whether there's any paparazzi hiding. We go up to the apartment, go out to the balcony with bottles of beer, and sit facing each other, trying to process this new era that our lives are entering. Richard reaches out to me and leads me to the living room.

"Photographers can also hide on roofs," he says, and we stretch out on the couch, our heads on the headrest, sipping our beers, laughing, and looking at each other. Richard kisses me, and the taste of beer mingles on our tongues. I lean my head back again, close my eyes, addicted to the feeling of his hand caressing my head and comforting me after the long day I've had.

"You should text Bill," he says suddenly.

"Despite what my father said?"

"Do you want him to dictate every move you make from now on?"

"No."

"So send Bill a message, and free yourself from these thoughts and worries."

I take his and Judith's advice, and text Bill Black: **They didn't give out the New York Times on First Ave today?**

We'll discuss everything at our weekly meeting, he responds a few minutes later, and I am trying to use my logical mind and not get sucked into interpretations and negative thoughts. I repeat some mantras that Judith taught me and I try to stay focused. If I can't handle this simple situation, how will I be able to deal with a campaign where there will definitely be intrigues, quarrels, scandals, and all the other evils of politics? I need thick skin, but thick skin is something needed by political players and dirty politicians. I associate myself with a different category, with energetic statesmen trying to change the world, working on a grander stage, where there is a different, much more practical consciousness. I share my thoughts with Richard, and at his advice, I decide to drop this and wait patiently for my meeting with Bill, which will take place in a few more days.

CHAPTER 14

Manhattan, Late-January

I need to learn to trust people, because the things I hope to do cannot be done alone. If I want to win this race, I have no choice but to learn to trust others. It's true, I'm letting the VP of finance run Olympia for me, but I'm not always able to control myself. I often intervene in discussions and stop him from running things the way he'd like to, even though I know I need to loosen my grip. It seems like this will be the lesson of my life: how to trust people; how to try to understand where they're coming from when they make decisions and accept the fact that there are different ways of doing things that may be no worse than my own.

The VP of finance, for example, comes from a completely different place than me: he grew up in Texas, on a farm, in what could certainly be considered an average family. He came by himself to New York, studied accounting and economics in college, paid for his own studies by working as an insurance agent, and spent a long time taking a variety of jobs as an accountant and economist. From the little I know about him, he has a good relationship with his parents and he's in a stable marriage. He sees things differently than I do, in all spheres. I understand this, and yet it's still hard for me to give him the space he needs in order to do what he needs to do. But I need to learn to trust him. I also need to let Glenn, my campaign manager, work as he sees fit. His reputation as a leading political PR strategist precedes him, and as such, he doesn't like it when people interfere with whatever strategy he decides to implement. I don't know if I'll be able to completely give myself over to him, if I'll manage to let him try to get me into the White House in whatever way he feels is best, without interfering, I actually know I probably won't be able to, but I know that I need to at least try.

He's already told me that if he's running my campaign, I can only speak according to clear, uniform messages. "Zero mistakes," he says. "Zero mistakes, especially when we're talking about a campaign as complex as yours." I'm not sure I agree with him. I've told him in our conversations that if he treats me like a problem, or as he likes to say, "a gay Jew," and asks me to appear as little as possible so that we have "zero mistakes," the voters will start to think that there really is a problem, and that will leave its mark on everything. If we treat it all like something normal, which it really should be in the twenty-first century, that's how the general public will accept it.

For now, I'm listening in at yet another Olympia meeting being run by the VP of finance. Even though I have something to say at every given moment, I'm holding myself back and staying quiet. He looks over at me every so often with a worried expression, waiting for the moment I decide to interrupt him and take over the meeting. But to both our surprise, and despite the fact that my disagreements continue, I am able to control myself.

The meeting ends with the VP of finance announcing that he'll make a decision and inform everyone about it soon. We leave the meeting room and I ask him to come into my office with me. Alexandra waves her phone receiver at me, and I walk over to her.

"Glenn's on the phone," she whispers. "He says it's urgent."

I take the phone from her hand.

"What's going on, Glenn?" I ask.

"This is for an in-person conversation," he responds, and we agree to meet up later on.

The VP of finance and I reach my door. I act like a gentleman, letting him in before me. I pour myself a glass of whiskey and offer him one as well, but he politely declines. I need to act logically. Maybe what Glenn considers urgent is not something I would.

Maybe he's trying to fabricate a crisis that's not really there, to show me that he can solve it. Strategic advisors are experts at this, after all. I decide to try to put it out of my head for now, until we meet.

"You ran that meeting well," I say, and he receives this with surprise and gratitude.

"I'm happy to hear it."

"I'm putting my trust in you. It's not always easy to trust people, but with you, I feel like it's the right move."

"I'm really happy to hear that," he says again, contemplating. "Can I ask you why you say there's a chance you may be absent for an extended period?"

I didn't expect him to bring this up. I was sure he'd wait patiently until I explained why I'd be gone, but I understand why he's asking.

"There are very few people who know what I'm about to tell you," I say. "I'm going to tell you, but it needs to stay between us. At this point, you can't tell a soul. Do you think you can manage to keep this secret?"

"Yes," he answers decisively, and I know I can trust him.

"If everything goes as planned, I'll be giving a press conference next week, in which I'll announce that I'll be running in the Democratic primaries for president of the United States," I say, and I watch as his expression changes to one of amazement.

"Wow!" he exclaims in utter awe, and I can see the sincerity on his face. "Good luck, Tom. I promise you that Olympia will be in good hands. I am here for you, and I will do everything the best way possible."

I am moved by his words.

"Thank you," I answer, and we part with a warm handshake. As I leave the Olympia offices, I ask Adam to come to my place later for a meeting with Glenn, and I head over to meet Jessica at a coffee shop that she likes.

"Tell me how your week's been," Jessica asks after we've ordered two cappuccinos, a slice of lemon pie, and some cheesecake.

I try to describe what's been going on, but I find myself unable to organize my thoughts, constantly changing subjects.

"I'm being very associative," I say.

"What's bothering you?" she asks.

"Nathan Glenn," I answer. "My campaign manager."

"What is it about him that bothers you?"

"I find I can't place my trust in him."

"Are you able to place your trust in the media advisor?"

"I don't know him well enough."

"And you do know Nathan Glenn well enough?"

"Jessica," I answer, annoyed. "I know it might not be logical that I've known them both for a short amount of time and I've already made up my mind about Nathan Glenn, but that's how I feel. It's my intuition. You know me. You know that I often make decisions based on my gut feelings, and we both know that more often than not, my feelings are right."

"If that's true, then you need to keep your cards close to your chest," she says. "Don't talk to him about personal things or sensitive strategic decisions, and don't let him know what you think about him. Keep things vague. Let him make an effort. He'll try to create the impression that he's the most professional one out there, and that he's the only one who understands what the right moves are. Let him think that when it suits you and be very careful about what you say when you're around him. If your opinion doesn't change, we'll need to deal with replacing him. The problem is that he can go to the press and sell you out if you do, so you need to be really careful and, in the meantime, don't tell him anything personal or talk about strategic moves or thoughts that you've considered."

"He's coming over to my apartment later. He called me and said he had something urgent to discuss with me, and that we couldn't talk about it over the phone."

"Are you worried?" Jessica asks.

"I'm concerned. I suspect that he might be trying to create a crisis, to drive things out of proportion and create a situation where I feel I can't do anything without him. I'm familiar with these tricks, and I don't like them."

"Listen to what he has to say, don't be too direct with him, don't break the trust you share, and the most important thing is not to do anything drastic. Give him a chance."

We wrap things up and go our separate ways.

I had asked Richard to be home when Glenn comes, to sit with us for at least a few minutes. The three of us sit in the living room. After a little while, the doorbell rings, and Adam comes in completely out of breath and apologizes for being late. Glenn turns pale. He asks to speak with me one-on-one. I propose we go to my study, and Richard invites Adam to join him on the balcony.

"So what's this urgent matter that couldn't wait?" I ask Glenn once we're in my study.

"You're not the only candidate that the party officials are backing," he says.

"What do you mean?"

"The governor of Montana…"

"They're backing him, too?"

"Yes. You're being played. They've convinced you to run and promised to help you, but their real plan is to have more candidates, so that the party elections will get some more attention. They're playing you," he says. "As you know, and as Bill Black told you, the party is in dire straits – there are conflicts and factions. There are no natural candidates suitable to replace the sitting president, and you know that Vice President Adamson has announced he's going to be retiring from politics at the end of his term."

"And this is all verified?"

"Yes," Glenn answers. "I have a source inside the party."

"Who's your source?" I ask, troubled.

"A senior official," he answers, with a sly smile that doesn't sit well with me. I decide to leave it alone.

"So, what do you think?" I ask.

"We need to hire a private investigator to look into the governor of Montana for us. I know Harvey Stone; he won't rest until we have every bit of dirt on him. We need to be prepared, too."

"Right," I say, not revealing my thoughts, keeping my cards close. "I'll think it over. I planned to run a clean campaign, one that would change American consciousness; a modest campaign, without mudslinging, without responding to every tweet, without spin, without sullying anyone's name, without digging up dirt. I just wanted to spread our message in a simple, receptive, and positive way."

"Maybe we still can do all that later," he says. "But for now, we have to get over the hurdle of the Montana governor, and then we can reassess the situation and see how we'll move forward with the campaign."

"I'll think it over," I say once again. We leave my study and find Adam and Richard sitting facing each other on the balcony playing chess. Glenn leaves. I walk him out, thank him, and shake his hand.

"The *New York Times* article was good," Bill Black says.

"So why haven't you called about it until now?"

"We were waiting to see what the implications would be and how the press would react. It made sense to wait a week, understand the trends, and speak about it all during our meeting," he says naturally and rationally, and I realize that for Bill, this wasn't as big a deal as I was imagining.

"And? What did everyone think?"

"Some of the senior officials got nervous and tried to back out of the decision to back you, claiming that America isn't ready for a gay Jewish president, but in the end, we're going for it, Tom," he tells me. "I want us to finalize the next step now."

"Before that next step," I say, straightening up in my seat. "I heard a rumor that I want to check with you."

"What rumor?"

"Is it true that you're also backing the governor from Montana, who will soon be announcing that he's going to run in the Democratic primaries?"

"No," he answers. "The governor from Montana decided on his own to run, and we can't prevent him from doing so. It's the Democratic Party, after all, right?" he smiles. "You are the only candidate that we are backing. We only recently heard that he's planning to announce his candidacy. The truth is that we're not worried about it at all. He has no real chances. He's sixty-eight, his time has passed, he has no serious electoral strength, and he has no fundraising capabilities. You are the future, and there's no one better than you to touch the American public and its hopes."

"I understand he plays dirty, like many politicians," I say.

"That's true. Nothing out of the ordinary," Black responds, closing the matter.

In Bill's mind, we need to be focusing more on the next step, which will come next week. "We'll want you to hold a press conference to announce your candidacy," he says. "Of course, we can't openly support you until the convention in the summer, but party officials have announced that they're backing you as candidate. We are sure you'll win at the Iowa Democratic caucuses, and definitely at the New Hampshire primaries, seeing as you're a Connecticut native. Soon, you'll begin traveling to all the states with a party stronghold. You'll speak at conventions and conferences. We'll help you build up strong field operations, and we'll also help get you good field workers. We believe the governor of Montana will announce his withdrawal from the race within a short period of time, and then we'll be able to focus on running against the Republican candidate."

"And another thing," he adds. "It's important that Richard is seen with you. He needs to be at your side, the way the candidates' wives usually are. Our strategy is to treat your relationship like any other. If anyone has an issue with it, that's their problem, not yours or ours."

★

Judith continues my lessons in all aspects of neo-humanology. According to her, we've been programmed over the years to think that society knows us better than we know ourselves, and we therefore depend on external feedback. A person needs to know who he is, from a logical rather than emotional place. In that way, he'll be dependent on his own energy instead of the energy of others. The ego, which mediates between a person and the world, is prepared to cheat and trample everything in its way in order to obtain the power that will ensure its energy.

The world today is in a bad place, Judith says. Violence keeps increasing, communication problems like autism, Asperger's syndrome, mental sickness, depression, anxiety, schizophrenia, are rapidly multiplying. The world is going to be forced to adopt a "mother plan" – a consciousness that is based on a rational mind and electrical energy that is supplied through the emotional mind's positive pole; the one that works independently of external objects and brings a person closer to unconditional love. Humanity is standing at the threshold of a new world. A change in your worldview can enable an evolutionary breakthrough. On the banner of humanity as a whole are emblazoned the words "unity and harmony." World wars will end, and quiet will once again prevail. Power struggles, petty politics, the corruption of politicians, tycoons who use public funds for their own profit, corrupt public and private monopolies, journalism that serves the powerful – these and other ills will find themselves outside the consensus.

I like the spirit of what Judith says, and I want to use it in my campaign. When I think about her words, it's hard for me to accept Nathan Glenn's proposal to hire a private investigator to build a case against the governor of Montana. I'm not naïve; I am very familiar with how politics works. I have been involved for years in political activity, and I've already seen all the moves, intrigues, and conspiracies that anyone could come up with. But I don't want to be a part of this dirty game and gain energy this way. I want to be a part of a different kind of politics altogether, a new kind of politics. I don't want to be lumped together with the political dealmakers and dirty politicians, but rather with the leaders and statesmen working towards unity and harmony. Following Richard's and Jessica's advice, I decide to keep Glenn on the campaign team for now. My gut feeling is telling me that he can't be trusted and that he is loyal only to himself and his reputation, but I won't do anything about it for now. Loyalty is a top value for me, and I have a feeling that in the end, Glenn and I will come to some sort of a head-to-head that will lead to a bombshell in our relationship, but for now, I'll wait to see what will happen.

In preparation for the press conference that I'm planning to give in a few days, I invite my campaign team over in the evening to formulate a strategy and even some sort of election slogan that I can present to Bill Black in advance.

As expected, Glenn is the first to arrive. He always makes sure to arrive a few minutes early in order to catch some one-on-one time with me, even if it's a really short conversation. He's followed by the rest of the campaign team, and we all gather in the living room. I tell them about my meeting with Bill Black and about my competitors at home, including the governor of Montana who is running "of his own volition," which I stress, as I look over at Glenn.

"According to Bill Black," I say, "his candidacy shouldn't be keeping us up at night. Even now, people from the party are working on neutralizing his already shaky power base. For now, we're continuing as if everything's business as usual, and our campaign launch doesn't need to relate to him in any way." Glenn doesn't seem satisfied with what I'm saying. The other team members agree, and we change topics to a number of points I've been thinking about over the past few days.

"We all know the story," I say. "In November 1932, after the Great Depression and the stock market crash three years beforehand, the Democratic party regained power with Roosevelt's New Deal policy. The Roosevelt administration brough to the forefront a group of people with characters that were totally different than what had been acceptable until that point. These people were young, energetic, optimistic, determined to change the world and leave their mark on it, and that is what I want to convey with our campaign. It's what I hope to convey at the Iowa caucuses and the New Hampshire primaries, and obviously also in the race against the Republican nominee.

"Like Roosevelt, I also want to surround myself with a group of young thinkers from different fields who'll be able to help me implement the changes I want to introduce into American government policy. One of my pillars, whose power I hope to be able to harness, is the creative class that Professor Richard Florida talks about. I hope you're all familiar with it. It's a class that is already changing the character of cities throughout the world. It's a leading socio-economic class whose choices are an astounding force in the shaping of urban life in the twenty-first century. Cities and countries that can manage to attract these creative people enjoy tremendous economic and cultural prosperity. Just like how the working class was the main class during the industrial era, the creative class is the economic engine in our society, and it will also be the solution for reducing gaps of societal inequality.

"I want you to map out the cities where young people, college students, and liberal minorities don't accept things as they are, and where they protest and try to change things. It doesn't matter if they're in cities that are mostly Democratic or Republican. We need to win them over. The creative class needs to connect with our ideas."

Mark Kurtz, the economist on our campaign team, asks to speak.

"The rise of a new economic rationality that addresses the development of human creativity is a good thing," he says, "but if we allow it to operate freely, it leads to massive inequality. We need to think about this. We need to build a new kind of creative society and draft a new social contract."

I accept this.

"Studies show that when you combine the creativity and knowledge of workers in a company, the employer's profits increase," I say. "The equation that lower salaries equal higher profits is incorrect. The right equation is that higher salaries lead to a more dedicated workforce, which then leads to higher profits. What's more, higher salaries enable workers to buy more consumer goods and therefore create more demand, which our economy needs. Henry Ford said that his workers needed to be paid wages that would be sufficient to enable them to buy the cars they made, and we need to understand that. It's not simple. During the thirties, there was a need for an economic depression, so that people could understand that industry workers needed to earn more and help society grow.

"Roosevelt, during his election campaign, emphasized the need for change, but he didn't say what change. The optimistic feeling that we're at the precipice of change is the spirit that will carry the public after it, and the idea that everyone is a part of this change will guide a young campaign that will strive for multi-culturalism, which is one of the cornerstones of the party. Unlike Roosevelt, I can't attack the sitting president, because he's from my own party. But I can speak about change and striving for a better America. The message needs to be that after eight years with our party in power, things in America will be better, but for now, we'll need to content ourselves with talking about the next four years."

"So that's your decision?" Glenn cuts me off. "You don't want to hear any other ideas?"

"Well, what do you propose?" I ask.

"The public isn't stupid," he tells me. "You can't fool it with general messages of change."

"I don't think it's stupid, but let's not ignore the fact that the situation now is way better than it was eight years ago, and we need to continue with the current spirit of change, just to strive for more. You want to ask me how? That's what you're here for."

"We need to come up with a way to hurt the Republican candidate's credibility and capability," Glenn insists. "That's how you win an election, and before the Republican candidate, we need to get through the governor of Montana, and who knows? Maybe someone else will pop up too."

"I should show how credible and capable I am by undermining someone else's credibility and capability? That approach is unacceptable to me," I say. "As a policy, I do not want to run a negative campaign."

"I can get in line with this campaign style," says Mandelbaum, the media advisor. "There are many examples of positive campaigns throughout the world that have succeeded. For example, the "No" campaign run by Chile's opposition in the eighties against the dictator Pinochet. The opposition party produced a positive election campaign. Simple logic demanded a negative campaign that would focus on the atrocities carried out by Pinochet's regime, to convince the public to vote against him, but contrary to logic, this campaign didn't speak about the regime's atrocities at all. It focused on a positive commercial direction, like a campaign that was marketing a good product. The campaign's symbol was colorful and happy. The slogan was 'Chile – Happiness is coming.' The jingle they used was catchy and people got swept away with it. There was no precise explanation for the feeling of change and happiness that was going to be coming, but the message of change and hope made it through, and against all odds, the opposition beat Pinochet in those elections.

"In a positive campaign, you can't get dragged into reacting," Mandelbaum continues. "The other side wants to drag us into dark corners, to spin the news about us, to take us out of a place of hope and change. And when we are provoked, we'll need to respond creatively, in a positive way. It's not easy, but it is possible."

"Thank you, Pete," I say, satisfied. "We need to build a campaign based on identifying voters who are on the fence as well, not only those who will definitely vote for us or definitely against us."

I turn to Adam and ask him to put together a team, to be set up in isolated offices in the southern part of the city. "You have whatever budget you need," I say. "I want to personally reach anyone who's undecided."

"When I talk about change, I'm also talking about returning to the party's values that were set down many years ago. I'm going back to Roosevelt because he knew how to emphasize the right values. We decided, and rightly so, to be an individualistic Western society, but somewhere along the way, we forgot some basic values like support for moderate capitalism and social welfare programs. I don't want to be a part of the piggish capitalism that has fragmented and divided our society."

"You'll be attacked for those kinds of statements," Glenn says.

"Why?"

"Because you're a part of that same piggish capitalism. Olympia is a part of it too. With your own two hands, you helped it become even more piggish in recent years. You chased after profits."

"Olympia has in fact increased its profits," I respond. "But it didn't fire the sailors and replace them with cheaper foreign sailors like other shipping companies did. It's ranked highly among the companies that pay the highest salaries to their employees, and the conditions offered are excellent. That's the legacy my father left – high salaries lead to satisfied and professional employees. And if they say that up until a few months ago, I was at the top of the list of piggish capitalism, there's nothing more credible than someone who was there and says we need to examine the pace of globalization and not forget the welfare state.

"There are economic empires today that have more economic power than entire countries. We need to find the golden path within these vast economic forces. I also want to be kept up to date on the prices of basic staples – milk, a carton of eggs, bread. I want to know how much it costs to ride an inner-city bus. I can't come off as out of touch. I need to get the average American to vote for me, and it's your job, Glenn, to translate this into the right messages I want to be sending, that will be catchy and convincing.

"I just want to remind you guys," I add, "that there is no one in our pocket. I'm Jewish and gay. As far as I'm concerned, we can't assume I'm going to get any automatic support, even from distinctly liberal states. A good job by the governor of Montana or by the Republican candidate can steal victory out from under us. I'm less worried about the governor, because he doesn't have the personal capital that I have, and he has no electoral power. He won't be able to leverage donations, and the donors will quickly realize he has no chance and will back out even if they pledged to donate to him. I also trust my father and Bill Black to do whatever's necessary. My father is an expert in applying discreet and pinpointed pressure on decision makers. He works behind the scenes and knows how to get the job done. He doesn't get involved in loud, public struggles. With him, everything's done quietly," I say, thinking with panic that I might have shown too many of my cards to Glenn and the others.

"At any rate, I will finance everything from my own personal capital. The public funds are intended for more important purposes, and I also don't want to be beholden to anyone. Remember – this election is about the future. The candidate who's able to best represent the public's hopes for the future will win." I've said my piece and now I'm examining everyone's faces.

Glenn's expression seems slightly horrified. There's no doubt that he disagrees with almost everything I've said.

At the end of the meeting, we go out to the penthouse balcony and help ourselves to Maria's pastries and beer that I pour out from the keg for everyone. I schedule a meeting with Glenn and Mandelbaum for the following day to prepare for the press conference we'll hold at the Plaza next week.

When everyone leaves, I hurry to the study where Richard's sitting.

I've missed him. I tell him all about the meeting that's just ended, and he tells me about a deal he closed at his New York branch, which will be bringing us five-hundred million dollars over the next five years. He pulls me over to the couch so we can watch his favorite late-night shows, and I rest my head on his thighs.

On Monday morning, I hold my press conference at the Plaza. None of the reporters have any idea why they're there. We managed to keep it all under wraps to surprise them, thus avoiding any unwanted obstacles. Since it was planned in advance that Bill Black would be there, we're not trying to hide the fact that this announcement is going to be something political in nature. But still, no one there can imagine what I'm about to declare.

We're sitting at a long table. I'm at the center, wearing a light blue button-down shirt and a blue jacket. The microphones and voice recorders from the leading media outlets are right next to me, and the many photographers crowding the room are taking nonstop pictures. Next to me are Bill Black and Howard Greenfeld, the party's new secretary for New York State. At 11 o'clock on the dot, Mandelbaum announces that the press conference will begin, and I start to speak.

I stick to the pre-arranged messages, and right at the bat, I declare in a calm, authoritative voice that I will be running in the

Democratic primaries for president of the United States. For a long while, cries of astonishment come from everyone in the room. I smile, examine the crowd of reporters and photographers for a few moments, and continue.

I give a brief overview of the main motives that led me to this decision, and I note the positions I've held over the years for the party, with special emphasis on my latest role as the sitting president's special envoy to the Middle East. Finally, I list the main points of my political, economic, and social platforms, and begin to plant the seed in the minds of those present about the kind of change that, in my humble opinion, the United States wants and needs: Strengthening welfare policies in this age of capitalism and narrowing the wage gaps, reforming the educational system, introducing a new economic logic that will lead to economic security and prevent the approaching economic slowdown, strengthening the creative class – these are only some of the ideas I focus on, and it seems that none of the reporters here were expecting any of it. I finish speaking and hand the floor over to Pete Mandelbaum.

He says that I will answer questions now and gives the reporter Mack the first question. "You could have given me that headline last time we met," she jokes.

"As an experienced journalist, I expected you to figure it out on your own," I answer, and I'm met with a wave of laughter. After her, Mandelbaum lets the rest of the reporters ask their questions, and I find most of them to be quite standard. Most of the questions are about matters of domestic security and global terror, the American economy, and American society.

One question is directed at Bill. A reporter from the *New York Daily News* asks him whether the United States is ready for a gay, Jewish president.

"The Democratic Party is liberal and diverse. We'd never prevent anyone who wants to run from running," Bill answers. "There are accepted election procedures, and Tom Gold will need to comply with them all. And then we'll know whether the United

States is ready or not. In any case, we don't define him as a Jewish man or a homosexual; to us, that's irrelevant. We view him as a talented, versatile man who has proven himself in key positions in the party and who can lead the United States and the entire world into a new era."

The press conference ends, and I understand that today, at 12 o'clock in the afternoon, something major has happened in my life, come what may. Bill and I part with a warm handshake as my cellphone rings. On the other end, I hear my father's voice. With his usual sharpness and coldness, he congratulates me on the press conference, which he watched live on TV. Now I am sure, more than ever before, that something huge has happened to me. My father and I are embarking on a new journey together.

★ *Part Two* ★

CHAPTER 15

One Year Before the Iowa Caucuses

Immediately after the press conference, I begin preparing for the journey of a lifetime. I keep up my weekly meetings with Judith in order to make sure I'm maintaining a positive mindset and not allowing fears, which can burst out whenever they see fit, take over.

The campaign team is working at full speed. We're all aware of the tight schedules. Adam is working with a small team that includes the Democratic Party liaison Ted Kravitz, our field work manager Leo Donaldson, our head of operations Lauren Lanter, and Simon Nelson, who's running the PR campaign, among others. Together, they've begun recruiting field workers and establishing our various volunteer headquarters. Bill Black and other senior party officials have been helping Adam, who is traveling nonstop from state to state, coordinating positions and explaining the main points of my platform, the campaign messages, and our field deployment. All the while, we're providing backup and support from our main headquarters in New York.

On a huge white board on the wall, we've mapped out every voting district in the United States, with even the most remote towns accounted for. As far as we're concerned, everyone is a potential voter. Next month, I'll begin my nationwide tour to lay the groundwork for the Iowa caucuses and the New Hampshire primaries, which will be held early next year. Party activists who are minorities in liberal states and others, college students, the creative class, the LGBTQ+ community, and first-time voters are the people we want to invest our field work efforts in, and I'm constantly on the phone with their leaders in order to strengthen my relationship with them. The heads of labor and trade unions, the leaders of strong communities, clergy – they're all important to us, and we are making earnest efforts to build trust with them, which will work in their benefit if I make it to the White House.

Barbara, my communications coach, is preparing me for the televised debates and I'm devoting myself to her methods and suggestions. When I get the green light from Adam, we fire the campaign's opening shot: we're touring the states, holding large support rallies, engaging in televised debates with the governor of Montana and two other candidates from the party, and we're following TV polls that influence voters and field workers alike.

In general, the national polls and focus groups are quite favorable to me, but that's not necessarily a good predictor of how the Iowa caucuses or New Hampshire Primaries will turn out. It seems Bill Black was right when he said the governor of Montana had no chance of gaining momentum and wasn't a threat; but still, commentators did declare him the winner of a debate on one of the leading networks after he went negative, attacking me with accusations and personal insults about my father's connection to the Democratic Party and many other positions of power in the country, but I refused to answer in kind. He spoke of my father's vast fortune, claiming he could buy anything he wanted. He spoke of his and other tycoons' control over the country's tax policy, hinting that my father could buy the presidency for me.

But in other debates, I was declared the winner, and according to polls of Democratic activists, I'm doing quite well. The debates with the governor are becoming more complex, but I still haven't agreed to Glenn's suggestion not to take part. I'll never agree to simply abandon the fight.

Mandelbaum was able to reach an agreement with the governor's people about the rest of the debates, including the debate in New York, my home field.

I really like the field work. I enjoy meeting with party activists in the various districts in the most remote of places. I feel as if I'm falling in love with my homeland. The plains, the Great Lakes, the South, the Rocky Mountains ... it all seems magical to me. Every night before I fall asleep, I imagine the announcer at the Iowa caucuses declaring me the winner. I can actually feel the excitement from the momentum I'll create at the caucuses coursing through my body, and this gives me the hope I need to go on. I can feel how badly I want to dedicate my life to my homeland's security, economic stability, and social resilience. And if I win, I'll also be able to use my power to help faraway Israel, where the roots of my people lay.

At the end of my months-long tour, I return to New York for a short stay, and prepare for the Iowa caucuses, where Richard will join me.

CHAPTER 16

Des Moines, Iowa; January –
One Year Later

As my private jet departs from JFK Airport, my official election campaign is launched into its next stage. The months spent on extensive field work and building infrastructure in all the states have now reached their climax, the Iowa caucuses, whose results will likely predict how the rest of the primaries will go. The whole campaign team is on the plane, and they can't help but be impressed by the luxury and comfort. The flight attendant serves everyone some Cordon Rose and we raise a glass to our success.

Since the press conference when I announced my candidacy, the American press has been very gracious to me, but I know that could easily come to a stop. The leading papers generally cover me in a positive light, and tend to focus less on my homosexuality and more on my political achievements until now: my time as the president's special envoy to the Middle East, the Democratic Party's secretary in New York, and – how could they not include this – the person chosen by the party to deliver the reaction to the Republican President's speech in the beginning of the 2000s, which is played on television constantly. My personal achievements leading Olympia are also covered favorably.

My sources tell me that the governor from Montana has already been in Iowa for weeks, and his representatives are working vigorously. In truth, he'd been planning this long before me, and he began his preliminary work far in advance. They tell me he's met with every voter in Iowa at least once. In that sense, he has an advantage over me. Like me, he understands the significance of the Iowa caucuses, since it's known to boost unknown candidates and give them the momentum to keep running. That's what happened with Jimmy Carter, for example. He was a complete unknown until that point, and the Iowa caucuses catapulted him onto the national stage, giving him the step up he needed to reach the Oval Office.

After takeoff, Richard and I go to the office on the plane. Adam and Glenn join us, and we go over the schedule of meetings that await me. I know I need to get through the Iowa caucuses to gain the momentum that I so badly need; I need to sweep all the voters up in excitement over the changes I want to make, so that I can also give the press an excuse to crown me as the leading candidate. Rumor has it that the governor from Montana has been attacking me personally, saying things like, "If you elect the spoiled billionaire with the shady past, the party will lose power," and "He'll be the end of us," and "Don't be fooled by his money; In our party, money can't buy you power."

I decide not to respond, and Glenn objects. He says that these kinds of statements will permeate and become accepted truth if I don't publicly come out against them. He thinks I should hold an urgent press conference in Iowa and start attacking the governor personally as well. He says I need to meet with the opinion makers as soon as possible to reveal his motives and interests, and send representatives to critical hotspots in Iowa to spy for me and update me on all political measures being carried out beneath the surface. I manage to keep my cool, and privately ask Richard what he thinks as we stand over the bar in my office on the airplane. Richard shares my opinion, and so I tell Glenn my final position on the matter – I will not let myself get dragged down into cheap political tactics. That's exactly the kind of old politics that my father represents, and I want to break away from it and create a significant alternative, a new, cleaner kind of politics.

Thinking about my father and his political involvement draws me back into memories of the past. Images from my youth and my twenties and thirties run uncontrollably through my mind. Memories of a time when I was a witness to the political measures my father made happen, things that ruined other peoples' lives. In my mind, these things were akin to a ruling on a capital case. Even then, I couldn't understand how my father wasn't afraid of payback from the universe, which would certainly come one day. Even back when we were completely disconnected, Bill Black would tell me about my father's political doings – playing divide and conquer, frame jobs, throwing people out in the trash in quite sophisticated ways, all without leaving a trace of evidence.

The pilot's announcement over the plane's PA system shakes me out of these memories. I feel dizzy, and there's a cold sweat dripping down my forehead. Richard can tell that something's up. He takes me by the hand and leads me to the in-flight bedroom.

"What happened?"

"It's my father," I answer, trying to stop the rage that threatens to rear its ugly head.

"Glenn's advice totally brought me back to some terrible memories of "my father, the dirty politician.""

"This is your chance to keep your promise that you'd never act like him," Richard says determinedly, and I hold my head in my hands.

"Don't get me wrong, Richard. I appreciate my father's help. For years, ever since I was a young boy, I waited for him to show me love once again. I'm overwhelmed with joy every time I see how much faith he has in me."

"Help is a wonderful thing," Richard answers. "Love is also a wonderful thing. So is a vote of confidence. But there is absolutely nothing connecting dirty politics to love, help, and expressing your faith in someone. Be careful, Tom. If you let him help you in his own way, you might very well earn his love again, but you'll lose your inner truth and betray your principles."

"You're right and I know it. But emotionally, it's hard for me to dismiss his support. It fills a void I've been carrying around for years. The feeling that my father loves me is something that's giving me strength now. For all those years, I dreamt of having a closer relationship with him."

"That's completely understandable, Tom, but still, you need to draw the line somewhere with these dirty politics. Don't give up!"

"Richard," I say, my voice shaking, but he stops me.

"Drink something, Tom," he hands me a glass of cold water, trying to help me calm my overexcited nerves.

An hour later, once I'm back in focus, I return to my meeting with Glenn and Adam, and we finish going over the schedule and the main talking points for me to stick to.

A bit later, Richard and I go back to the in-flight bedroom, each focused on our respective laptops. Suddenly, a wide grin spreads across Richard's face.

"Do you know anything about Roosevelt's vice president?" he asks, without looking up from his screen.

"Which one?" I ask.

"Henry Wallace," Richard answers. "He won the gay vote when he ran for president."

"Who told you that?"

"To prepare for this trip, I scheduled meetings with farmers in the Iowa plains. I studied up a bit on agriculture in the area, and I discovered that Wallace was born in Iowa, and that before he was vice president, he was Iowa's agriculture secretary. And then one of the farmers I'm in touch with randomly said something about this. I just Googled it, and he was right. Have you heard about the Mattachine Society?"

"Remind me," I say.

"Well, apparently this was an organization founded by a man named Harry Hay in 1950. It was in essence the first gay movement in the United States, and it sought to protect and improve gay rights. Whatever. The important thing here is that two years earlier, this same Harry Hay, along with some of his gay friends, established a support organization for Wallace called "Bachelors for Wallace."

"To support his presidential campaign?"

"It turns out that after he got involved in all sorts of shady affairs – for example when correspondence was uncovered between him and some Russian theo-sophist named Nikolai Roerich, in which he calls him 'Dear Guru' – Roosevelt decided to replace him before the 1945 elections and appointed Truman to take his place. And that is why, during the 1948 election, Wallace joined the American Progressive Party and ran for president, and Harry Hay's bachelors supported him."

"Meaning, there was a U.S. presidential candidate even back in the forties who was openly supported by gay voters?"

"Yes," Richard says. "Amazing, right? But I do hope you'll do better. Wallace only got 2.4 percent of the vote, and wasn't able to win a single state. When he lost, he moved to New York and went back to agriculture."

"In the end, I'll go back to sailing," I say, and we both laugh.

Over the PA system, the pilot announces that we will soon be landing at Des Moines International Airport, and Richard and I prepare for landing. I put on a blue suit with a light blue shirt and a blue tie with light turquoise lines and cufflinks that Richard bought me. For whatever reason, he decided to get dressed in some other room on the plane, and when we meet up again in the office, I see why. Richard appears wearing wool trousers and a blue sweater, with an amused expression.

"What are you wearing?" I ask in shock.

"The fashion of Richard the First," Richard answers. "I plan to be a fashion icon just like Jackie O. was, only for men. I won't be dressing like you, in suits and ties. I'm going to be just like the other candidates' wives who dress with their own feminine and personal style. I'll show them all my own personal, masculine style, as the 'first man,' standing at your side.

"You look amazing," I say, and we fasten our seatbelts.

★

Our campaign bus with my name splashed across the side is waiting for us at the airport. Immediately after we head out, I'm informed that there's a "welcome party" for me – a protest against same-sex marriage, apparently organized by the governor of Montana. At Mandelbaum's advice, I surprise the protesters. I go over and try to speak with them, but they were hired to do a job and the protestors are unreceptive and even aggressive towards me. The press has also arrived in droves, and I decide to leave.

In the afternoon, I have a meeting scheduled with Cliff Bergson, the Democratic Party Secretary in Des Moines, a key figure who can influence the caucuses that will take place throughout the state, and then at the convention. Beforehand, I meet with Bill Black, who has come here specially from New York, in a suite at the hotel where we're staying.

"You can relax," Bill says, as he takes a leisurely sip of his coffee.

"What happened?" I ask suspiciously.

"Iowa will soon be free of all disruptions."

"Explain yourself please," I say, even though I'm pretty sure I have a clue what he means.

"Your father is on his way here. He'll do whatever it takes to break the Montana governor's grip on the caucuses and the convention. We'll have people undercover at every school, community center, and public space, and even in the private homes where caucuses will take place. They won't stop working everyone they can until you have the support percentage we need."

"First you said there's nothing to worry about with the governor. Now we need to break his grip?" I ask, with a hint of curiosity. "And besides, what do you mean when you say, 'whatever it takes'?"

"Whatever it takes means whatever it takes."

"You guys are acting like amateurs!" I burst out in anger.

"Why do you say that?" Bill asks.

"Someone could find out about this and leak it to the press and then you'll be done."

"Not *you'll* be done. *We'll* be done," Bill corrects me.

"I'm not a part of this," I answer instinctively, in line with my inner contempt for these types of dirty games. "Right this minute, I'll call a press conference and announce my withdrawal from the race before it even begins," I slam my hand down on the table.

"What's wrong with you? Calm down. This is how it works in politics," Bill says. "This is how an election is won. You buy votes, promise jobs, break coalitions. Your father isn't reinventing the wheel here."

"Not my father, you. You're all cooperating with him, and I simply cannot agree to be part of a party that operates like this. As part of my platform, I'm promising the voters a new, cleaner, more creative, different kind of politics. I'm promising to bring change and I want to position myself as a statesman, not some slimeball politician. But you guys are all acting like every other sleezy politician out there. I will not be part of this dirty game. Your polls showed that I was winning among young voters and liberal minority groups. Give me the chance to win the way I want to."

"Come to your senses, Tom," Bill raises his voice. "If you want to win, this is how you do it. You're not operating in some vacuum. First, you play by the rules of the game, and after, if you win, you're welcome to change them."

I get up from my chair in a rage, and I leave the suite, slamming the door shut. I need to stay true to my principles.

"Tom," he calls after me, trying to calm me down. "Your father is an expert at these things. You know him. You know how he pulls strings without leaving a trace. I don't even want to tell you what sorts of things he did during the last election that no one will ever find out about. Noone wants to mess with Joseph Gold."

"I can't agree to any of these things, even if it's my father who's doing them."

"So what do you want me to do?" Bill asks.

"At this stage, nothing. I'll speak to him and demand that he puts a stop to everything he's planned. I'll tell him that I'm not willing to take part in any of it, and that I'll win by running my campaign the way I want to."

We part in a much warmer way than before, and I head over to my meeting with Cliff Bergson.

Cliff has a ton of influence over the party activists in Des Moines, and in the major cities and districts across the state. We meet at Grimmley's Restaurant, and he updates me on the chances of the other two candidates aside from me and the governor from Montana. He is very interested in my agenda, and I go over my platform; the nature of my campaign; my economic, social, and diplomatic worldview, and how I plan to implement them. We say goodbye two hours later, and agree to meet again the following day, when he'll bring fifty activists with him to meet me and convince them to vote for me.

Adam and I move on to our next meeting, with party activists and students from Des Moines University. The students are a major target audience for me. They're a part of the creative class that I want to enlist, and I honestly don't think it will be too hard for me. I believe they'll be able to create the buzz for me that I need at the caucuses so that I'll be able to win at the convention. They're determined and they believe in change. Nothing, not even the terrible Iowa weather, can deter them.

When I served as the party secretary in New York, I made sure to visit the universities once a year to meet with the party's youth and recruit new activists, and Des Moines University was one of the places I'd visit. The Democratic Party's university branch was headed in those days by Christopher Polk, currently a professor there. He's still a member of the Democratic Party, and he has a great deal of influence over the students and party members in various districts. He comes to greet me at the entrance to the university's administrative building. We were good friends in the past, and so he allows himself to ask me about Richard, and I feel free to tell him all about him.

Christopher has organized a number of large meetings for me at the university. He also plans on using his connections to get the students to the caucuses and the convention, even if they're not party members.

From Des Moines University, I continue on with my campaign team to some off-the-record meetings with the local press that's covering the election, in order to reinforce the unmediated relationship that I've developed with them. I know that I'm going to need them to help spread the buzz I'm trying to create, and I know that the reporters working for the leading papers have many ways to interpret the polls. I know the rules of the game, and I understand that they're waiting for me to tell them stories about the governor of Montana, as a response to things he's been telling them about me, but I decide to stay clean and matter of fact.

That evening, Adam's scheduled a meeting for me at a local bar with representatives of the city's LGBTQ+ community and with activists from the Jewish Democratic Coalition. The gay community throughout the entire country is excited about my campaign and has expressed overwhelming support and an eagerness to help me. *The first gay president of the United States*, I think to myself, and can't stop the smile from spreading across my face.

The Community is one of the best-known bars in Des Moines. It reminds me of The Silent Bartender, which I haven't' been to in quite a long time, but I'll always remember how it was a safe space for me for years. The Community is often visited by influencers affiliated with the LGBTQ+ community as well as leaders of the local Jewish Federations who were connected with the gay community as a result of large donations from the LGBTQ+ community in New York, which were in turn made in order to help the local federations adopt more gay-friendly, liberal, and open policies. To this day, no one knows that those donations came from me. It was important to me that gay Orthodox Jews could find allies in the Jewish Federations and have a say in their appointments to strengthen the liberal forces therein.

At a corner table, we get into a deep conversation about burning issues on the LGBTQ+ agenda: unemployed transgender people who are forced into prostitution, discrimination at work on the basis of sexual orientation, and measures taken to increase the enforcement of laws prohibiting such discrimination. I pledge that if I win, I'll help the LGBTQ+ lobby on Capitol Hill push supportive legislation, and I promise that I'll sponsor events promoting dialogue between the LGBTQ+ and other communities.

Adam continues discussing the specifics of the needed legislation with the people around him, as I drift into memories from the past. There's a local drag band performing on stage, and it's taking me back to Amy Patriot and her colorful performances at The Silent Bartender. I nod to myself. I am deeply moved, thinking about how far I've come from my days at that bar.

At midnight, after all my meetings are done, I've asked the entire campaign team to have dinner together at our hotel. Adam has booked a private room for us to eat, drink, and summarize our first day there. Glenn is noticeably dejected, having been excluded from some of my meetings today. I had no choice; hard as I try, I can't seem to trust him.

When dinner's over, Richard and I go up to our suite to gather strength for the busy day that awaits us tomorrow. Richard has a meeting scheduled with local farmers tomorrow, and I'm happy he's found his own interests on this campaign trail.

We sit down on the wide couch, sip some fine cognac, and I rest my head on his shoulder, which is my support literally as well as figuratively. Richard lifts my chin with his hand, and with my head tilted upwards, he looks me straight in the eyes. I return his glance with a penetrating one of my own, and feel my entire body tremble. Richard looks at me with his kind, loving expression, and I look back at him warmly, caressing his face, trying to convey my intense feelings for him through my touch. Our lips passionately seek each other's out. Richard tightens his hold on my lips. At a measured pace, we continue on our journey of pleasure. Richard removes his jacket, unties his tie, takes it off, and then turns to me to untie my own, all the while kissing me passionately, and I surrender myself completely to this divine pleasure. Naked, I lean over Richard, kiss him with intense heat, my hands in his hair, and he surrenders himself entirely to my desires. I turn him over onto his side and gently enter him. My nerve endings are stretched to complete pleasure. When we've finished, more connected than ever before, we snuggle together on the luxurious hotel couch.

The sound of an incoming text message is what finally gets me off the couch. I go over to the table, pick up my cellphone, and see that it's a message from my father.

I hope you've had a good day, he writes. **Good luck in your meetings tomorrow.**

I read it out loud to Richard, moved by what he's written, and sheer joy makes it hard for me to fall asleep.

The next day is dedicated to meetings in Des Moines, mostly one-on-ones with key influential figures, some of whom are friends of my father's. From our conversations, I gather that he's already managed to speak with them and make all sorts of promises, like district legislative changes and political favors.

That evening, I return to my suite to change into an outfit more suitable for the meeting Cliff Bergson has arranged for me with influential party members, ahead of the caucuses. Wearing a black suit, white button-down shirt, and red tie, I leave with Glenn, Mandelbaum, and Adam, but not before speaking with Judith about the internal battle being waged inside me between logic and emotions about my father, which is causing me to pop Tylenol almost nonstop. Judith explains to me that this struggle is robbing me of a great deal of energy. She says that I need to decide what exactly it is that I want, and act accordingly.

Cliff Bergson gives me a warm welcome at the entrance to the Floyd Auditorium in the city. He leads me inside. Every seat in the auditorium is taken. Behind a podium on the left side of the stage sits the moderator, who's waiting for us to take our seats. I sit in the middle of the first row, in a seat reserved for me. To my right is Bergson, and his deputy is sitting on my left.

First, the moderator invites Bergson to the stage, and he introduces me to the crowd. Because of all the news articles about me, everyone there is already aware of the details of my personal life, and I know from my previous conversations with Bergson and other party members that everyone is fine with it. I also know that the party has conducted several polls among its members throughout the country, and the relative openness to my sexual orientation has helped the party accept this as a positive.

I take the stage to thunderous applause. I feel my excitement rising, and I can sense the electrifying atmosphere of elections, the same feeling I remember from my days as the party secretary in New York when I would attend the conferences and conventions. I stand behind the podium, open my folder with the speech I've prepared, and raise my head to look at the audience. I see the signs that Adam had sent the campaign headquarters, which have my name in large print, and underneath, the slogan: "Yes to an Even Greater America."

After a stirring, hour-long speech interrupted by many bouts of applause, I thank the audience – most of whom will take part in the caucuses – for their faith in me and I ask them for their support. I leave the stage to a standing ovation. The campaign signs are waving in the air, and I know that I've done what I came here to do: I can feel the excitement in the air about the changes I'm hoping to make.

I had considered mentioning the fact that I'm gay and have a husband but decided to take Bill's advice and, in the end, I didn't bring it up. He keeps telling me that this whole thing is a way bigger deal in my mind than in the minds of the potential voters.

He's promised to let me know if it seems like an issue that could become a problem during the campaign, so that I can address it. He might be right. It could very well be that this is really just about me sticking to old, familiar patterns of defensiveness when that's simply no longer necessary.

The next day, we make our way from Des Moines to Waterloo. Once again, the entire campaign team crowds onto our bus, and it feels like we've already bonded as a group, with Richard right in the thick of it. Everyone else is talking amongst themselves and joking around, but I sit apart, next to a window, staring at the views outside. Just before we reach Waterloo, I see a billboard with a huge picture of me. "Gold," it says under my smiling face, "Yes to an Even Greater America." I know that I need to get used to seeing my picture everywhere I look, and that this is going to become quite a common sight during the campaign. But still, I can't help but get excited by the huge picture of me on an enormous billboard. It's as if, for the first time, I've truly internalized that I'm running in the Democratic primaries as a candidate for president of the Unites States. It's really happening. My logic is able to understand this huge achievement, but my emotions are still the dominant force. But right now, maybe for the first time in my life, a positive feeling of love and happiness about this great achievement takes over, taking the place of the negative feelings of my past.

The chairman of the Democratic Party in Waterloo, James Norton, welcomes me warmly, and we have a deep conversation. I get the impression that my field workers have been doing a wonderful job in Waterloo. He tells me that the governor of Montana has been investing a lot of effort in convincing party members in this and other cities not to support me, slandering me nonstop, but Norton thinks that they'll vote for me in the end. He's arranged a meeting for me that evening with a number of key figures, and we agree on the tone we'll take.

Our meeting ends earlier than I had planned, so I return to my volunteer headquarters in the city. On my way there, I read the morning papers. According to an extensive article about the Republican primaries, it seems that Robert Taylor is expected to gain momentum at the general assembly in Iowa and sweep New Hampshire. *Life in the Republican party is easier,* I think to myself. They have a leading candidate, and he's winning.

I meet up with Adam at the entrance to the volunteer headquarters. He tells me about his impressions from the headquarters and suggests I walk around a bit and get to know people.

"It'll do them good. It's important that you thank them for their hard work," he says, and I agree.

There are about 50 activists, mostly students, providing the field workers with round-the-clock support. My picture and slogan are everywhere I look, and I can feel the excited tension in the room with my arrival. Richard enters behind me, and in this moment, I feel everyone in the room looking at the two of us in astonishment. After all, the first ever gay American presidential couple might be standing before them. While I'm all buttoned up in my suit, Richard is standing next to me dressed in the fashion of Richard the First, wrapped in a camel hair coat with a black scarf dotted with shades of orange.

I walk around shaking hands, asking everyone for their names, where they're from, and what they do, and I personally thank each and every one of them for being there. Just before we leave, I gather everyone together and thank them once again. Afterwards, I have a chat with the head of the headquarters and tell him that he should feel free to call if he needs Adam at all.

We leave to make our way over to a large rally in a big assembly hall in the city, where I'm greeted by hundreds of my supporters – students, representatives of the LGBTQ+, Black, and Latin communities, who James Norton brought here for me. When our campaign bus passes the entrance to the assembly hall, I am filled with intense excitement as I see the long line of people waiting to get inside. As I stand before my supporters, after the applause finally subsides, I decide not to deliver the speech I'd prepared, and instead to hear from them about what kind of challenges they face in their lives. I listen intently, jotting down some of their comments and suggestions, and every so often I respond and also talk about my platform.

The rally ends with a standing ovation, which tells me once again that I have done my job. Glenn and Mandelbaum meet me backstage, clap and hug me, and it gives me further confirmation of what my gut feeling is telling me: this rally was excellent, far beyond what we'd expected.

"The college students are going to spread your message of change," Glenn says. "You won them over."

"Thanks," I answer. "We need to keep this up. We need to maintain this momentum until the convention. I'm sure the governor from Montana is investing in intensive field work as well."

"Don't be so sure," Glenn says. "He does tour around a lot, but he acts way more like a slimy politician. I'm sure he's busier closing deals and promising favors with the old guard. That won't work on the youth here, and you need to remember that there's a ton of potential for surprises in Iowa, since no one can predict how many voters will actually show up to the caucuses."

That evening, Richard and I, along with the campaign team, head over to a meeting with representatives of the local Jewish community and of the Jewish federations. We sit at round tables in a private room in a restaurant, and I speak with the senior Jewish figures about issues that are of importance to them. Ed Leibowitz, my enthusiastic supporter who came especially for this meeting and is hosting the evening, invites me to say a few words. This is like my home turf, and I'm really feeling all the love and encouragement from all around. I've been learning to enjoy the applause and I wait for the right moment to begin speaking without dampening the crowd's excitement. When I'm done speaking, we do a situation assessment, and I find that I'm expected to gain a ton of support in the district caucuses and the convention.

The next day, we drive an hour to Cedar Rapids, where I meet with the mayor – a party activist whose tentacles reach everywhere in Iowa. He had asked Bill Black to arrange a meeting with me to discuss how he could assist in setting up headquarters in the city ahead of the national elections. I appreciate his offer. Cedar Rapids is the largest city in Iowa, and I need to prepare accordingly.

Bill Black assured me that I could trust this mayor, but from the very first moments of the meeting, I feel differently. He passes himself off as a kind man, but under this displayed kindness he seems to me to be a coarse, self-interested man who can't be trusted. I try to put my concerns aside.

We sit for a long time in his office as he describes the main problems facing his city, the districts of Iowa, and the more remote towns, including reforms and amendments that they need. This is all in keeping with the perception he has as a veteran warhorse in the Democratic Party. Bill had sent him my platform, and he compliments me on the main points, but his compliments sound sticky-sweet to me, untrustworthy, and I'm unable to convince myself that he means a single word of it. He promises to arrange meetings for me with main party players in the city so I can ensure my victory at the convention, and we part with a warm handshake as he promises that his secretary will be in touch later that day in order to arrange these meetings.

When I leave city hall, I call Adam to discuss the rest of our day, and so I spend a few extra moments in the parking lot. Not far from me, a car stops, and the governor of Montana gets out and walks inside. I hang up with Adam and quickly call Bill Black. "The mayor can't be trusted," I tell him.

"Why not?" he shouts back.

"I just saw the governor from Montana enter city hall right this second, only a couple minutes after I left."

"Did the governor see you?" Bill asks, sounding panicked.

"Why are you so worried?"

"Why?" Bill asks, as if my question was ridiculous. "Because we don't want him to know that we're supporting you and giving you our full backing behind the scenes. This will also help us get loyal delegates to the convention in July. We treated the mayor like one of our own, and it seems like he might not be. We told him that we support you and that he can only help you. He can tell all that to the governor now."

"If this is your way of supporting me, we're definitely going to lose," I snap at him. "As soon as I entered his office, I knew he couldn't be trusted. That's what you call 'one of our own'? You should probably check the others, too, or this won't end well."

"You're exaggerating," Bill says. "Even if we failed in this case, we are all set with the others. We need to be practical now. Talk to him in the evening and let him know that you need to leave the city for Davenport. We're deployed there and well organized with meetings. Tell him you'll let him know when you plan to return, and that he shouldn't arrange anything for you in the meantime. I'm going to send a senior party representative from New York to Cedar Rapids and the other districts today, to work secretly. We'll look into the mayor. In the meantime, get this whole incident out of your head."

I take his advice and decide to call my father and ask him what he thinks about it all.

"Mayors can be fickle," he says. "They have a lot of interests related to the city. They have so many interests that they can't remember who's side they're on. I don't think you have anything to worry about with him. I'm taking care of things anyway. You keep moving forward."

"What do you mean, you're taking care of things?" I ask.

"This isn't an over-the-phone conversation," he says. "I'll tell you in person when I see you."

"When do you want to meet up?" I'm anxious to see him.

"I'll be waiting for you in New Hampshire," he answers.

I hang up the phone and can't help feeling angry about his involvement in my campaign. Aside from the fact that he uses playground tactics and drives the media networks crazy, I have no idea what he actually does behind the scenes. A phone call with Judith helps me feel whole with my decision about my father. The knowledge that he's still there, behind the scenes, does give me a certain sense of security, the kind that only a father can give his son. But still, I worry that what he's doing will tarnish this clean campaign that I'm striving for.

I text Adam that we're going to change course and he should organize whatever he needs to, and we agree to meet over lunch. We take a side table at a small chef's restaurant and begin analyzing what's happened. Over the past few days, Adam's been running back and forth between the various districts, meeting with activists and volunteers at our various headquarters, and so we've hardly seen each other. He's also managing the campaign staff and is essentially living and breathing Tom Gold all day and night.

"I'm happy we're meeting like this, just the two of us," I say. I want to treat him a bit warmer than I used to, but I don't always manage to.

"Me too," Adam responds.

"Sometimes, this race makes me lose track of myself. It's very important to me that I always have time to meet with you. When you're with me, I feel like I can go back to making sense of things and I can get everything back under control."

"Thank you," Adam says. "I want you to win so badly. I really believe the country needs someone like you." And now I'm the one saying thank you.

We clink glasses, and out of habit, start talking about Olympia.

I decide to call the VP of finance and see what's going on there. A short conversation with him gives me the sense that everything is under control, and I discover that my father called him a few days ago, asked him what's been happening there and even offered to come and help if he needed anything. I can't really blame him for calling. Olympia is his entire world. But I make sure to immediately clarify to the VP of finance that all decisions are still to go through me alone.

★

"Paranoid people are the only ones who can succeed in politics," I heard my father say many times in the past. Back then, I thought he was the one who was paranoid, and now I'm starting to think he was right.

Am I being paranoid, or is the governor of Montana actually having me followed and then meeting with every single person I meet with? This whole thing has shaken my confidence. How does the governor know who I'm meeting with? Did he hire a private investigator to have me followed? Or is there a mole on my campaign team? We make our way along Interstate 80 towards Davenport. At one point, I ask the bus driver to stop on the side of the road, and I ask Adam to step outside with me. The rest of the team gets the hint and stays on board.

"I have a bad feeling," I tell Adam.

"What happened?" he asks.

"I think there's a mole on our team."

"Is there any basis to this?"

"I hope not, but in politics, you need to keep your eyes open. It's not like in business. Dirty politicians have no limits." I get closer to him and whisper: "I suspect that it's Glenn. I have a feeling that his emotional intelligence is stuck somewhere at the age of three. I'm not giving him the independence he's used to as a campaign manager, and I think he's seeking revenge in these kinds of situations and will do anything he can to see me fail, so that he'll be able to say afterwards: 'You see? If you only listened to me, you'd have won.'"

"I think you might be overreacting a bit, Tom, but I can see where you're coming from. Maybe we didn't check him thoroughly enough. I hired him because of his reputation. Don't forget, every candidate he's worked for won their race. But if you're suspicious of him, we should probably stop this sooner rather than later. For your mental well-being and his."

"Listen, Adam. I was thinking of testing him. I can tell him something that only he'd know and see what happens. Then I'll have an indication. I have a feeling that after every meeting I have, the governor from Montana goes and meets with the exact same people and gathers whatever information he needs."

"I don't think the governor from Montana is focusing on your economic, social, and diplomatic ideas, but is trying to get everyone to focus on the fact that you're Jewish and gay, and he's hoping to convince them that those facts will make the party lose power. I must admit, it's a convincing enough argument, especially with certain people in certain states."

"So maybe I should focus on the polls that the party conducted, which showed that America is ready for a president who's Jewish and gay. Bill Black told me that explicitly."

"Did you see the polls with your own eyes?"

"No," I respond. "I'll ask Bill to show them to me."

"No, don't ask him. He won't understand, and he'll think you don't trust him or that you've lost confidence in yourself and your ability to win. Let's run our own polls without telling anyone on the campaign team."

"That's a great idea. But Glenn is something that needs to be dealt with first. And like I say, I'll give him a test. Do you have any ideas?"

"Maybe tomorrow you can tell him that you heard that the mayor from Cedar Rapids is being suspected of serious fraud," Adam suggests, "and that you can't tell him what it is, but that the whole story is going to come out soon. If he's really in contact with him, he'll definitely call him and ask what it's all about, and then the mayor will call you to try to get information. If he tells you he knows you're the source, you'll firmly deny it, but then we'll know that we have a mole."

We decide to go for it, and we get back on the bus. Everyone is looking at us. They know something must have happened for me to ask the driver to stop and so I could have a private one-on-one with Adam. Let them suspect something, I tell myself. It will only encourage them to work ever harder. I ask the driver to keep driving.

In the evening, I walk around the local park with Richard.

"The governor from Montana is everywhere," I tell Richard.

"Montana is alive and well," he answers, and we laugh. We walk together on the lit path, wrapped in our long wool coats and scarves, enjoying the fact that we were able to get away for some quality time, short as it may be, just the two of us.

"This has been hard on me," Richard suddenly says.

"What do you mean?" I ask in surprise. It dawns on me that I've really only been thinking about myself lately, and that I've considered Richard's presence here, by my side, as a given.

"I don't know if I have what it takes to be America's first lady – or, gentleman, or whatever they'd call me."

"Why haven't you said anything until now?"

"I don't think I really knew how I felt about it until now," he answers. "Today, I had lunch with Mandelbaum. He's really wonderful. He's someone you can really trust. He started talking about my role as the husband of the president. At first, he was confused and not sure what to call it. He said that in addition to my regular business, I'd need to find social issues I'd want to promote and think about the organizations where I'd want to volunteer, like the first ladies do. I was shocked. I suddenly realized that if we win, I'll lose my identity as a businessman and will need to adapt to a completely new kind of life. I'd no longer be able to devote myself to developing water technology. Even now, it's been hard for me to manage my company remotely, even though I trust the group's CEOs. It's fine for now, but I know that later on, I won't be able to give up on my business."

"I understand you completely, Richard," I caress his hand and apologize. I'm actually a bit embarrassed. "Without even consulting you, I started dreaming up all sorts of things you'd do as the first gentleman. I didn't think about your own empire, and what you'd do with it."

"And what did you decide I'd be occupied with?" Richard asks, amused.

"The global water crisis, particularly in Africa, and the plight of gays and lesbians in unenlightened countries."

"So basically, you tried to turn me into Tom. You knew that as president, you won't have time to work on those things, so you decided I'd do it instead."

"Yeah. Again, I apologize. Of course, you'll continue working on your own things, but at the moment I really need you here by my side. I need your support."

"It's all yours. And if you win, I promise I'll try to function at least in part as the president's first lady, or man, or whatever the hell we're supposed to call me. But I know that I'll need to continue with my business. We'll need to create a new model for presidential couples. I still don't know what it would look like. Hell, if you win, we'll be the first gay presidential couple in the world, but I know we'll be able to figure it out together."

Richard holds my hand. We continue walking, hand in hand, in silence.

Suddenly, a camera flashes at us out of nowhere, and a paparazzo flees on a motorcycle. Out of instinct, we drop each other's hands and walk faster. I call Mandelbaum and tell him what happened.

"Be prepared for the fact that your picture will be in all the local and probably even national papers tomorrow morning," he says.

This invasion of my privacy has me feeling outraged. Besides, I'm worried that the social-economic discourse I'm trying to inspire will once again be drowned out by a public discussion of my personal life and my marriage. I call Adam.

"Did Glenn know that Richard and I went for a walk in the park?" I ask him.

"Yes," he answers. "At dinner, the team was asking where you were, and I told them."

At 4 in the morning, I'm woken by the sound of an incoming text. I squint at my phone.

Nice picture, Bill Black writes.

What are you talking about? I write back, still half asleep.

The front cover of the New York Times. You and Richard walking hand in hand in the park in Davenport. I have to admit you guys look great together.

Thanks, I write back, and immediately open my laptop. I go to *The New York Times'* website. The picture of Richard and I, walking and holding hands in the park, is also on front page of the website. I'm furious. How could Mandelbaum not have known about this in advance. I call him. He answers with a sleepy tone.

"*The New York Times*, Pete. Front page," I tell him angrily.

"What's on the front page?" he says, fully awake now.

"The picture, Pete. The picture that the paparazzo took last night. I thought you were going to take care of it."

"I'll call you back in a few minutes," he says.

Indeed, a few minutes later, he texts me: **The New York Times bought the picture for 200,000 dollars.**

Two hundred thousand dollars, I think to myself. I look at the picture again and can't help but feel impressed by how flattering it is.

Stay on top of the morning programs online, and update me about everything, I text him back. I then wake Adam up and ask him to follow the story as well.

In the meantime, morning has made its way to Davenport. Apparently, every morning show today is very interested in the picture on the cover of *The New York Times*. Writers, intellectuals, and politicians are being interviewed nonstop, all trying to answer the question of whether America is ready for a gay presidential couple. Religious issues are also brought to center stage suddenly. I see that the governor of Montana has arranged some spin for me, in order to distract the public from any discourse on real issues and help him at the caucuses and the convention.

Your father was interviewed on "Good Morning America," Bill texts me.

Your father is being interviewed by New York Public Radio's morning show, Pete texts me. I get a similar text from Adam. I'm taken aback. What is he saying? I anxiously search for the stereo remote, but when I find it, the interview with my father is already over.

A few minutes later, I get a message from Bill.

He was amazing, he writes, and I finally exhale. I ask Adam to send me links to the morning programs that my father went on, and in the meantime, I call my father. I know that for him, my homosexuality is a wound that will never heal, no matter how many studies show that this is something you are from birth.

"What did you say on TV?" I ask him nervously.

"That you're the right man for the job. That America and the entire world need young leaders with a new perspective in order to solve problems, and that there is no one who can do this better than you," he says.

"Father, I meant about my personal life," I say, and he hesitates a bit.

"I said that I trust Americans not to let considerations of religion, race, gender, or sexual orientation get in the way of the real agenda anymore, now that we're in the second decade of the millennium," he answers, and I think it's not a bad answer actually. In one fell swoop, he's changed the constitution and added sexual orientation to religion, race, and gender, as if it's the most natural thing in the world.

"Thank you, Father," I say, wanting to say more but unable to.

"Stay focused," he says. "And don't worry about anything, because we're taking care of it all for you."

When I hang up, I go into the living room and find Richard sitting dejected, watching TV.

"Are you okay?" I ask.

"It's hard for me."

"What is?"

"All this exposure. I thought, as soon as you came out, that all the investigations into my private life were done, but here we go, a new wave has come. They just had some woman on who I don't know, claiming that she was once my girlfriend, and she started making up all sorts of lies about what I like and don't like. It's humiliating, and I can't take it. It's too much for me."

"I understand, Richard. Believe me, it's hard for me, too. I am sure there will be unpleasant moments like this still to come, but let's try to ignore it. It's just part of the whole thing."

"Maybe I'll only come to the main events."

"But you know that at the main events, you'll be the most exposed, right? And the press won't leave you alone, and they'll continue following you even if you're not with me on the campaign trail."

"But at least I'd have my life, and I'm sure that if I'm not in the spotlight all the time, they'll leave me alone even if only for a little bit. Maybe it will help your campaign too. They'll be less interested in us and more interested in you."

"I'll respect whatever you decide, and anyway, we don't have to decide anything right now."

I hold him close, caress his face gently, look him straight in the eye, and we hold our foreheads together for a long time.

Following a sweet afternoon nap that I made sure to make time for, I hold Richard's hand. The room is dark, and I light a scented candle, lending a romantic atmosphere to the whole room. My hand gently strokes his face, and my expression is one of love and admiration. I kiss him gently and feel his lips surrender to me. My other hand strokes his cheek, and he looks at me with a deep, penetrating gaze. I gently remove his shirt, longingly caress his chest, and embrace him tightly. Richard surrenders himself completely, and says quietly "stronger," three times in a row. When I hear this, I tighten my embrace, cradling Richard inside me stronger, stronger, stronger. In the tangle of sheets and pillows, with our palms entwined and our eyes not letting go, we make love. Our faces hold an identical expression of pleasure, and I'm able to see myself in Richard and Richard in me. Our intimacy has reached a whole new level. When we finish, Richard lies down on top of me. His head rests on my chest, and my arms hug him tightly, keeping him close to me. We stay like this for a while, with me covering Richard's forehead with light kisses.

"How much would it cost me to rent your arms?" Richard suddenly asks.

"What do you mean?" I ask, softly stroking his hair.

"When you'll be away, I'm going to miss these arms that are hugging me now," he says, amused.

"My arms are yours always, and they'll be with you forever."

Later, I leave the suite and head over to the meetings that have been scheduled for me with senior party members in Davenport. As I'm walking toward the downtown area, I get a text from Bill Black, who wants to speak urgently.

"What's up, Bill?" I ask him on the phone.

"The mayor of Cedar Rapids called me. He heard a rumor that there's a secret police investigation into his embezzlement of city finds. He wanted to know if I knew anything about it."

I burst out laughing.

"Do you know anything about this?" Bill asks me.

"I'm familiar with this rumor, because I started it," I tell him, still laughing. "I've been suspecting Nathan Glenn. Yesterday, I told him some nonsense I made up about this. He's the only person I told, and of course he told the mayor. Don't say anything to the mayor other than it's nonsense and he should ignore it."

I quickly call Adam. "Congratulations, we have a mole. I'm firing him tomorrow."

"Don't you dare," Adam says. "He'll get revenge. The press would undoubtedly have a field day with it if you fire him, and it could hurt us. Let's wrap up the Iowa caucuses and the New Hampshire primaries. We'll keep him out of everything important. We'll make it seem like we're consulting him, and we'll give him the feeling that he's a real partner. Let's not hold any more meetings with the entire campaign team. From now on, you'll only have one-on-one meetings, even with him. Let him think that he's the closest one to you. We're in too sensitive a place to be able to contain any vengeance he'd seek."

"I'm not scared," I say determinedly. "When we get to New Hampshire, arrange a one-on-one meeting for me and him. I need to put an end to this."

"Are you sure?" he asks weakly, trying to make me reconsider the decision I've just reached.

"Yes," I say decisively. My decision is final.

"Eyes straight at the lens," Barbara, my communication coach, instructs me, as we're rehearsing for my televised debate with the governor of Montana and two other candidates, and for my interview at the local Davenport station of a popular TV network. Her camera is attached to a tripod and connected to a monitor. She records the interviews she does with me, and then goes over the recordings with me. She explains to me what I need to improve and how, and we record another interview. Of course, I have a natural talent for TV interviews, and I'm photogenic, but Barbara makes sure to focus on the small details – the necessary body language, playing with the tone of speech, facial expressions – until I learn to be professional and completely aware, yet able to project credibility and humanity.

Our rehearsal time passes, and I leave with Mandelbaum and Glenn for the TV station. I go into a small, stuffy room by myself with a photographer, and I sit in front of the camera. The makeup artist powders my face and I adjust my tie, waiting for the program to start and the host to speak to me from the central studio. Five minutes later, I'm on the air. I know the talking points that I need to stick to, and I easily answer the professional questions.

"Before we conclude here, I want to ask you one more question," the interviewer says.

"Please."

"How is Richard dealing with the new role he may need to fill?"

The question makes me angry. Mandelbaum agreed with production that we wouldn't talk about Richard, and the interviewer violated this agreement, but I know I can't lose my temper.

"Step by step, in his own way," I respond.

"What would he be called? The first husband? The first gentleman? What is this position called when a man is filling it?"

"Fast and furious," I say, and the interviewer laughs. I also laugh, but only to wrap this up in a positive mood and get out of the studio.

I take the car I rented and pick Richard up. This way, we'll at least be able to spend time together on the way to Cedar Rapids.

The drive begins with tense silence. I glance over at Richard every so often, trying to get him to look at me.

"You've turned into your father," he suddenly says, and I know he's hinting at how I tested Glenn by pretending the Cedar Rapids mayor was under investigation.

"Richard," I defend myself. "I could never be like him. I lack the gene. I got carried away with Adam, and I have a bad feeling about this entire story. I hope it ends quickly."

"I'm happy to hear that," Richard says quietly. "It was strange seeing you act that way."

The mood in Cedar Rapids is different than it was the day we left. The mayor's been wasting his energy trying to prove his innocence, and the governor from Montana has already left, so the city is clean and ready for me. A phone call from Bill Black informs me that his people are spread out throughout this city, other central cities, and the nearby districts, and they're waiting for me. They've arranged meetings and rallies for me with very influential party activists. I know some of them from my previous party involvement and the meetings I've been having over the past few months in Iowa, ever since I announced my candidacy.

During the meetings, I feel like I'm on home court and getting rousing applause and cheers from the crowds. The walls of the conference halls are decorated with my picture and slogan, which I've finally gotten used to seeing. Late one evening, Adam, Richard and I meet up at a Japanese restaurant in the city's downtown area. We go over the results of the secret poll that Adam arranged, as I've only recently gotten the initial data. Indeed, without analysis or segmentation, this initial data is able to indicate a trend.

"It appears that the American people would be relatively welcoming of a gay president," Adam announces happily. "A gay and Jewish president is another matter, but you'd still get a bit of a positive attitude. In the more conservative states, it's a bit less encouraging. I also ordered a poll from a well-known polling company in Israel."

"And?" I ask, at full attention. Israel's attitude interests me greatly.

"The most interesting results are from among the big parties, rather than the general public. The public in Israel is definitely fine with the idea, but the large political parties are sure that the Americans will vote against you and then the Republicans will return to power, and so they're going to support the person they feel is the actual presumptive candidate more than they'll support you. Aside from religion and sexual orientation, they think you're too arrogant and independent, and that should the day come, African and Palestinian affairs will interest you more than Israeli interests. They think that because you're Jewish, you'll feel the need to prove to the world that Israel isn't your main consideration. That you'd overcompensate by supporting other causes in order to prove that you're not biased."

I feel completely discouraged. It's true that my philanthropic interests are very diverse, but my commitment to Israel has always been unequivocal and uncompromising.

"We need to organize a trip to Israel during the primaries," I say. "We need to coordinate strategic meetings. We can't let Jerusalem come out against me, making the Democrats worry about a loss of control. Arrange the trip. And add Berlin to the tour as well, so that we don't let on that we're on a special mission to resolve Jerusalem's position."

"That's not all," Adam suddenly adds. "Israel's cabinet minister asked me to let you know, discretely, that despite the pressure from the umbrella organization of American Jews on Israel's prime minister, he's decided, contrary to his advisors' opinions, not to support you. The prime minister plans to host the presumptive Republican candidate, with a warm and enthusiastic display. He's unofficially instructed all his people to help the Republican candidate with whatever he needs, and he's sent a message to the leaders of the Republican Jewish Committee that they shouldn't hesitate to contact his office for anything at all. The chairman of the Reform movement spoke to him discretely and said that American Jewry would find itself in an unpleasant position if Jerusalem didn't remain neutral about an American presidential election. He warned him about the implications, but the prime minister isn't changing his mind."

"Arik told you this directly?"

"Yes," Adam says. "He had a hard time trying to reach you and asked me to send the message along. He's a good friend," Adam adds with empathy.

"Yes, he's a good friend," I whisper, trying to digest the information that's just been given to me by Israel's cabinet secretary, and the shock that this information has caused me. Two glasses of red wine later, I'm able to get back into focus and pep myself up for the big rally in Cedar Rapids, which will take place later that evening. Bill Black informed me that polls of Iowa voters showed

I got a better score than the governor of Montana on leadership and credibility.

"The activists need to show incredible enthusiasm at the rally," I tell Adam, who's still munching on the sashimi platter we ordered.

"There are going to be tons of young people at this rally who've never voted in an election before. They'll light up the place with the explosive energy of change and they'll shock the establishment, which they trust less than ever before. I told them to fold up the chairs that were set up on the main floor where the rally will be. I think thousands will show up. The press needs to see how crowded it is, and needs to feel the enthusiasm, the winds of change, so that they'll also fight over broadcast positions at the rally."

"Excellent," I respond, and I know I can trust Adam. "Is the election day headquarters ready?" I ask.

"It's ready," he answers, firmly, and I know that everything is under control.

"The support networks will be reinforced?"

"They will," he answers.

The rally is a smashing success. I deliver a stirring, emotional speech befitting a visionary, about the change that America needs; the revolutions I'll lead in our society and economy; and the parts they'll all need to play in this equation. The thought occurs to me that I should pump up the crowd with aspects of neo-humanology, but I decide to end my speech with a critique of the growing disparities in our country in the era of piggish capitalism. I note that as the owner of Olympia, I know that I also have had a hand in this, and so I'll be indirectly responsible for a violent revolution, should one rise up if we can't figure out how to strengthen the creative class, the engine of the economy.

★

"Please welcome to the stage, presidential candidate Tom Gold!" the announcer's voice rings out, and I can hear the applause from backstage, where I'm standing next to a small staircase leading to the stage. I never believed I'd feel this excited. I close my eyes, count to ten, breathe, and try to get into the spirit of my speech. The crowd is going wild, and I know that we did good field work in Iowa. The campaign team is standing all around me, clapping and waving their flags. "Let's go, Tom!" they call, and my excitement mounts. I feel Richard's hand in mine. He squeezes it strongly. I look at him and see that he's feeling the excitement, too.

The electricity when my victory is announced, the applause and cheers, all increase the adrenaline in my body to levels I've only felt a few times in my life. Richard stands behind me and we get ready to get up on stage. I go up first, and the crowd is in a frenzy now. I raise my hand, turn around on the stage to give personal attention to the people there, just like Barbara taught me. I clap along with the crowd, who was handpicked by the campaign team, and I thank them for their support, which makes them cheer even louder. Richard is standing next to me and clapping as well, and the crowd loves him. We're standing side by side, both of us in blue suits, white shirts, and brightly colored ties, as if we've come straight out of a fashion catalog. Richard looks at me and smiles, and in his eyes, I can see his unconditional love for me. As planned, we make sure not to hold hands in public, and not to kiss, not even on the cheek. We're aware that various audiences might be sensitive about this, and we're trying to be patient with them and not offend people who might need some more time to digest this change.

I walk over to the podium at center stage to deliver my speech. The podium has my name on it, and there are activists everywhere waving my signs as high as they can. Richard is standing to my left. I begin my speech, which I know by heart. I start with just the right amount of dramatics, just like Barbara taught me. I remember the body movements I need to do, and the different ways that I need to play with my tone and volume.

Most of the people in the hall already know me from previous meetings, and they know my platform. That's why it's more important for me to show them that I'm a natural leader and an excellent public speaker. I manage to get them all fired up. My speech is interrupted every few moments with rounds of applause. When I finish my speech, everyone waves their signs, and the crowd is clapping at the same stirring rhythm. I thank them humbly, trying to capture this moment so I can remember it forever.

Richard and I come down from the stage, and my campaign team is standing in a row, clapping and bowing their heads in appreciation.

Later, we get the final results: I got just over 50% of the votes, which is enough points to win the first race. The governor of Montana got most of the remaining votes, with the other two candidates trailing farther behind. So not only is he still in the picture, he's breathing down my neck. I know that now is the time to make him slip up, so that his positions will seem too extreme for the political left.

CHAPTER 17

Concord, New Hampshire; Early February

"Your father did a great job," Bill Black says when we meet at a café in Concord, the non-conformist capital of New Hampshire.

"What now?" I ask. "I thought I made myself clear: no dirty games behind the scenes. I've already told you that I'm not willing to follow my father's lead. That whole blunder with the mayor from Cedar Rapids was more than enough for me, and it still haunts me. That's the whole reason why Richard went back to Manhattan. He didn't want to be part of the primaries. The paparazzi photos and everyone's preoccupation with talking about a gay president and his husband were too much for him. Add to that the fact that the love of his life had taken part in some really dirty tactics. It broke him and he returned home. And I'm having a really hard time without him. I even thought about withdrawing from the race. I'm not willing to lose him."

"You need to stay strong," he says. "There will be plenty more crises along the way. If this is how you'll respond each time, how will you be able to lead America for four years?"

"I'm not the leader of America yet, and we still have quite a ways to go until I even get there. I'm not breaking down, but I'll never agree to give up on my relationship with Richard for anything in the world."

"We'd never agree to that either," Bill says, surprising me. "In fact, Richard has an even more important role than you think in this campaign. You may be surprised to hear that the polls show unequivocally more support for a couple of men who can bring a new relationship model to the White House than there is for you alone. I apologize in advance for the political cynicism that I'm using here. But Richard and you have a lot of pull, and that's why people need to see you together. You guys are intriguing, different, and interesting, but that's about 'you guys,' not you alone. What I'm trying to get at is, tell me what we can do to get Richard back here with us."

"I'll talk to him. I wanted to give him space. I don't want to pressure him. He promised to come for voting day in New Hampshire, but he doesn't want any part in the assemblies and big events. It's the only way I can keep him by my side for this election."

"I understand," Bill says. "But he needs to stay in the picture. If the press catches wind that he's not attached to you during the election, they'll start wondering what's happening to your marriage. Is this couple stable? Can two men truly take on the roles of president and first spouse, or whatever we'll be calling it?" We laugh.

"At any rate, you're not going to get the model you wanted," I tell Bill. "Richard isn't going to be an Emily Zimmerman. He plans to continue working on his business. The model will need to change. If I win, Richard will open up a branch in Washington and work from there."

"So who's going to tackle the social issues and take on the traditional role of First Lady?"

"Richard will do it, but not full time. Simultaneous to his business, he'll also be busy with the water crisis in Africa and with assisting the LGBTQ+ communities in countries with anti-gay culture and legislation. I have been indebted to the community for years, and now's my chance to bring this matter to the forefront of public discourse in the United States. Anyway, I think we're putting our cart before the horse here. First, let's just see if I win."

"New Hampshire was the first state to appoint an openly gay Bishop," he says suddenly.

"Gays are suddenly popping up everywhere. It's like they've decided to lay the groundwork for me."

"Everything in its own time."

"But now, please tell me what you guys have planned with my father for New Hampshire, so I'll be able to stop it in time."

"We're not planning. It's already done."

"What did you do?" I ask angrily.

"We made a deal with the governor of Montana," he says, his body stiffening.

"You did *what?*"

"We made a deal with him. We offered him a job. It was the best way to make him withdraw from the race. Apparently, he has some secret major donor helping him gain momentum behind the scenes."

"This was my father's idea?"

"Yes," Bill answers. "You know your father. No one can say no to him."

"I really hope that whatever job you promised him, it's something as far away from me as possible."

"Guess again," he offers an embarrassed smile. "Your father's emissary offered him treasury secretary, should you be elected."

I stay quiet for a few moments, trying to digest what Bill's just told me.

"You know that I have social and economic policies that I plan to implement. How exactly am I supposed to do that with a treasury secretary like the governor of Montana?"

"He's an educated economist. He's the right guy for the job," Bill responds.

"Nonsense. My economic logic is based on a completely different way of thinking than his. And regardless, it won't make a difference. He'd always remember that he lost and I won, thanks to some deal no less. I have no need for a subversive fifth column by my side."

"So just make a special appointment that will place someone above him, in charge of implementing the economic-social program," Bill suggests, and I'm only getting more agitated.

"I'm not going to waste public funds for nonsense. Some of my economic plans are about stopping government offices from wasting public funds, and you're telling me to increase the waste?"

"Once you're president, you'll deal with the economy too. Things will work themselves out. Don't make a big deal out of it right now. You'll find some way to take away some of his power and remove some of his authority until he's neutralized in the job and won't be able to do a thing."

"Sure, things will 'work out,'" I say sarcastically. "I'll have a treasury secretary with no authority who's unable to do anything and it will all work out. It's no wonder that our country's economy is where it is if this is how the party acts."

I pick up my cellphone and decide that this time, I can take care of things by myself.

"Who are you calling?" Bill asks.

"My father," I answer.

"Tom, how are you?" my father asks, sounding quite satisfied.

"We need to meet. Now," I say.

"OK, Tom, come to Michelle Restaurant."

I make my way there quickly.

We clink our glasses of cognac in the restaurant's private room, and my father encouragingly tells me I should be very pleased.

"You won Iowa. That was a great achievement, and you did it your own way. Of course, the gap was a bit too narrow, but we'll fix that moving forward."

"What do you mean?" I raise my voice.

"Your reputation precedes you. You have nothing to worry about," he answers, letting me know in his own cynical way that there's no point in raising my voice.

"I don't want to keep playing this game, Father. Bill Black told me about what you're up to. How could you do this to me?"

"How could I do this to you, Tom? Instead of thanking me, this is what you have to say?" This time, he's the one raising his voice.

"I can't agree with the governor of Montana as my treasury secretary," I say, in a voice so decisive it surprises me too.

"Leave it alone, for now. What's important right now is that things stay quiet in New Hampshire, so that you can win the primaries there by a landslide."

"I can't agree to this. What you've done goes against my principles and against the new concept of politics that my entire campaign is based on."

"Tom, leave me alone with this nonsense of yours, this thing that you're calling 'new politics.' You decided to get into this game, so you had better play by the rules. But first, you need to earn the job. Once you're in the Oval Office, you can try out these new politics of yours. By the way, you also pulled some slick moves of your own with the mayor of Cedar Rapids."

"Don't remind me," I answer angrily. "My conscience has been tormenting me about it ever since."

My father tries, unsuccessfully, to control his laughter, but I decide to ignore him.

"I'm asking you, please don't do anything in South Carolina," I add.

"After we finish our meal, I'm heading over there," he says, signaling to the waiter to bring us the fillets we ordered.

"Father, let me do this job the way I know how. Everything you're doing behind the scenes, all the things you want to pretend no one knows about, those things will come back to bite us in the end, and they could hurt Olympia too."

"No one is going to come after us or hurt us. No one messes with Joseph Gold," he says, banging the table with his fist. "And now I'm asking you, golden boy, not to be afraid."

My entire body is tense. As I bite into a juicy piece of meat, I repeat to myself this sentence my father has just said. He's never told me before not to be afraid. It feels like he cares about me and is supporting me. For all my distaste for his actions, I can't help but feel moved that he's doing them for my sake. Slowly, I feel the rage that was so sharp when I directed it at Bill Black, fade away into another feeling that I haven't felt before. And as I sit here in this private room with him, our relationship is growing closer, despite our differences of opinion.

"So what's next?" I ask, softer now.

"You need to take New Hampshire by storm. We're coordinating with your campaign team and your field workers. Important meetings have been scheduled for you in the big cities. You'll meet prominent party players and key figures. Even if you already met them a few months ago when you were touring the states, it's important that you meet them again. Each meeting is a piece of the puzzle that will lead you to victory. The local press is interested in you and Richard. You've got some packed, hectic days awaiting you."

Outside the restaurant, on the busy sidewalk, my father approaches me and opens his arms to embrace me.

"What's going on?" he asks.

"I'm vehemently opposed to the offer you gave the governor of Montana, and I want us to put this entire story behind us right now."

"Think about it again, Tom."

"This is my final decision."

"Tom, the position of treasury secretary is the only one we were able to use to convince him to withdraw from the race soon and take his foot off the gas in the New Hampshire primaries, to enable you to gain the momentum you need."

"I'll manage. I'll beat him in Iowa, and I'll keep beating him after. And if not, then I won't. But I won't take part in this arrangement. Tell him the deal's off. I want a government that is free of conspiracy so that I can actually do what I plan to do. This is my final answer. You have until tomorrow to let him know that the deal is off," I say.

"The voters in Iowa and New Hampshire are white and homogeneous. In other states, it will be a lot more complicated to win. The best thing for us to do is to get him out of the race now," he says.

My father leaves, waving goodbye with his back to me.

In the evening, I call Richard from my suite in Concord. "I miss you," I say.

"I miss you too. A lot," he answers, and I feel an enormous relief just from hearing his voice on the other line.

"How's Manhattan?" I ask.

"It misses you also. We all do. Marta does too."

"How is she, really?"

"She's right here next to me, sending her love."

"Maybe you'll come join me here after all?"

"I'm going to try to push my trip up, but I must admit, Manhattan does me good."

I tell Richard what Bill Black told me about the polls, about how our relationship is a big factor in why I'm leading, and I mention Bill's concern that the press will speculate about Richard's absence.

"Don't let the press run your life," Richard says. "If they ask where I am, you can tell them I'm a successful businessman and that, just like any other especially talented spouse, I am able to multitask; I can run my business, and at the same time, support my husband in his run for office. You can promise them that I'll tell them all about what I'm up to when I get to New Hampshire. You know what? You can even promise a personal interview with me when I get to New Hampshire. I'll even provide them with a great headline."

"OK," I say, surrendering. "By the way, I just met with my father."

"How was it?"

"It was complicated. It's hard for me to just throw away the love and care he's showing me. For years, I hoped and prayed that we'd be able to sit together like we just did in a small room and talk, laugh, be angry, and love each other. And now, precisely when this dream is coming true, the conflicts are popping up and it's hard for me to make a decision."

"You need to separate the two things in your mind," Richard answers from the other end of the line. "Enjoy the love and your relationship, but don't give in. Protect your principles."

"That's what I did."

On the suite's balcony, I repeat my neo-humanology mantras, re-charging my batteries before my meeting with Nathan Glenn.

In the late evening, he enters the private meeting room in our hotel, and the tension coming from him is tangible. He sees me at the head of the long, mahogany table, where I'm slowly sipping cognac.

"You're firing me?" Glenn bursts out after I lay everything out for him. "I have never in my life been fired, certainly not by someone like you who wouldn't have gotten anywhere without his daddy."

I hand him a glass of cognac to help him calm down. He gulps it down, removes his glasses, and wipes the sweat from his forehead.

"Is that what you think of me?" I ask him.

"It's what they're saying," he responds.

"Who's saying?"

"They," he says. "People in the party. They say your dad and Bill Black are buying your victory, that you're a billionaire who's trying to take over politics."

"Why didn't you ever tell me?"

"Because those people are with the governor of Montana, so I didn't pay them too much attention. What difference could it even make, especially after their loss? It's easy for them to blame someone else rather than themselves, certainly after the deal the governor lost. Then it was obvious he'd go dirty."

"What deal?" I feign innocence.

"He was supposed to get the job of treasury secretary and pull out of the race so you'd win." He says.

"What?" I exclaim, realizing that in this very moment, I've just been handed further proof, straight from the source, of all my suspicions. How would he have known about this if he wasn't getting information from sources that don't support me? I also see that my father and Bill Black took me seriously.

"So why are you firing me?" he asks.

"Because I can't trust you. For both of our sakes, I recommend that you leave the position, and I'll make sure you get another job elsewhere."

"I don't need your help."

"I know that. And even though our contract allows me to let you go, I still think it's unfortunate that I'm putting an end to this when you're in the middle of the job that was promised to you. Also, in accordance with our contract, I must demand that you say you're leaving for personal reasons, without elaborating or giving any other information about me. I want us to part ways nicely and quietly."

Glenn holds his head between his two palms, rubs his eyes, and a few long moments later, without much choice, nods in agreement.

As soon as he leaves the room, I call Phil Brown, a well-known strategist from Connecticut and a close family friend, and ask him to be my campaign manager.

★

On the following afternoon, I leave Concord and head over to Nashua. There, I meet with leading activists and opinion makers and – this time, to my pleasure – am greeted by a demonstration that Adam's organized in favor of same-sex marriage. The meetings go really well and achieve the desired results. From my campaign team, I discover that the governor of Montana is here as well. I decide not to get too nervous and flee to some other city, like I did last time. Anyway, since Glenn has already been fired, I'm a bit less worried that the governor will be able to have me followed as closely this time.

After a few intense days in Nashua, we head over to Manchester, where I begin with a visit to the media situation room that Adam set up. The walls are entirely covered in plasma screens showing the news being broadcast on channels across the entire country. The analysts are analyzing the rating percentages and the effectiveness of my coming out based on secret formulas they developed, and they're able to show me at any given moment how media reports are positively or negatively influencing my popularity. Next to them sit some shadowy figures who are refining the messages in light of the results, handing them over to Mandelbaum, who in turn hands them over to the campaign staff working in the field, who then post all sorts of messages on my Facebook and Twitter pages.

The situation room manager is sitting with me and going over the reports from the local press, including those about my relationship with Richard. At my request, he also reviews reports in the local media that are about the governor of Montana. My popularity is far greater. The media sympathizes with me and tends to write a lot about my relationship with Richard, and the demonstrations that Adam coordinated in liberal New Hampshire are only helping. At the end of the briefing, in front of everyone there,

I recognize Adam's impressive organizational skills and I make sure to praise them all for their hard work and professionalism. I thank them for everything they've been doing, and I walk out to the sound of applause.

At the University of New Hampshire at Manchester, I meet students who are active in the Democratic Party. Thanks to internal polls that Adam commissioned, I know that I am way more popular among college students than the governor, and I can feel it in the enthusiastic reception I'm given. When I'm done speaking about my platform, I open the floor to any questions they might have. After a few standard questions, one student raises his hand, and Mandelbaum gives him the floor.

"Why did it take you so long to come out of the closet?" he asks.

I look over at Mandelbaum and Adam who are standing next to the stage. Ever since my interview with *The New York Times* before I began my campaign, no one's asked me such a direct question about this. Mandelbaum signals to me that he trusts me, and I decide to tell the truth.

"I come from a wealthy Jewish family, with a strong standing here, in New England, and in New York. My father has been an important figure in the Democratic Party, although in other senses he is quite conservative. From a very young age, I knew his thoughts on homosexuality, and I was sure that if I ever came out, he'd ostracize me. I'm a well-known businessman, I've been active in the Democratic Party, I am known in many countries around the world, and the truth is, I was scared that if I came out, it would hurt my family's reputation and my business.

"I lived in fear. I was in a serious state of distress. I couldn't understand why I wasn't happy. I had everything I could have dreamed of. I had enough money to buy anything I could ever want from anywhere on the planet. I had a great deal of satisfaction from my work. I was young and handsome. But something was missing. It's only recently that I understood that living a lie had been eating away at everything good inside me. When you can't be yourself and be proud of who you are, you wear away, even if you don't know exactly why." I suddenly feel a tear streaming down my face. I hurriedly wipe it away, stop speaking, and take a sip of water from the cup on the podium.

Suddenly, a thunderous applause erupts throughout the hall. The individual claps soon unify into a uniform rhythm, and it keeps going for quite a long time.

"I also came out recently," the student says after the applause dies down a bit. "And I understand what you're talking about. I felt like an enormous burden that I'd been carrying around for years was lifted right off my shoulders, and I suddenly felt like I could stand up straight, that I could be proud. I'll do everything I can to make sure that our community in New Hampshire supports you in the primaries and in the national elections," he promises, to a boisterous standing ovation.

From Manchester, we head up north to Rochester. There, I continue having meetings and I also give a personal interview, coordinated in advance, with the local TV station. I'm once again asked about my coming out, and I realize that the answer I gave at the university, which made its way to the local press, leant a sort of legitimacy to asking me questions of this sort. The interview goes well, and my media situation room informs me that today's green line – the line indicating positive, encouraging press coverage – has been record breaking.

From Rochester we travel to Dover, where I once again meet with important party activists and representatives of various influential committees throughout New Hampshire. In Dover, I set some time aside for myself to work with Barbara on my appearance before the televised debate that will be taking place later on in North Carolina, and for my speech on the day of the primaries.

My speech writer has prepared two speeches for me: a victory speech and a concession speech. After having gone over them and making some corrections, I've approved both. Adam made sure to print them out in huge font, and he and Mandelbaum are now holding them as I practice reading them out loud. I decide to only read my concession speech once. If I'll need to, I'll make sure to deliver it well to the absolute best of my ability. But I devote most of my energy to the victory speech. Barbara has brought a speaker's podium, and I'm standing behind it and practicing reading from the enormous font that Pete and Adam are holding before my eyes.

"Lower your chin a bit," Barbara says, watching me on the monitor. "Stop for a few seconds every time you see two lines after a sentence," she reminds me of the rules of correct speech reading and repeats for me what all the font colors mean: blue means authority, pink means sensitivity, and orange invites creativity and humor. Afterwards, we go over my posture, my gestures, my body language, and my inflections. We do another round of reading from the prompter. I follow Barbara's instructions like a diligent student. Although I do have experience with public speaking, it's important to me to come prepared, with no room for mistakes. Just to be on the safe side, I learn the speech by heart. From Dover, we move on to Merrimack, and from there to Londonderry. In all these cities, I continue meeting with important party players, activists on the college campuses, and representatives of the influential creative class with local economic leverage. I visit my HQs in all the cities and districts, I go over the media reports, I refine my messaging, and I have meetings with my campaign staff and field workers whom Adam has deployed impressively throughout all the cities.

When we return to Concord, I receive the results of our most recent internal polls. My race against the governor of Montana is a tight one. We analyze the polls and understand that nothing is definite here.

That night, I go to pick Richard up from the airport.

He flew here on our private plane, and I wait for him on the side of the runway. The door opens. Richard comes down the stairs, approaches me quickly, and we fall into each other's arms.

We stand there on the runway embracing each other for quite some time, not letting go. He's placed his hand on my neck and brings my head closer to his. But we need to refrain. Once we're in the car on our way to the hotel, I can finally be affectionate with Richard, my love.

Once the suite door closes behind us, we hurry to strip our clothes off. In bed, I curl up into Richard's body. His arms open up for me and receive me with love. My head rests on his arm, and his hand holds me tight. I try to channel my burst of energy into this warmth, in an effort to find the peace and quiet that can tame my adrenaline. It was worth going through all the hustle of the day just to be able to feel Richard's sincere warmth and love this evening. I feel like I belong here, like I'm wanted, and this feeling lifts my spirits indescribably.

This celebration of our love is joined by a gesture from my father, who's texted me that he hopes I had a good day and wishes me success for tomorrow. Moved, I read it out loud to Richard, and he hugs me even tighter.

We then sit at the table, enjoying some juicy steak. Richard looks at me, and his smile is warm and loving. Our eyes meet, and we laugh, this time out loud, the kind of laughter befitting a couple in love who share a friendship that's combined with intimacy.

The New Hampshire primaries have finally arrived. We begin our morning with breakfast in the suite, and Richard reads for me the headlines from the local papers and the results of the polls. We're both in our bathrobes and my legs are up on the table, my eyes closed tight. I start doing my self-soothing exercises and repeating my neo-humanology mantras, getting myself into a state of mind of victory. My victory speech, the only option as far as I'm concerned, is on repeat in my head. I open my eyes and look at Richard, joyful because today, for the whole day, he'll be with me everywhere I go.

In the evening, once the results are announced, he'll go up on stage with me and stand by my side. But for now, in the morning, we go down to the hotel parking lot, board my campaign bus, and begin our primary day journey in New Hampshire. Adam's made a playlist of songs with a great beat, and the driver is playing them for us at full volume. The mood inside the bus is electric. We're all singing, clapping, and getting into the spirit of the day.

The day begins with a visit to our Concord election headquarters. The people who work there are waiting for me, and when we go inside, they blast my campaign song and welcome me with rousing applause. We leave the headquarters, and the press stays with us. Mandelbaum is doing a great job maneuvering between the reporters and leads me to a live interview with an important local channel. I give a short interview and stick to my talking points. After that, I go with Richard and my entourage to the volunteer headquarters and the central polling stations.

In the evening, we gather for a situation assessment. Exit polls show us that there's no clear winner yet. I know it's impossible to rely on polls alone, but we're getting good feedback from our field workers and party emissaries throughout the capital. I'm hoping to win a large number of delegates before the convention.

My campaign bus stops on a side street. We all get out and enter through a back door to a room prepared in advance for me, on the side of a theater where hundreds of my supporters have gathered. My campaign team is there with me. Behind the walls, we can hear the songs being played in the theater, and the party activists clapping and cheering.

"Did you know we hired extras?!" Adam asks.

"You hired what?" I ask.

"Extras," he answers simply. "Like at the Oscars. Seat fillers," he tries to explain.

"Why do we need seat fillers?" I ask.

"To fill the place to capacity and create an atmosphere of support, to make noise in the streets and in this theater, like in a movie."

"Maybe we can stop with all this nonsense?" I say, directing my words at Mandelbaum, who has just now gotten a text saying that there's already a reliable, representative sample, but not mentioning any actual results.

A few moments later, there's a light knock on the door, and Bill Black enters the room smiling. He shakes my hand. Nervously, I look at his expression, and he tells me in a quiet voice, without any overexcitement, that it was a close race, but that I won.

"That's fantastic!" I exclaim in excitement, not understanding why he's acting so restrained.

"That's right," he responds. "We wanted an overwhelming victory. We wanted you to be the presumptive candidate at this stage already. You won by a very small margin, and a lot of the delegates to the convention in July are far from in the bag."

"We'll take it step by step," I say. "We got through Iowa, and now New Hampshire. We'll keep going until we win."

"If you hadn't nixed our deal, this would all be behind us already," he whispers.

"One step at a time," I say, opening the door and gently gesturing to him to leave.

Richard comes over to me, and we hug. My campaign team surrounds us. They are overjoyed. Barbara smiles at me, adjusts my tie, and wishes me luck for my speech. My makeup artist does a final touch-up, and I'm ready to go on stage.

My campaign team, Richard, and I are standing by the stairs that lead to the stage, waiting for my name to be announced. I can feel the electric energy in the theater and the echoes of something happening, indicating excitement there. I close my eyes and manage to sink into a meditative state where I can find some quiet, but the voice announcing the results manages to penetrate this state of mind.

The two trailing candidates received a few solitary percentage points, and before this was even announced, they had declared that they'd be returning to their home states to reconsider their election bids. The announcer then states that the governor from Montana has received 43% of the votes, and immediately declares me – with an exaggerated pronunciation of my last name – the winner. My captive audience there is going ballistic. The campaign team has surrounded me, clapping and jumping up and down in excitement.

"We did it!" they shout at me, as I walk up to the stage. "Show them what you're made of!"

Richard goes up on stage with me, and we both clap to the rhythm of the audience's applause as we walk towards the podium. Together, we lift our hands up in the air as winners. Richard goes over to one side of the stage, and I walk over to the other, as Barbara instructed us, and we show our thanks to the crowd. My campaign song is playing in the background, and the crowd is waving my banners high in the air. I take my place behind the podium, look out at the enthusiastic crowd with enormous emotion, and I see among them my campaign team, the heads of my headquarters, and my field workers, who hurried to the theater as well. For a few long moments, I'm unable to get a word out. My emotions are too strong. I swallow and look out at the audience, who sees how visibly moved I am and cheers even louder. I laugh. I wait for everyone to quiet down a bit, look at Richard, and then begin my speech.

As I leave the theater for the CNN broadcast set, I bump straight into the governor of Montana, and I extend my hand. He walks right past me with an angry look on his face, not looking at me or shaking my hand. He clearly wasn't pleased to hear that the deal was over. For a political wheeler-dealer like himself, this really is a big disappointment. He does seem motivated to win the race, but he knows as well as the party does that he has no chance of beating the Republican candidate.

CHAPTER 18

Columbia, South Carolina, February

"That's it," I say to Adam. "We won New Hampshire and got through the Nevada caucuses too, thanks in part to Jose's hard work with the large Hispanic community there. Tell the pilot to prepare for immediate takeoff back to New York. Tomorrow, I'm off with Mandelbaum and Jaqueline Stern for meetings in Jerusalem and Berlin."

"You need to go right now?" Adam asks, astonished. "We have a job to finish in South Carolina."

"We're doing well," I answer. "I'll spend one week in Jerusalem and Berlin, and then I'll come back to win South Carolina. The information that Arik shared has me really worried. It makes no sense that Jerusalem of all places views me as an obstacle and is supporting the Republican candidate behind the scenes. I need to reinforce my position as a leader of the free world, and strengthen my relationship with Jerusalem, too. This quick shuttle campaign should help. And while I'm there, Richard will be taking a short trip to Africa," I add.

"Africa?" Adam asks, shocked.

"Yes. Mandelbaum said that it would be good for the media to get pictures of Richard with starving children, against the backdrop of our philanthropic work there. He's the husband of the next president after all, isn't he?" I say with humor.

"How did you convince him?" Adam asks in amazement.

"Apparently, when you don't put too much pressure on and you loosen your grip a bit, things work themselves out. We've got a big job to do with the press in Jerusalem and Berlin as well.

I'll send you updates in real-time. Go to South Carolina today and make sure that the field work is going as planned. While I'm gone, I suggest you use Phil Brown, Leo Donaldson, and Ted Kravitz more."

Less than 48 hours later, we land at Ben Gurion International Airport in Israel. My first meeting is with the prime minister.

"Thank you," his media advisor says to the reporters and photographers, and our one-on-one meeting begins.

"You're full of surprises, Mr. Gold. At our last meeting, you didn't tell me of your plans to run for president. Your announcement came a very short time after."

"That's true. It all happened quite fast," I say, sensing his suspicion I had known I'd be running when we met and decided not to share it with him. He is as suspicious as they say he is, and I don't think I'll be able to convince him that the presidential race wasn't a consideration then. So I decide to change the subject.

"How are the talks with the Palestinians progressing?"

"We don't have a partner," the prime minister responds. "There's no one for us to talk with there."

"At this stage, you should put political agreements aside," I suggest. "Financial interim agreements can be a great solution right now. It could be an important step towards a better future. You'd win points. It could also be a great spin to help with your troubles at home. Spin for the short-term," I clarify. "Complete commitment for the long term. Without compromise. Go for it, it's sure to succeed."

"Young Mr. Gold, the apple fell right into the bag," the prime minister says, amused by his own joke. "You're just like your father. None of you in the Gold family have any inhibitions."

"I'll take that as a compliment, and you should think about what I said."

"Will it help you in the elections?" he asks me.

"If you were to announce something like that, it could help me with my platform of finding a solution to the Middle East conflict. But, as you know, I have an uncompromising commitment to the State of Israel," I emphasize, with a penetrating look straight into his eyes.

"It's very important to me," I continue. "Until now, you haven't expressed sufficient support for my candidacy. That could harm me personally as well as the American Jewish community in general. Now is the time for me to create momentum, and that's why your support is important to me. Central pillars of the American Jewish community support my candidacy and are excited by the fact that there could very well be a Jewish president in the White House. The Jewish front must remain united."

"Mr. Gold, what's important to me is to receive commitment and clear statements that you are uncompromisingly committed to the State of Israel, the core of the existence of the Jewish people. I've been given material indicating that within the framework of your involvement with the American Jewish Alliance and as a Democratic Party activist, you've never expressed absolute support for Israel's interests. Your statements about Israeli leaders who play the "Holocaust card" at every chance, who don't realize that the times have changed and Israel is no longer the only brand important to American Jews, have trickled down to me. The connection between the Holocaust and the very existence of the State of Israel needs to be something that flows through the blood of every Jew," he hurls at me.

In response, I tell him that at the Manhattan conference of the Corporate Heirs Club, I stated how very important the State of Israel is to me, how my parents are Holocaust survivors who decided not to live in Israel but that there's no doubt that they are major Zionists.

"I'll support you, my friend," he tells me, "but I want to hear unequivocal statements out of you in support of the State of Israel and the strategic partnership between Israel and the United States in such a difficult, problematic region like the Middle East. If you become president and you take measures that are in opposition with Israeli interests, you'll be attacked by the Republicans, Democrats, and the pro-Israel lobby alike." He pauses to take a sip from his water, and I take advantage of this pause to answer that the American Jewish community contributes greatly to the security of the State of Israel, and that I myself transferred millions of dollars to the cause. Actions speak louder than words.

After a long conversation, not devoid of differences of opinion regarding the best way to stop the spread of extremist terror, our meeting comes to an end. The prime minister makes sure to emphasize that the State of Israel has been taking great strides in its attitude towards the LGBTQ+ community, and notes the gay-identifying individuals in key positions in the political and diplomatic systems. "I myself worked hard to promote gay rights in Israel, and I am very proud of you, Mr. Gold, for your courage and the path you've embarked on."

Moved by these words of such a personal nature, I thank him warmly. When we leave the room, we're surrounded on all sides by photographers and reporters desperate for any morsel of information they can get about our exchange.

Accompanied by security guards, I leave for the Western Wall, where I embark on a tunnel tour at the site. I stand for a few long moments next to the enormous stones and concentrate on my innermost wishes.

In the evening, I call my father to tell him about my meeting with the prime minister and consult with him about the conditions he presented me with.

"Make a statement," he suggests unequivocally. "I'd also demand such a statement if I was Israel's prime minister. As a Jew and the son of Joseph Gold, you have an obligation to protect Jewish interests no matter what. You're well aware of my commitment to the State of Israel."

"And you're also aware of my position regarding Israeli occupation, Father," I say.

"Tom, I suggest you show empathy towards the Palestinians, while simultaneously protecting Israeli interests. We'll cross that bridge when we get to it. Where are you headed next, by the way?"

"Berlin," I answer, pained that I lack the courage to share with my father the traumas that I experienced in Berlin back in those darker years of my life.

Oh Berlin, you source of endless recollections. What a massive gap lies between whatever brought me here in the past, and the reason I'm here now. In my past, I'd come to Berlin, this free sex zone, dozens of times a year. My dark past here torments me now. I know I can't allow myself to delve into my memories of those days, to judge and criticize myself and in turn, waste the energy I need right now. I'm trying to mobilize my control mechanisms, just like Judith taught me, and I manage to silence the disturbing thoughts just enough to be able to look at the streets of Berlin with a fresh pair of eyes.

But should I tell Mandelbaum, who's sitting right next to me, about those dark years? After all, he's asked me to let him know about any skeletons in my closet that might come back to haunt me during the campaign, and I denied having any. For now, I'm remembering Bill Black reassuring me that everything in my past would remain between friends and that I had nothing to worry about. I'm trying to drive out these nagging thoughts and focus on the reason why I'm here.

In Bundestag, I meet with the President and representatives of the major factions. I go over the main aspects of my platform with them, especially those related to foreign policy and cooperation with the European Union. Everything is going as planned, and in the afternoon, I head to a meeting with the Chancellor, a friend of my father's and Bill Black's. He knows I need his support in order to position myself as the leader of the free world. I'm convinced that my acquaintances have done a good job briefing him and that I'll be able to provide Mandelbaum with the headlines he needs.

"Welcome," the chancellor greets me with a broad smile. I respond with a warm handshake, and we let the photographer that Mandelbaum invited take a picture of the two of us. The chancellor exudes a sort of discomfort with it, but he cooperates. I'm not convinced he would've taken this meeting with me had it not been for his friendship with Bill Black or my father, and I take full advantage of this.

After several more meetings with other influential figures in Berlin, Mandelbaum and I make our way to a café in one of the picturesque alleys of the eastern city for an interview with a senior political writer.

"East Berlin is magnificent," Mandelbaum says. "Just look at the alleys." We step towards an alley and walk inside. The café where the interview will be is right next to an ancient red brick building that houses a Jewish school. We all settle around a small wooden table in the café and the reporter and I begin with some polite small talk, in order to set a pleasant atmosphere for the actual interview. He is extremely interested in the aspects of my platform that relate to the creative class's contribution to the global economy of today, and how I view it as similar to how the working class contributed to the global economy during the industrial age. I manage to prove to this reporter how this societal class has revived remote cities where crime and unemployment had run rampant, and how this group will offer the solutions we need for reducing societal gaps. We delve into other issues related to the economy of Germany and the U.S., and three hours later, it seems the interview has gone quite well.

The next morning, over breakfast at the hotel, Pete is pleased to show me the laudatory article about me on the front page of the daily paper. We continue on to our next destination – the Holocaust Memorial across from the American embassy in east Berlin, in the place where Adolf Hitler's office was located during the Third Reich. I pause next to one of the concrete blocks that make up the memorial. These blocks are arranged like graves in a cemetery, and our designated photographer stages the photo that the Israeli press needs to spread so that I can please the prime minister after our tense meeting. Even if there is a hint of cynicism about this all, it is truly based in reality, and I feel myself surrendering to the dictates of politics.

The last stop on my tour of Berlin is a meeting with the American ambassador to Germany, someone I know well through the party's cooperation with the diplomatic corps. That's why I've allowed myself to relax a bit in his presence, cast aside the dictates of formality, bring up memories of the past, and find myself freely asking him about the relationship between the LGBTQ+ community in Berlin and Germany's political left. I'm reminded of the Mattachine Society that Richard told me about on our flight to Iowa.

On my way with Mandelbaum to the Brandenburg Gate – a place I wanted to see so that I could fulfill for one moment an old dream I had of delivering a speech there – it dawns on me that I should take a quick trip to Austria to visit the synagogue where my father's family used to pray before the Holocaust. Despite Adam's entreaties that I return as soon as possible, Mandelbaum and I take my private plane on a quick detour to Vienna. Donning a yarmulke and a prayer shawl, things that I always keep on board, I enter the Great Synagogue in Vienna's first district, which survived World War II. *"It's still hidden inside a building,"* I think to myself, but the splendor and beauty tug at my heartstrings. From the synagogue, Mandelbaum and I continue on to the nearby Jewish Community Cener, and the community rabbi briefs me on the history of Vienna Jewry. He's able to tell me a lot about my father's family, most of whom did not survive the Holocaust.

★

I remember South Carolina from my youth. My father used to visit often, as part of his Democratic Party involvement, and we sometimes joined him. In those days, my father was a senior Democratic Party official, and he was also a senator of Connecticut.

We used to take our family's private jet to Columbia City Airport. To this day, I can remember what it felt like to stand next to my father, holding his hand, and waiting excitedly for the airplane door to open and for us to walk down to the runway, where the local party leaders would be waiting to greet us with a great show of friendship and admiration for my father. His personality was different in those days. Unlike the toughness he'd display to everyone around us, he was patient and kind with me.

I chose to take my private plane to South Carolina as well, and this time I asked Philip to meet us at the airport with the Jaguar. I asked him to be my driver, at least for the first part of my trip here. I of course recognize the importance of traveling together with my campaign team, but I also need a bit of alone time, and I decided that I'd take a little break from the bus.

The gorgeous views through the Jaguar's windows evoke in me a sense of brightness, pleasantness, a feeling of simpler times from my childhood, and even from the days when I was growing up and came here as a student activist for the Democratic party. I open the window and let the wind caress my face. I close my eyes and let myself sink into those forgotten, reassuring feelings. "We've arrived," Philip's voice penetrates the pastoral feelings that have overtaken me.

"Just a little while longer," I implore, wanting to allow myself enough time to return calmly back to reality and get ready for my meeting with the head of the Democratic Party in South Carolina. We park in front of the building that I remember as the Democratic Party headquarters, from back when I used to come here with my father. It's a white, wooden building with blue and white stripes painted on it.

The Chairman of the Democratic Party in South Carolina is a good friend of my father's and used to welcome us at the entrance to this very building. There, they'd sit me down on a wooden window seat, so I could look outside and play with the chairman's antique toy car collection. He'd pour my father a stiff drink from a stylish crystal bottle that I always found impressive, and the two of them would start exchanging their whispers. Now that I understand life a tad better, I know that what they were doing was closing deals and finalizing agreements about all sorts of questionable moves that they'd both take to their graves.

"I used to love coming here with my father," I tell the local party chairman, and I'm rewarded with a warm handshake.

"I saw pictures of you and your father with Jacob Wyatt," he says. "It seems they were really good friends. Your father is revered in South Carolina. He was always committed to us here, and in exchange, we always welcomed him with a lot of warmth, love, and political support. Here in South Carolina, we value commitment and friendship, and Joseph Gold was always rewarded here for what he did for us. To this day, we're happy to repay the Gold family," he adds with a smile. "A few days ago, your father came here and was received very warmly indeed. That's how it'll always be for him and for any future generations."

The chairman leads me down a long corridor. I follow him and can't even imagine what awaits me behind the two large wooden doors at its end.

"Tom Gold!" I hear the announcer declare the moment the doors open, and the hundreds of people waiting in the convention hall are on their feet and clapping their hands. Above the stage, a huge sign is hung with the words: "Honorary degree for Mr. Tom Gold." And here I thought I was coming for a run-of-the-mill meeting with the local party chairman. I scan the crowd in search of a familiar face.

Is my father here? Is Richard? Where's my campaign team? None of them are here, and I quickly sit down in the seat that has a small sign bearing my name. The announcer explains to everyone there, myself included, that they had decided to surprise me in order to bestow upon me the title of honorary degree for my previous political action as part of my involvement with the Democratic Party.

In my youth, I used to travel to South Carolina under the auspices of a project I was running to improve the image of the public sector. I'd go from one high school to the next, explaining the importance of enlisting in the public sector and civil service. My work in Colombia gained momentum, and I was invited to come speak to the college students as well.

"We have an old debt we owe you," the announcer says. "Your contribution never received the recognition it truly deserved. And so we decided to take advantage of your visit here and grant you, albeit ten years late, an honorary degree on behalf of the Colombia Municipality, in the field of education." The crowd applauds enthusiastically.

The mayor and the local chairman of the Democratic Party are invited onstage to present me with this honorary degree, and beforehand, they each have some words to say. The mayor speaks first, describing the education system in Columbia and my contribution to the educational discourse there. After the mayor, the local party chairman speaks effusively about how much the Gold family has done for South Carolina. Finally, I am asked up to the stage, to rousing applause, and the local party chairman places the medal around my neck.

I deliver a short, off-the-cuff speech. I've noticed the local press there and assume they were briefed by people from the party to provide me with some flattering headlines. I come offstage to the sound of the audience's cheers, and I take my seat again next to the local chairman.

After the ceremony, we enter a room I used to go to with my father, for a meeting. Just like the previous party chairman used to do over 35 years ago, this one also pours me a glass of liquor from the same stylish crystal bottle, or at least one that looks uncannily like the one I saw when my father was poured a glass. The chairman presents me with a picture of me and my father. I look at it closely. He's standing upright, and as always, looks older than his age. I'm dressed in black pants and a striped sweater. He's looking straight at the camera, smiling, and holding my hand. The picture was taken before he changed his entire attitude towards me.

Two hours later, our meeting ends with an agreement to meet again the following day with key influential party activists. He walks me to the front door, and I get into the Jaguar, asking Philip to take me to the hotel. On the way, I call Richard.

"I just received an honorary degree in education from the Columbia Municipality," I tell him, amused.

"How exactly did that happen?" he asks.

"They arranged a sort of surprise party for me, a kind of welcome reception at the party headquarters, and said there was an old debt they owed me for all the educational work I had done here over a decade ago."

"Impressive," Richard says. "And it just so happens they remembered this debt right now?!"

"Sure. You know, to add some color to it all."

"To add some color, or to paint all of South Carolina in a 'Tom' shade of Gold?"

"Call it whatever you want. That's what happened," I say, starting to feel a bit angry.

"How much did your father pay for it?" he asks, and now I'm really pissed off.

"I don't know," I answer, trying to stay cool. I'm not in the mood for a fight with Richard when he's so far away.

"Tom, you're going to lose this election because of him. He's a dirty politician, and he's not immune. These things will all come out."

"My father was in South Carolina a few days ago, but I have no idea what he was doing here. And anyway, I got this award because of work that I really did do for education, which is a main part of my platform."

"And now is the time to give it to you? Moments before the primaries there? Isn't it obvious that the press will figure this out, and no good will come of it?"

"The Democratic party controls the local press, with or without my father."

"So now you're defending your father?" Richard asks angrily. "For over 30 years you hated the man, and now you're going to follow him blindly? You're going to lose because of him."

We hang up. I close my eyes and try to calm down. *Maybe it's better that Richard isn't here*, I think to myself. Maybe it's better not to share everything with him, because I could lose him. After all, here in South Carolina, I can't stop my father. His spirit would be here even if he wasn't here physically. What's more, my father might be right: First I'll win the election, playing by his old rules of politics, and then I'll be able to really apply the new politics that I want to inspire.

My black Jaguar is heading southeast to Charleston, on the Atlantic coast. My campaign bus is driving behind us. Out of the windows, I see magnificent views, and it occurs to me that I should call my father and tell him about how beautiful it is.

For the first time in my adult life, I've started enjoying this concept of "father." After about an hour's drive, we arrive at the port city. It's good that there's a port in Charleston. It will definitely be able to help ease my mood. I make my way to a meeting with the local Jewish community, which is considered one of the oldest and more important Jewish communities in the United States. On the way there, I text Richard.

There are Kings of England everywhere, I write.

I thought Richard the First was the only king for you, he replies.

You are truly the only one for me, I write back. **I'm in Charleston, named for England's King Charles the Second.**

As long as he's only the second, I'm okay with it, he replies.

I miss you a lot, I write.

I miss you too. But I'm busy right now.

His answer pierces my heart, and I hurriedly try to breathe. I can't be offended. There have been many times that I was busy and didn't have the time to text him.

See you in South Carolina, he writes, and I can't tell whether he wrote it dismissively, or because he's looking forward to it. Text messages can be a very problematic means of communication. I decide that when I'm done in South Carolina, before heading to Florida, I'll arrange a weekend for just the two of us in Miami. I need to find a way for our worlds to intertwine, even during this election campaign.

When my meetings and campaign rallies in Charleston are over, we're once again on the road, this time heading northwest to the city of Greenville. Again, I'm traveling separately, but this time I've invited Adam to ride with me in the Jaguar.

In Greenville, I meet with Edward Thompson, who's considered the strongest man in the district, and he treats me with a great deal of respect. He gives me a warm welcome, and from the very first moment, it seems we have good chemistry. We're about the same age. He's attractive. His blond Robert Redford hair makes him look like a Hollywood actor. He's tall, dressed in classic contemporary fashion, and he is definitely my type. I quickly realize that despite whatever the wedding ring on his finger is supposed to be communicating, he's a closeted gay man. I can recognize them, probably because I see something of myself in them.

Thompson pours me some more cognac and looks me in the eyes with a penetrating gaze. I feel the same excitement I used to feel when I'd stand in front of a man who I wanted, who I knew wanted me too. I'm even tempted to wink at him, to let him know that I want him too, but at the last moment an inner voice wakes me up, reminding me that I'm married and in the middle of the campaign of my life. As if all I need right now is a scandal like this.

I quickly thank him, cutting our meeting short. I think he noticed the panic that had overtaken me, but this is better than staying in his company. I leave, hurriedly closing the door of Jaguar, where Adam is still sitting.

"How was the meeting?" he asks me.

"Not now," I answer, trying to organize my thoughts and overcome the weakness that took over in that office and almost led me to betray Richard. I pour myself a whiskey from the car's bar, undo my tie, and wipe the sweat off my forehead.

"Is everything OK?" Adam asks me.

"Not now," I say again, impatiently, knowing that I need to get as far away from here as possible.

"Cancel my meetings in Greenville," I tell him.

"Why?" he asks.

"What's our next destination?" I ask, ignoring his question.

"Gaffney."

"How long?" I ask Philip.

"An hour and a half to two hours," he answers.

"So drive there," I instruct him, and I ask Adam to join the rest of the campaign team and make arrangements for my new plans.

During the drive, I call Richard.

"I miss you a lot," I say.

"I miss you too," he says. "You don't sound great."

"I'm not doing great."

"What happened?"

"I had an awful meeting in Greenville."

"Where's Greenville?" Richard asks, trying to distract me but I stay silent. "So what happened?"

"That Thompson guy is in the closet."

252

"Who?" Richard asks.

"Our strong man in the district."

"And you outed him?" Richard asks, still trying to be amusing.

"No, but I wanted to fuck him," I say angrily.

"Why are you telling me this?" Richard asks.

"Because honesty between us is important to me, and I'm ready to pay the price for it."

"OK, well, yesterday I really wanted to fuck a woman," Richard tells me.

"Anyone in particular?"

"No, but I had a strong urge to do it," he says, and pauses. "I wasn't going to do anything about it though."

"I didn't do anything either."

Richard is silent.

"We're growing apart," he says finally.

"I find it terrifying," I answer. "I had a complete panic attack, one like I haven't had in a long time. It reminded me of different days, bad days, the kinds I used to know before I met you."

"I'll come to Columbia in two days, and we'll talk."

"I love you," I say, and hang up.

I'm in Gaffney, I text Adam.

I'll arrive a bit later with the rest of the team. We got held up in Greenville, he replies, and I ask Philip to stop at a rest stop at the entrance to Gaffney so I can get us coffee.

There are a few truck drivers and a few more locals sitting in the café. The heavy chested barista behind the bar starts sending flirty looks my way the moment she sees me.

"Tom Gold," I hear someone behind me say. I turn around and find myself looking a tough guy in a cowboy hat straight in the face.

"With whom do I have the honor?" I ask.

"Zachary. Mark Zachary," he replies. I put out my hand trying to remember if I know this man, but he blatantly ignores the gesture.

"You're going to ruin our country," he declares. "Enough Jews and gays already control the money and culture. We don't need them to be our president, too." The people sitting around all nod in agreement. The barista continues sending me inviting glances.

"You're trying to tempt him?" he asks her. "You're wasting your time. He's a homo." With that, the other customers burst out laughing.

"Don't pay them any mind," she says, turning towards the coffee machine. "They're all dark and ancient. Looking for a fight. They're bored, and they're always trying to start something with anyone new who comes through the doors."

"Young billionaire homo Jew," Mark Zachary continues. "You and all your money bought up the media, the polling companies, everything you can buy in the country, and that's how you're controlling reality and the truth, as it's presented. You and your people are using your money to create an alternate truth, and you control it, and we're not able to fight back. Explain to me how it's possible that the polls all show America's in favor of a gay, Jewish president, the media supports you, and everything is going so well for you?" he asks, angry now.

I mutter something, take the coffee cups from the barista, and leave the café.

Once inside the car, I hand Philip his coffee. The Jaguar pulls out and I call Adam.

"The people here are backward," I tell him.

"Just don't let yourself get dragged into it," he replies from the other end of the line.

"I handled it professionally," I respond. "How were your meetings?"

"Greenville is ours. I think the governor of Montana is finally going to receive his first knock-out punch, here in South Carolina."

"It's about time," I say. "We'll knock him out in Florida, too, and end the game."

Josh Jordan, the chairman of a large farmers' union, is a senior leader of the Democratic Party in South Carolina and a good friend of my father's. He's invited me to his home in Gaffney, and we sit down in his study.

"I've arranged a meeting for you tomorrow with influential people in the districts here," Josh says. "It's important that you meet with them in person. When Bill Black spoke to me about the possibility of having a gay, Jewish candidate, I told him we're embarking on a dangerous adventure that could make us lose our power, but we knew that your secret weapon was your charisma, and you're really doing a great job here. I also spoke with a number of the super delegates here, and they support you too, but you can never know what they'll do in the moment of truth."

"What do you think the governor of Montana will do?"

"He's not going to pull out yet. It's still early days. There have been presidential candidates in the past who won the primaries even after suffering some knock-out blows. After you knock him out here and then in Florida, he'll be in trouble. His morale will certainly be. But even then, I'm not sure he'll pull out of the race. As far as we're concerned, we need to prepare for a close race up until the National Convention in the summer."

Josh invites me into the kitchen where he makes coffee for us.

"You've grown up," he says. "I remember when you'd come here as a boy, with your father. You have a special relationship with him. He's a very good, close friend of mine. I'm sure you know that once, during a crisis, he actually lived here with me for several weeks."

"When? Before he met my mom?" I ask, confused.

"No. Much later. He went through some big crisis, and he came here to try to take stock of everything. I tried to help him. I thought you knew."

"I didn't. What was the crisis about?"

"I don't really know. He refused to talk about it. Our conversations about it were vague. But he was in a bad state, your father. I'd never seen him like that before. And then one day, your mother showed up, they had a long talk, and he returned home."

"Do you remember when that was?"

"Sure," Josh says, doing the math. "It was when we were running Walter Mondale in the party's primaries."

"I was 12 years old," I say. "I didn't know a thing."

A murky wave of memories washes over me, and I'm no longer aware of Josh or of current reality. I remember that my father really had disappeared when I was 12, a few days after he had caught me and Sean kissing in the garage at Silver Bell. When I told Richard about it on our trip to London, I had forgotten that immediately after that, my father had left the mansion for a while. At the time, I thought he was on another one of his political or business trips. It never occurred to me that what happened could so badly hurt my father, who seemed invincible at the time.

The day after my father caught me and Sean kissing, I sat down at the breakfast table silently, like a thief. My father made a clear effort to completely ignore my presence. His silence was ear-splitting, and the way he ignored me contained something so hostile that I had never known before. I knew he'd never let this be something that he'd normalize, that he'd never forgive me, not until I married some woman.

"I'm done," I said quietly, wanting to slip outside because I felt like I was suffocating. I didn't know at the time that this threatening, foreign feeling that was taking over was actually my first panic attack, something that would quickly become a constant companion of mine.

"Wait," my father commanded in a steely voice. "Arthur will drive you to school." There was no point in arguing or telling him that I wanted to ride the bus like everyone else. I nodded in agreement and quietly waited for him to get up from the table. Every morning, he'd read *The New York Times* from cover to cover. To this day he still does it, and I've adopted the same habit. At 7:30 on the dot, he finished reading the last page, put the paper down on the table, and got up from his chair. I walked behind him to the estate's parking area.

Arthur was waiting next to the Rolls Royce, said, "Good morning," to my father, and closed the door after him. I ran to the other side of the car and took my place in the back seat, next to my father. I sat as far away from him as I could. I clung to the door, terrified. I was sure he was going to beat me. I actually wanted him to hit me, to punish me, to let out all his anger so we could leave this ugly story behind us and move forward, but he remained silent. For me, there was nothing worse than that silence.

"Stop at Tom's school," my father instructed Arthur, and off we went.

With the push of a button, he lifted the partition between us and the driver, turned to me, stared at me intently, and uttered one of the harshest things I've ever been told in my life. "You're no longer my son," he said. "I'll make sure to provide for you, because you're still your mother's son, but don't expect anything from me any longer."

I started to shake all over. The words were so harsh that my cries got stuck in my throat and wouldn't come out. Only tears streamed from my eyes, washing my cheeks.

"Sorry, Father," I said in a quiet, choked voice, but he ignored me. He lowered the partition, signaled Arthur to turn on the radio, took a paper out of his bag and began to read it.

I remember how I sat shrinking in silence, looking out the window trying to hold back the tears, because I didn't want Arthur to see me cry. When we reached the school entrance, I fled out of the car with my head down, but instead of entering the school I ran to a side street and from there to some public park and sobbed. I howled like a wounded animal. It took me a long time to calm down.

I didn't go to school that day. I wandered the streets. In the end, I found myself next to the hiding place I used to hide in as a kid, near my old preschool. When Maria would come pick me up in the afternoon, I'd often manage to drag her to this very spot, get her to sit inside with me and play pretend with me.

I went inside, between the bushes, and sat down on the ground. I was all cried out, but I started imagining life without my father. After some time, I started to calm down and my thoughts finally left my father and wandered towards other realms. I thought about school, about my language and writing class that was starting right then. I loved those classes and my teacher Miss Olivia. I suddenly realized she'd probably call my mother that afternoon to ask why I wasn't in school that day. I left my little hiding place in a panic and ran all the way home. I got there at the time I usually came home from school.

Mother was busy with her own things, Maria was preparing lunch, and I realized that Miss Olivia hadn't called yet.

I went up to my room and sat right next to the phone so that I'd be able to answer it as soon as the teacher called. I had an excuse ready for her: my throat hurt that morning. I had a low fever, but now I was feeling much better and would be back in school tomorrow. I continued sitting in my room next to the phone for over an hour, but in the end, hunger won out and I went down to the kitchen to eat lunch.

Mother suddenly entered the kitchen.

"Don't irritate your father," she said.

"How did I irritate him?" I played dumb, trying to gauge whether he told her anything about what had happened.

"He said you're not acting nicely. He's very mad at you."

"Do you think I'm not acting nicely, Mother?" I asked sweetly, smiling the most enchanting smile that I could muster.

"You're a wonderful boy, Tom, but do what your father tells you to do, and don't upset him," she said, running a finger over my nose and letting Maria know that she was going out to meet up with her friends. And the moment she left, the danger that she'd answer the call that might come from my teacher passed, and I decided to go outside. Before doing so, I made sure to ask Maria to say I was at the doctor's office and would be back at school tomorrow, if my teacher called. Maria didn't love this plot I'd conjured up but agreed to cooperate.

I got on my bike and rode without any actual destination in mind, but my feet took me to Sean's house. I knocked on the door and, as usual, his mother answered, greeting me affectionately.

"Sean's in his room," she said.

I went up to the second floor and found Sean reading a comic book.

"Tom," he called out in excitement at seeing me and leapt up from his bed. "Are you OK?"

"My father will never forgive me for what he saw us doing," I told him.

"Do you think he'll tell my father about it?" he asked, worried, and I was a tad disappointed in his reaction.

"Of course not. He's so ashamed by what happened, he'll never speak of it with anyone. He'll take this with him to the grave and never forgive me."

"You're exaggerating," Sean said. "Of course he'll forgive you. After some time, he'll forget all about it. That's how parents are."

"I'm not so sure," I said quietly. "You don't know my father."

"It will also be our secret, for the rest of time," Sean said, coming closer to me.

For some time after, I avoided going to Sean's house, a place that had been like a second home to me before "the incident." We'd see each other in school, but there, we could avoid our forbidden actions. I hoped this might help me wean myself off of my fantasies, but they only grew stronger, filling my mind constantly. Those were the weeks my father disappeared. Now I know where he went. When he returned, he decided to keep me away from Sean, and under the guise of promoting his father at Olympia, he made sure that Sean's family moved to West Africa, where his father was now the manager of the company's local branch.

And that's how I was cut off from my good friend Sean, and was left all on my own. I remember sitting during recess and during classes that I skipped, with my Walkman headphones in my ears, escaping to other worlds that were created for me by Pink Floyd and David Bowie. Maria was also a sort of refuge for me, a sort of substitute mother, and she made sure to welcome me every afternoon. She'd sometimes even wait for me at the entrance to the mansion. She couldn't ignore how coldly my parents treated me, and she tried to make up for their behavior. That's how I found myself spending long hours in her company, walking with her around the house and the yard, sharing my thoughts with her, and she'd tell me about her family, her childhood and teenage years, while carrying out her various household duties. I never dared mention to her the way I felt about other boys; at that time, I was also sure those feelings would one day pass.

In order to speed things up and also in order to please my parents, I started to show interest in girls, as it were. At school, I became friends with Andrea, a smart and funny girl. She had a rich and fascinating inner world that reminded me of my own. I enjoyed talking to her and spending time with her, and I made sure to invite her over and introduce her to my parents. Mother liked her a lot. Father looked at her and our relationship with suspicion, but it seems that he was also pleased when she'd show up at our house. When our relationship ended, I started bringing over Amanda, a beautiful and charismatic girl who got along great with my parents.

I celebrated my sixteenth birthday in Jacksonville, Florida, where I'd been spending time as part of a delegation of the Jewish Agency. We were a bunch of young Jews from Israel and America. That's where, to my great surprise, I once again met Sean. After my father exiled Sean's family to West Africa, he had decided a few years later to move them to Chicago. That's why Sean was able to be part of the delegation. For the four years that followed "the incident," I never had any sexually suggestive encounters with a guy. I never managed to overcome my sexual desires, which only swelled to monstrous proportions since there was never any real outlet for them, but I tried to deal with them by using alcohol and drugs, which were my best friends in those days.

I kept myself in check for four years, until one night when Sean entered my hotel room. Jacksonville is where I had my first real sexual experience. Sean had also come with very little experience, and the feeling of liberation and discovery that overtook the two of us was unimaginable for us. It filled us with a joy that was both enormous and temporary, but a joy that came back every night when we'd meet in secret, until we needed to return to our respective homes.

We stayed together on and off for five years, meeting under the guise of ideological activists at Jewish Agency events across America, until one day when Sean decided he wanted to enlist in the U.S. Army and severed all contact. Our final meeting was at his funeral. Sean's airplane had plunged into the sea immediately after taking off from the aircraft carrier where he had served. At his funeral, I met his mother, who had always been so lovely to me. I hugged her tight, trying to comfort her but also trying to feel Sean – who had disappeared from my life forever in one instant – through her.

★

There's a knock on the hotel suite door and I open it, annoyed, not understanding why any of my campaign team would permit themselves to come to my room without warning.

The sight of Richard standing there facing me sends a wave of pleasant warmth throughout my entire body. In one moment, I forget everything – our fight, the governor of Montana, the primaries – and I grab his hand and pull him towards me, holding him close to my own body, feeling myself managing to breathe once again as long as Richard is with me. The night air on the suite's rooftop reminds me of our wedding night. I take his hand, hold it close to my chest, and lead him towards the bedroom. In a tangle of sheets and pillows, Richard lies on his side and I penetrate him, our palms intertwined and our gazes refusing to let go. Once we've finished, Richard snuggles into me for a long while.

The next morning, we make our way to the central volunteer headquarters in Columbia. We're in a great mood. Hundreds of activists have gathered, and I thank and encourage them, which in turn rewards me with applause and cheers.

Adam briefs me on our field deployment and the election day timetable. He takes me to a private room prepared for me, where I'll be able to call the party's key activists, but I decide to give up the room and instead sit among my volunteers, making phone calls together with them. Every now and then I lift my head, look around, and see my own face smiling back at me from every direction. I'm still not used to this.

From the volunteer headquarters, I make my way to the important polling stations that Adam has chosen for me. Richard makes sure to stand by my side throughout the entire day, and I can see how right Bill Black and all the others are. Along with Richard, the positive attention and reactions I'm getting are making me soar to higher heights than I've ever known.

In the late evening, Richard and I rest in the hotel before the results are announced, and then we make our way to the city's arena, where activists and campaign staff are waiting for us.

I'm sitting with Adam and Richard in one of the back rooms. Despite the good feelings we have, we're waiting anxiously for the results. I suddenly feel how badly I want to win; how badly I want to give my father what he wants; how badly I want to see this journey to its end.

Josh Jordan enters the room.

"Congratulations," he exclaims with a fatherly smile, inviting me in, and I fall into his arms and give him the strong embrace that is essentially intended for my actual father. He hands me a small note that has "78%:22%" written on it.

"I got 78%?" I ask.

"Yes," he answers and laughs, his cheeks red in excitement. "It's even better than we'd hoped for."

We can hear applause and cheers from the hall.

"Please welcome to the stage, South Carolina's clear winner, Tom Gold!" the announcer declares, dragging out my name until he's out of breath. I'm standing backstage, surrounded by my campaign team cheering me on. The excitement is palpable. I walk over and hug each and every one of them.

To the sound of the song *Live is Life*, I jog up on stage, go towards the front, towards the crowd that's waving my signs in the air, and I cheer and thank them. Suddenly, all the applause and cheers increase at once. I turn around and see Richard getting up on stage, and the crowd adores him.

My victory speech is short and sweet. I'm having a hard time finishing it because of all the enthusiasm in the audience and the great joy in the hall. "Thank you, thank you, thank you!" I finally say, overtaken by emotion, as I make my way offstage. My election jingle is playing in the background, and this setting has brought me back to my twenties, to the days when I'd attend the big conventions and imagine that one day I'd be standing on stage and delivering my victory speech.

Suddenly, we can hear people near the stage shouting out "How much did it cost your daddy to buy you the primaries?" My heart skips a beat, even though it's obvious that these are the Montana governor's people who managed to sneak into our closed event. I'm fully aware of the sincere efforts I made that led me to victory, and I get offstage with a full heart. Together with Richard and my campaign team, I go outside to the campaign bus, where a huge crowd of photographers and reporters attack us from all sides.

"Good night," I say to all the press there, letting them shoot a few more pictures of me and Richard, and then I board the bus. I wave to them from the bus door and bid farewell to South Carolina.

CHAPTER 19

Palm Beach, Florida, Mid-February

Richard gets up from his sunbed and runs after me on a path covered by overgrowth that leads to the beach. We make our way through this tangled vegetation that I remember from my family vacations at my parents' weekend home on Palm Beach. My mother suggested we take the house for the weekend to have a break from the campaign, and I agreed. I have good memories from this place.

Suddenly, the breathtaking beach appears before us. I take Richard to the white wooden bridge that leads to the deck floating on the water. We lie down on the deck as it moves gently on the waves, and we rest. Every now and then, I steal a glance at Richard and enjoy looking at him. I stretch my hand out toward him and caress his cheeks.

"Tom," he murmurs.

"I can't hold back," I say, bringing my rejected hand to my chest. Maybe he's right; maybe even here on this beach in February, there's a paparazzo hiding who'll document our entire weekend together.

"There's a price to living a public life. Everything's no longer permitted. Not for you or me."

"I didn't know you were so affected by all this."

"After the paparazzi pictures and all the noise surrounding them, I've put a lot of thought into what I do, so that I don't get caught, even on little things."

"Do you feel like you're suffering because of it?"

"I'm not suffering but I'm also not enjoying. I'm a private person. Given the choice, I'd prefer avoiding the primaries and political life in general, but I love you and your success is important to me."

I'm silent. I knew this was how he felt, but it's hard for me to hear that he needs to tolerate all of this for my sake.

"And you? Are you enjoying yourself?" Richard asks.

"Sometimes yes, sometimes no. There were some amazing moments during these primaries. I've discovered things I didn't know about myself. It's been challenging. I've also had my fair share of failures, but I've managed to stay focused on my goal and emotionally balanced."

"Great," Richard says. "If one of us can manage to enjoy this, we're off to a great start," and we both laugh.

About two hours later, we're climbing up the path back towards my parents' summer home. Mother has recently renovated it, since she's getting it ready for sale, and you can see her good taste everywhere. Richard gets out of the shower and stands facing a large glass wall overlooking the sea. The sun is setting, and the view is painted in deep shades of red.

"This house is perfect," Richard says.

"It's for sale."

"Let's buy it," he suggests, "I'd be happy to come here for vacation."

"Fine," I say in a joyful tone, and we shake hands and wink at each other. When it's only the two of us there, safe from the prying eyes of the public, I can pull Richard towards me, remove his towel, embrace him, and lead him towards our bed. My entire body is tense with excitement, and my sexual organ is cocked and ready. After some quick coitus, I roll onto his lap for some lovey musings.

"I miss our little talks like this," he says.

"I also miss them a lot," I answer, and we hold each other tight and fall asleep.

In the morning, I get up early, before Richard. I make our breakfast and he joins me in wool pants and a matching sweater.

"So you've totally switched over to wool clothes now?" I ask him, amused.

"It's the morning line of Richard the First fashion," he answers with a smile. "I've been trying all sorts of ways to get used to the idea, including external remedies. I bought an entire collection for myself in Manhattan."

"So maybe you are enjoying this a bit after all. When did you manage to buy all these clothes?"

"I didn't manage. Lisa did."

"Lisa?"

"Lisa, my personal shopper. Like all the First Wives before me, I too have a personal shopper."

"But I'm not the president yet."

"We need to be optimistic," Richard says. "I have a good feeling. Look at how you took South Carolina by storm. And remember how you won in Iowa," he adds, taking a jab at me for going along with the dirty deals my father and his friends made. He begs me to understand that I have no one but myself to blame for it. "If you want to put an end to that, you need to tell him outright."

"You're right," I tell Richard. "But it's not so simple."

"I'm just worried about you," Richard says. "That's all. I'm afraid that his dirty games will knock you down in the end. Political wheeler-dealers are no suckers. Your father may be the wizard of political deals and games, but he's not the only one. I saw how your supporters got swept up in all their excitement about you. I saw how the college students in Iowa admired you. For them, you symbolize something new, a change, hope, a different kind of America. You got them all swept up, you're different from the establishment that they are fed up with. You can touch people's hearts and win them over without your father making his deals."

"The people's hearts aren't what we need to be thinking about right now," I say a bit angrily to Richard, not sure whether this anger is directed towards him or myself and the position I'm in. "First, I need to win the Democratic primaries, and the hearts of party members won't be enough. That's what I'll need to focus on later, in the national elections. Here, within the party, there are heartless dirty politicians, and you need to know what moves to make when they're involved. Maybe not my father's moves, but it's clear that I'm going to need to do something. He who draws first wins."

We finish our breakfast. Richard glances at his watch and gets up from the table.

"Good luck," he says, coming over to kiss me on the forehead. I pull him close, stroke his hair, close my eyes, and take a deep breath to fill my lungs with his scent. When I loosen my hold a bit, we look at each other for a while, and Richard is the first to look away. He gently slides his hand out of mine and begins walking out the door, taking his bag and leaving for Manhattan.

I remain seated, looking out at the view from the window, already longing for Richard's body and his manly presence.

On my way to Miami, I make two important phone calls. The first is to my father, who is pleased to hear my voice and congratulates me on my victory in South Carolina. "I want to thank you for your assistance, Father," I say, taking a deep breath.

"I'm glad you're starting to understand the rules of the game. Politics is politics. It has many sides. Its essence is doing the impossible. Within all this chaos, you need to know how to conduct yourself. Sometimes it's dirty, but then you make up for it elsewhere. The secret to it all is balances and brakes. Not everything is black and white, there's also a lot of grey, and I suggest you start getting used to it."

"We must not lose this momentum," he adds. "The governor is doing a great job in Florida, and I'm already less strong there as is. My contacts tell me that he's been there for several months over the past year. Of course, he planned his presidential run long before you and managed to get a lot done in the important states. Unlike you, who entered the race at the very last moment. Your field workers need to motivate the young people and minorities to vote at the primaries."

"Despite all his hard work, I managed to win three states so far." I can hear the smile in his voice when I say this. "I'll win Florida too. Leave it to me. I'll use the momentum from South Carolina, and I need to do it my way."

My father is silent. I interpret his silence as agreement.

"I met Josh in South Carolina, and we had an interesting conversation about the past."

"We'll discuss it when we meet," my father cuts me off immediately, understanding what I'm talking about.

We say goodbye, but not before he warns me once again that the governor of Montana will do everything he can in Florida to knock me down. "It's his last chance, after all the blows he's taken."

I hang up, ponder what was said for a few moments, and decide to call the governor.

"Mr. Stone?" I ask.

"Yes," the governor answers in his usual stern voice.

"Tom Gold."

"Yes," he replies coldly.

"Last time I saw you, you wouldn't shake my hand."

"You don't break agreements, Tom," the governor proves me right.

"I agree with you, but I wasn't a part of that agreement, and I am opposed to that kind of a deal. Besides, I can't see how you'd be the treasury secretary in a government of mine. I have a very clear economic agenda, and I'm not sure you'd agree with it."

"You and your father don't speak?"

"We do. Why?"

"So let him update you. People approached me on his behalf and offered me to serve as your treasury secretary. When I agreed, I was sure it was with your approval. You two should coordinate with each other," he says angrily.

"I called you to ask if we can maintain the norms of decency and integrity – me towards you and you towards me. Our fight is clear and understandable, but there's a respectable way to do it."

"Florida isn't South Carolina," he declares, refusing to end our conversation respectfully. "It would be good for you to remember that. Your father is weak here, and no one even counts you. After I knock you out here, if you still want to maintain fair and respectful ties, I'll agree."

"Good luck," I say, ending the call with a sense of despair. I hope I didn't make a huge mistake with this phone call. Maybe I really am naïve and maybe my father was right.

I ask Philip to stop on the side of the road. My campaign bus stops behind us, and I get out of the Jaguar and walk over to the bus so I can ride with my team. Now that Glenn's no longer with us, I can do so without worry. When I get on, it seems like my presence has interrupted some sort of joyful vibe that blossomed among the campaign team when I was away. They receive me with surprise, like small kids who were caught doing something wrong. That's what happens when the boss is gone for too long. I tell them why I haven't been traveling with them lately, making sure to clarify that I trust them and am forever grateful for everything they do. Despite what I've said, there's a heavy atmosphere on the bus. Maybe they're worried that I'm paranoid and suspect their integrity as much as I suspected Glenn's – albeit justifiably.

"So where are we headed?" I ask Adam, trying to break the tense silence.

"To the University of Miami. You'll meet with the president of the University, who's also a political activist. After that meeting, we've planned a conversation for you with hundreds of college students, most of whom are active in the Democratic Party. We researched the more prominent people you'll be meeting with." Adam hands me an orderly document.

I scan the document and, to my surprise, need to make quite a lot of corrections. "Please include what I wrote by hand," I tell Adam, giving him back the document. "In the future, please go over these things a few days in advance rather than at the last minute. We can't be complacent. Our victory in South Carolina doesn't mean anything yet. There could be surprises along the way. We need to be vigilant until it's all over. I think Miami has given you guys a deceptive sense of freedom, so let's get back to business."

"Is everything okay with them?" I quietly ask Adam later.

"Everything's good," he says. "They're great. Don't discourage them. They've been away from home for a long time, they're devotedly running after you from place to place, and they deserve kind words. You spent the weekend with Richard in Palm Beach and came back on a high. You need to come back down to earth, Tom. Besides, after firing Glenn, you need to let them see that you trust them completely. If you're going to go far, you need to nurture the team, take care of it, and protect it."

Adam's right, of course. Without a loyal team, I have no chance of winning, not in the primaries and not in the elections themselves.

We arrive at the University of Miami. My meeting with the president goes well, for the most part, but something about him doesn't sit well with me. Something in his eyes has my guard up. We part with a handshake, and I head over to my conversation with the college students. The president doesn't accompany me, as is generally done, and this also raises my suspicions, but I decide to put it out of my mind for now and focus on the students, lecturers, and activists who've crowded into the auditorium.

The announcer calls my name. I go up on stage using my presidential walk that I've recently developed and approach the podium. I get a standing ovation. I know my speech by heart. I describe the dilemmas that I'll face as a new president trying to deal with the problems they are facing, and I list the solutions I'd offer in detail. I'm speaking to them as equals. I don't make any promises I won't be able to keep and I don't throw a bunch of empty slogans at them. I go over the main points of my economic proposals and review Olympia's economic achievements. From there I move over to political ideas I'd like to push forward in various regions, mainly using diplomacy.

Slowly but surely, I'm weaving them into my web, where I'll trap them in my network, and indeed they reward me with thunderous applause.

"Come and show me how much power you all have. Who here is a member of the Democratic Party?" I raise my voice, and an enormous roar fills the auditorium as hundreds of students jump up and wave the party flags.

"I want you all with me!" I call out, which whips them up into an even bigger frenzy. I really do need them, more than ever before, and a wave of panic takes over for a moment. The cheers and applause subside, and one of the students wants to ask a question.

"My name is Samayon Rodriguez," he says, and the name sounds familiar to me. "I want to know how you can claim to know what's going on with me and my friends. After all, you were born with a silver spoon in your mouth, a billionaire from day one. Together, you and your husband are worth several billion dollars. You two are an entire economy in and of itself. You can't truly understand what it's like for minorities who can't find their way to the status that you never once needed to work for."

I suddenly realize where I know him from. He's a friend of Jose, Maria's son, and he's been to my house a few times when Jose needed to see his mother for whatever reason. He's seen the kind of luxury I live in, and I can see where he's coming from.

"Samayon, my friend," I say. "You're Jose's friend, right? Samayon is friends with my housekeeper's son," I explain to everyone else there, and a proud smile starts to spread across Samayon's face that he's unable to hide. "Samayon's been to my house in Manhattan a number of times with Jose who, by the way, is my campaign advisor on Hispanic affairs. So he knows what he's talking about. Samayon, I understand why you asked that question, and I'm actually glad you did. You're absolutely right. I never lacked for money, but I did inherit a company that was worth a billion dollars and managed to turn it into a company worth four billion. Because I know how to make money, I know which moves to make, and I know how to look ahead and identify what the market will do before anyone else.

"But it's important to remember that my skills and the fact that I was born rich don't mean that I'm insensitive to the plight of others. You decided to focus on my money only, but the hardships of life are more complex than that, and sensitivity and compassion for others are not the exclusive property of members of any one socio-economic status. I've faced many obstacles, in my family and in my personal life, and I bring that to any situation I face. Franklin Delano Roosevelt didn't come from a poor family either, but that didn't stop him from enacting the New Deal. He'd also never been an army general, yet he still managed to courageously lead the war against Nazi Germany. You don't need to experience everything in the world in order to understand it. A good leader must act with a kind of sensitivity towards humanity that enables him to see someone beyond the hard facts, and I have that kind of sensitivity. The circumstances of my life forged it within me, and I promise you, Samayon, that I know how to use it. Just give me the chance to prove it to you. Vote for me."

I get a standing ovation. Samayon claps too. I go down the stairs leading to the backstage area to the sound of the crowd chanting my name in unison. There, I meet Adam.

"You were excellent," he says. "There's a small hiccup but it's under control. Mandelbaum is taking care of it."

"What's going on?" I ask, and in that one second, I go from soaring high to landing with a thud.

"In a few minutes, the governor of Montana will be holding a joint press conference with the president of the university. It turns out they are very close. Florida is his territory, and he's not going to let anyone take it. They're going to be bad, Tom. After your success with the college students now, they're going to be even worse, but we'll be fine."

Despite his reassuring words, his expression shows he's worried.

"I take it the press has arrived."

"In droves," Adam answers. "It seems they were promised a good story."

"Have you been able to figure out what this is all about?"

"As we speak, Mandelbaum is talking to his friends in the press. It seems it might be connected to the treasury secretary deal," Adam says, and I know we're in trouble. The media is going to present this as election fraud, and it could mark the end for me. I sit down to the side, wanting to call Richard, but I don't feel like hearing "I told you so" right now.

Mandelbaum joins us.

"What do you suggest?" I ask him.

"That we show restraint," he answers. "We don't need to jump at the opportunity to respond to everything anyone says. We can't play into the governor's hands, and we certainly can't act like rookies falling for the story he's trying to spin. He knows he can't lose Florida, and he's going to do everything in his power to deflect the fire over to you, to force you to waste time dealing with nonsense so that he can use that time for what he needs."

"So how will we respond?" I ask Mandelbaum.

"I'm not sure we will," he says confidently. "Let's hear what they have to say, and then we can decide what to do next. The reporters aren't stupid. They recognize spin, tricks, and fake news. In the end, they know if someone's playing games with them or telling the truth. Let him be his own ruin."

"But there really was a deal," I say.

"What deal?" Mandelbaum asks, shocked.

"There was a deal, Pete. My father was behind it. I don't even know how it all happened, but I know that the party offered him treasury secretary if he'd pull out of the race. They might have offered him money too, maybe to cover his campaign expenses until now. I don't know, but something like that definitely happened."

"And you were involved?" Mandelbaum asks, and I can see the disappointment in his eyes. It's the exact same disappointment that will be felt by everyone who believes in the new, clean politics I've been talking about.

"Of course not," I answer dismissively.

"Then there's no problem here. We'll direct the press to Bill Black. He can answer to this, as a senior party official," he suggests, and I agree and call Bill.

A short time later, the press conference begins at the office of the president of the University of Miami. The office is too small to contain all the reporters who managed to push inside. First, the university president speaks. He stands behind the microphone with a serious expression. "The University of Miami prides itself on serving as an example for proper conduct and maintaining the values of democracy, including integrity, fairness, transparency, and morality," he says, his beady eyes darting across the room.

"Today, the University of Miami hosted both presidential contenders from the Democratic Party. I held one-on-one meetings with both, and was impressed by both of their capabilities. But during my meeting with the governor of Montana, I was made aware of attempted political dealmaking and election bribery that he's had to contend with. I convinced the governor to hold this press conference here today to share with you what Tom Gold means when he speaks of a new kind of politics. Mr. Stone?" the president says, handing the microphone over to the governor.

"Good afternoon," the governor says, and endless camera clicks can be heard in the background.

Look at how much screen time he's getting, I think to myself. *What a jackpot he's trying to win at my expense.*

"I received a phone call today from Tom Gold. He asked if the two of us could act with integrity and fairness towards each other and maintain clean politics. I wondered to myself why he'd call me in the middle of this race, after having gained good momentum in South Carolina, to ask me to act with integrity. Maybe he did it because he himself wasn't acting with integrity," he announces, sending significant glances towards the reporters. "Maybe he did it because new politics don't actually walk hand in hand with Tom Gold, if he's sewing up deals and making dirty moves behind the scenes and then criticizing others, asking them to use integrity? I'll clarify just what I'm talking about. I was recently approached, on behalf of Tom Gold, to pull out of the race in exchange for money and a position."

A wave of whispers washes over the room.

"I was offered to serve as the next treasury secretary of the United States, under President Tom Gold, should he win the national elections. I was also offered a nice sum of money to cover my campaign expenses until now. It goes without saying that I rejected this offer vehemently. After my meeting today with the president of this university, I decided to share with you what Tom Gold has done."

"Liar!" I shout at the screen. "He didn't reject it, he accepted it with open arms. But I canceled the deal as soon as I heard about it, a few days after it was made."

I can see the shock in all the campaign team members' faces, because they had all thought the entire story was made up. Their shock turns to disappointment, and I know they think I've betrayed their faith in me. I hurriedly whisper to everyone near me that I'll explain everything after the press conference.

"How much money was mentioned?" a report asks the governor.

"A lot of money," he replies. "In cash, no tax involved," he adds in order to make it all sound even more nefarious.

"Mr. Gold himself offered you this deal?" another reporter asks.

"No. Senior party officials offered it to me on Mr. Gold's behalf."

"Were you shown polls showing that your chances are negligible?" a third reporter asks.

"I asked to see them, but they never did show them to me, and that's why I immediately understood that this was a dirty game and I refused."

The press conference ends after a while. The governor enjoyed a lot of precious airtime and managed to sully my name. *Just don't panic,* I try to calm myself down. *Don't shoot from the hip.*

Mandelbaum is flooded with reporter inquiries. After consulting together, we decide not to respond to the governor's claims but instead direct everyone to Bill Black, with whom we've coordinated our positions. In the evening, while the media continues covering this story, a press release is sent out on behalf of Bill Black:

We were sorry that the governor of Montana decided to attack the leading candidate in the internal elections of the Democratic Party and bite the hand that's been feeding him for years. It is clear that the timing of his press conference didn't happen by chance. We are deep into our primaries, and the governor of Montana is obviously hoping for a decisive win.

However, the party's polls are showing that he's losing ground and has been unable to gain the momentum he'd need. It was due to these assessments that he was offered to serve as the next treasury secretary should the Democratic Party win the elections. He was also offered to have the party cover his expenses until now, a common practice in such cases. We are sorry that he is not telling the truth and claiming that he refused the offer, when in reality, he accepted it enthusiastically.

It should be noted that none of these measures were coordinated with Tom Gold, and as soon as he heard about the offer, he insisted that it be negated. Mr. Gold's cancellation of the offer angered the governor of Montana, which made the latter decide to continue his presidential bid. We wish him well and ask that he maintain integrity and fairness.

"It's a good response," Mandelbaum says. "We'll follow this story and see how the wind blows. You come out strong here. You didn't know about it, and as soon as you did you put an end to it."

"Nicely done," I say to Mandelbaum. "If I win, you'll be my White House Press Secretary." He is quite moved to hear this. From the situation room in Miami, we're updated that Bill Black is being interviewed on radio shows and getting harsh criticism by the media.

"Harsh criticism?" I ask.

"Yes," Mandelbaum explains. "Because of the offer for a candidate to pull out of the race in exchange for a job and having his expenses covered. They're claiming that it was unethical, as if the party was trying to arrange an easy win for you. It was too early on in the elections and there wasn't any real way to assess whether the governor had any real chance of winning, so it looks like they did it merely to make things easier for you, to turn you into the presumptive candidate way too early on. Which is true," he says.

"This is bad," I say.

"It's not good, but it's also not your problem. The media hasn't connected you to the story. They're attacking Bill Black and the party. The governor went out against his own side, against the party that raised him. He exposed things the party does behind the scenes and showed the party's naked truth, with all its divisions and conflicts. The party's senior officials won't forget this. I assume he'll grow weak in the party because of it. The discussion will now revolve around the parties' elections conduct. It's a discussion of principles and philosophy, but it's unrelated to you. The situation room has updated me that your name has not been tied to this story. In the few cases where it has, it was in a positive way, because you cancelled the deal as soon as you heard about it."

I get a text from my father: **By tomorrow, it will already start dropping from the headlines.** I smile to myself in frustration. If he hadn't done anything, it wouldn't have reached the headlines in the first place.

Thanks for the encouragement. Who's idea was it? I write back.

You're doing a good job with the media, he types, choosing to ignore my question. **Don't respond and don't do anything else. The media will busy itself with trying to find out more for a few hours, and if the governor doesn't bring them anything new, the whole story will get dropped soon.**

Does he have anything new to give them? I text my father back.

Nothing from me, he responds, adding: **It won't be simple like it was in South Carolina. Good luck.**

The time has come to call Richard. I've been wanting to call him for a while, but I waited until things got a bit clearer. The nagging question keeps popping up in my head, why hasn't he called me? Maybe he's so busy that he isn't even aware of this media circus around me, I try to reason with myself.

"Have you seen?" I ask as soon as he answers.

"Of course, I haven't been able to peel myself away from the TV."

"So why haven't you called me?" I ask, angry.

"I was with you in the situation room in Iowa and I know the kind of pressure you're under right now. I didn't want to bother you. I sat in my office and haven't stopped praying that everything will be OK and work in your favor. I love you."

"I love you too. I'm sorry I got upset."

"I think you're going to come out of this OK. You put everything on our friend Bill Black."

"I didn't put anything on him. He was behind the whole thing, so he should deal with the consequences."

"It was your father's idea, and it would be good if you could remember that, Tom. This time, you came out OK. But next time, you could fall. Make sure your father doesn't intervene in Florida."

"Don't worry, he won't," I say.

"Maybe he isn't such a political genius after all," Richard mumbles.

"If I hadn't cancelled the deal, it's safe to say it would never have come out," I respond like someone who knows these political games well.

"Richard is quiet for some time, and then says, "I'm leaving today on business for Europe. I originally thought about sending my CEO, but I need to go myself. There are agreements that need to be signed with me personally. I won't be able to be there for the primaries."

"You what?" I ask angrily, feeling myself start to lose control after everything that's happened today. "Richard, we had an agreement. You don't need to go everywhere with me, but you come to the primaries' announcement events. You're not changing this on me now. I'm not built for this. I need you by my side for political reasons too, unrelated to how much I love you."

"I'm really sorry, Tom, but this is my business, and the bottom line is that I have no choice," he says in a weak but decisive voice, and we hang up.

Two days later, we leave Miami, and the press leaves us and the governor's press conference in peace. No one came out a winner from the whole thing, and the Democratic Party, who had a lot of its skeletons outed from the closet, lost in a major way.

From Miami, we're going to head northwest to Tampa, but on the way, I have a visit scheduled at the Miami port, connected to my previous job. I've missed Olympia, and that's what led me to plan this visit to one of our ships that docks there frequently. We pass through the enormous entrance gate. I'm received by Olympia's branch manager at the port, who leads me to the dock slip where a cargo ship that exports raw goods throughout the world is moored. A crew member opens the Jaguar door for me. I get out of the car, walk the ship's ramp in excitement, and make my way inside its belly. It's been a while since I was on board a ship, and the familiar scent immediately brings me back to memories spanning from my childhood through the past few years.

I meet the ship's captain. He leads me to an elevator, and we go up to the seventh floor where I'm invited into the hospitality suite that, in keeping with the custom of sailors, has at its center a long table loaded with food: trays of both sweet and savory pastries, smoked fish, various salads, and platters of meat, all prepared by the ship's cook. I can feel my spirits lifting. I ask to invite the cook to the suite and then make some small talk with the captain and his officers. The captain pours us whiskey and offers me a cigar from his last voyage to South America. I sit back in my chair and think to myself that I'd be happy to spend a few days here instead of pounding the pavement chasing after supporters from among the Florida democrats and trying to clean up the slime that the governor of Montana leaves wherever he goes.

The ship's cook enters the suite. I shake his hand and thank him for his efforts. It is important to me to thank him and give attention to all the crew members. "The pleasure is all mine," he answers. "We're happy to welcome guests to our ship, and we want them to feel at home, even though for you it really is home in every sense of the word." He leaves the room, and I follow the captain toward the command bridge and sit at the wheel. The captain describes the ship's new equipment, which we purchased as part of some strategic measures we undertook two years ago to upgrade all the technical and mechanical equipment on board our ships.

After looking at Miami from the deck, I walk back toward the ship's ramp accompanied by the senior crew members, and regrettably say "goodbye." A moment before I get back into my car, I take one last deep breath of the port air. After that, I continue on to Tampa, where I have some meetings scheduled with senior party officials and opinion leaders in the city.

A few days later, at first light, Adam and I take my Jaguar to head from Tampa to Orlando, where I have some early-morning meetings scheduled. I haven't spoken with my father or Bill Black, so I have no way of knowing how I'm doing, and I don't even have a gut feeling one way or the other about it. And somehow despite that, I feel calm. The goal is to get through Florida, and after that, we'll do a situation assessment.

"Turn here," I tell Phillip when we pass a sign pointing towards Disney World. It's still early and the amusement park isn't open yet. I get out of the car. When we'd go with my father on his political trips to Florida, we used to stay at one of the hotels inside the park. Those were still the good old days for me and my father, and he always made sure to set aside time in his busy schedule to take me and my siblings to the Magic Kingdom. I go towards the enormous entrance gate. I wish I could go inside.

Adam stands next to me, and I glance at him.

"Nostalgia," I say.

"I don't know this side of you."

"I don't either, but it's been peeking out lately."

"Should we get going?"

"Should we go inside?"

"It's not open yet," Adam says.

"And still..."

"You can't be serious."

"I'm totally serious. I feel like going in."

"It'll end up in the headlines. The press conference wasn't enough for you? Now you want them to write about how you snuck into Disney World?" He looks at me and sighs. "Just wait a minute," he says, taking out his phone and walking away. A few moments later he's back.

"They'll open it up for us," he says.

"How did you manage that?" I ask in amazement.

"I have my ways," he answers with a smile.

A tall man covered in tattoos with a pierced nose appears inside, opens up a side gate for us, and tells us we have an hour to walk around. Adam and I walk side by side without a word. There is tremendous power in seeing this enormous place, usually bursting with life, standing empty and still. The only people we see are the maintenance people preparing the facilities for the action-packed day ahead. A lot has changed since my times here with my father, but the atmosphere has remained exactly the same. The empty park allows me to leave my memories and the sense of security I had felt in my father's presence among all the rides, grounds, and pathways. I take a selfie and send it to Richard.

"Don't stop for him again, even if he asks," Adam says to Philip when we're back in the car. About a half hour later we've started the round of meetings in Orlando.

From there, two days later, we continue on to Jacksonville.

I first went to Jacksonville as a kid, as part of the Jewish Agency's youth camp. It's where I was when I met Sean for the second time, and had my first sexual experience. It's also where I met Arik Gonen, Israel's cabinet secretary. In truth, I had a bit of a crush on him, but he never knew. Even then, at 16 years old, I was already into drugs and alcohol. Arik definitely knew about that. He even smoked a joint with me once or twice. To him, a good boy who grew up in an Israeli farming town in the eighties, this was exciting American authenticity. It was just like what he saw in the movies. He didn't know about my sexual orientation. He didn't know that it was actually all I ever thought about. My unfulfilled sexual desire for men drove me crazy. The huge excitement that accompanied my sexual encounters with Sean slowly faded away, and then I was filled with pangs of conscience that led to panic attacks.

In those days, I wasn't truly living. I was buried deep in the closet, hopeless. Aside from Sean, my partner in crime, there was no one in the world I could share my troubles with. There was one woman, Julietta, a fortune teller that my friends in New Haven used to go to. I also went to her, just so that someone would notice me and offer me some words of hope and encouragement. I tried to hint to her what was bothering me, thinking maybe she'd understand, but she was mostly interested in taking advantage of my weak state and my wealth. There were days I'd stop by her place more than once a day, just to hear something nice. She knew why I was there and would put on a show of forced warmth, telling me about the rosy future that awaited me. I could sense the deceit in our relationship, but I didn't care. Given the icy coldness my parents directed at me, I was willing to settle for this.

Until one day, when I got fed up with it all. All I needed to do was acknowledge that she was taking advantage of me, because the truth is that I had known it for a while, and I cut off all contact with her. During my last visit to her, just before I took off, I stole a book off her shelf that had always grabbed my attention, *The Way to Happiness*, written by a man whose name, L. Ron. Hubbard, I didn't yet recognize.

I brought the book with me to the Jewish Agency camp and started reading it there. I quickly found myself trying to implement in my own life the 21 moral precepts that he preached as the way to happiness: take care of yourself, be temperate, don't be promiscuous, love and help children, honor and help your parents, set a good example, seek to live with the truth, do not murder, don't do anything illegal, support a government designed and run for all the people, do not harm a person of good will, safeguard and improve your environment, do not steal, be worthy of trust, fulfill your obligations, be industrious, be competent, respect the religious beliefs of others, try not to do things to others that you would not like them to do to you, try to treat others as you would want them to treat you, flourish and prosper.

"Is everything OK, Tom?" Adam asks me, noticing how I'm lost in thought.

"Jacksonville brings back memories of my youth, from when I'd come here with the Jewish Agency," I respond.

"I need you to focus, Tom. This evening is the televised debate with the governor, and you need to be totally prepared. He's going to be bad. Worse than ever. I need you to be at your very peak. Put aside all the sensitive, nostalgic thoughts that have taken over you recently, and be here, in the present, please."

He's right. I need to put aside everything that's been going on and focus on the energy that spurs me to action. Once I win the national elections, I'll have time to reflect on the past.

"OK. You're right," I sit up straight in my seat.

My first meeting in Jacksonville is with representatives of women's organizations, all members of the Democratic Party. From there I hurry to meet up with Barbara and Mandelbaum to practice for the debate, which is going to be televised on Fox News.

"Richard won't be coming tomorrow," I tell Mandelbaum.

"Why not? We need him by your side when you win Florida," he says with confidence, as if there isn't even a chance I might lose.

"I know, but he's working on an important deal and he can't come. It's a one-time thing," I promise, hoping that's true and Richard won't actually decide to stop being part of this campaign.

"The press is going to ask why he's not here," Mandelbaum says. "They're used to seeing you together at these important events. It's going to stand out."

"I know," I repeat. This whole thing is hurting me and making me nervous too. I'm in no mood to keep talking about it. "But that's what's happening, and we'll win anyway."

"Fine. We'll cross that bridge when we get to it. Have you gone over the talking points?"

"Yes."

Adam's expression shows that he knows I'm lying.

"Just a moment, Mandelbaum," he says, signaling for me to leave the room with him. "What's going on?" he asks me.

"I don't know. I'm finding it impossible to recalibrate. But it'll be fine. Give me the talking points so Mandelbaum doesn't catch me." Adam laughs, and a few minutes later we're back in the room. Barbara is ready with the camera. Mandelbaum gets ready to act as the moderator, and Adam is standing in for the governor. Everyone is ready, except for the star of the show. I stand behind the podium, near Adam's, or rather, near the governor's. Mandelbaum throws out some provocative questions, and I begin enjoying myself.

"What mistake did you make just now?" Barbara suddenly cuts me off.

"I shouldn't have told a joke?"

"Telling a joke is wonderful," Barbara says. "It shows your creative side and conquers the crowd's heart. The problem is that you're not making eye contact. You don't look at the governor when you're talking to him, you don't look at the camera when that would make sense, and you don't look at the moderator when you should. It's like you're floating in your own little bubble, amused by yourself and this whole situation. You need to be serious and follow the rules I taught you. We've done tons of debate prep. I want you to be at your best," she says, and I try to collect myself and follow her instructions.

After about an hour, I go up to my suite to try to rest a bit before the debate. I lay down in the suite bedroom, trying without success to fall asleep. I know that I'm angry at Richard for not making the effort to come and be by my side when the results are announced. That was our agreement. He wouldn't need to come with me on my shuttle diplomacy trip, but he'd come for all the big events and votes. That was his word, and he should have stood by it, certainly here in Florida where nothing is certain.

With all my strength, I enlist my logical mind to help me push aside the negative emotional one. Maybe Richard really had no choice. After all, there's a specific timing for when business deals need to be signed. No one knows that better than me. I take deep breaths in and out to help calm my nerves before the debate. I lift my hands and place them on my pillow, rest my head on them, close my eyes, and try to relax. The phone in the room rings, and I pick it up.

"Where are you?" Adam calls over from the other line.

"I'm resting a bit," I mumble.

"We're going to be late for the debate! Come downstairs quickly. Everyone's waiting for you."

I get up from the bed, put on my watch and pants, wash my face, and quickly go down to the bus.

"You didn't change your clothes," Adam says.

"Get off my back all of you," I say, signaling that I'm not going to listen to any other notes.

"Can I get you fixed up?" Veronica, my makeup artist, asks me.

"Sure, Veronica," I say, finding comfort in her intoxicating scent, her gentle touch, and her smile. Veronica combs my hair, puts on some makeup, and conceals the obvious fatigue in my face.

"May I?" she asks gently, and I nod my consent. Her hands undo my tie and remove it from my neck. She adjusts my collar and reties the tie in a new, more precise knot this time. Every now and then I look at her and we smile at each other. She is the best thing that could have happened to me in this moment.

"He's ready," she finally says, and Mandelbaum comes over to me. I signal "no" with my hand, and he understands that I'm not willing to speak any more about the talking points or the debate. I'm sitting quietly at the front of the bus, calm, and no one dares approach me. About an hour later I somehow find myself already inside the TV studio. The debate has begun, and I'm having trouble extracting myself from my head and floating back to reality.

"Tom Gold is a corrupt man, a man involved in dirty deals and slimy politics," the governor of Montana declares when it's his turn to speak, completely evading the moderator's actual question.

"Please answer the question you were asked," the moderator requests, but to no avail. "If that is the case, I'll move over to the next question, and you won't be given the chance to respond to the substance of the matter," the moderator, who is losing his patience, informs the governor. It is clear that he's surprised by the audacity of the governor, who has completely ignored all the rules of the debate and is doing whatever he feels like.

"Fine," the governor responds. "To the substance of the matter –Tom Gold has zero political experience. His platform includes things that he has no understanding of. That is something that should concern every American citizen. 'Change.' 'Economic reform.' To him these are simply meaningless buzzwords to throw around."

The moderator turns to me. "Mr. Gold, can you explain what's behind your platform, and expand a bit on the economic reforms you propose?"

I have a complete blackout. A cold sweat washes over me, and a huge wave of panic, which I thought was behind me, is threatening to crash over me right this moment, when I need to be at my very best.

"The economic reforms are mainly there to ensure the prevention of government waste and large deficits, like you see in Montana, for example," I say, even though I'm finding it impossible to recall the details of the briefing Adam gave me about the problems of the administration in Montana.

"That is certainly a topic that we might get to later on," the moderator says. "But what I'd like to know is, what are the foundations of the economy that you propose?" he sharpens his question, and I feel lost. I can feel the beads of sweat collecting in my collar, and I feel like I'll suffocate unless I loosen my tie.

"The economy that I'm proposing will no longer allow for the randomness that exists today. We will not be dragged down into market crises like we saw in 2008. We will have more control over the results of globalization and may even work to slow its rate, in order to prevent the high unemployment rates that can harm the economy," I answer, unable to understand exactly what I'm saying.

"That's complete nonsense," the governor interrupts me. "Slow the pace of globalization? Does that sound logical at all? What luck I had to refuse the opportunity to serve as your potential future treasury secretary." And thus, with his characteristic crudeness, he changes the subject.

"I must ask that you observe the rules," the moderator admonishes him. "I will not accept outbursts, Mr. Stone. The press already covered that issue, and it is clear that Mr. Gold had no connection to that campaign deal. I ask that you observe the rules of conduct for this debate. Each of you will answer questions in turn. You can deal with your spin campaign afterwards."

"The work of the righteous is done by others," I think to myself, and begin liking the moderator whose name I can't remember. Mandelbaum gave me all the information about him so that I'd be able to better interact with him, but for now, I can't remember a thing. I start counting to ten, trying to calm myself, to regain control and balance.

"The next question is for the governor," says the moderator, whose words still sound like distant background music to me. The debate continues, but I can't grasp anything that I'm saying. It's all sentences atop sentences that I've thrown together without actually understanding them.

As soon as the debate is over, I hurry to thank the moderator, muttering something that will hopefully excuse my speedy departure from the studio.

I pass Adam, Mandelbaum, and Barbara, all looking at me in confusion, and I make my way out, fleeing through the long black corridors to the street, and they follow me. In a narrow alley, I bend over with my hands on my knees, fill my lungs with air, and suddenly vomit. Adam signals to Mandelbaum and Barbara to return to the hotel. I sit on the side, drinking from the water bottle that Adam brought me and try to calm down. I take off my jacket and loosen my tie. My shirt is wet with sweat, and I unbutton it a bit, trying to get some air.

"What happened?" Adam asks me.

"A panic attack," I respond.

"Why'd it have to happen right now? Nothing happened that we weren't prepared for. In our rehearsals for today's debate, we asked you much harder questions, and you answered perfectly. You even managed to incorporate humor. What happened? We still have a ways to go. We're lucky the moderator was protecting you."

"You felt it too?" I ask, surprised, and the thought crosses my mind that my father might have had a hand in this.

"Of course I felt it. I only hope the public and the press didn't, and that tomorrow's headlines won't hint at it. I feel like I need to be honest with you and tell you that your performance tonight was not good."

"You don't need to apologize. I know I was terrible. It's a miracle that I managed to stand there despite losing all control."

"I want you to meet with a psychologist," Adam says. "Or we'll attach a personal coach to you for the rest of the campaign. We can't take any chances. This shouldn't have happened today. You were ready for this debate and could have easily answered all the questions and all of the governor's provocations."

I can't help but agree with him. I must not allow my emotional upheaval to attack me in Florida, or let Richard's decision not to be with me on voting day undermine me so dramatically. I suddenly remember the clinical psychologist that Adam added to the campaign team in order to analyze the characters of the people I may run against. Perhaps the time has come to use him, too, in addition to Judith.

"Please ask the clinical psychologist you recruited to our team, Joe Green, to come to Florida," I say to Adam. "Explain my situation to him. After all, he needs to uphold doctor-patient confidentiality."

After that, we return to the hotel together. The campaign team is waiting for us in the lobby. I thank them for their understanding and assistance and take my leave to go to my room. After two glasses of whiskey in a row, I call Judith.

"I apologize for the late hour," I say, in a choked voice.

"You should feel free to call me at any hour," Judith warms my heart. "What's going on?"

"I totally bumbled the televised debate with the governor of Montana. I hope the price won't be too heavy. I had a panic attack in Jacksonville if you can believe it.

"Jacksonville, what a funny name! Where is Jacksonville?"

"I'm in Florida, Judith, and I'll say it again. I had one of the worst panic attacks I've ever had. I have no idea what I said or how I answered questions. I completely blacked out. I can't even reproduce a second from the debate. I am sure that tomorrow, the press will announce the governor's victory. I'm out. I lost Florida," I say, trying to get a bit of empathy and encouragement out of her.

"Tell me how it happened, and why you think it happened."

"Waves of memories from my past washed over me. I remembered how I used to come here, as a lost teen, looking for drugs and sex with Sean, so that I could fulfill my sexual fantasies that had reached monstrous proportions in those days. I'm done for, Judith."

"Why do you think you're done for?"

"Because I've lost Florida!"

"How many times have you won until now?" Judith brings me back to the facts and data, managing to get me once again to focus a bit.

"Three," I answer.

"You've won three times and you might lose one. That's what you call being done for? You're winning, Tom! You need to focus on the facts! See reality as it is, without interpretation. Focus on what you have, not on what you don't. Don't be critical of yourself. Apply logical control using your rational mind and move forward. As you know, your negative, emotional mind is quite cunning, and has managed to drag you back to the unhelpful patterns of your past. Despite the work we've done and your wonderful progress, it managed to get its claws back in and regain control. It's hard for it to lose primacy to the rational mind, and so it will try to regain dominance at every opportunity. That's only natural. Don't get worked up over it. Think of what happened as a small setback and keep moving forward. Repeat the five rules of neo-humanology and repeat your mantras. You must raise your energy level and maintain a positive state of mind. You can't make a victory happen unless you maintain positive thinking about winning." I promise her that I'll follow the rules and repeat the mantras, and the second our conversations ends, I begin repeating them without pause, as I lie exhausted on the armchair in my Jacksonville suite.

"Mr. Harvey Stone has won the Florida primaries." One of my field workers tells me the announcer has just declared at a huge party organized by the governor in a luxury hotel in Miami. A few hours beforehand, Bill Black called to let me know that I lost. Even though I had a landslide victory in South Carolina, the gap between our results in Iowa and New Hampshire wasn't big enough, and so I now found myself quite far from the knockout punch I'd wanted to deliver. I'm alone in the room, leaning on the back of a chair and trying to digest the news. I jump at a knock at the door. Adam enters. "Here's your concession speech," he tells me, handing me a sheet of paper. I take it, unable to actually look at it.

"I'm not going to give a speech this time."

"You have to," Adam says, agitated. "These are the rules of the game. You can't speak to your many activists and supporters only when you win, and then hide when you lose. If you don't want to read the speech, that's fine, but you need to get up on stage and say something to the people who are supporting you."

I accept this. I stand up straight, adjust my suit, and button my jacket.

"I take it the governor is celebrating?"

"Yes," Adam responds. "It's his first victory and he's taken as much advantage of it as he can."

"Is he talking about me?"

"For now, no, and I doubt he'll even mention you in his victory speech. It wouldn't be right. Get him out of your mind for now. In any case, you need to get ready to get back on stage. They're going to call you up soon. Thank everyone for their help and support. Get them excited about the victories we expect on Super Tuesday. Don't let it seem like you're deflated. As far as you're concerned, nothing happened here. One loss is feasible, and everything is still under control. It is important that you convey optimism to your campaign team and field workers."

My whole team is waiting for me near the stairs that lead up to the stage, and they welcome me with applause and encouragement. I go up on stage and I'm met with enthusiastic cheers from the crowd that's waving my banners high, and in that very moment, I'm reinvigorated with the fighting spirit and the thrill of the primaries. Facing the excited crowd, I understand that this loss is not going to break us and that we will definitely keep moving forward. I smile to the crowd, thank them, say goodbye, and leave the stage.

From there, we go straight to Miami International Airport to fly back home to New York.

It's not a good situation, Bill Black texts me. **We were sure you'd be the presumptive candidate after Florida.**

I hope that will be the case after Super Tuesday, I text him back.

We're worried that what will happen will be something that hasn't happened since the seventies, he replies.

What happened then?

I'll tell you in person, he replies. **By then, we'll have the results from our internal polls** he adds in a separate text.

Renaissance, next week, I write. All the optimism I felt when I left the stage after my concession speech has completely dissipated, and I'm in a terrible mood as I board my private plane. I fasten my seat belt and we take off.

CHAPTER 20

Manhattan, Late-February

"Where's Richard?" I ask Maria as soon as I return home, after receiving a warm welcome from her.

"He's out running in the park," she reassures me. "He's missed you very much. It was really hard for him to sit and wait, so he went out to let off some energy."

"Since when does Richard go jogging?" I ask in surprise. The last time we went running together, and that was quite a while ago, he was out of breath after only a few minutes.

"Ever since he got back to Manhattan. I think it's got something to do with his missing you, too. Go, surprise him in the park."

I got out to the balcony to relax after so many weeks away, trying to make the moment last because I'm excited to see Richard, but I'm nervous about it too.

I take one more little breath of the cold Manhattan air and then get myself ready to go to the park, hurrying toward my regular running route, which has become Richard's as well. A few minutes later, I see him from afar. As I get closer, I slow my pace a bit and appear next to him, running at first without glancing at him, as if I haven't noticed him at all. Richard looks at me, a few fractions of a second pass until he realizes it's me, and he jumps to the side in shock. We stop, wanting to hug each other but avoid doing so. We don't even hold hands so as not to tempt any negativity towards us. Excited, we run side by side to the small café on the edge of the park.

Richard suggests we go in, and we sit at a small round table, drinking coffee and speaking only a little, so that the words don't ruin the strong feeling that accompanies our being together once again at long last. The evening has arrived. Quiet background music is playing inside the café and colorful lights have turned on above us. We're surrounded by other couples of all ages. This place is calm and peaceful, enveloped in a sweet ambiance. Some of the couples are quietly talking to each other, while the others are mostly quiet, like us.

When I was younger, I felt a disdain towards couples sitting at cafes or restaurants in silence. I was sure they were bored, that there was nothing left for them to say to each other, that that's how they'd spend the rest of their days, bored and wasted. I didn't know that quiet can also come from a sense of intense closeness, something I want to believe exists between me and Richard. Often, words can actually be spoken for the purpose of concealing problems between two people.

We pay and leave, walking along the winding paths towards our apartment, and at this point we're talking too. Our conversation drifts into many subjects but avoids sensitive topics surrounding our relationship.

"I cooked an indulgent dinner for you guys," Maria tells us just before she leaves the apartment.

We thank her and each kiss her on the cheek. She offers us her motherly smile, and we wait with her by the door for the elevator to come.

A little bit later, we sit down to eat the dinner she prepared for us: beef casserole with root vegetables and mashed potatoes with touches of sweet potato, as only Maria knows how to make. I open a bottle of Masi Amarone, and we eat in silence. Again. Now I'm beginning to worry about this silence that keeps insisting on settling between us. The wine bottle is empty. I open another. "Music," Richard says to the room, and the sound system selects some Elvis Costello to play for us. The ambiance all around us is perfect, but something's still off. It's like something has broken down, and it's now clear that in our silence, we're both afraid of touching the crack that's been growing between us. Richard takes out two cigars and we go out onto the balcony, to breathe the cold Manhattan air. I sit down on the balcony's sofa, my legs spread apart, smoking the cigar and sipping my wine. I look over at Richard and blow clouds of smoke at him, trying to make him laugh.

"You know, two years ago, we didn't even know each other," I finally say.

"That's true," he answers. "Would you have fallen in love with me if we'd have met before?"

"Of course."

"And now, after having gotten to know me completely?"

"Even more so."

"So come with me for a moment. I want to show you something," Richard says, leading me toward our bedroom. He smiles at me, and I wink back. We're holding hands. I come closer to him, standing between his spread legs as he sits at the foot of the bed. Slowly, gently, I bring my head closer to his and we kiss. I take off my shirt, stand close to him, and he licks and kisses my chest.

"Why can't we enjoy each other like this during the primaries?" I murmur.

Richard pushes me away.

"Don't you start with that now!" he shouts. "Everything is always about you, your career, your success, your life, your self-realization. You never notice anyone else when you want to achieve something. You use everyone to get what you want."

"Why are you doing this?" I ask.

"It's hard, isn't it?" he asks angrily.

"What's hard?"

"To hear the truth and deal with it."

"I love you, Richard."

"You're not going to solve this by saying that," he spouts out at me.

"Fine," now my voice is showing its irritation as well. "What truth are you having me face?"

"That you only notice yourself. You don't care about my career. You don't care how important it is to me that my New York branch succeeds; that I'm conducting worldwide business through it. You want to take that away from me now, you want me to leave everything and go off with you on a months-long journey all over America."

"Wow," I say. "I knew I was a bit focused on myself, but I didn't know how much."

"I'm trying to cope," Richard says. "When I met you, I knew what it would mean to live with Tom Gold. I was wounded when we met, and I was everything to you, a lover, friend, partner. Now everything's changed. I'm happy that your relationship with your father is growing stronger. I understand the significance of the primaries. I'm happy that things are going well for you, but that's no reason for you to ignore everyone else, including me, your beloved.

"I can't be the First Lady. I'm not built for it. You need to understand this. You can't ask me in every phone call wherever I am in the world to drop what I'm doing and be with you. I know that you miss me, but you only see your side. You never ask me how my work is going, or if I can leave for a few days and come. You're only concerned with yourself, with what's difficult for you, with how my behavior is screwing up the elections for you, with how the journalists will screw you in the press. It's all about Tom Gold. Have you ever thought about what I need?" He gets up and leaves the room, and a few moments later, I hear the door slam shut behind him.

I remain sitting on the edge of the bed. I hold my head in my hands, take a deep breath, and try to calm down. I never expected an outburst like that. A few moments later, I hear the door open, and Richard is once again in the room.

"You know what?" he says angrily. "I'll tell you what the distance between us has done to me. Yesterday, I was with a woman."

"What?!"

Richard sits down in the armchair.

"I didn't sleep with her," he says. "I stopped it beforehand."

"Do I know her?"

"No," he says quietly, his head lowered. "She was my neighbor in my last apartment. She's had her eye on me since the first time she saw me in the building, and she flirted with me. She's not someone I would ever have taken seriously, even if I was single. She's someone it would be nice to fool around with a few times, but nothing beyond that."

"What were you doing in your apartment?"

"I went over to get some things. She saw me in the lobby and knocked on the door a few minutes later. I was happy to see her. She's smiley, blond, tall, she looks like a Barbie doll. She's not particularly smart, but she's nice. We were talking and she started coming closer to me and suddenly she kissed me." He's quiet for a moment. "I'll admit there was a sort of comfort in that kiss." Richard looks at me, trying to decipher my expression.

"Why are you telling me all this?" I'm angry.

"I'm telling you the truth. Just like you, I don't want there to be any secrets between us. Even if I made a mistake, you'll forgive me if you love me."

"That's not how this works. There's a very fine line between love and hate. With stories and descriptions like this, I could start to hate you in a moment," I say, but Richard decides to ignore my last comment, justifiably. Even if he told me worse stories, I could never hate him.

"When she pressed her body against mine, I suddenly realized what I was doing. I jumped away in shock and sat at the edge of the bed. I felt like I was suffocating. I felt disgusted with myself and was immediately filled with guilt. After all, you're the only one I love. I love speaking with you, spending time with you, being with you, making love with you. I don't want to destroy this.

I continued sitting there on the bed, and she started to rub my back to help me calm down. I told her that I'm married to a man, and she said she knew, that she had read about us in the paper and knew that I was bisexual. I explained that it doesn't matter because I have a spouse, but that didn't seem to bother her and she stayed there, lying naked on the bed trying to seduce me. I brought her clothes to her and asked her to go. I got dressed quickly and waited for her by the door. I wanted to treat her with respect. I had no intention of hurting her. She simply caught me off guard in a moment of loneliness and sadness. I said bye to Emily, and she quietly left."

"Her name is Emily?"

"Yes."

"Emily what?"

"I don't know."

My body suddenly tenses up.

"It's Emly Zimmerman," I declare, in anger. "Don't you get it? They tried to set up a trap, to throw us out with the trash. They wanted you to cheat on me. After that, they would have taken it to the press and bingo! Another juicy story about Tom Gold."

"Tom, please calm down. You're going off the rails and being paranoid again. Politics does this to you. Once again, you're immediately thinking only about yourself. But this time, it's not about you. It's about me. It's not Emily Zimmerman. I know her. I've met her. She was even at that meeting of the corporate heirs at the Plaza and in Maine. And regardless, they'd have no reason to use Emily Zimmerman. Why would she even agree to it? Anyway, she was my neighbor way before I ever met you. You can relax, everything is fine. This wasn't a trap. Just stop thinking only about yourself all the time."

We're both quiet.

"By the way, I didn't technically cheat on you. I stumbled for a moment but then put a stop to the whole thing. I'm sure life still has many more tests in store for us."

"We're fighting instead of enjoying our time together," I say to Richard, coming closer to him. Richard is sitting on the edge of the bed. I go between his legs, bringing his head close to my stomach. Richard kisses me, and we throw ourselves onto the bed, snuggle into each other's arms, and lay like that together, trying to calm down.

"I have a few more days in Manhattan," I say after some time. "After that, I need to continue on my campaign tour. I really don't want us to fight during these days."

"What do you have in mind?"

"I'll have a lot of political things to deal with, and I want you to understand that. But in between, when you also have time, of course, I want us to have a lot of sex. I want us to go see a movie and have a corned beef sandwich at Corn Bake and go bowling and go running in the park and sit on our balcony and smoke cigars and watch your favorite TV shows."

"I want to wake up in the morning and have sex with you," Richard says. "Go out for breakfast, come back home and fuck until the afternoon. Go to a restaurant for lunch, come home, and fuck until the evening. Go out for dinner, come home …"

"I get you," I cut him off. "I'm in favor."

"So what now?" he asks me, and I can tell he's quite pleased with himself.

"Sex, of course."

In the morning, we pamper ourselves in bed with the breakfast that Maria prepared for us, and we read the morning papers.

"To me, it feels like you're on your honeymoon now," Maria says. "You guys don't get the chance to indulge much together lately. I want to take care of you just like you're taking care of my Jose."

"As if you wouldn't be taking care of us anyway," Richard says, and Maria laughs.

"You're right," she agrees.

"Jose's doing a wonderful job with the Hispanic community," I say. "I'm really happy we hired him for the campaign. Because of him I feel even more committed to Hispanic issues. If only I get the opportunity."

"You'll get the chance," Maria says. "You're the right one for the job. And anyway, your father will help you."

"That's exactly what we're worried about," Richard tells her. "When he's too involved, it can end badly." The three of us laugh.

"Joseph is Joseph and there is none other like him. He's a man of the world. There are things he can do that only he knows how to, and he never fails," Maria says. "It's like the spirit of God is watching over him. He has a lot of luck in the stars. Someone up there is always looking after him. I saw many things on that estate in Connecticut, and I know what I'm talking about. Don't worry about him or any moves he may make. It always works out for him, certainly when you're talking about a presidential race. After all, through you, he's fulfilling the dream he had for himself, and he won't let it fail this time."

"This time?" I ask.

"You didn't know?" Maria asks me.

"I didn't know what?"

"When you were a young boy, your father considered contending in the Democratic primaries for resident of the United States. I can still remember the meetings in the lounge at Silver Bell. So many things were discussed there. I'd find excuses to go in so I could hear what they were talking about. But back in those days, the spirit of God was definitely not with your father. He was diagnosed with blood cancer. You were five years old, I think. He and your mother flew to Europe so he could get a special treatment there. His blood was replaced. They literally cleaned the cancer out of him. Your mother didn't want you or your siblings to worry, so she just told you they were going on a trip to Europe, and I stayed with you guys.

"They came back three weeks later. Your father was thin and exhausted, but the doctors said he was healthy. He truly had recovered, but he gave up on his presidential dreams. Your mother was always claiming that the cancer was a result of dirty politics, and she didn't want him to be involved anymore. As you know, that didn't really work for her. Since then, he's held all sorts of jobs and became one of the most influential people in the United States."

Richard looks at me. "You could also get cancer from these dirty politics."

In the afternoon, I go over the morning papers and read the op-eds in *The New York Times* about the crisis within the Democratic Party, articles that are definitely not complementary to us. I put the paper down and join Richard on the balcony. In the evening, we walk together to Corn Bake. I've missed our beloved café. A few camera flashes greet us outside the window, but Richard and I have gotten used to this, and we simply ignore the paparazzo stationed on the sidewalk outside.

"What's your route going to be?" Richard asks.

"We'll start in Minnesota. Adam's already there. I don't actually remember the order of the states, but I know we'll be in Vermont, Massachusetts, Texas, Virginia, Tennessee, Alabama, Georgia, Colorado, Arkansas, Oklahoma, and a lot more places that I'm sure I'd never have seen in this beautiful country of ours that, I must admit, I'm falling in love with. Will you be joining me?" I smile, worrying for a moment that Richard won't take my words in the good spirit that I intend.

"No," he answers in a shy voice. Maybe he's embarrassed by his extreme reaction earlier.

"On the private plane, there's a special room just for us," I try to tempt him, but he doesn't respond.

"Fine," I sigh, "But you'll come for the Democratic Convention in July."

"I'm coming for Super Tuesday too."

This fills me with joy.

The next morning, I meet Bill Black at Renaissance.

"Everything could have been behind us already," he says after we've given the waiter our orders.

"Meaning?" I ask impatiently.

"If you hadn't undone the deal, you would already be the presumptive candidate, and we'd be done with all these rotten primaries already."

"You're stuck in the past. There is no point in rehashing something that has already happened and can't be undone. You need to be practical. We've already spoken about this countless times, and I have no intention of repeating myself. This deal would never actually have been carried out. No one closes deals for me, not even my father."

"For that alone you deserve to win. You are the only person on the planet who's ever managed to stop Joseph Gold."

"I want a different kind of politics, and I really mean it. The governor would be like a fifth column trying to subvert any government of mine. I want a loyal government that believes in a common goal, without camps, without intrigues, and without any tricks up anyone's sleeves. I want people who want to work, and to work together. By the way, what did you mean in your message about the seventies?"

"As far as I can recall, the last time the party actually decided who the presidential candidate would be at the National Convention was in 1972," Bill says. "Since then, it's served mostly a ceremonial purpose, and the decisions were made way beforehand, during the primaries. But it looks like history is repeating itself. We'll need to wait until the summer to know who will actually be the party's candidate. I can no longer say with any degree of certainty that it's going to be you, even more so if you continue insisting on your new politics."

"I'm planning to deliver a knock-out punch on Super Tuesday," I tell him. "I will do everything necessary, but in a clean way."

"We'll hope for the best," he says, with a hint of despair. "The party is split. We didn't bank on the governor fighting at full speed and we didn't expect him to raise as many funds as he did and stay in the game. If we had known, we'd have prevented his candidacy from the start. Tom, if he wins, it's all over for us. The party's national committee doesn't want him to be our candidate in the national elections, and we have ways to prevent it from happening," he adds, sending me a look, waiting for my response, but I choose to ignore those last few words.

"I'm leaving today for my tour of the country," I say. "The activists and volunteers are working in the field. Help them with whatever you can, but without any dirty tactics. That's my decision, it's my gut feeling, and I won't change it."

"This is for you," he suddenly says, handing me a thick bound notebook.

"What is it?" I ask.

"You'll have time to read it while you're running from state to state. It includes reforms, legislative proposals, updated amendments, the promotion of construction complexes, and all sorts of other things. We won't have a choice, we'll need to fulfill our promises to all the people who are helping us," he says, lowering his gaze. "But once you're in the White House, it will be easier."

"There's a Congress and a Senate," I say, not believing we're even having this conversation.

I take the notebook and leave the restaurant in anger.

Super Tuesday has arrived. Over the past few days, I've been jumping around between the many states taking part in the primaries today. Adam and Mandelbaum were attached to me throughout the entire long, emotional journey, and the campaign team worked in the field with the activists and volunteers. The bulk of their efforts were invested in the larger states, but we didn't forget the others.

As I sit among the volunteers who are calling party members and encouraging them to come out and vote, in my mind's eye I can see myself becoming the presumptive candidate. I imagine the news broadcasts opening with this story and the newspaper headlines describing my achievements until now, my skills, and my charisma, and I know that I need to increase my energy in order to manifest what I want. But the noise all around me brings me back to the reality of the volunteer headquarters, and I hasten to take one of the phones and call another party member to encourage her to go out and vote, for me of course.

From there, I continue on to the field tours, I meet with operatives, and I pose for any photographers who ask. Richard is right there with me. His skills of persuasion are impressive, and he's managed to use his charm on the press and on potential voters, and to strengthen the volunteers' spirit. In the late afternoon, we get to my Washington D.C. headquarters for a meeting I've scheduled with representatives of the Jewish Federations and AIPAC, and after that, I get ready to fly to Virginia for a watch party with my supporters, to observe the Super Tuesday results coming in. This was organized by Lauren Lanter, my campaign's manager of operations.

I sit at the head of the table in a side room at the headquarters, surrounded by key activists, with Richard next to me. Unlike the previous times, I still haven't gotten any sampling results from Bill Black. I'm actually trying to call him, but he's not answering me. The campaign photographer is immortalizing us in a few more photos, until the moment of truth comes, and the broadcasts begin.

I look anxiously at the map of the United States projected on screen, and the Super Tuesday results start coming in. States voting for me are colored yellow and those voting for the governor are purple. Vermont is mine, Massachusetts is mine, Colorado is his, Minnesota is his, Georgia is his, Virginia is mine, Arkansas is his, Texas is mine, and so on and so forth. I soon realize that neither of us has gotten a decisive win, neither of us has won enough delegates for that.

"There's no decisive winner," I whisper to Richard, trying not to betray the frustration taking hold of me. I slowly begin to digest it all. The commentators on TV are still calculating the number of delegates to the summer convention that each candidate has won, but I already calculated them for myself, and I know that neither of us has won unequivocally. The primaries will continue on into more states, and everything is still wide open. Richard and I leave the room and enter one of the empty offices that we find along the corridor.

"I can't manage to win this campaign. I feel like I'm losing control. I wanted it all to be done with today," I confess in anger. He tries to console me, approaches me, touches me gently, and tries to help calm my nerves. "Fine," I say, taking a deep breath. "We're continuing. I want to go back to the activists and cheer them on."

"Let's go to them together and give them a shot of encouragement," he says. "We'll continue in the primaries until there's a decisive vote, and if it won't happen now, then fine, it's just not the right time. Maybe someone up above wants you to remain alert and not become complacent."

"That means that in the coming months, I'll be on the road again and we'll be apart again."

"I'll help you," Richard promises me. "I won't be able to accompany you throughout the entire tour, but I'll come and help when I can." These words reassure me and give me strength. I feel like, as long as Richard's by my side, everything will be OK. We come close to each other and embrace. It's a different kind of embrace. A more mature one. A ripe one. I walk towards the activists, with Richard behind me.

"Smile," I request, and clap in encouragement, even though my heart isn't fully in it. "We won a lot of states. We got more votes than the governor. It's still not enough, but we'll win."

"Let's continue in full force!" the head of my Virginia headquarters cries out passionately, and he begins clapping. Soon, all the other activists join in. I'm also clapping, but this moment is a difficult one for me and I know that up until the painful loss in Florida, I'd never felt anything like this. After all, I had never lost anything before. I don't know how to lose. I met every challenge I had ever set for myself in the business world. I'm not familiar with this sensation of needing to comfort myself, and be comforted by what other people are saying, and it's making me feel resistant. I remember something Judith once told me when we had spoken about the lives of people who achieve everything easily and at a young age. She claimed that it comes at a cost, and I understand that I'm paying that cost now. I try to console myself with the fact that, if I actually win in the end, I'll have managed to experience a feeling that I never would have otherwise, as well as a much greater satisfaction than I have ever known; a true victory and one not taken for granted.

"Let's keep going," I say, this time with real passion. I wait for them to call my name, I go up on stage to encourage my activists, and I am rewarded with loud cheers.

Later that night, Richard and I board our private plane and return to Manhattan for a few days of rest.

CHAPTER 21

Manhattan, Mid-March

I need to meet with you ASAP, Mandelbaum texts me early in the morning.

I'll see you at our ten o'clock meeting, I text back, still half-asleep.

No! he responds. **I need to meet you right now!**

Come over to my house, I write back. I sit up in bed, panicked. What could possibly be so urgent? I look over at Richard, who's still sleeping, and I decide not to wake him. I drag myself out of bed and get into the shower.

"Good morning," Maria greets me on her way in. She's surprised to find me already sitting in the breakfast nook with my coffee and laptop this early in the morning.

"Good morning," I answer glumly.

"You're up early," she says, looking at me in concern.

"Everything's fine, Maria. Just campaign stuff."

"Do you want your usual breakfast?" she asks with a smile, trying to cheer me up.

"Yes. Mandelbaum's coming over, so make enough for him too."

A short while later, the doorman informs me that Mandelbaum has arrived. When I open the door, I find Pete standing in front of me, white as a ghost.

"What happened?" I ask.

"We're in trouble."

I lead him over to the breakfast nook and pour him some coffee.

"The editor of *The New York Times* has asked for a response by noon tomorrow," he says, taking a sip of coffee.

"A response to what?"

"They're planning on publishing an investigative piece about you next week. A bad one. A very bad one."

"OK," I say, taking a few deep breaths. "What's it about?"

"About your wild twenties." He pauses.

"Go on."

"It's hard for me to say it out loud."

"You'll have to get over that."

"They're going to write that you were addicted to drugs and alcohol, that you belonged to the Church of Scientology, and that you hired male prostitutes."

I hang my head, silent.

"Is it true?" he asks, hoping I'll flatly deny the accusations.

I nod.

"All of it?"

"Yes, all of it," I say in a whisper. I start talking, hoping it will prevent my mind from processing what he's said. "Those were my twenties. I was in the closet, deep in the closet. I wasn't coping well. I was completely cut off from my father. I was afraid that I'd damage my family's reputation, my father's business, my budding political career. I lived in constant fear. I was lonely. Drugs and alcohol were a refuge. It started back in high school."

"What drugs did you take?"

"Weed, cocaine," I respond. "I came across Scientology by chance, after reading L. Ron Hubbard's *The Way to Happiness*. Once I got involved, I stayed active in one way or another for a few years. Scientology was what helped me get off drugs and alcohol. I've been drug-free for years, I don't get drunk, and I don't pay for sex.

"Also, not that it matters, but I never paid male prostitutes for sex; I paid them for their silence. Once they realized this, some of them tried to squeeze more money out of me, but I didn't care. It's possible some of them may actually have worked as prostitutes, but that wasn't how I found them. I never had a problem getting sex.

I was good-looking, and gay men were always hitting on me. But I was afraid that one of those men would leak something to the media. I was petrified of my father, so I paid them for their silence. That was my deal with them, and for a number of years it worked."

"I already asked you to tell me about any skeletons in your closet," Mandelbaum says, "And you said there weren't any. Is there anything else you're hiding from me that could get you in trouble later on?" His voice is gentle, and I know he has my best interests at heart.

"I've invested in markets around the world. Including in some Arab states."

"Iran?" he asks nervously.

"Not directly, but it's possible that some of the companies I invest in – in Saudi Arabia, Qatar, and the UAE – might invest in Tehran. I have no idea."

"I'll have Adam check that immediately." He sounds tense.

"But if we find out that they do invest in Iranian companies, should I withdraw the money? I don't think that would look good. As things stand now, I can still claim ignorance."

Mandelbaum stands up and starts pacing the room.

"What are my options?" I ask him.

"First of all, call your father and ask him to help us behind the scenes. Do you think he'd be willing to help?"

"What do you mean?"

"Anything that he can do about *The New York Times*. We have to prevent the article from getting published. It would destroy everything we've achieved so far. All the media outlets would focus on the article and on the questions it raises. Add that to the fact that you're Jewish, and you've got yourself a big mess. We won't be able to control the snowball effect. Once it starts, it's not going to stop, not for a long time, maybe not ever. Elections are lost over articles like this. I was thinking that we could threaten a libel suit, but if everything's true, there's no point. I was sure it was all made up and we'd be able to get rid of the story right away."

"Who do you think leaked all this to the *Times*?"

"Who leaked it? The governor of Montana, who else?"

"How would he know all of these things about me?"

"Good investigative work. We could publish a piece about him, too, if we wanted. Everybody has skeletons in their closet. But your skeletons are huge," he says, and he hangs his head. "And you still haven't answered my question about your father," he adds, knowing how sensitive this subject is for me.

"What are our other options?"

"We could respond to the editor of the *Times* by noon tomorrow, saying that these things happened years ago, at a difficult time in your life, and try to leverage it. We can come up with some new spin so the press will focus on that rather than on you. But journalists aren't suckers. They recognize spin when they see it, and it might end up making things worse. What else? We can see what we can dig up on the governor and leak it to the media, so they'll focus on him instead of you."

"We can't be certain that it's him," I say, in what I realize is a futile attempt to avoid dirty politics when that's exactly what's threatening my political career right now.

"We can ask the editor to meet with us and beg him not to print the article," Mandelbaum continues. "We can try to convince him of what an achievement it is for humanity and the world that there's a candidate who is both gay and Jewish. Or," he says, "we can call a press conference and tell them the truth. Allow the public to judge you and accept their judgement with love."

"That sounds good," I say, trying to persuade myself. "I'll be able to win over the public."

"You're being naïve, Tom. They won't be convinced them that easily. But you'd at least be able to demonstrate how honest and open you are."

"I choose the third option," I say. "Call a press conference."

"Before the *Times* article comes out? You'd be taking a risk if, for whatever reason, the article never gets published in the first place. Listen to me and try to relax. I'm here for you, and we'll get through this together. But there's something else I have to ask you. Does Richard know about this part of your life?"

"No. I never told him. I had a whole life of my own before we met, as did he. There are things we haven't spoken about."

"You need to tell him."

"I will."

"He needs to support you now. If he doesn't, it will be yet another PR disaster."

"I understand and I'll take care of it."

"One last thing," he says. "I think we should maintain a state of ambiguity with the *Times*. We still have some time before noon tomorrow. We can even ask for a small extension if we want."

"OK. And by the way, about my father, bringing him in could be dangerous. They may end up uncovering the things he's done, too."

"You have a point," Mandelbaum says. "If we can't prevent the article from being published, we'll call a press conference as soon as it comes out. You'll speak honestly, straight to the hearts of the people."

"OK," I answer submissively. As I escort him to the door, we bump into Maria.

"I thought you said Mandelbaum was staying for breakfast," she says.

"No, it turns out he has more important things to do," I say. He and I exchange bitter smiles.

When Mandelbaum leaves, I know that I should go wake Richard and tell him everything. Instead, I go back to the breakfast nook and wait for him. After a while I hear noise from the bedroom; Richard is humming to himself. He's woken up in a good mood. Little does he know that I'm about to ruin his whole day. Or worse.

"I need to speak with you," I tell him as soon as he enters the room.

"What happened, Tommy?"

"A lot," I say. "We need to talk."

I pour him some coffee. He picks up his mug and stands next to me. I pause for a minute, then speak.

"The New York Times is about to publish a very bad investigative report about me. About things I used to do in my twenties. Mandelbaum came by at seven o'clock. We've been asked to respond by noon tomorrow, and we've come up with a plan of action." I pause again. "This isn't going to be easy to hear, Richard. These are things I never told you about."

"Tell me, Tommy. I can take it." He pulls a chair next to mine and sits down.

I know that there's no point in hiding anything, and the words come tumbling out of me. When I'm finished, I try to catch my breath.

"And The New York Times is going to publish all this?" Richard asks.

"Yes. More or less. I don't know if they know everything, but they know enough."

"Why didn't you tell me sooner?"

"Because I was afraid you'd leave me."

"What are you talking about?" he says, but his voice sounds distant. "You have nothing to worry about. I'll stand by you. We'll get through this."

We're both quiet for a few moments.

"Why do you sound like that?" I ask.

"How do I sound?"

"Cold. Distant. Look at you, you're afraid to even touch me."

Richard places his hand on my thigh, with restraint. The artificiality of his gesture infuriates me, and I jump up.

"If that's what you call touching me, I'd rather you not touch me at all," I shout in anger.

"I don't understand. What do you want from me?" He raises his voice. "What exactly do you expect me to do?"

I can't speak; the words are caught in my throat. I feel so ashamed of what I've done and of the childish anger that I'm projecting at Richard, but I can't stop myself and I walk out of our apartment slamming the door behind me.

I feel like I'm going to burst into tears, and I use every tactic I can think of to stop that from happening. I walk aimlessly along Fifth Avenue, stumbling over my feet looking like a drunk. When I reach the park, I sit down on a bench near the fountain. Once I finally calm down, I realize that I treated Richard terribly and I hurry back home to apologize, only to find that he's already left. I go back outside and continue wandering aimlessly for another hour until I find myself outside Judith's apartment.

"What happened?" Judith asks, worried, when she sees me slumped over and listless.

"I lost," I tell her.

"The race is still open" she says. "I've been following the results."

"*The New York Times* is planning to publish an exposé of my past, about how I belonged to the Church of Scientology when I was in my twenties."

"You were in Scientology?!" Judith repeats. "You never told me about that. Sit," she says in her maternal voice, as she leads me to the armchair in her office. "Tell me about what happened back then." I lean back in the chair and close my eyes. Waves of vague, long-suppressed memories rise up and wash over me.

One night, I was woken up by a loud banging on the door of my Greenwich Village apartment. God only knows what time it was. My head was pounding, and I barely managed to stand up and walk to the door. Collin, my dealer, came inside.

"If you don't turn your life around, you're going to die," he says.

"As if you care about me. You're living in luxury thanks to me."

"I do care about you. I don't know why, but I do. You're still in your twenties. I have enough clients to keep me living my life of luxury until the end of my days, and rest assured, I've never told any of them to turn their lives around."

"I care about you," I repeated mockingly, and invited him into the living room.

"You don't believe anyone could care about you?"

"Maybe, but not you. You I don't believe."

"How much have you had to drink?"

"You were late, and I didn't have any meth, so I downed a bottle of vodka and then some." I held my head in my hands and massaged my temples, then got up and went to the kitchen.

"Sit," Collin says, blocking my way with his outstretched arm. I sat. "I'll make us some coffee." A few minutes later, he reappeared with two double espressos.

"Drink." He pushes a pill in my direction.

"Is it anything good?" I joked morbidly.

"It's for your headache, you idiot. I'm trying to help you, not make things worse."

"Thanks," I said. I tilted my head back, trying to rest.

"Do you want me to leave you the stuff?"

"Yes." I didn't have to think twice; I couldn't imagine getting through the day without it.

He placed three small plastic bags filled with beautiful crystals on the table, and I gave him a fat roll of dollar bills in exchange. On his way out, he handed me a slip of paper. "Take it," he said. On the paper was the phone number of someone named Peter.

"Who's Peter?"

"He'll help you turn your life around."

"I'd rather you get me someone new to fuck," I answer, defiantly.

"Whatever." Collin turned around and left. I closed the door behind him and sat down at the kitchen table. I took out a few crystals, ground them into powder, arranged it in lines, and snorted them one by one. Within seconds, I finally felt like I was back in control. Nothing could stop me. The world had turned into one big amusement park, all within arm's reach.

The next day, Collin sent over a young man. "Follow me," I said to him, leading him to my bedroom. "What's your name?"

"Solomon."

"Wait here a minute." I went into my study, snorted a line, and returned to the bedroom with the glorious feeling that my senses were about to explode. The guy was still standing there. I was sure he'd be waiting for me in bed, naked.

"Collin had only good things to say about you," he said. "How do you know him?" I didn't bother to answer. I told him to take off his clothes, and I pounced on him. I played with his body for a bit, fucked him hard from behind until I came, and then laid down in bed and lit a joint. I looked at him; I'd already forgotten his name. I asked myself if I wanted to go another round, but I wasn't into him anymore. I passed him the joint; he took a few puffs and handed it back to me. I took out a roll of bills from my drawer, counted out five one-hundred-dollar bills, and gave them to him.

"I didn't come here for money," he mumbled, embarrassed. I wasn't sure if he really meant it or if Collin had told him to say that.

"If you were a prostitute, I wouldn't be paying you five hundred dollars for half an hour. I'm paying you to keep quiet. And it'll be worth your while. There's a good chance I'll ask Collin to send you again," I lied, "and that way you'll be able to get both me and the money once again."

He thanked me and asked me if I wanted another round.

"No. Go home."

He got up, got dressed, and left. I tried to sleep, but after tossing and turning for a long time, I gave up. I went to my study and tried to get some work done for the Democratic Party conference that I was organizing, but I couldn't concentrate. I went out into the living room, turned on the stereo, cranked the volume all the way up, and drank whiskey straight from the bottle. When I was finally tired, I lay down on the couch, and woke up the next morning with yet another awful headache.

I went to the Democratic headquarters at ten the next morning, after having taken energy pills and an assortment of vitamins to keep me on my feet and get me through another day of work. In the afternoon, I wandered through Manhattan, tired, dejected, and full of self-loathing, so I hurried home to do some more meth, and felt back in control again. Bill Black, a senior member of the DNC, called me. I took a deep breath and tried to sound lucid, even though the freedom and lightness I was feeling made me want to break out into song and laughter.

"Meet me at seven," he said. "It's urgent." I agreed in an authoritative tone, using all my power to conceal my actual condition.

I pause to take a sip of the water that Judith has placed in front of me.

"Go on," she says softly.

That evening, I sat with Bill Black at our usual table at Renaissance. A had a huge smile plastered across my face; I was high as a kite. I ordered some fine whiskey for us and struggled to suppress the bouts of laughter.

"What's going on with you lately?" he asked me compassionately. "I'm worried about you. I asked you here because the party chairman in New York wants to revoke all your official duties."

"He can go fuck himself," I blurted out, and downed another shot of whiskey.

"You have a brilliant future ahead of you, Tom." Like any good father would, Bill chose to ignore my outburst. "It would be a shame to throw it all away. Josh told me that you and your father aren't speaking, and I understand that you're going through a difficult time right now, but this isn't the way to deal with it. I know your father and I know how rigid and cruel he can be, but drinking your way to oblivion won't get you anywhere."

I was relieved to see how certain he was that my only problem was drinking. *Do you have any idea how much I drink?* I wanted to shout in his face. *Do you know about all the drugs I do? How many men I fuck?*

"I understand," I responded softly. "This has really been a difficult time for me, but soon everything will sort itself out. I trust you'll be able to convince the party chairman that I'm OK, that I was under pressure and now I'm fine." I hurriedly took a sip of my drink. I had a hard time swallowing it because another wave of laughter was threatening to explode and I could picture it making me spit the whiskey straight into Bill's face, which made it all the more challenging to restrain myself.

After dinner, I got into my BMW, lowered the roof, and drove slowly towards my apartment in the Village. I was out of focus. I was seeing double, and everything looked hazy and strange. I sang at the top of my lungs. It was as if my voice was stabilizing me. A blurry figure standing on the nearby sidewalk signaled for me to stop. I made a crude gesture in return, burst into laughter, and continued driving, until I could hear a police siren and a firm voice through a megaphone ordering me to stop. I knew this wouldn't be good.

I sat in the waiting room of the police station, my head cradled between my hands, and tried to make sense of what happened. The policeman was insisting on a urine test, and I waited for my friend Mark to come and get me out of this mess. Mark Shuster was a lawyer who had gone to college with me. He was studying law, I was studying business management, and we became friends. When he came into the waiting room, there was a look of panic on his face.

"Are you OK?" He sounded worried.

"I'm fine. Skip the drama, please, and just get me out of here. I'll tell you all about it when we get outside."

"Alright," he said. He straightened his tie and turned to the police officer, trying, as always, to please me.

"They won't budge on the urine test," he told me quietly when he came back.

"Would money help?"

"Are you out of your mind?" he yelled. Then, quieter, "I'm a lawyer. I can't offer a bribe. I'd be disbarred."

"So I'll do it. I just want to know if it could help."

"I'm not sure," he said, and I could sense how hopeless he felt.

"They can't find out that I was drunk. If this comes out in the papers, I'm done for. If they arrest me, it'll be the end of me. I need to get out of this. Wait here." I walked over to the officer on duty.

"I'm sorry about what happened, officer," I said. "Let me go, and I promise it will never happen again."

"I can't, sir," he said indifferently. "There are rules I have to follow."

In response, I decided to make a deal with him the way I knew best.

"Listen," I said. "A urine test isn't going to change anything. It took a while for my lawyer to get here, and by now you won't find anything in my urine anyway. Let me go, and I promise I'll join AA."

The officer, still chewing his gum, sat up in his chair and shot me a penetrating look. Holding his gaze, I studied his piercing eyes and his impressive moustache. Then he extended his hand and gave me back the cup for the urine sample.

"Go away," he barked. I backed away from the desk and went into the bathroom, where I called Josh. My last hope.

"I'm at the police station," I told him. Now that the drugs had worn off, I was on the verge of tears.

"What happened?" I could hear the fear in his voice.

"Nothing. They're just making too big a deal out of a couple of beers."

"Are they going to arrest you?"

"I don't know, but if I have to spend one more minute here, I'm going to lose my mind. Not to mention the fact that my father will lose *his* mind if this gets out."

"Lose his mind?" Josh exclaimed. "That would be the best-case scenario. Leave it to me."

I left the bathroom and saw Mark trying to convince the officer to let me go, but again, he was unsuccessful.

"I don't think you have a choice," he whispered.

"Give it a minute. It'll all be sorted out soon."

Mark looked at me. He assumed I was still drunk and decided not to reply. We watched the officer sitting behind the desk. Suddenly, the desk phone rang. He picked it up, listened silently, and, after a couple of moments, hung up, and called Mark over. They shook hands and exchanged a few words.

"Let's get out of here," Mark said, dragging me out of the station. "That was the mayor of New York on the phone. He's the one who got you released."

"I told you it would all work out," I said, bursting into laughter. I invited him to have a celebratory drink with me. After a few drinks with Mark, I went back home and called Josh. When he sleepily answered the phone, I immediately burst into tears like a little boy.

"Maybe we should take a break," Judith suggests, but I refuse.

"You have to understand, Judith. That whole episode at the police station was the lowest point of my pathetic life. After that, I didn't want to leave the house. I didn't want to see anyone. Not even the men who'd show up at my door every night. I told Collin to stop sending them until further notice. I spent my evenings sitting in the living room, in the dark, smoking joints, drinking, and sinking deeper and deeper into depression, stuck in one long panic attack.

"Finally, one evening, I couldn't take it anymore. I looked for the note that Collin had given me, and I called Peter."

"I'd like to meet with you," I told Peter over the phone.

"Come by tomorrow morning at nine. Call Tracy and she'll tell you how to get here." The next morning, when I showed up at the address Tracy had given me, I found myself standing outside the Church of Scientology. My brain was in a fog after a sleepless night. My body had been poisoned with drugs and alcohol, and the damage they had done even after leaving my body was substantial. Before I left the house, I snorted a short bump, hoping to lift my spirits and energize my body.

I went inside. The interior of the building, which was in the Theater District on Broadway, filled me with awe. Everything around me was opulent in an exaggerated way. The entryway was adorned with tall gold columns that were reminiscent of a building in ancient Rome. It led to a gigantic hall that looked like the lobby of one of the most luxurious hotels I'd ever seen, and I'd certainly seen a few. Two well-groomed young men, who looked like they had stepped out of the pages of a fashion magazine, came over to greet me.

"Tom, you have arrived at the Church of Scientology," they informed me. "Our mission is to improve mental clarity and aptitude, and to make us better spiritual beings. Have you ever heard of the religion of Scientology?"

"Yes," I said quietly. "Actually, when I was a teenager, I came across L. Ron Hubbard's book, *The Way to Happiness*." They continued smiling and nodding like robots, but the positivity that radiated from them felt nice, even if it was artificial.

"And did you read it?" a female voice asked. A woman sat down next to me and introduced herself as Tracy.

"Did I read it?" I repeated. "More times than I can count. It was my bible. The twenty-one precepts helped me a lot. I was on drugs at the time, and the book gave me the strength I needed to put them aside. And for many years, drugs stopped being the center of my life."

"Why did you need drugs at that age?"

"Personal reasons," I said. Tracy passed me a form, which she described as a personality questionnaire.

"Once you've filled it out, you can meet Peter. Not everyone gets to meet him, but when it comes to Tom Gold, that's another story."

"How do you know my last name?"

"Collin told me," she said, as if it were obvious. "I'm leaving now, but I'll be back soon. If you need anything, use the intercom on the desk."

I sat up in the chair, took off my jacket, and paged through the questionnaire. There were dozens of questions, and I tried to focus and answer them properly. When I was all done, I pressed the button and Tracy appeared immediately. She handed it over to be checked and then led me to the office of Peter, the director of the Church of Scientology in Manhattan.

Before she left, Tracy asked me if I wanted anything else to drink, and I shook my head. She closed the door behind her.

"What brings you to us?" Peter asked me.

"Collin suggested I get in touch with you. We've known each other for years. He feels I've been a bit weak lately and he thought you might be able to help me."

"Did you know who you were calling?"

"No, but when I got here this morning, I realized it was a church. I told Tracy that when I was younger, I was really into L. Ron Hubbard's book."

"Interesting," Peter said, then went on as if what I had just told him wasn't of interest to him, all the while keeping the smile pasted on his face and nodding in endless understanding, just like Tracy.

"We can help you, Tom. I can offer you a course of treatment that will free you of your addictions and will cleanse you both physically and mentally. You don't need those drugs. You come from the noble Gold dynasty, and it would be a shame for you to destroy your life."

"The noble Gold dynasty," I repeated, chuckling at the absurdity. "What can you possibly know about the noble Gold dynasty?"

"Not very much, just what I read in the papers." He studied me, and for a moment the smile left his face. "Tom, do you want to help yourself?"

"Yes," I answered. I'd come this far, and I wasn't about to stop now. Moreover, Hubbard's twenty-one precepts had a warm place in my heart. They'd helped me before; maybe they'd work this time, too.

"Wonderful. In that case, let's move forward. Starting tomorrow, we'll meet regularly for two months. One-on-one meetings. This treatment is called 'auditing,' and it is practiced with the help of something called an 'E-meter.' Have you ever heard of an E-meter?"

I shook my head.

"The E-meter is a tool developed by Mr. Hubbard that helps us isolate sources of spiritual distress or depression that exist beneath one's current consciousness. Once these problematic areas are uncovered, we can examine them without the subjective influences that exist within the spiritual counsel offered by other religions. The E-meter doesn't offer a diagnosis or a cure, it just monitors your emotional state and any changes that may occur therein, and helps us pinpoint the specific issues that need to be addressed.

"With the help of the E-meter, you'll discover hidden emotional baggage that has been affecting you without your knowledge, causing you to behave in irrational ways and endangering your wellbeing. Over the course of the treatment, this baggage will gradually disappear, until it no longer has any influence over you. Our sessions are basically confessionals; I will keep a personal file of everything you confess. Before we start, you'll have to sign a waiver stating that you won't ask to see the file and you won't ask me to give it to you. All of this is, of course, for your own benefit, as part of the healing process."

While those last conditions didn't sit well with me, at that moment I truly believed that they would help me with my recovery.

"Our goal is to help you attain complete freedom, or what we call a 'state of Clear.'" When he saw the confusion on my face, he explained. "That is what we call the absence of a 'reactive mind.' When a person is in a state of Clear, he has no aberrations. He is completely rational, and makes good decisions based on data and his own personal perspective. He reaps maximum joy from the present and the future. The path to Clear is the path to complete freedom. There are several stages, and each of them helps a person achieve a new and improved state of being. The process of purification also includes liberating yourself from the destructive influences of the drugs and the toxins that have been accumulating in your body over the years, toxins that can result in an undesirable physical state and stand in the way of spiritual freedom.

"You will go through objective processes to help orient you to your physical environment in the present," he continued, "along with an alcohol and drug rehabilitation program to free you from their mental influence. Then you'll undergo a happiness assessment, and then some more stages during which you'll identify the source of your problems and be able to eliminate them. You'll be free of the bitter disappointments of the past and be better equipped to cope with the future, until you finally reach the state of Clear. Needless to say, we can help you. We'll make sure that your passage through and between the stages is smooth."

At home that evening, I snorted three lines of crystal meth, and finally felt truly good at the end of that strange day. The false sense of satisfaction and joy brought on by the drugs was worth everything. The feelings of self-confidence, hyperactivity, and energy never lost their thrill. I invited Danny – a man I already knew, and even liked – to come over. I fucked him for over an hour, then kicked him out. He already knew the rules. He took my money and left content.

Towards morning, I was pacing the house again, unable to settle down. Despite the sleeping pills I took, I couldn't fall asleep. I must have drifted off eventually, because I woke up in the late morning and realized I was late for my first auditing session.

"What happened during the auditing sessions?" Judith asks, and I continue with my story.

During our sessions, Peter would hook me up to the E-meter and ask a lot of questions. The first meeting was followed by many others, and I found myself confessing everything: events, thoughts, fantasies, things I never dreamed of sharing with other people. He was good at his job; he knew how to get everything out of me that he wanted, and it felt good to purge myself of all the filth that had built up inside me. It was so purifying and revitalizing, in fact, that I actually forgot what it truly meant to tell all these things to someone who was virtually a stranger, especially one who worked for a cult that was known to be problematic.

I didn't talk only about myself; I told him about the corrupt and criminal acts that were taking place in the Democratic Party. I told him about my father and my mother and God knows who else. Over the months, I climbed the Scientology hierarchy, and by the time I reached the third stage I had paid the church a hundred thousand dollars. Eventually, I figured out the basic operating principle of the cult: if you didn't have money, you couldn't move up in the hierarchy. Regular people spent years doing all sorts of jobs within the church in order to progress, while I could acquire my high status with money. My escrow account, which my mother had opened to pay for my education and to allow me to live a life of luxury, was emptied in inverse proportion to my confessional file, which continued to grow thick. I became completely dependent on Peter. He knew everything about me, and I was at his mercy. Over time, I was rehabilitated. I stopped taking drugs, cut back on alcohol, resumed my studies at Harvard's MBA program, and did a lot of athletic activity, which improved my attitude and restored my energy. And one day, after I had reached the seventh stage at the church and had paid hundreds of thousands of dollars for the privilege, I told Peter it was time for us to go our separate ways.

"But you haven't reached Clear yet," he said. "You can't leave in the middle of the process."

I thanked him again for all he had done for me and told him I was willing to take my chances.

That evening, a man came to my door. He introduced himself as a member of the Church of Scientology and asked me to state my name. When I confirmed that I was indeed Tom Gold, he handed me a letter from Peter and left. The letter, which was printed in large font, was loaded with threats. "We'll boycott you. We'll declare you an 'oppressive person.' We won't leave you in peace for a single day. We'll come after you. You can never leave the Church. It's your home."

Peter's letter and behavior – especially after I'd paid him such enormous sums of money – infuriated me. This anger gave me the courage I needed to turn my back on the church. A short while later, I heard that a famous singer, a beautiful young woman who I'd occasionally see at the church, had committed suicide. What had prompted her to take her own life? Had they blackmailed her the way they tried to blackmail me? Had they threatened her when they found out that she wanted to leave? What if it wasn't suicide at all?

I arranged a meeting with Peter. In return for a promise to leave me alone, I transferred hundreds of thousands of dollars into his account, and, for extra protection, made him sign a letter on church stationery promising not to publish my confession file. I asked him to give me the file, but he refused, reminding me of the waiver I'd signed. I realized that even if he did give it to me, he could still make a copy, so I left it alone. One of the precepts of Scientology is "start, change, stop." And that is just what I did: I stopped, albeit not in the way they hoped I would.

"So what happened to your file?" Judith asks, concerned.

"It's still inside the Church of Scientology in Manhattan. And I'm wondering what Peter will do with it when the article comes out in the *Times*. My hope is that my file is sitting empty in an archive somewhere, along with countless others. That the church is just holding it over our heads like some kind of doomsday weapon, trying to intimidate us into staying. So, what do you think now?" I ask sarcastically. "You need to stay positive," she says. "Look, Tom, if the cult has already released the information, it's out of your hands, and dwelling on it is just a waste of energy. By the way, is there anyone else who knows these things?"

"Margaret, my former psychologist. But she's bound by doctor-patient confidentiality."

"It's all for the best. There's something comforting in the fact that all your skeletons are coming out of the closet. You've essentially freed yourself of all the darkest parts of your life. That will help you reach a permanent state of calm, and you'll no longer live in fear that these stories might come out. Embrace this with love. You just have to make it through this stage. It's an excellent test for you – a chance to practice my methods."

After another hour of discussion, accompanied by mental exercises to prepare me for what's to come, I leave her townhouse. I continue wandering aimlessly through the streets of Manhattan until I find myself sitting at the bar of The Silent Bartender, just like in the old days. The shouts of encouragement and support from the people around me warm my heart, and I know that whatever the future holds, I've already accomplished more than I ever thought possible.

CHAPTER 22
Manhattan, Mid-March

I take my Porsche out of the parking lot and drive wildly through the streets of Manhattan. I'm angry, frustrated, and feel like I'm losing everything: my good name, the presidential race, and Richard.

The car leaves the city and I soon realize I'm making my way towards Silver Bell, towards my father. In these critical moments, I find I'm seeking his protection. I'm aware of how childish this is, and I know it goes against my principles, but this is an emergency and I feel like this is exactly what I need right now. Father opens the door, as if he knew I was coming.

"What's going on?" he asks, examining me with a closed expression.

"Something horrible," I say, not knowing how or where to even begin.

My father invites me in and closes the door behind me.

"Are you upset because an investigative report about you is going to come out?"

"How did you know?!" I ask in shock.

"Don't be so naïve. I've already told you to get this idea of a cleaner, newer politics, or whatever you're calling it, out of your head."

"OK. You win. But how do you know about the article?"

"I don't know about a specific article, but I'm not surprised. They've been gathering material about you for a while now, and I assumed they'd be using it at the last minute."

"Who's been gathering material about me?" I ask in annoyance.

"Come," he says, leading me to the large living room. "Sit."

I sit down next to the fireplace, and he pours me a generous amount of whiskey. "We need to be practical. Leave your nerves and anger for later. What paper are we talking about?"

"*The New York Times.* They sent Mandelbaum a request for comment. We need to respond by noon tomorrow."

"What is it about?"

"A certain period in my life."

"I need more information than that."

"Before I give you details, I want you to tell me who's after me. Is it the governor of Montana?"

"Tom, who else would it be?" Father asks. "Really, you need to stop being so naïve."

"It could also have come from the Republican party."

"The Republicans are preoccupied with themselves, and for now, they're staying quiet about you. Don't forget that I'm an old fox," he says. "I know politics from all sides. I know its bad sides and its worse sides. The moment you announced you were running, I knew they'd come after you and try to take you down. As far as politicians are concerned, you're a strange bird. They've been preparing for the job for years, and then here you come along, the billionaire son of Joseph Gold, extremely talented, extremely strong, and extremely successful – and on top of all that you're also gay and Jewish. It's too much for them, and they'll use everything they can to try to ruin you. Since they have nothing to discredit you with on the professional side, they decided to go personal, where you're vulnerable. All they care about is knocking you down, at any cost. And because I know who we're dealing with and predicted that they'd do this, I decided to do a little sniffing around of my own."

"What do you mean 'sniffing around'?"

"I'm expecting you not to get mad. Not now."

"Father, what have you done?"

"At the beginning of the race, I ordered a wiretap on the governor, on Robert Taylor who I assumed would be the leading

Republican candidate, and at a certain stage, on Nathan Glenn too," he says in a quiet, cold voice. "I hope you can understand. It was my only way to protect you. Politics is war, Tom, and you can't win a war without good intelligence."

"Wiretapping is a criminal offense," I say, just to put that out there on the table.

"It's nothing the Police Commissioner can't fix," he says and pauses, examining my face. "We're not going to be able to prevent the article from getting published."

"What does that mean?" I ask angrily, getting up on my feet. "I'd expect you of all people to use all your contacts to make sure it doesn't get published. Your friends Black and Josh told me there's nothing you can't do. Now is the time for you to prove to me that that's true."

"Sit down," my father says in a soft and loving tone that I had never heard before. "Sit down and calm yourself." He pours us both a glass of cold water. "Put victory aside for a minute. There are things that are far more important."

"What's wrong with you?" I exclaim in anger and astonishment. "Until this morning, everything was just fine. If you take down the article, everything will stay just fine."

I know I'm acting like a child, but I don't care.

"I understand," Father says. "But first and foremost, I need to know that you're living a healthy life. That you're as happy as you can be, that those things from your past are truly behind you."

"How do you know what was in my past?"

"I know," he says quietly. "I read the transcripts of the governor's recorded phone calls. I know everything."

I hang my head in shame. "It was a long time ago," I mutter. "It was a dark period in my life, but I'm fine now."

"Every day, I'd wait for the transcripts from the private investigators who gave me the information that the governor's investigators collected about you," he continues. "I couldn't help myself. I read it all. I wanted to know about your life, the life my son led during the long period that I didn't really know him. There's a huge black hole that I wanted to fill. On the days they told me there weren't any intercepted calls, I was disappointed, because I felt I was missing out on a day in your life."

He's sitting on the sofa, unmoving like stone, but continues on bravely.

"I never imagined that such difficult things had happened to you. I didn't know you had suffered so much, that you needed to fall so low. I failed you as a father and a person. I was sure that my harshness towards you, the distance I put between us, would force you into becoming a man. That's the truth. In politics, I never hesitate to confront the most difficult situations, but in real life…" he pauses. It seems that one minute more and he'll burst into tears, but he stops himself.

"I'm also pained by all the years we lost," I say. "I often think about all the missed opportunities, about the fact that we didn't have a normal relationship. But how does that help us now? We can't turn back time. All we can do is look ahead."

Father looks at me with a smile. He seems grateful for those words. As far as he's concerned, he's just asked for my forgiveness, and I granted it, and for the moment, all our problems are forgotten.

I go to the kitchen and make us some coffee. When I return to the living room, I sit down next to him on the sofa.

"Let's do something today that your mother would never let us do," Father laughs, lighting us each a cigar. "Bring some brandy too."

"Just a second ago we were drinking whiskey."

"What difference does it make?" he asks. "We'll pour it into our coffee, like sailors do. There's a well-known café in La Spezia that the sailors flock to when they dock there. They serve black coffee with brandy and whipped cream."

"So let's be sailors," I say, going back to the kitchen to bring the can of whipped cream from the fridge.

We're both quiet for some time, smoking our cigars and drinking our sailors' coffees.

"Let's get back to business," Father suddenly says.

"Let's," I answer.

"Listen, Tom," he says. "There are things that are more important than this race, and if you want, you can pull out. This is politics. The more you succeed and the more power you accumulate, the more they'll be looking for ways to destroy you. You need thick skin, otherwise there's just no use. And I don't want you to get hurt. You've been through enough."

"This hasn't been easy for me, but I don't want to withdraw. I'll accept the word of the people with love, but I'm not going to withdraw. Only cowards quit."

"What about Richard?" he asks.

"I don't know. I have no idea how he'll deal with it all. I don't even know what's going to happen after our explosion this morning, after I told him everything."

"You can't afford to lose Richard," he responds. "Your life together is way more important than anything else. If you think this could ruin your relationship, that's one more reason to withdraw."

"That's assuming I didn't already ruin it this morning."

"A relationship based on love cannot be destroyed so easily. Trust me, I know what I'm talking about. Your mother and I also went through some crises in our lives, and we managed to overcome them. If you're going to stay in the race, you and Richard need to sort these things out quickly, or else the press will have a field day over it."

"What do you mean?" I ask. "You're really not going to stop the story from getting published?"

"I won't be able to. I don't know anyone in the entire world who'd be able to stop it. If anything in it wasn't true, we'd be able to threaten a libel suit, and even then, I'm not sure we'd have managed to stop it from getting printed. I read the transcripts. They have hard facts. Men you had sex with have agreed to testify, without even hiding their identity. They found your drug dealer and he's also agreed to talk in exchange for a lot of money, of course, and they found a couple people who were in Scientology with you. We're going to have to deal with this."

"How is it possible that you don't have a single creative solution?" I ask in despair. "You're supposed to be the expert in these sorts of things."

"Don't get worked up Tom," he says in his familiar cold voice that is somehow calming me down now. "I have a solution, but I won't be able to prevent the article from getting printed. No paper in the world would agree not to publish it, especially when everything is backed up with proof."

"I don't understand how they managed. No one in the world knows all these things about me. I always maintained secrecy. Even if they spoke with everyone who knows me at Olympia, or at The Silent Bartender, they wouldn't be able to get all this information."

"Does the name Margaret mean anything to you?" he asks.

"Margaret? Yes of course. But she's bound to patient-doctor confidentiality."

"It seems you can't even trust psychologists these days."

"I'll ruin her!" I shout out in anger. "I'll bury her in the courts."

"Later on, you can do whatever you want, but it won't change the situation you're in right now. We're busy trying to save your career, not ruin hers."

"How did the governor even get to her?"

"She got to him."

"What?" I ask, flabbergasted.

"It seems she was having some financial trouble and called him. She offered juicy information about you and received three million dollars in exchange."

"Three million dollars, that's what my life story is worth," I say, and we let ourselves chuckle a bit. "How does the governor even have three million dollars?"

"It took me some time to understand. In the transcripts, the same code name kept being repeated, and when I did some digging, I saw that these were my old enemies from the past, trying to settle the score now, at your expense.

"As for Margaret, the governor won't expose his source. If I expose it, everyone will know that I listened to his phone calls, which is also a crime, so for now, we can't sue a soul. We have no choice but to stay quiet. And I promise you, she'll pay for what she's done."

"Well, what now?" I ask.

"I put together a file on the governor."

"Meaning?"

"When he started gathering information about you, I decided to have one made on him. Why should he be the only one enjoying himself?" my father asks with a mischievous smile.

"Did you find anything?"

"A ton."

"And if it comes out that they were bugged and that we hired private investigators to dig into his past?"

"Tom," my father says with self-important self-awareness, "Joseph Gold doesn't get exposed. Certainly not on such small matters."

"I understand. Well?"

"The governor of Montana was a regular at a brothel in Texas. Not only did he enjoy the sexual services there and cheat on his wife, including in bi-sexual orgies, but he was also a business partner and made a ton of money there, but lost it all gambling. This all happened while he held public positions in the Democratic Party. I will add to this for reasons of my own, and there we have it. A perfect scoop," my father says in great pride.

"What do you plan to add?"

"That he had a child out of wedlock with one of the prostitutes."

"Did he?"

"Again with the naivety," he chuckles. "I don't know, but I'm sure that once it's published, someone will appear. Don't worry. Your psychologist isn't the only one with money troubles."

Father looks pleased with himself. I feel much less so.

"And what if this gets us into trouble?"

"It won't. There's nothing to worry about."

"What do we do about *The New York Times*?"

"We'll give them a response by noon tomorrow. Nothing can prevent it from getting published, but you can demand that your response be published in full. You need to mentally prepare yourself for this. Once it's published, every media outlet in the United States and the world is going to cover it. We'll need to remain calm. We won't respond beyond what we give the *Times*, and we'll need to hope that interest dies down quickly so that we can make sure the story about the governor is published soon after, throwing the spotlight on him instead."

"The party will suffer, naturally."

"It will suffer, but it's not the end of the world. The party will get over it. The main thing for us to do is remain standing on our feet."

"A day after the article is published, I'll call a press conference," I say.

"What for?" he asks dismissively. "It's unnecessary. What will come of it? More headlines, more pictures."

"I want to maintain my credibility. A response in the paper won't be enough to clear my name. I want to hold a press conference and tell the truth. Explain that this all happened a long time ago, that I was going through a very difficult period in my life that I can't even recognize any more. I want to be honest with the American people and let them judge me."

"The American people can be harsh judges," he says. "Be careful what you say, so we don't get into any more trouble. If you feel you need to hold a press conference, do it. Our story about the governor is strong. That's the main thing. A press conference here, a press conference there, it doesn't really make much of a difference. And one more thing," he says, his expression turning serious. "You need to reconcile with Richard. He needs to fully support you on this. Without him, it will be very hard for you to make it out of all this."

"I could never make any commitments on Richard's behalf, certainly not now."

"You have no choice. He'll need to find it in himself to accept this and make peace with it. He is married to you, and he needs to deal with everything, just like your mother does," he laughs. "It's not easy living with Joseph Gold."

"I don't want to pressure him. I want to give him time."

"There isn't any time," Father says. "Call him now. Tell him that I want him to come here. That your father is asking him to come. He'll need to respect that."

There's a knock at the door.

"I'll get it," Father says, leaving the living room.

"Hello, Richard," I hear him say warmly.

"Hello, Mr. Gold," Richard answers.

"Call me Joseph," Father says.

"Hello, Joseph," Richard answers, and I can hear the smile in his voice. They enter the living room. Father leads Richard in. We smile to each other, but I can see the anger in Richard's eyes over my childish behavior.

"Sit down," Father offers, pointing to the gold armchair and patting him on the shoulder. He then takes his place back on the white sofa. "Helena," he calls, and she comes running.

"Yes, Mr. Gold?"

"Call me Joseph," he says, and she looks at him in shock. She's been working in my parents' house for twenty years and has never called him anything other than Mr. Gold.

"Yes, Jospeh?" she asks with a degree of embarrassment.

"Please bring us glasses and the cognac from my desk," he asks.

"Right away, My. Gold, I mean, Joseph," she blushes. My father asks Richard about his business, mustering all his charm – and he has a lot to muster when he wants to – until she comes back into the room. A few moments later, there are three glasses and a bottle of cognac on the table. Richard volunteers to pour for everyone.

"Take a whiff," my father instructs Richard, who sniffs with a big inhale, takes a small sip, washes it around his mouth, and then pours for us too. First, he hands a glass to my father. When he comes closer to me, I can feel the tension between us, but it's clear that the basis of this tension is positive, despite the anger. We both want to go back to being close to each other, but we don't know how.

"The cognac is excellent," Father says, taking another sip. "Richard, I want you to feel at home here," he adds, and I understand he's using his political mediation skills to try and help us reconcile. I still can't tell whether he's doing it for political reasons or whether he actually cares about us, and I must say, I don't really care.

"I hoped this would happen one day," Richard replies.

"It took me some time," Father admits.

"I understand," Richard says. "My father died many years ago. If he was alive, you'd be around the same age, and I don't know how he would have reacted to this marriage. Every time I wanted to judge you for your behavior, like when you didn't show up to our wedding, I thought about him and understood that this is no simple matter for your generation and that I really can't judge you."

"It is wise of you not to judge," my father answers. "Just know that I thought about you two a lot that day."

"My father worked at Olympia," Richard suddenly says.

"I know."

"You looked into me?" Richard asks with a supposedly accusatory tone, managing to get a small grin out of my father.

"I looked into you the moment you and Tom started getting serious. I'm used to looking into people. Looking into everything about everyone." All three of us laugh and Father calls for Helena again.

"Please bring the brown file that's on the desk in my study," he asks her.

"Every Holocaust survivor who came to America and worked at Olympia was invited to a personal meeting with me," Father tells us as we wait for Helena to return. "It's what I used to do in those days. It was important to me to get to know my fellow survivors personally. I felt like we were flesh and blood. I was happy and proud to be able to provide them with work and a livelihood, to give them the foundation for their new lives. That was the main significance Olympia held for me, and it's the reason it remains so important to me even now."

Helena enters the room with a small file that she hands to my father. He thanks her and she leaves.

"So, in the beginning, I never dreamt that Olympia would turn into this vast empire. I just wanted to raise my family respectfully and help others, and one of those others was your father." He gives Richard the file with an old Olympia sticker on it.

"I asked for this to be brought to me from the company archives and I've been waiting for the right moment to give it to you."

Moved, Richard opens the file and I go over to where he's sitting. "That's my father. He must have been around twenty years old then."

"And that's my father," I say. The picture shows my father and Richard's at the Olympia shipyard. My father's arm is rested on Richard's father's shoulder, and they're both smiling.

"I documented those meetings. I wanted to give the Holocaust survivor employees the warmest treatment possible, so they'd feel at home at Olympia."

"You certainly succeeded," Richard says. "My father definitely thought of Olympia as home. It was his whole world. I'm one of the thousands of children who were dubbed "Olympia's kids," he says, and I can see from my father's expression that he enjoys remembering that period. "As young kids, we'd come with our parents to visit the ports, and they'd let us on the large ships and spoil us all day long. It was a powerful experience. We all felt like sailors, and at the end of the day, the real sailors gave us their own hats."

"There's something else in that file," Father says, and indeed, there's another picture under a sheet of tissue paper. I look at it and almost choke.

"When was this taken?"

"When we dedicated the new shipyard, I invited some of the Jewish families for a celebratory dinner. It was a really important moment for me, and I wanted other people to be able to enjoy it too. The Silverman family was among those invited."

"Your mother was really beautiful," I tell Richard, as he passes his hand over his face. In the picture are our two families standing together, smiling, and we're in the picture too. Richard and I are all dressed up and standing next to each other. I'm leaning on my father and Richard is leaning on his mother in her black satin dress cascading down her body, her hair done up in two braids that join at the top of her head.

"Looks at us," Richard says to me. We look at each other and smile.

"Thank you very much," Richard thanks my father, his voice full of emotion. He puts his glass of cognac on the table and, slightly hesitant, goes over to my father and hugs him. A few moments later, they sit back down. My father's matter-of-fact expression shows that we're now getting to business. "The article will be published in *The New York Times* in the next few days," he says, without any segue.

"There's no way to prevent it?" Richard asks.

"Why do you want to prevent it from being published?" I ask him.

"I don't understand," he says, visibly confused.

"Do you want to stop it because you're embarrassed by the things that will come out about your husband, or in order to increase my chances of winning?"

"That's not the point right now," my father cuts me off. "For now, we need to focus on what actions we need to take. Each of us has a job to do."

"Father, for me, it's the entire point," I say. "I need to know what Richard thinks about the things I told him."

"He's very surprised both by the things themselves and the fact that you never told him about any of it before," Father is speaking on Richard's behalf. "But he will get over it and he is here with us now, waiting to hear what his job will be."

"Joseph," Richard stops him. "I don't need a spokesperson, thank you."

"Fine," my father says, "but we don't have any time to lose. We're on a tight schedule and your behavior is going to be critical, even if you will only be acting."

"I'll deal with this however I chose. You can't manage me."

My father sighs with clear impatience, but Richard ignores his sudden change in demeanor. Father examines his face for a few moments, nods to himself, and looks thoughtful.

"I understand," he finally says. "Helena?" he calls out in a strict tone.

I'm observing this exchange between Richard and my father and for a moment, I've forgotten that it's actually about me. Never in my life had I ever heard anyone speak that way to my father or disagree with him. They're both filling me with pride: Richard, for daring to speak that way to him, and my father, for managing to accept his behavior with understanding.

"Yes, Mr. Gold," Helena says as she hurries into the room, not daring call him by his first name.

"Bring us each a cappuccino and a slice of cheesecake," he instructs her, and I see that harsh, matter-of-fact Mr. Gold has re-entered the room.

"Tom had a whole life before he met you," Father tells Richard. "It's natural for there to be things you wouldn't have known, as I'm sure there are things that he doesn't know about you."

"There are no skeletons in my closet," Richard says like a stubborn child. "My deepest, darkest secrets are that I sometimes copied off other kids in school or that I'd skip school without telling my mother."

"A boring life," my father declares, and you can see he's amused with himself. "But now, you need to present a unified front, to support each other just like when the wives of public figures do even when scandals come out. There's nothing you can do about it. It's the way the game is played."

"I don't need to play this game. I'm different from those wives. I despise them for standing by their husbands at all costs. They are cynical politicians with political ambitions, and they are addicted to power. But for me, success doesn't heal the wounds like it does for those women. This whole idea of 'let's just win the elections and then everything will be fine' makes no sense to me," Richard says. "I have a hard time with politics and all the struggles it demands of me. Whoever runs for office needs to know that their skeletons don't remain in their closets, and they need to get them all out beforehand. You took a gamble, Tom. You should have exposed everything," he says to me.

"If he had let it all out from the beginning, he wouldn't have even been able to start the race," my father says, insisting on continuing to defend me.

"So maybe he shouldn't have started," Richard says angrily. I get up and ask to leave the room, but my father's booming voice stops me.

"Enough!" he says. "Sit down," he instructs me, and I obey.

"Now listen to me, the both of you. Tom is so close to victory he can taste it. A Jewish, gay candidate. Who would have ever believed it possible? Let's just say for a moment that a gay candidate was feasible. But a Jewish president? You can rest assured that neither I nor your father, Richard, who had come to this country as a Jewish refugee, would ever have believed that something like this could happen. And now this story has sprung on us without warning. People go through crises and are pushed into places they never wanted to be in the first place. That's what's happened to Tom back then, and I hope you never find yourself in the terrible situation he was in, which made him fall as low as he did. But Tom managed to overcome it all and turn into the man you met and fell in love with.

"You need to remember that Tom never committed any crimes against anyone else, only against himself. He never raped or murdered or robbed. He destroyed himself, that's what he did, but he also managed to overcome it. Tom was a victim then and he's a victim now: a victim of the ugliest kind of political smear campaign, a victim of his greedy psychologist who sold everything he told her. And if you love Tom, Richard, you need to protect him with all your might."

Richard looks at me in astonishment.

"Son of a bitch," he mutters, hurrying to get up and hug me. "You and Tom keep insisting on misunderstanding me," Richard says. "I'm talking about politics, the campaign, the price that he and I need to pay. I'm not mad at him and I don't blame him for anything. I love him and I only want to help. When he told me what happened, my heart broke, and I was filled with rage over the price he's paying for this disgusting race. You're telling me that I need to protect him? That's all I want to do. I just need to be convinced that me joining the campaign will protect him and not actually harm him anymore. Tom," he turns to me. "You can walk away from all of this if you want. Your life is as full as a president's even if you don't run."

"I can't," I reply. "I can't give up now. I can't let them destroy me over my past. I overcame it back then and I'll overcome it now. Even if I lose, I need to keep trying until the end. I see now, more than I ever have before, that I have a lot of power. And after the article is published, I'll have even more power. I'll be invincible because I won't have anything left to hide. The secrets that I've fled from all my life weakened me, but as of tomorrow, they won't be able to hurt me anymore."

I'm standing at the front of the conference hall full of members of the press. Although my campaign team, Richard, and even my father said they wanted to be there with me to support me, I preferred to stand and face the media alone. Only Mandelbaum, who's there to run the press conference, is with me in Olympia's conference hall, which was chosen so that I'd be able to speak from my home turf.

Before me lies the speech I wrote as soon as the article came out in *The New York Times*. During the night I learned it by heart, and I'm now reciting it in a steady voice, making sure to look directly at the cameras. I'm nearing the end. There is a heavy silence in the hall, broken only by the clicking of cameras.

"This is me, Tom Gold, and I'm leaving the choice in your hands. That was my life almost twenty years ago, and you can decide whether you're able to accept the mistakes I made in my previous life with understanding, or not. People make mistakes and need to pay for them. I paid a hefty price for my mistakes every day during that dark period in my life. Today, I can truthfully say I am a different man. Family values are important to me; friendship, honesty, reliability, fairness, and love are sacred to me. I am dedicated to my moral values, to my husband, and to America, which I love with all my heart. Thank you all very much."

No one in the room dares utter a single word. Mandelbaum announced at the beginning of the press conference that we wouldn't be taking any questions, but I was sure the reporters would pounce on me anyway. Shortly after, they turn to their cameras and microphones to summarize my speech, as I leave the stage and then the conference hall, accompanied by Mandelbaum.

"You were wonderful," he tells me. "Authentic and real. I can't say how everything will turn out, but we did what we came here to do. How do you feel, Tom?"

"Honestly, it's a huge relief to have made this statement. If I had gone into hiding, the rumors would never have ceased. At least now, everyone knows the truth. In any case, we're not offering any more responses or statements on the matter, regardless of how the headlines may read. We're going to focus on action."

"We've prepared material about the things you've been doing in the U.S. and throughout the world, in order to encourage positive coverage about you in the coming days. The press will understand that this is our attempt to divert attention elsewhere, but we're going to try to create a new agenda nevertheless."

"I'd like to go back to normal and meet with as many potential voters as possible."

"I'm not sure that's the right move," he says. "The press will be at the events. They could ask questions, harass you. We won't always be able to say, 'no comment.' Maybe it would actually be wise to keep a low profile for the near future. Adam can manage the campaign with the activists and volunteers until this wave passes, and you can work behind the scenes. It might be time to let the press know that the popular and talented governor of California, Aiden Connor, is your choice for VP. That might help us score some points and redirect the fire elsewhere. We can even use Connor for the rest of the campaign until you return."

"When is *The Washington Post* going to print its investigative report on the governor of Montana?

"I didn't want to tell you before the press conference," Mandelbaum says quietly. "I wanted you to be cool and collected for it. *The Washington Post* decided not to publish for now. They're claiming that by the time they'd manage to corroborate everything, the primaries would already be over. If the governor beats you, they'd have more of an interest in those details, but at that point, the Democratic Party would no longer want the paper to print the story. They were also unconvinced that this wasn't merely a revenge move."

"You chose an unreliable leak," I scold him.

"I gave them Sam Marvin. There's no one more reliable."

"Could Sam bring it to a different paper?"

"I don't think he should. The convention is almost here. Another paper would also need to do its fact-checking. This could actually work in our favor. Who knows who's pulling the strings there? This way, you're the clean candidate that the other side is trying to incriminate, the victim in the best sense of the word. Let's wait patiently for the governor to make every possible mistake."

During the day, the news programs don't stop playing my statement. The media coverage is mostly cynical, and there are only a few reporters treating me with any degree of empathy. The question of whether a candidate with a turbulent past is fit to lead the United States does not stop being asked. None of the articles we tried to encourage manages to penetrate the media's wall of opposition. It's all about the slimy headlines. The people wanting to get revenge on my father have launched a huge online campaign: "Tom Gold, for an America you can be ashamed of."

I decide to take Mandelbaum's advice and keep a low profile. I hold my weekly meeting with Bill Black in my home. He's supportive of my press strategy and tries to encourage me. He promises that he's still backing me, and that he has no intention of giving in to any demands to support the governor of Montana instead of me.

"We'll get through this," he tells me. "We're going to keep moving on."

I'm trying my best to move on, but it's no simple task. I leave my house only to go to Olympia, and I manage to escape the reporters waiting for me, both at the entrance to my building and next to my office. My employees are warm and friendly, and that is really comforting to me. I've gone back to spending most of my time in my office, getting regular updates from Adam and Aiden Connor who've been racing to every state the governor of Montana has been to, in an attempt to clean up the filth he's left in his wake. From time to time, I find refuge in my previous occupations and in running the company.

One day, I notice a large gathering outside my window. I come closer and see the words "Tom Gold" emblazoned on enormous banners painted in my campaign colors and the colors of the American LGBTQ+ flag. The demonstrators are waving these signs high. I stand close to the window, trying to decipher the text on the signs, but the distance makes it hard for me. I excitedly call Alexandra into the room.

"Can you make out what it says on those signs?" I ask, and she suggests we go downstairs. We hurriedly put on our coats and I decide to add an old, wide brimmed hat of my father's that was left behind in one of the offices here.

"Are you worried they'll see you?"

"Come," I say, letting her see that she's right.

From a side corner of Rockefeller Center, we manage to understand the meaning of this demonstration. The people standing opposite the entrance to my office are holding improvised signs in support of me. This spontaneous show of support moves me. I still can't tell who's behind it all, but all the signs contain the same one sentence: "On second thought, Tom Gold for president."

Alexandra grabs my hand and pushes me towards the lobby of the building. "Let's go back up," she suggests, and with us both suddenly feeling like we're in some detective movie, we flee towards the elevators. I hurriedly call Adam, who's currently in North Dakota, and tell him everything.

"I imagine your father is behind this," he says.

"I hadn't thought about that, but it really moved me to see all those people standing at the entrance to my office, all bundled up and shouting in support of me."

"I'll try to figure out who was behind it, so we can expand it," Adam, who remains decisive in any situation, even after the crisis we just got through, concludes. "The situation in North Dakota isn't good, Tom," he says gently, and I decide to ignore this and focus on what I've just seen with my own eyes.

In the evening, when Philip and I drive past the entrance to my building, I notice another large group of people standing there. They have the same signs I saw earlier, and they are shouting the same slogans: "On second thought, Tom Gold for president!" I ask Philip to stop the Jaguar, consider going out to the demonstrators, but decide against it a few seconds later. I still don't feel ready for this kind of encounter.

"Get a photographer over to my apartment ASAP," I excitedly tell Mandelbaum over the phone. "There's a big demonstration to support me for president here." I keep peeking under my wide brim. From the moment I put it on my head, I haven't wanted to take it off. It once belonged to my father, and I feel closer to him through wearing it.

"Take the back entrance to the parking lot," I tell Philip, since I don't want them to notice me, but as soon as the car passes the demonstrators, a handful of them notice me and I can hear them shouting words of love to me. Full of excitement, I thank them by waving my black-leather-gloved hand.

Later, Maria and I go out to my penthouse balcony and watch what's happening. The group of demonstrators keeps growing, and the passers-by from the Park Avenue neighborhood embrace the noise that has overtaken the area. *My New Yorkers*, I think to myself, realizing just how much I love this city.

To my astonishment, the demonstrations supporting me keep increasing from day to day, even outside New York State, and it's clear that this is a large group of people being led by liberal minority groups and members of the LGBTQ+ community.

In interviews, they tell the media that despite the crises from my twenties, I am the only figure they don't identify with the old

349

guard, and I'm the only one who'll be able to clean all the corruption out of Capitol Hill. I'm the only one who can lead to change.

Change, I think to myself with satisfaction. In the end, this word caught on. Certainly among the college students, the creative class, and the LGBTQ+ community, all of which are behind this huge campaign. And this is what's enabling me to lift my head back up and continue my race.

CHAPTER 23

The Democratic National Convention

Denver, Colorado, July
"The executive committee of the DNC is meeting again," Adam informs me. "They're holed up in one of the meeting rooms. The singularity of this situation is tangible. Everything is rumbling beneath the surface."

"Above the surface," I correct him.

"Black wants to meet with you," he tells me, leading me to a side room.

"Listen closely," Black says as soon as I've entered the room and closed the door behind me. "The first round was inconclusive, even though we were careful in choosing the convention delegates. Your father is doing the hard work now with the superdelegates associated with the establishment. There's a problem with some of the senators from the Blue Dog Coalition, but it seems your father will soon explain to them in his own way that supporting the governor from Montana will make the party lose power, and that they can take their conservatism and shove it," Bill says angrily. Aside from them, we still need 50 more delegates in order to win. But losing is not something we plan on doing in this contested convention.

"You've done a wonderful job so far. The wave of support for you is at a huge peak, but there are other groups in the U.S. aside from the liberal minorities, students, and the creative class. We need to break the conservative establishment's support for the governor of Montana. Promises, jobs, money – for now, it's all on the table. Let me be clear: Neither you nor your new politics interest us for now. I'll never recognize the governor of Montana as president, not for all the money in the world!" he declares. Ecstasy has overtaken him. He slams his fist on the table and his face turns red. "I and the other senior members of this party will not accept him. If disaster strikes and he somehow gets the majority of delegate votes, we'll boycott him.

"Later, I'll settle the score with the tycoons who supported him as a way to get revenge on your father, but for now, all I care about is your victory. Your father and I worked together to decide who we'd approach to buy the delegates whose votes we want to change, based on our close personal relationships. There's nothing to worry about."

"Father won't let his dream remain unfulfilled yet again," I say, finding it difficult to hide the bitterness in my voice. Bill ignores this.

"Josh is here too," he says.

"He also has a dream?" I ask cynically.

"No, but Martin Luther King had a dream, and I hope we're at the start of a new age for civil rights in the United States," he says, and I don't know whether he actually means it or is just trying to make me happy. A few moments later, Josh shows up in the room and lets us know that he's gotten commitments from the owners of Impression, one of the most influential lobbies in Congress, his close personal friends, that the representatives of Louisiana at the convention will now be voting for me.

"How much did that cost us?" Black asks, as if he really cares, only minutes after he told me that all options were on the table.

"Not now," Josh says, deciding to keep me out of it. He adds that I'm not particularly beloved in Louisiana. The governor of Montana is considered "a man of the people," Black insists on explaining to me, as if I didn't already understand.

"It's not enough. Keep working," Black goes back to the task at hand, giving a shot of encouragement to Josh. He nods and leaves the room, and I shift uncomfortably in place without saying a word.

"The governor's people are without a doubt doing the exact same things as us," I say to Black, but I'm actually trying to encourage myself.

"They're doing this, you can be sure of that. Your father has reliable sources telling him what the governor's people are doing. Based on that, we're offering the delegates some more attractive solutions," Black phrases it, "in order to change their minds. In any case, the governor's people don't know how to do what we're doing."

"And what is it that we're doing?"

"You don't need to know the details. It's best to keep you out of this. Let's just say we're fixing the mistakes caused by your new politics." He picks up the phone and goes back to the slimy politics that he's so well-versed in. "Get me George," he tells his assistant, and I know that in the next few minutes, I'm about to witness another crooked move.

"How are you, George? It's done, right?" and he returns the phone to its place smiling to himself.

"Who's George?" I ask.

"It doesn't matter who George is, but rather what he did."

"And what did George do?"

"George is a wonderful man, the chairman of the North America Construction Workers' Union. He owes a lot to your father. Without Joseph Gold, he'd never have gotten his position. He knows why it's worthwhile for him to use all his contacts and make every promise necessary to ensure that some of the Oklahoma delegates change their minds."

I can feel the beginnings of a panic attack starting to rear its ugly head inside my chest, but I manage to silence it.

"What was he promised in exchange?"

"He wasn't promised, he was given," Black says. "We're doing this all for you. But like I said, it's better that you don't know what he was given so that, if necessary, you'll be able to deny any knowledge about it and it won't be a complete lie. But there's no chance there will ever be a need. What's happening now is bigger than any of us, Tom."

I know that these are the final moments of truth, and I decide not to intervene. Black presses the button on the intercom and asks his assistant to come in. She hurries in and he hands her an envelope. "This needs to get to the representative from Michigan," he tells her, and she leaves the room with the envelope in her hands.

Adam and I look at each other, understanding that within a few minutes, the delegates from Michigan will be changing their minds as well. "In Detroit now, the only thing that works is money," Black murmurs quietly, trying to explain what he's just done and debating whether to include me or keep me out. "The leaders of the Industrial Workers Union in Detroit understand that we're the only ones who'll be able to help them in their current situation. You're the only one who'd sign orders to transfer grants that the industry in the city still needs."

"What orders?" I ask confused, and immediately feel myself starting to lose control. I shout at Black, "What the hell are you even talking about?" at the exact moment my father enters the room.

"Come," I say to Adam, and we get ready to leave the room.

"Tom," my father calls over to me, and I stop at the doorway. "Come back in and close the door," he instructs, like the lead actor in a play that only he'd be able to write. It seems it's impossible for him to do anything without drama. It's the source of his energy, and I only recently learned how to prevent it from entering my life.

"We are close to victory," my father says in a serious tone, standing behind the old desk in this back room of the convention hall that was reserved for me. "I've spoken with party members who are gathering in the convention hall. You're the one with the image of an honest, professional, high-quality person who could bring change. The winds of change are blowing, Tom. Be proud of yourself for what you've achieved in your own way. You did excellent fieldwork. Activists who met you talk about you with admiration, and the excitement in the field is tangible. If you can keep this up, you'll win the national elections too.

"It would be a shame to give up on this massive achievement just because of some delegates who are not fans of the winds of change, due to some narrow political and personal considerations. Don't be naïve, Tom. These delegates get tons of money from tycoons who've been my business rivals for years. Some of them are upset that I took their properties away from them. Some managed to reaccumulate capital, mostly through dubious ways that still aren't out in the open. And now, they've decided to get their revenge on me. But as always, Joseph Gold has the upper hand."

"Still aren't out in the open – you mean to say that the legal authorities still haven't figured them out?" I mock my father.

"The legal authorities have their interests too," my father answers, without elaborating. "I really do hope you'll bring change, Tom," he suddenly adds in a serious tone that contains a touch of faith and hope.

"But what would happen if the things you've done come out?" I ask.

"When you know what others have done, you'll see how I was justified," he answers with a grin. He's managed to amuse himself. "Signing orders in Detroit is no big deal. Don't make it a big deal."

As I get up once again to leave the room and have my hand on the door handle, I feel it being grasped at the same time on the other side. When the door opens, I find myself standing opposite three very large Native Americans.

"Come in!" my father calls out to them joyfully, coming over to bring them into the room. My rational mind begs me to leave the room, but it feels as if something stronger than me is forcing me to stay put and see what will unfold. My father and the three Native Americans share a powerful embrace and pat each other hard on the back.

"It's been a while," the oldest looking of the three says. To me, they look like a father and two sons. They're all dressed in new dark jeans; blue, green, and red button-down shirts; and a small blue handkerchief tied in a sort of bowtie around their necks.

Hanging from their leather belts are beaded chains in matching shades, as if their outfits were all coordinated. They share looks of appreciation and admiration with my father, and it seems they share many secrets too.

"That's one of New Mexico's biggest tycoons, the sheriff of San Juan County, and the mayor of Farmington," Black whispers in my ear. "They owe your father their careers," he adds, and a look of amazement washes over my face.

"What do you need?" one of them asks my father.

"The delegates from New Mexico. We need them to change their votes in the second round. How did we even get here, where they're supporting the governor of Montana?" he asks them in shock, as if New Mexico belongs to him personally.

"Interests," the man answers. "Representatives of the governor made huge promises to the coal miners' union and the coal companies who've been hurt by the situation in China."

"Everything they promised, I can promise you more," my father says. "Speak with the delegates who've been sent here. Promise, in my name, anything you can think of. I will guarantee anything," he says, and these men understand that his word is worth its weight in gold, but this time, I'm the one who'll need to fulfill those promises. My father pours everyone some cognac. With an Indian blessing that only they understand, they raise their glasses and then retire for a short conversation on the other side of the room.

"New Mexico is ours," Black summarizes, as if I couldn't understand what's just happened before my very eyes.

"Come," I take Adam by the hand, and we walk out, behind the convention hall, to smoke.

"It seems victory is mine," I say, "but I find this final chord extremely jarring."

"Put it aside," Adam says decisively. "The governor is also doing everything in his power right now. From what we heard now with the Native Americans, you can see he's been doing just that.

Leave all the nonsense to the side for now," Adam says, as if he's made peace with it all and nonsense is all it is. "After everything we've been though over the past few months, we can't give up now over 50 delegates who would be voting for you anyway had it not been for whatever the governor promised them," he asserts, trying to encourage himself as much as me. "Tom, there's a huge movement following you. Mandelbaum just updated me that the polls are showing widespread support for you in the national elections, because of who you are. Politics is an emotional business, and the people love you."

"I believe you that it's because of who I am, but what I saw just now truly isn't me. The movement can change direction in a second if my voters find out that I know about everything we just witnessed."

"No one will know. The people who went to see your father are close personal friends. And anyway, you were kept out of a lot of it. You don't actually know what orders they're talking about, what was promised to the coal miners' union or the owners of the coal companies in New Mexico or anything else. What happened today was an important lesson for the governor: Anyone who tries to build a case against another candidate will lose in the end. That's how it is, plain and simple. Lucky for you, Black and Josh and your father are on your side. When you're president, you'll be able to continue implementing your new politics."

"I'm not the president yet. I still have a long way to go."

"A long but good way," he says, and we continue sitting quietly on the low stone wall until I get a text from Bill.

Come, he writes, and we hurry back to the room where he and my father are.

"It's all signed and done," he says happily, and I see my father speaking on the side of the room with the head of the NFL. I can see that he's irritable. He pounds the table with his fist a few times to clarify what will happen if he doesn't get what he wants. I have no idea what this man owes my father and what he's doing at the convention, but he'll know how to push the delegates we need to change their minds and vote for me. When the head of the NFL leaves the room, he notices me, but walks past me, knowing the rules of the game dictating that I need to be kept out of all of it. *Everyone's protecting me*, I think to myself in frustration, trying to find solace in Adam's encouraging words.

Just when I thought that no one else would come to this side room of ours, my mother suddenly appears in all her glory, with a huge smile on her face. Father also tends to keep her out of things, too. She's pure in his eyes. He's never wanted her to witness any dishonesty, even though in Silver Bell, when he was the senator of Connecticut, she witnessed much, sometimes against her will. If Father told her to come here from the hotel where they're staying, I'm sure he's convinced I won.

Out of the corner of my mother's eye, I see a tear. She walks over to my father, and they embrace. They've always shared a strong bond, despite all the crises they went through. For them, love will always conquer all.

"My darling Tom," she comes over to me and places her hand on my cheek, hugging me and whispering in my ear how much she loves me and how proud she is of me. I take advantage of this moment, hugging her back in a strong embrace and surrendering my whole self to her love, which I had been missing so terribly.

"Tom," my father says after my mom lets go. We're standing facing each other, very close. "Even if you didn't love what you saw earlier, the day will come that you will forgive me for it. I'm convinced that once you're sitting behind that desk in the Oval Office, you'll thank me for everything. But that's not what's important right now. Soon, we'll all go out to the convention hall, we'll cheer for you, and we'll hear the long-awaited declaration that you are the official presidential candidate of the Democratic Party, and that the governor of California is your running mate," he says dramatically, and shivers run down my spine.

"But before that happens," he says, his voice shaking, "I'd like to ask whether you can ever forgive me for the awful years that we weren't in touch." My mother wipes tears from her eyes, and I know she's had a hand in this. "That's all I care about right now, Tom. I accept you as you are, with everything that means. All the rest is nonsense," he repeats, and this time, I see tears in his eyes as well.

"I forgive you, Father," I answer emotionally, giving him a look that is both forgiving and full of love.

"Forgiveness is righteousness," my father says, coming closer to me. "I love you, Tom," he says. He hasn't said anything like this to me for decades. We hug, and I feel my mother's hand grasping onto my shoulder and joining in.

"Get a stirring speech ready," my father says. "Radiate happiness. Get rid of this crestfallen face. You've won. I want to see an exciting, charismatic leader. None of the activists outside knows about what we've done here. Josh, Adam, Black, and I are the only ones who know, and we also know what loyalty truly is. We're a fortress. Not a word of this will get out. Rest assured.

"And besides, you should be proud of yourself, Tom. Put aside those last delegates, think about all the ones you managed to enlist the way you wanted, despite all the screws in your tires, despite the risk in having a gay, Jewish presidential nominee. Just focus on your enormous victory, Tom," he concludes by clapping his hands, trying to lift my spirits. "I hope that I'll get to see this new politics of yours in my lifetime," he adds in a tone that's a mix of faith and skepticism.

"Call Barbara," I say to Adam, more determined than ever. "I want to prepare for an epic victory speech."

"Tom Gold," the announcer declares in excitement, "is the Democratic presidential nominee!"

I'm overcome with emotion as I go up on stage. The cheers from the activists are so loud they're shaking the walls of the convention hall. My campaign banners are flying high, and a soul singer welcomes me on stage. The excitement is like nothing I've ever felt before. I look out at the massive crowd cheering joyously, I thank them, and when another wave of excited cheers fills the air, I know that Richard has come up on stage too. He stands next to me and we hold our hands in the air to the sounds of the audience's thunderous applause and enthusiastic cheers. Finally, I walk toward the podium with Richard by my side.

"We've certainly kept you on the edge of your seats until the last minute," I say playfully, and am rewarded with another round of applause. "I promise it won't have been for nothing." Again, more deafening cheers fill the entire convention hall. I begin my acceptance speech, applying the rhetoric that I successfully developed, and the crowd is swept up in excitement. I'm giving Bill Black and the party leaders exactly what they wanted – a young, exciting, and charismatic leader. I finish my speech by thanking the crowd. I then stand up straight for the singing of the national anthem, close my eyes, and thank God for this moment, which I will hold in my heart forever. Something makes me open my eyes and look to the side. There, next to the stage, I see my parents and siblings looking at me with pride, tears streaming down their faces.

A Few Months Later

After a night of disturbed sleep, I discover that Richard isn't in bed. It's five in the morning. I get up, go out into the corridor, and walk towards the kitchen. Richard and Maria are sitting comfortably and having a chat.

"Tom never told you how we met?"

"No," Maria says. "He never told me much."

"Well, it was in May. I had just moved to New York. I bought an apartment in Tribecca, but I had been morose for a while already. That morning, I started to get ready for a meeting with the Corporate Heirs Club, even though it was the last thing I wanted to do. Talking about the Holocaust and the security of Israel didn't quite suit me that day, and I'm not even a corporate heir. I was only asked to join the club because of my fortune."

"Coffee?" Maria asks.

"Thanks," Richard responds. She pours him a mug and he takes a sip. "Excellent coffee," he says. Pretty soon, the smell of the coffee reaches me too, but I hold myself back so I can hear the rest of this story without interruption, and Richard continues. "I felt utterly empty that morning, and I went out to my balcony hoping that sensing the city waking up on that spring morning would help get me going. Everyone is in love with Manhattan, and I hoped that maybe out of this great nothingness, I'd be able to find a bit of love. A live recording of Simon and Garfunkel's 'Mrs. Robinson' was playing in the background, and I thought to myself that just like Dustin Hoffman, I might meet someone exceptional today who'd take me on some adventure that I had never dreamed of. It was one of those fantasies that you forget the moment it's over, but I decided that if something like that were to happen, I'd give it a chance.

"My driver let me off at the entrance to the Plaza. Someone named Ed Leibowitz, who I had only ever met over the phone, was waiting for me there and led me through the long corridors to Columbia Hall. I was the last inside and found the seat with my name on it, and suddenly I saw Tom sitting across from me. It felt like there was a bright aura all around him. He was very well dressed. I can still remember it to this day: a blue suit, white shirt, and light blue tie. I remember thinking that he looked like a Greek god, but what struck me the most were his eyes, which truly spoke to me. I don't even know how to describe it, Maria. His eyes spoke to me."

"Cookies?" Maria offers and Richad nods. "Not even Columbia Hall could contain all his charisma," Richard continues. "And yet, he radiated the warmth and sympathy of a real person. I felt that something big was about to happen. When I'd stand on my balcony, it never occurred to me that all this would happen, but when I saw Tom, I understood that I'd need to change the role of Mrs. Robinson into a man's part. In retrospect, I know I was always attracted to men, but I repressed it and made up all sorts of excuses for myself. At any rate, when Tom started to speak, I could tell he had something to say and that he knew how to say it. In one moment, he had all the other people in that room eating out of the palm of his hand, until Ed Leibowitz and Israel's Diaspora minister began to sweat.

Maria laughs. "He always knew how to speak. Ever since he was a little boy."

"And then," Richard continues, "in the lounge during brunch, he came over to me, gave me his business card, and we exchanged glances. To this day, I can remember how he looked at me. After he left, I knew I needed to see him again. After that, I went to visit my mom in Chicago, and I was supposed to meet with Tom as soon as I returned, but before we got the chance, it was time for the annual Corporate Heirs Club meeting in Maine. That's where our romance began, and that's where I fell in love with him. It quickly became clear that I wanted to live the rest of my days by his side, and it never occurred to me what surprises he'd have in store for us, for all three of us," he says with a laugh.

I decide to get up from my armchair and enter the kitchen. Maria and Richard are sitting by the counter. She's wiping away tears. I wink at Richard, and he smiles back at me.

"Coffee?" Maria asks me through her tears.

"Sure," I answer happily.

After breakfast, I get ready for my first day on the job. Richard takes Roxy, the dog we adopted, out to play in the Rose Garden. I go out after my husband, drawn to him like a magnet, with my security detail following close behind.

Printed in Great Britain
by Amazon

46187683R00209